THE GIRL IN THE SPIDER'S WEB

"Fans of Stieg Larsson's captivating odd couple of modern detec-
_____ _____ hacker Lisbeth Salander and her
_____ _____list Mikael

_____

just as compelling as ever ___ __.

"Larsson died before his wildly popular *The Girl with the Dragon
Tattoo* came out, but the publisher chose wisely in tapping David
Lagercrantz to continue the series with *The Girl in the Spider's
Web*. Not only do the matter-of-fact style and intricate plotting
and sexy, chilling atmosphere feel very true to the original novels,
but Lagercrantz transcends the source material. He's the better
writer. He worked as a crime reporter and knows our journalist
protagonist, Mikael Blomkvist, and Sweden's troubles well. In this
version: A brilliant scientist is murdered. Corporate and government Web sites are compromised. Cybercriminals lurk in the
sordid corners of the night and the Internet. And a severely autistic
savant might hold the key to a mystery. It's a dark, thrilling novel
that channels our very real digital vulnerabilities as people, businesses, and nations" BENJAMIN PERCY, *Esquire*

"One devours Larsson's books for the plots, the action, the anger, and most of all for Lisbeth Salander, a character who resembles Sherlock Holmes or James Bond in being so powerful because she is a brilliantly realised myth rather than a psychologically convincing character study. Lagercrantz has caught her superbly, and expertly spun the sort of melodramatic yarn in which she can thrive" JAKE KERRIDGE, *Daily Telegraph*

"Last seen vanquishing her half-brother by punching nails through his feet, Lisbeth Salander, the heroine of Stieg Larsson's Millennium Trilogy, is making a comeback – but now with a new author. Since the posthumous publication [in Sweden] of the first book *The Girl with the Dragon Tattoo* in 2005, sales of Larsson's Millennium Trilogy have exceeded 80m copies. Now David Lagercrantz has stepped into the original creator's shoes to bring the tattooed, vengeful hacker Lisbeth back to life . . . Mr Lagercrantz displays an innate understanding of the world Mr Larsson created, and has stayed true to the characters of Salander and Blomkvist, who remain impervious to authorial change" *Economist*

"A skilled novelist in his own right – his books include *Fall of Man in Wilmslow*, about the tragic British computer pioneer, Alan Turing – Lagercrantz has constructed an elegant plot around different concepts of intelligence . . . Lagercrantz's continuation, while never formulaic, is a cleaner and tighter read than the originals, although he follows the template in building the plot slowly and methodically. He is, technically, a more adept novelist than Larsson, smoothly switching viewpoint in two sections where characters come under threat from assassins. Without ever becoming pastiche, the book is a respectful and affectionate homage to the originals" MARK LAWSON, *Guardian*

"Mr Lagercrantz definitely shares Larsson's love of Lisbeth Salander, the punkish, tatted waif and hacker whose chief talent is to remind us that revenge is a dish best served piping hot. He keeps her offstage for the opening chapters, but when the dragoness enters the story she speeds it up nicely . . . But the novel's overarching evil is greed. A Swedish security cop shudders 'at the creeping realization that we live in a twisted world where everything, both big and small, is subject to surveillance, and where anything worth money will always be exploited.' This kind

̶ ̶v̶e̶r̶y̶ much in the Stieg Larsson spirit: The

ney and fewer

asked him to w̶r̶i̶t̶e̶ Salander. He has carried it out with intelligence a̶n̶d̶ ̶ Girl in the Spider's Web conveys the essence and atmosphere of Larsson's Millennium novels. He has captured the spirit of their characters and devised inventive plots . . . On the evidence of Spider's Web, most Millennium fans will want to continue following their Lisbeth" MARCEL BERLINS, The Times

"The plotting is similar to Larsson's. There is a slow burn, punctuated by bursts of action before a page-turning finale. However, the book never strays into the dark descriptions of violence that punctuate the originals . . . Lagercrantz could not have fulfilled the commission any more efficiently. The novel leaves much to be said between Salander and Blomkvist and so surely increases the chances of the sequence continuing on towards the ten books that Larsson is said to have originally imagined" NICK CLARK, Independent

David Lagercrantz

THE GIRL IN
THE SPIDER'S WEB

MACLEHOSE PRESS
QUERCUS · LONDON

First published in Great Britain in 2015 by MacLehose Press
This paperback edition first published in 2016 by

MacLehose Press
An imprint of Quercus Publishing Ltd
Carmelite House
50 Victoria Embankment
London EC4Y ODZ

An Hachette UK company

Det som inte dödar oss © David Lagercrantz & Moggliden AB,
first published by Norstedts, Sweden, in 2015
Published by agreement with Norstedts Agency

English translation copyright © 2015 by George Goulding
Maps © Emily Faccini

The moral right of David Lagercrantz to be
identified as the author of this work has been
asserted in accordance with the Copyright, Designs and Patents Act, 1988

George Goulding asserts his moral right to be identified as
the translator of the work

A CIP catalogue record for this book is available
from the British Library

ISBN (PB) 978 1 84866 778 5
ISBN (e-book) 978 1 84866 777 8

17

Designed in Cycles by Libanus Press Ltd
Typeset by Palimpsest Book Production Ltd, Falkirk, Stirlingshire
Printed and bound in Great Britain by Clays Ltd, St Ives plc

CONTENTS

GAMLA STAN

Stads-
biblioteket
Handels-
högskolan

Birger Jarlsgatan

Observatorie-
lunden

Sveavägen

NORRMALM

Stureplan

Konserthuset

① Slottet
② Järntorget
③ M.Trotzigs gränd
④ Österlånggatan

Stadshuset

**GAMLA
STAN**

HOLMEN

Riddarholmskyrkan
RIDDARHOLMEN

SALTSJÖN

Tavastgatan

Bellmansg.

SLUSSEN

Stadsgårdskajen

Katarinavägen

S:t Paulsgatan

Götgatan

Hökens ga.

Fiskarg.

Mariatorget

↑Mosebacke torg

SÖDERMALM

Synagogue
S:ta Maria Magdalena kyrka

**MEDBORGAR-
PLATSEN**

Ringvägen

Ingarö
Saltsjöbaden

↓ Ⓣ SKANSTULL

Rådhuset *Court House*	Stadsbiblioteket *City Library*
Konserthuset *Concert Hall*	Tantolunden *Tantolunden Park*
Stadshuset *City Hall*	Nationalmuseum *National Museum*
Handelshögskolan *School of Economics*	Polishuset *Police Headquarters*
Observatorielunden *Observatory Park*	Slottet *Royal Palace*

CHARACTERS IN THE MILLENNIUM SERIES

LISBETH SALANDER

an exceptionally talented hacker with tattoos, piercings and a troubled past.

MIKAEL BLOMKVIST

an investigating journalist at *Millennium* magazine. Salander helped him to research one of the biggest stories of his career, about the disappearance of Harriet Vanger. He later helped to clear her of murder and vindicate her in a legal battle over her right to determine her own affairs.

ALEXANDER ZALACHENKO

also known as Zala, or his alias Karl Axel Bodin. A Russian spy who defected to Sweden and was protected for years by a special group within Säpo. He is Lisbeth Salander's father, and used to violently abuse her mother, Agneta Salander. He was also the head of a criminal empire.

RONALD NIEDERMANN	Salander's half-brother, a blond giant impervious to pain. Salander arranged for his murder.
CAMILLA SALANDER	Salander's twin sister, from whom she is estranged.
	Salander and Camilla's mother, ... a nursing home at
DRAGAN ARMANSKY	Salander's former, now occasional, employer, the head of Milton Security. Another of the few she trusts.
PETER TELEBORIAN	Salander's sadistic child psychiatrist. Chief prosecution witness in Salander's incompetency trial.
IRENE NESSER	a woman whose Norwegian passport has fallen into Salander's hands, allowing Salander to assume her identity.

HANS-ERIK WENNERSTRÖM	a shadowy magnate who tricks Blomkvist into publishing an unsubstantiated defamatory article about his business, landing Blomkvist in prison. Salander uses her talents to empty his bank accounts in retribution.
ERIKA BERGER	editor in chief of *Millennium* magazine, occasional lover of Blomkvist.
GREGER BECKMAN	Erika Berger's husband.
MALIN ERIKSSON	managing editor of *Millennium*.
CHRISTER MALM	art director and partner at *Millennium*.
ANNIKA GIANNINI	Blomkvist's sister, a lawyer who represented Salander in her trial.
HARRIET VANGER	scion of a wealthy industrial family, who disappeared as a girl and was found by Blomkvist and Salander at the behest of her great-uncle, Henrik Vanger. She became a shareholder in *Millennium*.
SVAVELSJÖ M.C.	a motorcycle gang closely associated with Zalachenko.

Members of the gang were seriously injured by Salander.

HACKER REPUBLIC   a coalition of hackers, among whom Salander, who goes by the handle "Wasp", is the star. Includes Plague, Trinity and Bob the Dog.

the Swedish security police,

the team investigating the Salander case. Now promoted to chief inspector. Known as "Officer Bubble".

SONJA MODIG   a police officer who works closely with Bublanski.

JERKER HOLMBERG   a police officer who, in Bublanski's eyes, is perhaps the best crime scene investigator in the Swedish police force.

HANS FASTE   a Stockholm policeman who clashed with Bublanski and leaked information to

Prosecutor Ekström during the Salander investigation.

RICHARD EKSTRÖM   the prosecutor who brought the case against Salander, now chief prosecutor. A manipulative and venal man, believed within the police to be interested only in self-advancement.

PROLOGUE
One Year Earlier

This story begins with a dream, and not a particularly spec-

_____ ___ at that. Just a hand beating rhythmically and

PART I

THE WATCHFUL EYE

1 – 21.xi

-with Internet and telephone traffic. Time after time its powers have been increased, and now it monitors more than twenty billion conversations and messages every twenty-four hours.

CHAPTER 1

Early November

was having a ~~long~~ partner, Lasse Westman.

So Balder had given up his job in Silicon Valley, got ~~on a~~ home and was now standing at Arlanda airport, almost in shock, waiting for a taxi. The weather was hellish. Rain whipped into his face and for the hundredth time he wondered if he was doing the right thing.

That he of all self-centred idiots should become a full-time father, how crazy an idea was that? He might as well have got a job at the zoo. He knew nothing about children and not much about life in general. The strangest thing of all was nobody had asked him to do it. No mother or grandmother had called him, pleading and telling him to face up to his responsibilities.

It was his own decision. He was proposing to defy a long-standing custody ruling and, without warning, walk into his ex-wife's place and bring home his boy, August. No doubt all hell would break loose. That bloody Lasse Westman would probably give him a real beating. But he put that out of his mind and got into a taxi with a woman driver who was dementedly chewing gum and at the same time trying to strike up a conversation with him. She would not have succeeded even on one of his better days. Balder was not one for small talk.

He sat there in the back seat thinking about his son and everything that had happened recently. August was not the only – or even the main – reason why he had stopped working at Solifon. His life was in turmoil and for a moment he wondered if he really knew what he was getting himself into. As the taxi came into the Vasastan neighbourhood it felt as if all the blood was draining from his body. But there was no turning back now.

He paid the taxi on Torsgatan and took out his luggage, leaving it just inside the building's front entrance. The only thing he took with him up the stairs was an empty suitcase covered with a brightly coloured map of the world, which he had bought at San Francisco International. He stood outside the apartment door, panting. With his eyes closed he imagined all the possible scenarios of fighting and screaming, and actually, he thought, you could hardly blame them. Nobody just turns up and snatches a child from his home, least of all a father whose only previous involvement has consisted of depositing money into a bank account. But this was an emergency, so he steeled himself and rang the doorbell, fighting off the urge to run away.

At first there was no answer. Then the door flew open and there was Westman with his piercing blue eyes and massive chest and enormous fists. He seemed built to hurt people, which was why he so often got to play the bad guy on screen, even if none of his roles – Balder was convinced of this – was as evil as the person he played in real life.

"Christ," Westman said. "Look what we have here. The genius himself has come to visit."

"I'm here to fetch August," Balder said.

"You what?"

"I'm taking him with me, Lasse."

6

"You must be joking."

"I've never been more serious," he tried, and then Hanna appeared from a room across to the left. True, she was not as beautiful as she had once been. There had been too much unhappiness for that and probably too many cigarettes and too much drink as well. But still he felt an unexpected wave of affection, especially when he noticed a bruise on her throat. She seemed to want to say something welcoming, even under the circumstances, but she never had time to open her mouth.

"... f a sudden?" Westman said.

... stable

... doub...

A shiver ran through him as ...

his mighty bulk and his pent-up rage. It was crushingly cle...

he would have no means of resistance if that madman let fly. The whole idea had been insane from the start. But the strange thing was that there was no outburst, no scene, just a grim smile and then the words, "Well, isn't that just great!"

"What do you mean?"

"That it's about time, isn't it, Hanna? Finally some sense of responsibility from Mr Busy. Bravo, bravo!" Westman clapped his hands theatrically. Afterwards that is what Balder found the most frightening – how easily they let the boy go.

Perhaps they saw August only as a burden. It was hard to tell. Hanna shot Balder some glances which were difficult to read and her hands shook and her jaw was clenched. But she asked too few questions. She should really have been cross-examining him, making thousands of demands, warning him and worrying that the boy's routine would be upset. But all she said was:

"Are you sure about this? Will you manage?"

"I'm sure," he said. Then they went to August's room. Balder had not seen him for more than a year and he felt ashamed. How could he have abandoned such a boy? He was so beautiful and strangely wonderful with his curly, bushy hair and slender body and serious blue eyes, engrossed in a gigantic jigsaw puzzle of a sailing boat. His body seemed to cry out "Don't disturb me!" and Balder walked up to him slowly, as if approaching an unknown and unpredictable creature.

He nonetheless managed to get the boy to take hold of his hand and follow him out into the corridor. He would never forget it. What was August thinking? What did he imagine was happening? He neither looked up at him nor at his mother and of course he ignored all the waving and the words of farewell. He just vanished into the lift with Balder. It was as simple that.

August was autistic. He was most likely also mentally disabled, even though they had not received unequivocal advice on that point and anyone who saw him from afar might easily suspect the opposite. His exquisite face radiated an air of majestic detachment, or at least suggested that he did not think it worth bothering with his surroundings. But when you looked at him closely there was something impenetrable in his gaze. And he had yet to say his first word.

In this he had failed to live up to all the prognoses made when he was two years old. At the time, the doctors had said that August probably belonged to that minority of autistic children who had no learning impairment, and that provided he was given intensive behavioural therapy his prospects were quite good. But nothing had turned out as they had hoped and Balder had no idea what had become of all that remedial care and assistance or even the boy's schooling. Balder had run away to the U.S.A. and lived in his own world.

He had been a fool. But now he was going to repay his debt and take care of his son. Right away he ordered up casebooks and called specialists and educational experts and one thing became immediately apparent: none of the money he had been sending had gone towards August's care, but instead had trickled out to pay for other things, probably Westman's extravagances and gambling debts. The boy seemed to have been left pretty much to his own devices, allowed to become set in his compulsive ways, and probably worse – this was also the reason why Frans had come home.

policeman whom he knew privately. Even if they were not able to confirm his fears with any degree of certainty he grew more and more angry and set about submitting a series of formal letters and reports. He almost forgot all about the boy. He realized that it was easy to forget him. August spent most of his time sitting on the floor in the room Balder had made ready for him in the house in Saltsjöbaden, doing his exceedingly difficult jigsaws, assembling hundreds of pieces only to break them up and start afresh.

At first, Balder had observed him in fascination. It was like watching a great artist at work, and sometimes he was taken by the fantasy that the boy would glance up at any moment and say something grown-up. But August never uttered a word. If he raised his head from the puzzle it was to look straight past Balder towards the window overlooking the sea and the sunshine reflected in the water, and eventually Balder just left him alone. Balder seldom even took him outside into the garden.

From a legal point of view he did not have custody of the boy and he did not want to take any chances until he had sorted this out. So he let the housekeeper, Lottie Rask, do all the shopping – and all the cooking and cleaning. Balder was no good at that side of things. He understood computers and algorithms but not much else, and he immersed himself in them even more. At night he slept as badly as he had in California.

Lawsuits and storms loomed on the horizon and every evening he drank a bottle of red wine, usually Amarone, and probably that did little good either, except in the short term. He began to feel worse and worse and fantasized about vanishing in a puff of smoke or taking himself off to some inhospitable place, somewhere remote. But then, one Saturday in November, something happened. It was a cold, windy evening and he and August were walking along Ringvägen in the Södermalm district, feeling frozen.

They had been having dinner at Farah Sharif's on Zinkens väg. August should have been asleep long since, but dinner had gone on late and Balder had revealed far too much. Farah Sharif tended to have that effect on people. Balder and she had known each other since they read computer sciences at Imperial College in London and now Farah Sharif was one of the few people at his level in Sweden, or at least one of the few who was by and large able to follow his thinking. It was an incredible relief for him to meet someone who could understand.

He also found her attractive, but despite numerous attempts he had never managed to seduce her. Balder was not much good at seducing women. But this time he had received a farewell hug that almost turned into a kiss, which was a big step forward. He was still thinking about it as he and August passed Zinkensdamm sports centre. Maybe next time he should get a babysitter and then perhaps . . . Who knows? A dog was barking some way off and there was a woman's voice shouting behind him, hard to tell if she was upset or happy. He looked over towards Hornsgatan and the crossroads where they could pick up a taxi or take the Tunnelbana down to Slussen. It felt as if it might rain. Once they got to the crossing the light turned to red and on the other side of the street stood a worn-looking man in his forties who seemed vaguely familiar. At precisely that moment Balder took hold of August's hand.

He only wanted to make sure his son stayed on the pavement, ~~felt it:~~ August's hand tensed as if the boy were reacting ~~look~~ was intense and clear, as though ~~had been magically~~

the scene, ~~and~~
emotion, which he found ~~so~~
not even an especially bright or joyful one
distant bell, stirred something long dormant in his memory,
the first time in an age he felt hopeful.

CHAPTER 2

20.xi

Mikael Blomkvist had slept for only a few hours, having stayed up late to read a detective novel by Elizabeth George. Not a particularly sensible thing to do. Ove Levin, the newspaper guru from Serner Media, was due to present a strategy session for *Millennium* magazine later that morning and Blomkvist ought really to be rested and ready for combat.

But he had no desire to be sensible. Only reluctantly did he get up and make himself an unusually strong cappuccino with his Jura Impressa X7, a machine which had been delivered to his home a while ago with a note saying, "According to you, I don't know how to use it anyway". It stood there in the kitchen now like a memorial to a better time. He no longer had any contact with the person who had sent it.

These days he was hardly stimulated by his work. Over the weekend he had even considered looking around for something new, and that was a pretty drastic idea for a man like Mikael Blomkvist. *Millennium* had been his passion and his life, and many of his life's best, most dramatic events had occurred in connection with the magazine. But nothing lasts for ever, perhaps not even a love for *Millennium*. Besides, this was not a good time to be owning a magazine dedicated to investigative journalism. All publications with ambitions for greatness were bleeding to death, and he could not help but reflect that while his own vision for *Millennium* may have been beautiful and true on some higher plane, it would not necessarily help the magazine survive. He went into the living room sipping his coffee and looked out at the waters of Riddarfjärden. There was quite a storm blowing out there.

From an Indian summer, which had kept the city's outdoor restaurants and cafés open well into October, the weather had turned hellish with gusts of wind and cloudbursts, and people hurried through the streets bent double. Blomkvist had stayed in ~~~~~~~~~~~~~~~ only because of the weather. He had been

had been through a ~~~~~~~~~~~~~~ cial journalist William Borg had written a piece in ~~~~~~ *Business Life* magazine under the heading: MIKAEL BLOMKVIST'S DAYS ARE OVER.

The fact that the article had been written in the first place and given such prominence was of course a sign that Blomkvist's position was still strong. No-one would say that the column was well written or original, and it should have been easy to dismiss as yet another attack by a jealous colleague. But for some reason, incomprehensible in retrospect, the whole thing blew up. At first it might have been interpreted as a spirited discussion about journalism, but gradually the debate began to go off the rails. Although the serious press stayed out of it, all kinds of invective was being spewed out on social media. The offensive came not only from financial journalists and industry types, who had reason to set upon their enemy now that he was temporarily weakened, but also from a number of younger writers who took the opportunity to make a name for themselves. They pointed out that Blomkvist was not on Twitter or Facebook and should rather be seen as a relic of a bygone age in which people could afford to work their way through whichever strange old volumes happened to take their fancy. And there were those who took the opportunity to join in the fun and create amusing hashtags like #inblomkvistsday. It was all a lot of nonsense and nobody could have cared less than Blomkvist – or so he persuaded himself.

It certainly did not help his cause that he had not had a major story since the Zalachenko affair and that *Millennium* really was in a crisis. The circulation was still O.K., with 21,000 subscribers. But since advertising revenue was falling dramatically and there was now no longer additional income from their successful books, and since one of the shareholders, Harriet Vanger, was not willing to put up any more capital, the board of directors had, against Blomkvist's wishes, allowed the Norwegian Serner newspaper empire to buy 30 per cent of the shares. That was not as odd as it seemed, or not at first sight. Serner published weekly magazines and evening papers and owned a large online dating site and two pay-T.V. channels as well as a football team in Norway's top division, and it ought not to be having anything to do with a publication like *Millennium*.

But Serner's representatives – especially the head of publications Ove Levin – had assured them that the group needed a prestige product and that "everybody" in the management team admired *Millennium* and wanted only for the magazine to go on exactly as before. "We're not here to make money!" Levin said. "We want to do something significant." He immediately arranged for the magazine to receive a sizeable injection of funds.

At first Serner did not interfere on the editorial side. It was business as usual, but with a slightly better budget. A new feeling of hope spread among the editorial team, sometimes even to

Blomkvist, who felt that for once he would have time to devote himself to journalism instead of worrying about finances. But then, around the time the campaign against him got under way – he would never lose the suspicion that the Serner Group had taken advantage of the situation – the tone changed and they started to apply pressure.

Levin maintained that of course the magazine should continue with its in-depth investigations, its literary reporting, its social fervour, all of that stuff. But surely it was not necessary for all the .... financial irregularities, injustices and political .... Blomkvist did not .... the time. Six months earlier he had himself written a long .... about the paparazzi industry, and as long as he could find a serious angle then he was content to profile just about any lightweight. In fact he always said it isn't the subject that determines if it's good journalism, it's the reporter's attitude. No, what he objected to was what he sensed was there between the lines: that this was the beginning of a longer-term assault and that, to the group, *Millennium* was just like any other magazine, a publication you can damn well shift around any which way you want until it becomes profitable – and colourless.

So on Friday afternoon, when he heard that Levin had hired a consultant and commissioned several consumer surveys to present on Monday, Blomkvist had simply gone home. For a long time he had sat at his desk or lain in bed composing various impassioned speeches about why *Millennium* had to remain true to its vision: there is rioting in the suburbs; an openly racist party sits in

Riksdagen, the parliament; intolerance is growing; fascism is on the rise and there are homeless people and beggars everywhere. In so many ways Sweden has become a shameful nation. He came up with lots of fine and lofty words and in his daydreams he enjoyed a whole series of fantastic triumphs in which what he said was so relevant and compelling that all of the editorial team and even the entire Serner Group were roused from their delusions and decided to follow him as one.

But when sobriety set in, he realized how little weight such words carry if nobody believes in them from a financial point of view. Money talks, bullshit walks, and all that. First and foremost the magazine had to pay its way. Then they could go about changing the world. He began to wonder whether he could rustle up a good story. The prospect of a major revelation might boost the confidence of the editorial team and get them all to forget about Levin's surveys and forecasts.

Blomkvist's big scoop about the Swedish government conspiracy that had protected Zalachenko turned him into a news magnet. Every day he received tips about irregularities and shady dealings. Most of it, to tell the truth, was rubbish. But just occasionally an amazing story would emerge. A run-of-the-mill insurance matter or a trivial report of a missing person could be concealing something crucial. You never knew for sure. You had to be methodical and look through it all with an open mind, and so on the Saturday morning he sat down with his laptop and his notebooks and picked his way through what he had.

He kept going until 5.00 in the afternoon and he did come across the odd item which would probably have got him going ten years ago, but which did not now stir any enthusiasm. It was a classic problem; he of all people knew that. After a few decades in the profession most things feel pretty familiar, and even if something looks like a good story in intellectual terms it still might not turn you on. So when yet another squall of freezing rain whipped across the rooftops he stopped working and turned to Elizabeth George.

It wasn't just escapism, he persuaded himself. Sometimes the best ideas occur to you while your mind is occupied with something completely different. Pieces of the puzzle can suddenly fall into place. But he failed to come up with anything more constructive than the thought that he ought to spend more time lying around like this, reading good books. When Monday morning came and with it yet more foul weather he had ploughed through one and a half George novels plus three old copies of the *New*

of hell out there.

Icy, heavy, wet squalls bit into his bones as he hurried down towards Hornsgatan, which lay before him looking unusually grey. The whole of Södermalm district seemed to have been drained of all colour. Not even one tiny bright autumn leaf flew through the air. With his head bent forward and his arms crossed over his chest he continued past Maria Magdalena kyrka to Slussen, all the way until he turned right on to Götgatsbacken and as usual he slipped in between the Monki boutique and the Indigo pub, then went up to the magazine on the fourth floor, just above the offices of Greenpeace. He could already hear the buzz when he was in the stairwell.

An unusual number of people were up there. Apart from the editorial team and the key freelancers, there were three people from Serner, two consultants and Levin, Levin who had dressed down for the occasion. He no longer looked like an executive and had picked up some new expressions, among others a cheery "Hi".

"Hi, Micke, how's things?"

"That depends on you," Blomkvist said, not actually meaning to sound unfriendly.

But he could tell that it was taken as a declaration of war and he nodded stiffly, walked on in and sat down on one of the chairs which had been set out so as to make a small auditorium in the office.

Levin cleared his throat and looked nervously in Blomkvist's direction. The star reporter, who had seemed so combative in the doorway, now looked politely interested and showed no sign of wanting to have a row. But this did nothing to set Levin's mind at ease. Once upon a time he and Blomkvist had both temped for *Expressen*. They mostly wrote quick news stories and a whole lot of rubbish. But afterwards in the pub they had dreamed about the big scoops and talked for hours of how they would never be satisfied with the conventional or the shallow, but instead would always dig deep. They were young and ambitious and wanted it all, all at once. There were times when Levin missed that, not the salary, of course, or the working hours, or even the women and the easy life in the bars, but the dreams – he missed the power in them. He sometimes longed for that throbbing urge to change society and journalism and to write so that the world would come to a standstill and the mighty powers bow down. Even a hotshot like himself wondered: *Where did the dreams go?*

Micke Blomkvist had of course made every single one of them come true, not just because he had been responsible for some of the big exposés of modern times, but also because he really wrote with that passion and power that they had fantasized about. Never once had he bowed to pressure from the establishment or compromised his ideals, whereas Levin himself . . . Well, really *he* was the one with the big career, wasn't he? He was probably making ten times as much as Blomkvist these days and that gave him an enormous amount of pleasure. What use were Blomkvist's scoops when he couldn't even buy himself a country place nicer than that little shack on the island of Sandhamn? My God, what was that hut compared to a new house in Cannes? Nothing! No, it was he who had chosen the right path.

Instead of slogging it out in the daily press, Levin had taken ̶ ̶ ̶ ̶ ̶ ̶nalyst at Serner and developed a personal rela- ̶ ̶ ̶ ̶lf, and that had changed his ̶ ̶ ̶ ̶ ̶ ̶ ̶ ̶ ̶ournalist

but still. He wa̶ ̶ ̶ ̶ ̶ ̶ ̶ ̶ ̶ Blomkvist, and that was probab̶ly̶ ̶ ̶ ̶ ̶ for the group to buy a stake in *Millennium*. A little bi̶r̶ ̶ him that the magazine was up against it and that the editor-in-chief, Erika Berger, whom he had always secretly fancied, wanted to keep on her two latest recruits, Sofie Melker and Emil Grandén, and she would not be able to do so unless they got some fresh capital.

In short, Levin had seen an unexpected opportunity to buy into one of the most prestigious brands in Swedish media. But Serner's management was not enthusiastic, to put it mildly. On the contrary, people were heard to mutter that *Millennium* was old-fashioned and had a left-wing bias and a tendency to end up in fights with important advertisers and business partners. The plan would have come to nothing if Levin had not argued his case so passionately. But he had insisted. In a broader context, he argued, investing in *Millennium* represented a negligible amount, which might not yield vast profits but which could give them something much greater, namely credibility. Right now, after the cutbacks and blood-letting, Serner's reputation wasn't exactly their prime asset. Taking a stake in *Millennium* would be a sign that the group did after all care about journalism and freedom of expression, even if Serner's board was not conspicuously keen on either. This much they were able to understand, and Levin got his acquisition through. For a long time it looked like a winning outcome for all parties.

Serner got good publicity and *Millennium* kept its staff and was able to concentrate on what it did best: carefully researched, well-written reportage, with Levin himself beaming like the sun and even taking part in a debate at the Writers' Club, where he said in his usual modest way, "I believe in virtuous enterprise. I have always fought for investigative journalism."

But then . . . he did not want to think about it. At first he was not really bothered by the campaign against Blomkvist. Ever since his former colleague's meteoric rise in the reporting firmament, Levin had rejoiced secretly whenever Blomkvist was sneered at in the media. This time, though, his joy did not last. Serner's young son Thorvald became aware of the commotion – social media made a big thing of it – even though he was not a man who took any interest in what journalists had to say. But he did like power and he loved to intrigue, and here he saw a chance to score some points or simply to give the older generation on the board a good drubbing. Before long he had encouraged the C.E.O. – who until quite recently had not concerned himself with such trivial matters – to declare that *Millennium* could not be given special treatment, but would have to adapt to the new times like all of the other products in the group.

Levin, who had just given Berger a solemn promise that he would not interfere in the editorial line, save perhaps as a "friend and adviser", all of a sudden felt that his hands were tied and he was forced to play some intricate games behind the scenes. He did everything he could to get Berger, Malin Eriksson and Christer Malm at the magazine to buy into the new policy, which was never in fact clearly expressed – something that flares up in a panic rarely is – but which somehow entailed making *Millennium* younger and more commercial.

Naturally Levin kept repeating that there could be no question of compromising the magazine's soul and provocative attitude, even if he was not sure what he meant by that. He only knew that to keep the directors happy he needed to get more glamour

~~~~~~~~ and reduce the number of lengthy investiga-

~~~~~~~~~~~~~~~~~~~~~~~~ dvertisers

wearing ~~~~~~~~
head office. He had instead opted for jeans, a white ~~~~~ dark-blue V-necked pullover which was not even cashmere. His long curly hair – which had always been his rebellious little gimmick – was tied in a ponytail, just like the edgiest journalists on T.V. But most important of all he kicked off in the humble tone he had been taught to adopt on his management courses.

"Hello, everybody," he said. "What foul weather! I've said it many times before, but I'm happy to repeat it: we at Serner are incredibly proud to be accompanying you on this journey, and for me personally it amounts to more even than that. It's the commitment to magazines like *Millennium* which makes my job meaningful; it reminds me why I went into this profession in the first place. Micke, do you remember how we used to sit in the Opera Bar and dream about everything we were going to achieve together? And we weren't exactly holding back on the booze, ha ha!"

Blomkvist did not look as if he remembered. But Levin was not to be put off.

"Don't worry, I'm not going to get all nostalgic," he said, "and there's no reason to do so. In those days there was much more money in our industry. Just to cover some piddling little murder in the middle of nowhere we would hire a helicopter and book an entire floor at the poshest hotel, and order champagne for the after party. You know, when I was about to go off on my first overseas trip I asked Ulf Nilson, foreign correspondent at the time, what the deutschmark exchange rate was. 'I have no idea,' he said, 'I set my own exchange rate.' Ha ha! So at the time we used to pad our expenses, do you remember, Micke? Maybe we were at our most creative back then. In any case, our job was just to knock out some quick copy and we still managed to sell any number of issues. But a lot has changed since then – we all know that. We now face cut-throat competition and it's not easy these days to make a profit in journalism, not even if you have Sweden's best editorial team, as you do. So I thought we should talk a little bit today about the challenges of the future. Not that I imagine for one moment that I can teach you anything. I'm just going to provide you with some context for discussion. We at Serner have commissioned some surveys about your readership and the public perception of *Millennium*. Some of it may give you a bit of a fright. But instead of letting it get you down you should see it as a challenge, and remember, there are some totally crazy changes happening out there."

Levin paused for a moment and wondered if the term "totally crazy" had been a mistake, if he had tried too hard to appear relaxed and youthful, and whether he had started off in too chatty and jocular a vein. As Haakon Serner would say, "It is impossible to overestimate how humourless underpaid journalists can be." But no, he decided, I'll fix this.

I'll get them on my side!

*

Blomkvist had stopped listening more or less at the point when Levin explained that they all needed to reflect on their "digital maturity", and so he didn't hear them being told that the younger generation were not really aware of *Millennium* or Mikael Blomkvist. Unfortunately that was precisely the moment at which he decided he had had enough and went out to the coffee room. So he had no idea either that Aron Ullman, the Norwegian ...te openly said, "Pathetic. Is he so scared that he's

...d Blomkvist less at that

...surveys

felt right an...
was blowing. For a time h...
how long it would take before Berger ca...

The answer was about two minutes. He tried to ca... angry she was by the sound of her heels. But when she was standing next to him she only gave him a dejected smile.

"What's going on?" she said.

"I just couldn't bear to listen."

"You do realize that people feel incredibly uncomfortable when you behave like that?"

"I do."

"And I assume you also understand that Serner can do nothing without our agreement. We still have control."

"Like hell we do. We're their hostages, Ricky! Don't you get it? If we don't do as they say they'll withdraw their support and then we'll be sitting there with our arses hanging out," he said, loudly and angrily. When Berger hushed him and shook her head he added sotto voce, "I'm sorry. I'm being a brat. But I'm going home now. I need to think."

"You've begun to work extremely short hours."

"Well, I reckon I'm owed a fair bit of overtime."

"I suppose you are. Would you like company this evening?"

"I don't know. I honestly don't know, Erika," he said, and then he left the magazine offices and went out onto Götgatsbacken.

The storm and the freezing rain lashed against him and he swore, and for a moment considered dashing into Pocketshop to buy yet another English detective novel to escape into. Instead he turned into Sankt Paulsgatan and as he was passing the sushi restaurant on the right-hand side his mobile rang. He was sure that it would be Berger. But it was Pernilla, his daughter, who had certainly chosen the worst possible time to get in touch with a father who already felt bad about how little he did for her.

"Hello, my darling," he said.

"What's that noise?"

"It's the storm, I expect."

"O.K., O.K., I'll be quick. I've been accepted on the writing course at Biskops Arnö school."

"So, now you want to be a writer," he said, in a tone which was too harsh and almost sarcastic, and that was unfair in every way.

He should have simply congratulated her and wished her luck, but Pernilla had had so many difficult years hopping between one Christian sect and another, and from one course to another without finishing anything, that he felt exhausted by yet another change of direction.

"I don't think I detected a whoop of joy there."

"Sorry, Pernilla. I'm not myself today."

"When are you ever?"

"I'm just not sure writing is such a good idea, given how the profession is looking right now. I only want you to find something that will really work for you."

24

"I'm not going to write boring journalism like you."

"Well, what are you going to write then?"

"I'm going to write for real."

"O.K.," he said, without asking what she meant by that. "Do you have enough money?"

"I'm working part-time at Wayne's Coffee."

"Would you like to come to dinner tonight, so we can talk about

Pappa. It was just to let you know," she said,

the positive side in her

across

existence where he

fingers to the bone. For a brief mom...

place up. There were magazines and books and clo...

where. But instead he fetched two Pilsner Urquells from the fridge and sat down on the sofa in the living room to think everything through more soberly, as soberly as one can with a bit of beer in one's body.

What was he to do?

He had no idea, and most worrying of all was that he was in no mood for a fight. On the contrary, he was strangely resigned, as if *Millennium* were slipping out of his sphere of interest. Isn't it time to do something new? he asked himself, and he thought of Kajsa Åkerstam, a quite charming person whom he would occasionally meet for a few drinks. Åkerstam was head of Swedish Television's "Investigative Taskforce" programme and she had been trying to recruit him for years. It had never mattered what she had offered, and how solemnly she had guaranteed backing and total integrity. *Millennium* had been his home and his soul.

But now . . . maybe he should take the chance. Perhaps a job on "Investigative Taskforce" would fire him up again.

His mobile rang and for a moment he was happy. Whether it was Berger or Pernilla, he promised himself he would be friendly and really listen. But no, it was a withheld number and he answered guardedly.

"Is that Mikael Blomkvist?" said a young-sounding voice.

"Yes," he said.

"Do you have time to talk?"

"I might if you introduced yourself."

"My name is Linus Brandell."

"O.K., Linus, how can I help?"

"I have a story for you."

"Tell me."

"I will if you can drag yourself down to the Bishops Arms across the street and meet me there."

Blomkvist was irritated. It wasn't just the bossy tone. It was the intrusion on his home turf.

"The telephone will do just fine."

"It's not something which should be discussed on an open line."

"Why do I feel so tired when I talk to you, Linus?"

"Maybe you've had a bad day."

"I *have* had a bad day. You're right about that."

"There you go. Come down to the Bishop and I'll buy you a beer and tell you something amazing."

Blomkvist wanted only to snap: "Stop telling me what to do!" Yet without knowing why, or perhaps because he didn't have anything better to do than to sit in his attic apartment and brood over his future he said, "I pay for my own beers. But O.K., I'm coming."

"A wise decision."

"But, Linus . . ."

"Yes?"

"If you get long-winded and give me a load of wild conspiracy theories to the effect that Elvis is alive and you know who shot Olof Palme, then I'm coming straight home."

"Fair enough," Brandell said.

CHAPTER 3

20.xi

Edwin Needham – Ed the Ned, as he was sometimes called – was not the most highly paid security technician in the U.S., but he may have been the best. He grew up in Dorchester, Boston, and his father had been a monumental good-for-nothing, a drunk who took on casual work in the harbour but often disappeared on binges which not infrequently landed him in jail or in hospital. Yet these benders were the family's best time, a sort of breathing space. When Ed's father could be bothered to be around he would beat his mother black and blue. Sometimes she would spend hours or even whole days locked inside the toilet, crying and shaking. Nobody was very surprised when she died from internal bleeding at only forty-six, or when Ed's older sister became a crack addict, still less when the remains of the family stood teetering on the brink of homelessness soon afterwards.

Ed's childhood paved the way for a life of trouble, and during his teenage years he belonged to a gang who called themselves "The Fuckers". They were the terror of Dorchester, and engaged in gang warfare, assault and robbing grocery stores. There was something brutal about Ed's appearance from an early age and this was not improved by the fact that he never smiled and was missing two upper teeth. He was sturdy, tall and fearless, and his face usually bore the traces of brawls with his father or gang fights.

Most of the teachers at his school were scared to death of him. All were convinced that he would end up in jail or with a bullet in his head. But there were some adults who began to take an interest in him – no doubt because they discovered that there was more than aggression and violence in his intense blue eyes.

Ed had an irrepressible thirst for knowledge, an energy which meant that he could devour a book with the same vigour with which he could trash the inside of a public bus. Often he was _____ at the end of the school day. He liked to stay _____ logy room, where there were _____ A physics

He began to ex_____ and distinctions and eventually _____ of the odds against him – he went on to study Electri_____ and Computer Science at M.I.T. In his doctoral thesis he explored some specific fears around new asymmetric cryptosystems like R.S.A., and he then went on to senior positions at Microsoft and Cisco before being recruited by the National Security Agency at Fort Meade in Maryland.

He did not have the ideal C.V. for the job, even leaving aside his criminal behaviour as a teenager. He had smoked a lot of grass at college and flirted with socialist or even anarchist ideals, and had been arrested twice for assault – nothing major, just bar fights. He still had a volcanic temper and everyone who knew him thought better of crossing him.

But at the N.S.A. they recognized his other qualities. Besides which it was the autumn of 2001. The American security services were so desperate for computer technicians that they hired pretty much anybody. During the ensuing years nobody questioned

Needham's loyalty – or patriotism, for that matter – and if anyone thought to do so, his advantages always outweighed his shortcomings.

Needham was not just amazingly gifted. There was an obsessive streak to his character, a manic precision and a furious efficiency which boded well for a man in charge of building I.T. security at America's most highly classified agency. Nobody was damn well going to crack his system. It was a matter of personal pride for him. At Fort Meade he quickly made himself indispensable, to the point where people were constantly lining up to consult him. Not a few were terrified of him and he was often verbally abusive. He had even told the head of the N.S.A. himself, the legendary Admiral Charles O'Connor, to go to hell.

"Use your own busy fucking head for things you might just be able to comprehend," Needham had roared when the admiral attempted to comment on his work.

But O'Connor and everyone else let it happen. They knew that Needham screamed and yelled for the right reasons – because colleagues had been careless about security regulations, or because they were talking about things beyond their understanding. Not once did he interfere in the rest of the agency's work, even though his level of clearance gave him access to pretty much everything, and even though in recent years the agency had found itself at the centre of a heated storm of opinion with advocates of both the right and the left seeing the N.S.A. as the devil incarnate, as Orwell's Big Brother. As far as Needham was concerned, the organization could do whatever the hell it wanted, so long as his security systems remained rigorous and intact. And since he did not yet have a family he more or less lived at the office.

Apart from the occasional drinking session, during which he sometimes turned alarmingly sentimental about his past, there was no suggestion that he had ever told outsiders what he was working on. In that other world he remained as silent as the grave and, if ever questioned about his profession, he stuck to a well-rehearsed cover story.

It was not by chance, nor was it the result of intrigue or manipulation, that he had risen through the ranks and become the N.S.A.'s most senior security chief. Needham and his team had tightened internal surveillance "so that no new whistle-blowers ... up and punch us on the nose" and during countless sleep-... thing he alternately called "an unbreakable ..."

... in there

... had put on quite a ... the coffee machine in his charac... seniority he completely ignored dress codes. He w... jeans and a red-checked lumberjack shirt, not quite buttoned at the waist, and he sighed as he settled down at his computer. He was not feeling great. His back and right knee hurt and he cursed the fact that his long-time colleague, Alona Casales, had managed to persuade him to come out for a run the night before. Sheer sadism on her part.

Luckily there was nothing super-urgent to deal with. He only had to send an internal memo with some new procedures for those in charge of C.O.S.T., a programme for cooperation with the large I.T. companies – he had even changed the codenames. But he did not get far. He was just beginning to write, in his usual turgid prose:

```
<So that no-one will be tempted to fall back
into idiotic habits again, but instead to
keep you all on your toes as good paranoid
```

```
cyber-agents, I would just like to point
out...>
```
when he was interrupted by one of his alerts.

He was not particularly worried. His warning systems were so sensitive that they reacted to the slightest divergence in the information flow. It was going to be an anomaly, a notification perhaps that someone was trying to exceed the limits of their authorization, or some minor interference.

As it turned out, he never had time to investigate. In the next moment something so uncanny happened that for several seconds he refused to believe it. He just sat there, staring at the screen. Yet he knew exactly what was going on. A R.A.T. had got into the NSANet intranet. Anywhere else he would have thought: *Those fuckers, I'll crush them*. But in here, the most tightly closed and controlled place of all, which he and his team had gone over with a fine-toothed comb a million times just this last year to detect every minuscule little vulnerability, here, no, no, it was impossible – it could not be happening.

Without realizing it he had closed his eyes, as if hoping that it would all vanish so long as he wasn't watching. But when he looked at the screen again, the sentence he had begun was being completed. His `<I would just like to point out>` was continuing on its own with the words `<that you should stop with all the illegal activity. Actually it's pretty straightforward. Those who spy on the people end up themselves being spied on by the people. There's a fundamental democratic logic to it.>`

"Jesus, Jesus," he muttered – which was at least a sign that he was beginning to recover some of his composure.

But then the text went on: `<Chill out, Ed. Why don't you stick around for a ride? I've got Root>` at which point he gave a loud cry. The word "Root" brought down his whole world. For about a minute, as the computer raced through the most confidential parts of the system at lightning speed, he genuinely believed that he was going to have a heart attack. He was only vaguely aware that people were beginning to gather around his desk.

There was not much of a crowd down at the Bishops Arms. The weather was not encouraging people to venture out, not even to the local pub. Blomkvist was nevertheless met by shouts and laughter, and by a hoarse voice bawling:

"Mikael Blomkvist,

Arne and his friends laughed as if Blomkvist the biggest joke of all.

"Got any good scoops?" Arne said.

"I'm thinking about blowing wide open the whole murky scene at the Bishops Arms."

"You reckon Sweden's ready for a story like that?"

"No, probably not."

In truth Blomkvist quite liked this crowd, not that he ever talked to them more than in throw-away lines and banter. But these men were a part of the local scene which made him feel at home in the area, and he was not in the least bit offended when one of them shot out, "I've heard that you're washed up."

Far from upsetting him, it brought the whole campaign against him down to the low, almost farcical level where it belonged.

"I've been washed up for the last fifteen years, hello to you brother bottle, all good things must pass," he said, quoting the poet Fröding and looking around for someone who might have had the gall to order a tired journalist down to the pub. Since he saw no-one apart from Arne and his gang he went up to Amir at the bar.

Amir was big and fat and jolly, a hard-working father of four who had been running the pub for some years. He and Blomkvist had become good friends. Not because Blomkvist was an especially regular customer, but because they had helped each other out in completely different ways; once or twice when Blomkvist had not had the time to get to the state liquor store and was expecting female company, Amir had supplied him with a couple of bottles of red wine, and Blomkvist in turn had helped a friend of Amir's, who had no papers, to write letters to the authorities.

"To what do we owe this honour?" Amir said.

"I'm meeting someone."

"Anyone exciting?"

"I don't think so. How's Sara?"

Sara was Amir's wife and had just had a hip operation.

"Complaining and taking painkillers."

"Sounds like hard work. Give her my best."

"Will do," Amir said, and they chatted about this and that.

But Linus Brandell did not show up and Blomkvist thought it was probably a practical joke. On the other hand there were worse tricks than to have someone lure you down to your local pub, so he stayed for fifteen minutes discussing a number of financial and health-related concerns before he turned and walked towards the door, and that was when Brandell appeared.

Nobody understood how Gabriella Grane had ended up at Säpo, Swedish Security Police, least of all she herself. She had been the sort of girl for whom everybody had predicted a glittering future. Her old girlfriends from the classy suburb of Djursholm worried that she was thirty-three and neither famous nor wealthy nor married, either to a rich man or to any man at all for that matter.

"What's happened to you, Gabriella? Are you going to be a police officer all your life?"

Most of the time she could not be bothered to argue back, or point out that she was not a police officer but had been head-hunted for the position of analyst, and that these days she was writing far more challenging texts than she ever had at the Foreign Ministry or during her summers as a leader writer for

~~...~~ from which, she was not allowed to talk

~~...~~ quiet and

who went after ~~Kurds~~

racist reasons, and who had no qualms about committing

crimes or infringements of civil rights in order to protect former senior Soviet spies. And indeed sometimes she was on their side. There was incompetence in the organization, and values that were unsound, and the Zalachenko affair remained a major blot. But that was not the whole truth. Stimulating and important work was being done as well, especially now after the shake-out, and sometimes she had the impression that it was at Säpo, not in any editorial or lecture hall, that people best understood the upheavals that were taking place across the world. But of course she often asked herself: *How did I end up here, and why have I stayed?*

Presumably some of it was down to flattery. No less a person than Helena Kraft, the newly appointed chief of Säpo at the time, had contacted her and said that after all the disasters and bad press they had to rethink their approach to recruitment. We need to "bring on board the real talents from the universities and, quite honestly Gabriella, there's no better person than you," and that was all it had taken.

Grane was hired as an analyst in counter-espionage and later in the Industry Protection Group. Even though as a young woman, attractive in a slightly proper sort of way, she got called a "daddy's girl" and "snotty upper-class bitch", she was a star recruit, quick and receptive and able to think outside the box. And she could speak Russian. She had learned it alongside her studies at the Stockholm School of Economics, where needless to say she had been a model student but never that keen. She dreamed of something bigger than a life in business, so after her graduation she applied for a job at the Foreign Ministry and of course was accepted. But she did not find that especially stimulating either – the diplomats were too stiff and neatly combed. It was then that Helena Kraft had got in touch. Grane had been at Säpo for five years now and had gradually been accepted for the talent that she was, even if it was not always easy.

It had been a trying day, and not just because of the ghastly weather. The head of division, Ragnar Olofsson, had appeared in her office looking surly and humourless and told her that she should damn well not be flirting when she was out on an assignment.

"Flirting?"

"Flowers have been delivered."

"And that's my fault?"

"Yes, I do think you have a responsibility there. When we're out in the field we have to show discipline and reserve at all times. We represent an absolutely key public agency."

"Well, that's great, Ragnar dear. One always learns something from you. Now I finally understand that I'm responsible for the fact that the head of research at Ericsson can't tell the difference between normal polite behaviour and flirting. Now I realize that I should blame myself when men indulge in such wildly wishful thinking that they see a sexual invitation in a simple smile."

"Don't be stupid," Olofsson said, and he disappeared. Later she regretted having answered back.

That kind of outburst rarely does any good. On the other hand, she had been taking shit for far too long. It was time to stand up for herself. She quickly tidied her desk and got out a report from G.C.H.Q. in Britain about Russian industrial espionage against European software companies, which she had not yet had time to read. Then the telephone rang. It was Kraft, and that made Grane happy. She had never yet called to complain or moan. On the

. . . . . . call from

on the person who . . . . .
way, says that she knows you."

"Put me through."

It was Alona Casales at the N.S.A. – although for a moment Grane wondered if it really *was* her. When they had last met, at a conference in Washington D.C., Casales had been a self-assured and charismatic lecturer in what she somewhat euphemistically described as active-signals surveillance – hacking, in other words. Afterwards she and Grane had gone out for drinks, and almost against her will, Grane had been enchanted. Casales smoked cigarillos and had a dark and sensuous voice well-suited to her punchy one-liners and frequent sexual allusions. But now on the telephone she sounded confused and sometimes unaccountably lost the thread of what she was saying.

Blomkvist did not really know what to expect, a fashionable young man, presumably, some cool dude. But the fellow who had arrived looked like a tramp, short and with torn jeans and long, dark, unwashed hair and something slightly sleepy and shifty in his eyes. He was maybe twenty-five, perhaps younger, had bad skin and a fringe which concealed his eyes and a rather ugly mouth sore. Linus Brandell did not look like someone who was sitting on a major scoop.

"Linus Brandell, I presume."

"That's right. Sorry I'm late. Happened to bump into a girl I knew. We were in the same class in ninth grade, and she—"

"Let's get this over with," Blomkvist interrupted him, and led the way to a table towards the back of the pub.

When Amir appeared, smiling discreetly, they ordered two pints of Guinness and then sat quietly for a few seconds. Blomkvist could not understand why he felt so irritated. It was not like him; perhaps the whole drama with Serner was getting to him after all. He smiled towards Arne and his gang, all of whom were studying them keenly.

"I'll come straight to the point," Brandell said.

"That sounds good."

"Do you know Supercraft?"

Blomkvist did not know much about computer games. But even he had heard of Supercraft.

"By name, yes."

"No more than that?"

"No."

"In that case you won't know that what makes this game different, or at least so special, is that it has a particular A.I. function that allows you to communicate with a player about war strategy without being really sure, at least to begin with, whether it's a real person or a digital creation that you're talking to."

"You don't say," Blomkvist said. He couldn't care less about the finer points of a damn computer game.

"It's a minor revolution in the industry and I was actually involved in developing it," Brandell said.

"Congratulations. In that case you must have made a killing."

"That's just it."

"Meaning what?"

"The technology was stolen from us and now Truegames are making billions while we don't get a single öre."

Blomkvist had heard this line before. He had even spoken to an old lady who claimed that it was actually she who had written the Harry Potter books and that J.K. Rowling had stolen everything

Brandell hesitated.

"Yes?"

"Nothing. But even the Security Police were involved – you can talk to Gabriella Grane there. She's an analyst and I think she'll back me up. She has also mentioned the incident in a public report published last year. I have the reference number here . . ."

"In other words, this isn't news," Blomkvist interrupted.

"No, not in that sense. *New Technology* and *Computer Sweden* wrote about it. But since Frans didn't want to talk about it and on a couple of occasions even denied that there had been any breach at all, the story never went very far."

"But it's still old news."

"I suppose so."

"So why should I be listening to you, Linus?"

"Because now Frans seems to have understood what happened. I think he's sitting on pure dynamite. He's become completely manic about security. Only uses hyper-encryption for his phones and email and he's just got a new burglar alarm with cameras and sensors and all that crap. I think you should talk to him – that's why I got in touch with you. A guy like you can perhaps get him to open up. He doesn't listen to me."

"So you order me down here because it seems as if someone called Frans may be sitting on some dynamite."

"Not someone called Frans, Blomkvist, it's none other than Frans Balder; didn't I say that? I was one of his assistants."

Blomkvist searched his memory: the only Balder he could think of was Hanna Balder, the actress, whatever might have become of her.

"Who's he?" he said.

The look he got was so full of contempt that he was taken aback.

"Where've you been living? Mars? Frans Balder is a legend. A household name."

"Really?"

"Christ, yes!" Brandell said. "Google him and you'll see. He became a professor of computer sciences at just twenty-seven and for two decades he's been a leading authority on research in artificial intelligence. There's hardly anyone who's as far advanced in the development of quantum computing and neural networks. He has an amazingly cool, back-to-front brain. Thinks along completely unorthodox, ground-breaking lines, and as you can probably imagine the computer industry's been chasing him for years. But for a long time Balder refused to let himself be recruited. He wanted to work alone. Well, not altogether alone – he's always had assistants whom he's driven into the ground. He wants results, and he's always saying: 'Nothing is impossible. Our job is to push back the frontiers, blah blah blah.' But people listen to him. They'll do anything for him. They'll just about die for him. To us nerds he is God Almighty."

"I can hear that."

"But don't think that I'm some star-struck admirer, not at all. There's a price to be paid, I know that better than anyone. You can do great things with him. But you can also go to pieces. Balder isn't even allowed to look after his own son. He messed up in some unforgivable way. There are a lot of different stories, assistants who've hit the wall and wrecked their lives and God knows what. But although he's always been obsessive he's never behaved like this before. I just know he's onto something big."

"You just know that."

"You've got to understand, he's not normally a paranoid

probably thought that we should get to work on something that we liked. But his A.I. program was also right for that business. It was a perfect testing environment and we got fantastic results. We broke new ground. It was just that—"

"Get to the point, Linus."

"The thing is that Frans and his lawyers wrote a patent application for the most innovative parts of the technology, and that's when the first shock came. A Russian engineer at Truegames had thrown together an application just before, which blocked our patent, and that can hardly have been a coincidence. But that didn't really matter. The patent was only a paper tiger. The interesting thing was how the hell they had managed to find out about what we'd been doing. Since we were all devoted to Frans even to the point of death, there was actually only one possibility: we must have been hacked, in spite of all our security measures."

"Is that when you got in touch with the Security Police and the National Defence Radio Establishment?"

"Not at first. Balder is not too keen on people who wear ties and work from nine to five. He prefers obsessive idiots who are glued to their computers all night long, so instead he got in touch with some weirdo hacker he had met somewhere and she said straight away that we'd had a breach. Not that she seemed particularly credible. I wouldn't have hired her, if you see what I mean, and perhaps she was just talking drivel. But her main conclusions were nevertheless subsequently borne out by people at the N.D.R.E."

"But no-one knew who had hacked you?"

"No, no, trying to trace hacker breaches is often a complete waste of time. But they must have been professionals. We had done a lot of work on our I.T. security."

"And now you suspect that Balder may have found out something more about it?"

"Definitely. Otherwise he wouldn't be behaving so strangely. I'm convinced he got wind of something at Solifon."

"Is that where he worked?"

"Yes, oddly enough. As I told you before, Balder had previously refused to let himself be tied up by the big computer giants. No-one has ever banged on as much as he did about being an outsider, about the importance of being independent and not being a slave to commercial forces. But out of the blue, as we stood there with our trousers down and our technology stolen, he suddenly took up an offer from Solifon, of all companies, and nobody could understand it. O.K., they were offering a mega-salary, free rein and all of that crap: like, do whatever the hell you want, but work for us, and that probably sounded cool. It would definitely have been cool for anyone who wasn't Frans Balder. But he'd had any number of offers like that from Google, Apple and all the others. Why was this suddenly so interesting? He never explained. He just took his clobber and disappeared, and from what I've heard it went swimmingly at first. Balder continued to develop our technology and I think the owner, Nicolas Grant, was beginning to fantasize about revenues in billions. There was great excitement. But then something happened."

"Something that you don't actually know so much about."

"No, we lost contact. Balder lost contact with pretty much everyone. But I understand enough to know that it must have been something serious. He had always preached openness and enthused about the Wisdom of Crowds, all that stuff: the impor-

the whole Linux way of

seems to be under pressure and who doesn't care what he looks like – though it's not clear how the neighbours can see that, if he never goes outside?"

"Yes, but I think—"

"Listen, this could be an interesting story, I get that. But unfortunately it isn't for me. I'm no I.T. reporter – as someone so wisely wrote the other day, I'm a caveman. I'd recommend you contact Raoul Sigvardsson at the *Svenska Morgon-Posten*. He knows everything about that world."

"No, no, Sigvardsson is a lightweight. This is way above his head."

"I think you underestimate him."

"Come on now, don't chicken out. This could be your comeback, Blomkvist."

Blomkvist made a tired gesture towards Amir, who was wiping a table not far from them.

"Can I give you some advice?" Blomkvist said.

"What . . .? Yes . . . sure."

"Next time you have a story to sell, don't try to explain to the reporter what's in it for him. Do you know how many times people have played me that tune? 'This is going to be the biggest thing in your career. Bigger than Watergate!' You'd do better with just some basic matter-of-fact information, Linus."

"I just meant . . ."

"Yes, what actually *did* you mean?"

"That you should talk to him. I think he would like you. You're the same uncompromising kind of guy."

It was as if Brandell had suddenly lost his self-confidence and Blomkvist wondered if he had not been unnecessarily tough. As a general principle, he tended to be friendly and encouraging towards people who gave him tip-offs, however weird they sounded, not just because there might be a good story even in something that sounded crazy, but also because he recognized that often he was their last resort. There were many who turned to him when everyone else had stopped listening. He was the last hope, and there was never any excuse to be scornful.

"Listen," he said. "I've had a really bad day and I didn't mean to sound sarcastic."

"That's O.K."

"And you know," Blomkvist said, "there is actually one thing which interests me about this story. You said you had a visit from a female hacker."

Alona Casales was not one to become nervous easily and she rarely had trouble staying on topic. She was forty-eight, tall and outspoken, with a voluptuous figure and small intelligent eyes which could make anybody feel insecure. She often seemed to see straight through people and did not suffer from a surfeit of deference to superiors. She would give anyone a dressing down, even the Attorney General if he came calling. That was one of the reasons why Ed the Ned got on so well with her. Neither of them attached much importance to status; all they cared about was ability.

Nevertheless, she had completely lost it with the head of Sweden's Security Police. This had absolutely nothing to do with Helena Kraft, it was because of the drama unfolding in the open-
... office behind her. Admittedly they were all used to Needham's
... But something told her right away that what
... different scale.

... blurting

... say
to Gabriella Grane,
met and tried to seduce in Washing...
not succeeded in taking her to bed, she had been ...
feeling of pleasure.

"Hello, my dear," she said. "How are you?"

"Not so bad," Grane answered. "We're having some terrible storms, but otherwise everything's fine."

"I really enjoyed that last time we saw each other."

"Absolutely, it was nice. I was hungover the whole of the next day. But I don't suppose you're calling to ask me out."

"Unfortunately not. I'm calling because we've picked up signs of a serious threat to a Swedish scientist."

"Who?"

"For a long time we had trouble understanding the information, or even working out which country it concerned. The communication was encrypted and used only vague codenames, but still, using a few small pieces of the puzzle we managed . . . what the *hell* . . .?"

"What?"

"One second . . .!"

Casales' computer screen blinked, then went blank, and as far as she could see the same thing was happening all over the office floor. For a moment she wondered what to do, but carried on the conversation; it might just be a power outage, after all, although the overhead lights seemed to be working.

"I'm still here," Grane said.

"Thanks, I appreciate it. Sorry about this. It's complete chaos here. Where was I?"

"You were talking about pieces of the puzzle."

"Right, yes, we put two and two together, because there's always one person who's careless, however professional they try to be, or who . . ."

"Yes?"

"Um . . . talks, gives an address or something, in this case it was more like . . ."

Casales fell silent again. None other than Commander Jonny Ingram, one of the most senior people in the N.S.A. with contacts high up in the White House, had come onto the office floor. Ingram was trying to appear as composed as usual. He even cracked some joke to a group sitting further away. But he was not fooling anyone. Beneath his polished and tanned exterior – ever since his time as head of the cryptological centre on Oahu he was suntanned all year round – you could sense something nervous in his expression, and now he seemed to want everybody's attention.

"Hello, are you still there?" Grane said on the other end of the line.

"I'm going to have to leave you unfortunately. I'll call you back," Casales said, and hung up. At that moment she became very worried indeed.

There was a feeling in the air that something terrible had happened, maybe another major terrorist attack. But Ingram carried on with his soothing act and, even though there was sweat on his upper lip and forehead, he kept repeating that it was nothing serious. Most likely a virus, he said, which had found its way into the intranet, despite all the security precautions.

"To be on the safe side, we've shut down our servers," he said, and for a moment he really did manage to calm things down. "What the hell," people seemed to be saying. "A virus isn't such ~~a big deal.~~

~~...~~ started spouting such vague statements that ~~...~~ shouting:

~~...~~

"Is it the Iranian ~~...~~

"We think—" Ingram said.

He got no further. Ed Needham, the one who should ~~...~~ standing there in the first place, explaining what was happening, interrupted him brusquely and got to his feet, a bear of a man, and at that moment there was no denying that he was an imposing sight. Gone was the deflated Ed from a minute before; he now exuded a tremendous sense of determination.

"No," he hissed. "It's a hacker, a fucking super-hacker, and I'm going to cut his balls off."

"The female hacker doesn't really have anything to do with this story," Brandell said, nursing his beer. "She was probably more like Balder's social project."

"But she seemed to know her stuff."

"Or she was just lucky. She talked a lot of rubbish."

"So you met her?"

"Yes, just after Balder took off for Silicon Valley."

"How long ago was that?"

"Almost a year. I'd moved our computers into my apartment on Brantingsgatan. My life was not great, to put it mildly. I was single and broke and hungover, my place looked like hell. I had just spoken to Balder on the telephone, and he'd been going on like some boring old dad. There was a lot of: don't judge her by how she looks, appearances can be deceptive, blah blah and hey, he said that to *me*! I'm not exactly the ideal son-in-law myself. I've never worn a jacket and tie in my entire life, and if anyone knows what people look like in the hacker community, then I do. Whatever, so I was sitting there waiting for this girl. Thought that she would at least knock. But she just opened the door and walked in."

"What did she look like?"

"Bloody awful . . . but then, she was also sexy in a weird way. But dreadful!"

"Linus, I'm not asking you to rate her looks. I just want to know what she was wearing and if she maybe mentioned what her name was."

"I have no idea who she was," Brandell said, "although I did recognize her from somewhere – I had the feeling that it was something bad. She was tattooed and pierced and all that crap and looked like a heavy rocker or goth or punk, plus she was as thin as hell."

Hardly aware that he was doing it, Blomkvist gestured to Amir to pull him another Guinness.

"What happened?" he said.

"Well, what can I say? I guess I thought that we didn't have to get going right away, so I sat down on my bed – there wasn't much else to sit on – and suggested that we might have a drink or some-thing first. But do you know what she did then? She asked me to leave. She ordered me out of my own home, as if that was the most natural thing in the world, and obviously I refused. I was like: 'I do actually live here.' But she said, 'Piss off, get lost,' and I didn't see what choice I had so I was out for a while. When I got back she was lying there on my bed, smoking, how sick is that? And reading a book about string theory or something, and maybe I gave her some sort of dodgy look, what do I know. She just said that she wasn't planning on having sex with me, not even a little. 'Not even a little,' she said, and I don't think she looked me in the eye even once. She just announced that we'd had a Trojan, a R.A.T., and that she recognized the pattern in the breach, the level ~f ~riginality in the programming. 'You've been blown,' she said.

was very clear that you couldn't draw any ~~conclus~~
and that however much he searched through our computer he couldn't find any old spyware. But still his guess was – Molde was his name, by the way, Stefan Molde – that we'd been hacked."

"This woman, did she ever introduce herself in any way?"

"I did actually press her, but all she would say, and pretty surly she was too, was that I could call her Pippi. It was obvious that that wasn't her real name, but still . . ."

"Still what?"

"I thought that it suited her somehow."

"You know," Blomkvist said, "I was just about to head home again."

"Yes, I noticed that."

"But now everything's changed in a pretty major way. Didn't you say that your Professor Balder knew this woman?"

"Well, yes."

"In that case I want to talk to him as soon as possible."

"Because of the woman?"

"Something like that."

"O.K., fine," Brandell said thoughtfully. "But you won't find any contact details for him. He's become so bloody secretive, like I said. Do you have an iPhone?"

"I do."

"In that case you can forget it. Frans sees Apple as more or less in the pocket of the N.S.A. To talk to him you'll have to buy a Blackphone or at least borrow an Android and download a special encryption program. But I'll see to it that he gets in touch with you, so you can arrange to meet in some secure place."

"Great, Linus. Thanks."

CHAPTER 4

20.xi

"I'm sorry it took a while," Casales said. ~~~~~
morning. Total chaos."

"Here too," Grane said politely, but looking at her watch.

"But I do have something important to tell you, as I said, at least I think I do. It isn't that easy to analyse. I just started checking out a group of Russians, did I mention that?" Casales said.

"No."

"Well, there are probably Germans and Americans involved as well and possibly one or more Swedes."

"What sort of group are we talking about?"

"Criminals, sophisticated criminals who don't rob banks or sell drugs any more. Instead they steal corporate secrets and confidential business information."

"Black hats."

"They're not just hackers. They also blackmail and bribe people. Possibly they even carry out old-fashioned crimes, like murder. I don't have much on them yet, to be honest, mostly codenames and unconfirmed links, and then a couple of real names, some young computer engineers in junior positions. The group is active in suspected industrial espionage and that's why the case has ended up on my desk. We're afraid that cutting-edge American technology has fallen into Russian hands."

"I understand."

"But it isn't easy to get at them. They're good at encryption and, no matter how hard I try, I haven't been able to get any closer to whoever leads them than to catch that their boss goes by the name of Thanos."

"Thanos?"

"Yes, derived from Thanatos, the god of death in Greek mythology, the one who's the son of Nyx – night – and twin brother to Hypnos – sleep."

"Real cloak-and-dagger stuff."

"Actually, it's pretty childish. Thanos is a supervillain in Marvel Comics, you know that series with heroes like the Hulk, Iron Man and Captain America. First of all it's not particularly Russian, but more than that it's . . . how shall I put it . . . ?"

"Both playful and arrogant?"

"Yes, like a bunch of cocky college kids messing around, and that really annoys me. In fact there's a whole lot that worries me about this story, and that's why I got so worked up when we learned through our signals surveillance that someone in the network may have defected, somebody who could maybe give us some insight – if only we could get our hands on this guy before they do. But now that we've looked more carefully at this, we realize it wasn't at all what we thought."

"Meaning what?"

"The guy who quit wasn't some criminal, but the opposite, an honest guy who resigned from a company where this organization has moles, someone who presumably happened to stumble on some key information . . ."

"Keep going."

"In our view this person is now seriously under threat. He needs protection, but until recently we had no idea where to look for him. We didn't even know which company he'd worked at. But now we think we've zeroed in," Casales said. "You see, in the last few days one of these characters mentioned something about this guy, said that 'with him all the bloody Ts went up in smoke'."

". . . bloody Ts?"

. . . the advantage of being

"We're talking . . ."

"We think so. At least it felt like everything . . . place, so we began to investigate who had left Solifon recently. The company always has such a high staff turnover, it's actually part of their philosophy – that talent should flow in and out. But then we started to think specifically about those Ts. Are you familiar with them?"

"Only what you've told me."

"They're Grant's recipe for creativity. By tolerance he means that you need to be open to unconventional ideas and unconventional people. Talent – it doesn't just achieve results, it attracts other gifted people and helps create an environment that people want to be in. And all these talents have to form a team. As I'm sure you know, Solifon's been a remarkable success story, producing pioneering technology in a whole series of fields. But then this new genius popped up, a Swede, and with him . . ."

". . . all the bloody Ts went up in smoke."

"Exactly."

"And it was Frans Balder."

"Exactly. I don't think he'd previously had any problem with tolerance, or with teamwork for that matter. But from the beginning there was apparently something toxic about him. He refused to share anything, and in no time at all he managed to destroy the rapport among the elite researchers at the company, especially when he started accusing people of being thieves and copycats. There was a scene with the owner too. But Grant has refused to tell us what it was about – just that it was something private. Soon after, Balder gave notice."

"I know."

"Most people were probably relieved when he took off. The air at work became easier to breathe, and people began to trust each other again, at least up to a point. But Grant wasn't happy, and more importantly his lawyers weren't happy either. Balder had taken with him whatever he had been developing at Solifon, and there was a rumour – maybe because no-one really knew what it was – that he was on to something sensational that could revolutionize the quantum computer, which Solifon was working on."

"And from a purely legal point of view, whatever he'd produced belonged to the company and not to him personally."

"Correct. So even though Balder had been going on about theft, when all was said and done he himself was the thief. Any day now things are likely to blow up in court, as you know, unless Balder manages to use whatever he has to frighten the lawyers. That information is his life insurance, he says, and it may well be true. But in the worst-case scenario it could also be . . ."

". . . the death of him."

"That's what I'm afraid of," Casales said. "We're picking up stronger indications that something serious is getting underway, and your boss tells me that you might be able to help us with the puzzle."

Grane looked at the storm that was now raging outside, and longed desperately to go home and get away from all this. Yet she took off her coat and sat down again, feeling deeply uneasy.

"How can I help?"

"What do you think he found out?"

"Do I take that to mean that you haven't managed either to bug him or hack him?"

"................ answer that one, sweetheart. But what do

him. I didn't take ....

was talk in-house of getting him some form .. ..

met him a couple of times more. His transformation over the last few weeks was actually incredible. Not only because he had shaved off his beard, tidied up his hair and lost some weight. He was also mellower, even a little bit unsure of himself. I could tell that he was rattled, and at one point he did say that he thought there were people who wanted to harm him."

"In what way?"

"Not actually physically, he said. It was more his research and his reputation they were after. But I'm not so sure that, deep down, he believed it would stop there, so I suggested that he get a guard dog. I thought a dog would be excellent company for a man who lived out in the suburbs in far too big a house. But he wouldn't hear of it. 'I can't have a dog now,' he said rather sharply."

"Why's that, do you think?"

"I really don't know. But I got the feeling that there was something weighing on him, and he didn't protest too much when I arranged for a sophisticated alarm system in his house. It's just been installed."

"By whom?"

"A company we often use, Milton Security."

"Good. But my recommendation is to move him to a safe house."

"Is it that bad?"

"We think the risk is real."

"O.K.," Grane said. "If you send over some documentation I'll have a word with my superior right away."

"I'll see what I can do, but I'm not sure what I can get my hands on. We've been having . . . some computer issues."

"Can an agency like yours really afford to have that sort of thing?"

"No, you're right. Let me get back to you, sweetheart," she said, and hung up. Grane remained quite still and looked out at the storm lashing against the window with increasing fury.

Then she picked up her Blackphone and rang Balder. She let it ring and ring. Not just to warn him and see to it that he move to a safe place at once, but also because she suddenly wanted to know what he had meant when he said: "These past few days I've been dreaming about a new kind of life."

No-one would have believed that at that moment Balder was fully occupied with his son.

Blomkvist remained sitting for a while after Brandell had left, drinking his Guinness and staring out at the storm. Behind him, Arne and his gang were laughing at something. But Blomkvist was so engrossed in his thoughts that he heard nothing, and hardly even noticed that Amir had sat down next to him and was giving him the latest weather forecast.

The temperature was already down to -10°C. The first snow of the year was expected to fall, and not in any pleasant or picturesque way. The misery was going to come blasting in sideways in the worst storm the country had seen for a long time.

"Could get hurricane-force winds," Amir said, and Blomkvist, who still was not listening, just said, "That's good."

"Good?"

"Yes . . . well . . . better than no weather at all."

"I suppose. But are you alright? You look shaken up. Wasn't it a useful meeting?"

that there's even an end to eternity.

"What did he mean by that?"

"I think he was talking about love everlasting. It was shortly before he left my mother."

Blomkvist chuckled. "I haven't been so good at everlasting love myself. On the other hand . . ."

"Yes, Mikael?"

"There's a woman I used to know – she's been out of my life for some time now."

"Tricky."

"Well, yes, it is. But now I've had a sign of life from her, or at least I think I did, and perhaps that's what's got me looking a bit funny."

"Right."

"I'd better get myself home. What do I owe you?"

"We can settle up another time."

"Great, take care, Amir," he said. He walked past the regulars, who threw a few random comments at him, and stepped into the storm.

It was a near-death experience. Gusts of wind blew straight through his body, but in spite of them he stood still for a while, lost in old memories. He thought about a dragon tattoo on a skinny pale back, a cold snap on Hedeby Island in the midst of a decades-old missing-person case and a dug-up grave in Gosseberga that was nearly the resting place of a woman who refused to give up. Then he walked home slowly. For some reason he had trouble getting the door open, had to jiggle the key around. He kicked off his shoes and sat at his computer and searched for information on Frans Balder, Professor.

But he was alarmingly unfocused and instead found himself wondering, as he had so many times before: where had she disappeared to? Apart from some news from her one-time employer, Dragan Armansky, he had not heard a word about her. It was as if she had vanished off the face of the earth and, although they lived in more or less the same part of town, he had never caught a glimpse of her.

Of course, the person who had turned up at Brandell's apartment that day could have been someone else. It was possible, but not likely. Who other than Salander would come stomping in like that? It must have been Salander, and Pippi . . . that was typical.

The name by her doorbell on Fiskargatan was V. KULLA and he could well see why she did not use her real name. It was all too searchable and associated with one of the most high-profile trials the country had ever seen. Admittedly, it was not the first time that the woman had vanished in a puff of smoke. But ever since that day when he had knocked on her door on Lundagatan and given her hell for having written a personal investigation report about him which was much too thorough, they had never been apart for so long and it felt a little strange, didn't it? After all, Salander was his . . . well, what the hell was she, in point of fact?

Hardly his friend. One sees one's friends. Friends don't disappear like that. Friends don't only get in touch by hacking into your computer. Yet he still felt this bond with Salander and, above all, he worried about her. Her old guardian Holger Palmgren used to say that Lisbeth Salander would always get by. Despite her appalling childhood, or maybe because of it, she was one hell of ———— there was probably a lot of truth in that. But one ————————— woman of such a background, and ————————— really had lost

there was ——— Salander and, with the help ——— sentimentality.

Among other things, Armansky told Blomkvist that his company, Milton Security, had supplied a number of personal alarms to a nursing home in Högdalen. Good equipment, he said.

But not even the best equipment in the world will help you if the electricity goes off and nobody can be bothered to fix it, and that is precisely what happened. There was a power outage at the home late one evening, and in the course of that night one of the residents, a lady called Rut Åkerman, fell and broke her femur, and she lay there for hour after hour pressing the button on her alarm to no avail. By the morning she was in a critical condition and, since the papers were just then focusing heavily on negligence in care for the elderly, the whole thing became a big deal.

Happily, the old lady pulled through. But she also happened to be the mother of a senior figure in the Swedish Democrats party. When it emerged on the party's website, Unpixelated, that

Armansky was an Arab – which incidentally he was not at all, although it was true that he was occasionally called "the Arab" in jest – there was an explosion in the posted comments. Hundreds of anonymous writers said that's what happens "when you let coons supply your technology" and Armansky took it very badly, especially when the trolling affected his family.

But then suddenly, as if by magic, all those posts were no longer anonymous. You could see the names and addresses of those responsible, their job titles and how old they were. It was beautifully neat – as if they had all filled in a form. You could say that the entire site had been unpixelated, and of course it became clear that the posts did not just come from crackpots, but also from many established citizens, even some of Armansky's competitors in the security business, and for a long time the hitherto-anonymous perpetrators were completely powerless. They could not understand what had happened. Eventually someone managed to close the site down. But nobody had any idea who lay behind the attack – except for Dragan Armansky himself.

"It was classic Salander," he said. "You know, I hadn't heard from her for ages and was convinced that she couldn't give a damn about me, or anybody else for that matter. But then this happened, and it was fantastic. She had stood up for me. I sent an effusive thanks by email, and to my surprise an answer came back. Do you know what she wrote?"

"No."

"Just one single sentence: 'How the hell can you protect that creep Sandvall at the Östermalm clinic?'"

"And who's Sandvall?"

"A plastic surgeon to whom we gave personal protection because he'd been threatened. He'd pawed a young Estonian woman on whom he had performed breast surgery and she happened to be the girlfriend of a known criminal."

"Oops."

"Precisely. Not such a clever thing to do. I answered Salander to say that I didn't think Sandvall was one of God's little angels any more than she did. But I pointed out that we don't have the right to make that kind of judgement. Even male chauvinist pigs are entitled to some degree of security. Since Sandvall was under serious threat and asked for our help, we gave it to him – at double the usual rate."

"But Salander didn't buy your argument?"

"... didn't reply – at least not by email. But I suppose ... sort of answer."

the most te...,

"Jesus!"

"That's putting it mildly. Stark staring mad. I mean, thing like that in front of so many witnesses, and in a doctor's office to boot. And of course there was a huge fuss afterwards – a lot of brouhaha about lawsuits and prosecutions and the whole damn thing. You can just imagine: breaking the fingers of a surgeon who's lined up to perform a string of lucrative nips and tucks . . . It's the kind of thing that gets top lawyers seeing dollar signs everywhere."

"What happened?"

"Nothing. It all came to nothing, apparently because the surgeon himself didn't want to take things any further. But still, Mikael, it was insane. No person in their right mind steams into a top surgeon's office in broad daylight and breaks his fingers. Not even Salander."

Blomkvist actually thought that it sounded pretty logical, according to Salander logic, that is, a subject in which he was more or less expert. He did not doubt for one second that that doctor had done far worse than grope the wrong girlfriend. But even so he could not help wondering if Salander hadn't screwed up in this case, if only on the score of risk analysis.

It occurred to him that she might have *wanted* to get into trouble again, maybe to put some spice back into her life. But that was probably unfair. He knew nothing of her motives or her current life. As the storm rattled the windowpanes and he sat there in front of his computer Googling Frans Balder, he tried to see beauty in the fact that they had now bumped into each other in this indirect way. It would seem that Salander was the same as ever and perhaps – who knows? – she had given him a story. Linus Brandell had irritated him from the word go. But when Salander dropped into the story, he saw it all with new eyes. If she had taken the time to help Frans Balder then he could at least take a closer look at it, and with some luck find out a bit more about Salander at the same time.

Why had she got herself involved in the first place?

She was not just some itinerant I.T. consultant after all. Yes, she could fly into a rage over life's injustices, but for a woman who had no qualms about hacking to get indignant about a computer breach, that was a little bit surprising. Breaking the fingers of a plastic surgeon, fine! But hackers? That was very much like throwing stones in glass houses.

There must be some backstory. Maybe she and Balder knew each other. It was not inconceivable and so he tried Googling their names together, but without getting any hits, at least none that had any relevance.

He focused on Frans Balder. The professor's name generated two million hits but most of them were scientific articles and commentaries. It did not seem as if Balder gave interviews, and because of that, there was a sort of mythological gloss over all of the details of his life – as if they had been romanticized by admiring students.

Apparently it had been assumed that Balder was more or less mentally disabled as a child until one day he walked into the headmaster's office at his school on Ekerö island and pointed out a mistake in the ninth-grade maths book to do with so-called imaginary numbers. The mistake was corrected in subsequent editions and the following spring Balder won a national mathematics competition. He was reported as being able to speak backwards and create his own long palindromes. In an early school essay which was later published on the net he took a critical view of H. G. Wells' novel *The War of the Worlds* on the grounds that he

in every way could

Institute of Technology in Stockholm and was Swedish Academy of Engineering Sciences. These days he was regarded as a world authority on the hypothetical concept of "technological singularity", the state at which computer intelligence will have overtaken our own.

In most photographs he looked like a dishevelled troll with small eyes, his hair standing on end. Yet he married the glamorous actress Hanna Lind. The couple had a son who, according to evening newspaper coverage, under the headline HANNA'S GREAT SORROW, was mentally disabled, even though the boy did not – at least not in the picture accompanying the article – look in the least bit impaired. The marriage fell apart and, amidst a heated custody battle in Nacka district court, the *enfant terrible* of the theatre, Lasse Westman, stepped into the fray to declare aggressively that Balder should not be allowed to look after his son at all because he cared more about "the intelligence of computers than that of children". Blomkvist concentrated his efforts on trying to understand Balder's research, and for a long time he sat engrossed in a complicated text about quantum processors in computers.

Afterwards he went into Documents and opened a file he had created a year or so earlier. It was called LISBETH STUFF. He had no idea whether she was still hacking into his computer, but he could not help hoping that she did and wondered if he should not after all type out a little greeting. Long, personal letters were not her thing. He would do better to go for something brisk and a little bit cryptic. He wrote:

```
<What should we make of Frans Balder's arti-
ficial intelligence?>
```

CHAPTER 5

20.xi

was not an obvious setting
coups.

It felt more like a place where a social welfare case might hang out. Plague lived on Högklintavägen in Sundbyberg, a markedly unglamorous area with dull, four-storey, faded brick houses, and the apartment itself had nothing much going for it. It had a sour, stale smell, and his desk was covered in all sorts of rubbish, McDonald's containers and Coca-Cola cans, crumpled-up pages from notebooks, unwashed coffee cups and empty sweet packets. Even though some had actually made it into the wastepaper basket – which had not been emptied for weeks – you could hardly take a step in the room without getting crumbs or grit under your feet. But none of this would have surprised anyone who knew him.

Plague was not a man who normally showered or changed his clothes much. He spent his whole life in front of the computer, even when he was not working: a giant of a man and overweight, bloated and unkempt, with an attempt at an imperial beard that had long since turned into a shapeless thicket. His posture was dreadful and he had a habit of groaning when he moved. But the man had other talents.

He was a wizard on the computer, a hacker who flew unconstrained through cyberspace and was probably second only to one person in the field, a woman in this particular case. The mere sight of his fingers dancing across the keyboard was a joy to behold. He was as light and nimble on the net as he was heavy and clumsy in the other, more material world, and as a neighbour somewhere upstairs, presumably Herr Jansson, now banged on the floor, he answered the message he had received:

```
<Wasp, you bloody genius. They ought to put
up a statue to you!>
```

Then he leaned back with a delighted smile and tried to run through in his mind the sequence of events, savouring the triumph for a little while longer before going on to pump Wasp for every detail, and to ensure that she had covered her tracks. No-one must be able to trace them, no-one!

This was not the first time they had been messing with a powerful organization. But this was on a new level, and many in Hacker Republic, the exclusive fellowship to which she belonged, had actually been against the idea, Wasp herself most of all. Wasp could take on just about any authority or person you could care to name, if it were necessary. But she did not like to pick a fight for its own sake.

She disliked that sort of childish hacker nonsense. She was not someone who hacked into supercomputers merely to show off. Wasp wanted to have a clear objective, and she always damn well analyzed the potential consequences. She weighed long-term risks against whatever need was being satisfied in the short term, and from that point of view it could not be said it made sense to hack into the N.S.A. Still, she let herself be talked into it. Nobody could quite understand why.

Maybe she was bored and wanted to stir up a little chaos so as not to die of tedium. Or else, as some in the group claimed, she was already in conflict with the N.S.A. and therefore the breach amounted to little more than her personal revenge. But others in the group questioned even that and maintained she was looking for information, that she had been on the hunt for something ever since her father, Alexander Zalachenko, had been murdered at Sahlgrenska hospital in Göteborg.

But nobody knew for sure. Wasp had always had her secrets and actually her motives were unimportant, or so they tried to

ization did not confine itself to eavesdropping on terror potential security risks, or even just foreign heads of state and other powerful figures, but listened in on everything, or nearly everything. Millions, billions, trillions of communications and activities on the net were spied on and archived, and with each passing day the N.S.A. went further and further and pried deeper and deeper into every private life, and had become one immeasurable, watchful, evil eye.

It was true that nobody in Hacker Republic could claim the moral high ground here. Every single one of them had made their way into parts of the digital landscape where they had no business being. Those were the rules of the game, so to speak. A hacker was someone who crossed the line, for better or for worse, someone who by virtue of their occupation broke rules and broadened the frontiers of their knowledge, without always being concerned about the distinction between private and public.

But they were not without ethics and above all they knew, also from their own experience, how power corrupts, especially power without control. None of them liked the thought that the worst, most unscrupulous hacking was no longer carried out by solitary rebels or outlaws, but by state behemoths who wanted to control their populations. Plague and Trinity and Bob the Dog and Flipper and Zod and Cat and the whole Hacker Republic gang had therefore decided to strike back by hacking the N.S.A. and messing with them in one way or another.

That was no simple task. It was a little bit like stealing the gold from Fort Knox, and like the arrogant idiots they were they did not content themselves with breaking into the system. They also wanted superuser status, or "Root" in Linux language, and for that they needed to find unknown vulnerabilities in the system, for what was called a Zero-day attack – first on the N.S.A.'s server platform and then further into the organization's intranet, NSANet, from which the authority's signals surveillance went out across the world.

They began as usual with a little social engineering. They had to get hold of the names of systems administrators and infrastructure analysts who held the complex passwords for the intranet. It would not do any harm either if there was a chance that some careless oaf was being negligent about security routines. In fact, through their own contacts they came up with four or five names, among them a Richard Fuller.

Fuller worked in the N.I.S.I.R.T., the N.S.A. Information Systems Incident Response Team, which supervised the intranet, and he was constantly on the lookout for leaks and infiltrators. Fuller was a decent sort of fellow – a Harvard law graduate, Republican, former quarterback, a dream patriot if one were to believe his C.V. But through a former lover Bob the Dog managed to discover that he was also bipolar, and possibly a cocaine addict.

When he got excited he would do all sorts of stupid things,

such as opening files and documents without first putting them in a so-called sandbox, a required security protocol. Furthermore he was very handsome, though a little smarmy, and someone, probably Bob the Dog himself, came up with the idea that Wasp should travel to his home town in Baltimore, go to bed with him and catch him in a honey trap.

Wasp told them all to go to hell.

~~~~~~~ ~~jected their next idea, that they would compile a ~~~~~~ ~~rmation which looked like dynamite, ~~~~~~~~ ~~~at head office in Fort ~~~~~~ ~~taining an

so worke~ ~~~~~~
plan at all – it could take ~~~~~~
without an active breach that migh~ ~~

Wasp said that she was not going to sit around wa~~~~ blockhead Fuller to put his foot in it. She did not want to have to rely on other people making mistakes and was being generally contrary and bloody-minded, so no-one was surprised when she suddenly wanted to take over the whole operation herself. Even though there was a certain amount of protest, in the end they all gave in, but not without issuing a series of instructions. Wasp did carefully write down the names and details of the systems administrators which they had managed to obtain, and she did ask for help with the so-called fingerprinting: the mapping of the server platform and operating system. But after that she closed the door on Hacker Republic and the world, and Plague had no reason to think that she paid any attention to his advice, for example that she should not use her handle, her alias, and that she should not work from home but rather from some remote hotel under a false identity, in case the N.S.A.'s bloodhounds managed to track her down. Needless to say, she did everything her own way and all Plague could do was sit at his desk in Sundbyberg and wait, his nerves in tatters. Which is why he still had no idea how she had gone about it.

He knew one thing for certain: what she had achieved was legendary, and while the storm howled outside he pushed aside some of the rubbish on his desk, leaned forward and typed on his computer:

```
<Tell me! How does it feel?>
```
<Empty>, came the answer.

Empty.

That was how it felt. Salander had hardly slept for a week and she had probably also had too little to drink and eat, and now her head ached and her eyes were bloodshot and her hands shook and what she wanted above all was to sweep all of her equipment to the floor. In one sense she was content, though hardly for the reason Plague or anyone else in Hacker Republic would have guessed. She was content because she had been able to get some new information on the criminal group she was mapping out; she had found evidence of a connection which she had previously only suspected. But she kept that to herself, and she was surprised that the others could have imagined that she would have hacked the system for the hell of it.

She was no hormone-fuelled teenager, no idiot show-off looking for a kick. She would only embark on such a bold venture because she was after something very specific, although it was true that once upon a time hacking had been more than just a tool for her. During the worst moments of her childhood it had been her way of escaping, a way to make life feel a little less boxed in. With the help of computers she could break through barriers which had been put in her way and experience periods of freedom. There was probably an element of that in the current situation too.

First and foremost she was on the hunt and had been ever since she woke up in the light of early dawn with her dream of that fist beating rhythmically, relentlessly on a mattress on Lundagatan. Her enemies were hiding behind smokescreens and this could be the reason why Salander had been unusually difficult and awkward of late. It was as if a new darkness emanated from her. Apart from ⟨…⟩ loudmouthed boxing coach called Obinze and two or three ⟨…⟩es, she saw hardly anyone. More than ever she ⟨…⟩ was straggly, her eyes threatening, ⟨…⟩ effort she had not

⟨…⟩ since she had ⟨…⟩ rate it or make it homely. ⟨…⟩ furniture, placed seemingly at random, ⟨…⟩ a stereo system, perhaps because she did not unders⟨…⟩ She saw more melody in a differential equation than in a piece by Beethoven. Yet she was as rich as Croesus. The money she had stolen from that crook Hans-Erik Wennerström had grown to a little more than five billion kronor, so she could afford whatever she wanted. But in some way – which was typical of her – her fortune had not made any mark on her personality, unless perhaps it had made her yet more fearless. She had certainly done some increasingly drastic things of late.

She may have crossed a line by wandering into N.S.A.'s intranet. But she had judged it necessary, and for several days and nights she had been totally absorbed. Now it was over she peered out of tired, squinting eyes at her two work desks, set at right angles. Her equipment consisted of the regular computer and the test machine she had bought, on which she had installed a copy of N.S.A.'s server and operating system.

She had run her own fuzzing program, which searched for errors and tiny vulnerabilities in the platform against the test computer. She then followed that up with debugging and black-box penetration testing and various beta test attacks. The outcome of all that formed the basis of her rootkit, including her R.A.T., so she could not afford to neglect a single point. She was scrutinizing the system from top to bottom and that was why she had installed a copy of the server here at home. If she had set to work on the real platform, the N.S.A. technicians would have noticed it immediately.

This way she was able to work on without distraction, day after day, and if she did happen to leave the computer then it was only to doze off for a while on the sofa or to put a pizza in the microwave. Apart from that she kept at it until her eyes hurt, especially with her Zero-day Exploit, the software which exploited the unknown security vulnerabilities and which would update her status once she had actually got in. It was completely mind-boggling. Salander had written a program which not only gave her ownership over the system, but also the power to control remotely pretty much anything on an intranet of which she had only patchy knowledge. That was the most extraordinary part.

She was not just going to break in. She was going further, into NSANet, which was a self-contained universe barely connected to the ordinary net. She might look like a teenager who had failed all of her subjects at school, but give her source codes in computer programs and a logical context and her brain just went click, click. What she had created was nothing less than wholly new and improved malware, an advanced Trojan with a life of its own.

She found the pay-as-you-go card she had bought from T-Mobile in Berlin and put it into her telephone. Then she used it to go onto the net. Maybe she should have been far away in another part of the world, dressed up as her alter ego, Irene Nesser.

If the security people at the N.S.A. were diligent and on top of things, they just might be able to trace her to Telenor's base station here in the block. They would not get all the way through, at least not with the technology now available, but it would still be close and that would be very bad news. Yet she reckoned the advantages of sitting here at home outweighed the risk, and she did take all the security precautions she could. Like so many other hackers, she used Tor, a network along which her traffic bounced about

thousands and thousands of users. But she also knew that

tertight – the N.S.A. used a program called

so she spent a long time

did she

had been given and

creating a bridge between the ser

none of which was simple, not by any means. No wa

or anti-virus programs must be allowed to start ringing. In the end she used the identity of a man called Tom Breckinridge to penetrate NSANet and then . . . every muscle in her body tensed. Before her eyes, her overworked, sleepless eyes, the magic unfolded.

Her Trojan took her further and further in, into this, the most secret of the secret, and she knew exactly where she was going. She was on her way to Active Directory – or its equivalent – to upgrade her status. She would go from unwelcome little visitor to superuser in this teeming universe, and only once that was done would she try to get some sort of overview of the system. It wasn't easy. It was more or less impossible, in fact, and she did not have much time either.

She worked fast to get a grip on the search system and to pick up all the passwords and expressions and references, all the internal gibberish. She was on the point of giving up when finally she found a document marked TOP SECRET, NOFORN – no foreign distribution – not particularly remarkable in itself. But together with a couple of communications links between Zigmund Eckerwald at Solifon and cyber-agents at the Department for the Protection of Strategic Technologies at the N.S.A., it turned into dynamite. She smiled and memorized every little detail. Then she caught sight of yet another document that seemed relevant. It was encrypted and she saw no alternative but to copy it, even if that would set alarm bells ringing at Fort Meade. She swore ferociously.

The situation was becoming critical. Besides, she had to get on with her official assignment, if official was the right word. She had solemnly promised Plague and the others at Hacker Republic to pull down the N.S.A.'s trousers, so she tried to work out who she should be communicating with. Who was to get her message?

She settled for Edwin Needham, Ed the Ned. His name invariably came up in connection with I.T. security, and as she quickly picked up some information about him on the intranet, she felt a grudging respect. Needham was a star. But she had outwitted him and for a moment she thought twice about giving the game away.

Her attack would create an uproar. But an uproar was exactly what she was looking for, so she went ahead. She had no idea what time it was. It could have been night or day, autumn or spring, and only vaguely, deep in her consciousness, was she aware that the storm over the city was building up, as if the weather was synchronized with her coup. In distant Maryland, Needham began to write his email.

He didn't get far, because in the next second she took over his sentence and wrote: <that you should stop with all the illegal activity. Actually it's pretty straightforward. Those who spy on the people end up themselves being spied on by the people. There's a fundamental democratic logic to it>, and for a moment it felt as if those sentences hit the mark. She savoured the hot sweet taste of revenge and afterwards she dragged Ed the Ned along on a journey through the system. The two of them danced and tore past a whole flickering world of things that were supposed to remain hidden at all costs.

It was a thrilling experience, no question, and yet . . . when she disconnected and all her log files were automatically deleted, then came the hangover. It was like the aftermath of an orgasm with ~~~~ner, and those sentences that had seemed so abso- ~~~~ to sound increasingly childish ~~~ddenly she

of victory ~~~ Defiance perhaps.

She drank and drank while the storm roared and ~~~ whoops came streaming in from Hacker Republic. But none of it touched her now. She hardly had the strength to stay upright and with a wide, hasty movement she swept her hand across the desktops and watched with indifference as bottles and ashtrays crashed to the floor. Then she thought about Mikael Blomkvist.

It must have been the alcohol. Blomkvist had a way of popping up in her thoughts, as old flames do, when she was drunk, and without quite realizing what she was doing she hacked into his computer. She still had a shortcut into his system – it was not the N.S.A., after all – and at first she wondered what she was doing there.

Could she care less about him? He was history, just an attractive idiot she had once happened to fall in love with, and she was not going to make that mistake again. She'd much rather get out of there and not look at another computer for weeks. Yet she stayed on his server and in the next moment her face lit up. Kalle Bloody Blomkvist had created a file called LISBETH STUFF and in that document there was a question for her:

```
<What should we make of Frans Balder's arti-
ficial intelligence?>
```

She gave a slight smile, in spite of it all, and that was partly because of Frans Balder. He was her kind of computer nerd, passionate about source codes and quantum processors and the potential of logic. But mostly she was smiling at the fact that Blomkvist had stumbled into the very same situation she was in, and though she debated for some time whether to simply shut down and go to bed, she wrote back:

```
<Balder's intelligence isn't in the least bit
artificial. How's your own these days?
And what happens, Blomkvist, if we create a
machine which is a little bit cleverer than
we are?>
```

Then she went into one of her bedrooms and collapsed with her clothes on.

had shaved or taken a sho...
hours the world and the storm outside had ceased t...
and he even failed to notice what was going on at his feet. They
were small, awkward movements, as if a cat or an animal had crept
in under his legs; it was a while before he realized that August was
crawling around under his desk. Balder gave him a dazed look, as
if the stream of programming codes still lay like a film over his
eyes.

"What are you after?"

August looked up at him with a pleading, clear look in his eyes.

"What?" Balder said. "What?" and then something happened.

The boy picked up a piece of paper covered in quantum algorithms which was lying on the floor and feverishly moved his hand
back and forth over it. For a moment Balder thought the boy was
about to have another attack. But no, it was rather as if August
were pretending to write. Balder felt his body go tense and again
he was reminded of something important and remote, the same

feeling as at the crossing on Hornsgatan. But this time he understood what it was.

He thought back to his own childhood, when numbers and equations had been more important than life itself. His spirits rose and he burst out, "You want to do sums, don't you? Of course, you want to do sums!" and the next moment he hurried off to fetch some pens and ruled A4 paper which he put on the floor in front of August.

Then he wrote down the simplest series of numbers he could think of, Fibonacci's sequence, in which every number is the sum of the preceding two, 1, 1, 2, 3, 5, 8, 13, 21, and left a space for the next number – 34. Then it occurred to him that this was likely too simple, so he also wrote down a geometric sequence: 2, 6, 18, 54 . . . in which every number is multiplied by three and the next number should therefore be 162. To solve a problem like that, he thought, a gifted child would not need a great deal of prior knowledge. Balder slipped into a daydream that the boy was not disabled at all, rather an enhanced copy of himself; he, too, had been slow to speak and interact socially, but he had understood mathematical relationships long before he uttered his first word.

He sat beside the boy for a long time and waited. But nothing happened. August just stared at the numbers with his glassy look. In the end Balder left him alone, went upstairs and drank some fizzy water, and then settled down again at the kitchen table to continue to work. But now his concentration was gone and he began absent-mindedly to flick through the latest issue of the *New Scientist*. After half an hour or so he went back downstairs to August, who was still sitting on his heels in the same immobile posture in which he had left him. Then Balder noticed something intriguing.

A second later he had the sense of being confronted by something totally inexplicable.

*

78

Hanna Balder was standing in the kitchen on Torsgatan smoking a filterless Prince. She had on a blue dressing gown and worn grey slippers, and although her hair was thick and beautiful and she was still attractive, she looked haggard. Her lip was swollen and the heavy make-up around her eyes was not there purely for aesthetic reasons. Hanna Balder had taken another beating.

It would be wrong to say that she was used to it. No-one gets used to that sort of abuse. But it was part of her everyday existence and she could scarcely remember the happy person she once had

... had become a natural element of her personality and

... sixty cigarettes a day

would make ...

expenses for some educational expert or remedi...

obviously the funds had never gone anywhere near. That's what made it so odd. Why had he given up all of that and let Balder take the boy away?

Deep down Hanna knew the answer. It was hubris brought on by alcohol. It was the promise of a part in a new detective series on T.V.4 which had boosted his confidence still further. But most of all it was August. Westman found the boy creepy and weird, even though to Hanna that was incomprehensible. How could anyone detest August?

He sat on the floor with his puzzles and did not bother anyone. Yet he had that strange look which was turned inwards rather than outwards, which usually made people smile and say that the boy must have a rich inner life, but which got under Westman's skin.

"Jesus, Hanna! He's looking straight through me," he would burst out.

"But you say that he's just an idiot."

"He is an idiot, but there's something funny about him all the same. I think he hates me."

That was nonsense, nothing more. August did not even look at Westman or at anyone else for that matter, and he surely did not have it in him to hate anybody. The world out there disturbed him and he was happiest inside his own bubble. But Westman in his drunken ravings believed that the boy was plotting something, and that must have been the reason he let August and the money slip out of their lives. Pathetic. That at least was how Hanna had interpreted it. But now, as she stood there by the sink smoking her cigarette so furiously and nervously that she got tobacco on her tongue, she wondered if there had not been something in it after all. Maybe August *did* hate Westman. Maybe he *did* want to punish him for all the punches he had taken, and maybe . . . Hanna closed her eyes and bit her lip . . . the boy hated her too.

She had been having these feelings of self-loathing ever since, at night, she had been overcome by an almost unbearable sense of longing, and she wondered whether she and Westman might not actually have damaged August.

It was not the fact that August had filled in the right answers to the numerical sequences. That sort of thing did not particularly impress a man like Balder. No, it was something he saw lying next to the numbers. At first sight it looked like a photograph or a painting, but it was in fact a drawing, an exact representation of the traffic light on Hornsgatan which they had passed the other evening. It was exquisitely captured, in the minutest detail, with a sort of mathematical precision.

There was a glow to it. No-one had taught August anything at all about three-dimensional drawing or how an artist works with shadow and light, yet he seemed to have a perfect mastery of the techniques. The red eye of the traffic light flashed towards them and Hornsgatan's autumn darkness closed around it, and in the middle of the street you could see the man whom Balder had noticed and vaguely recognized. The man's head was cut off above the eyebrows. He looked frightened or at least uncomfortable and troubled, as if August had disconcerted him, and he was walking unsteadily, though goodness knows how the boy had managed to capture that.

"My God," Balder said. "Did you do this?"

August neither nodded nor shook his head but looked over towards the window, and Balder had the strangest feeling that his

general.

She scrolled through her contacts two, three times, in the hope that a new name would come up. But of course there were only the same old people, and they were all tired of her. Against her better judgement she called Mia. Mia was her agent and once upon a time they had been best friends and dreamed of conquering the world together. These days Hanna was Mia's guilty conscience and she had lost count of all her excuses. "It's not easy for an actress to grow older, blah, blah." Why not just say it straight out?: "You look worn out, Hanna. The public doesn't love you any more."

But Mia did not answer and that was probably just as well. The conversation would not have done either of them any good. Hanna could not help looking into August's room just to feel that stinging sense of loss which made her realize that she had failed in her life's most important mission – motherhood. In some perverse way she took comfort in her self-pity, and she was standing there wondering whether she shouldn't go out and get some beer after all when the telephone rang.

It was Frans. She made a face. All day she had been tempted – but did not dare – to call him to say that she wanted August back, not just because she missed the boy, still less because she thought her son would be better off with her. It was simply in order to avoid a disaster.

Lasse wanted to get the child support again. *God knows what would happen*, she thought, *if he were to turn up in Saltsjöbaden to claim his rights*. He might even drag August out of the house, scare him out of his wits and beat Frans to a pulp. She would have to warn him. But when she picked up and tried to say that to Frans, it was impossible to get a word in edgeways. He just went on and on about some strange story which was apparently "totally fantastic and completely amazing" and all that sort of thing.

"I'm sorry, Frans, I don't understand. What are you talking about?" she said.

"August is a savant. He's a genius."

"Have you gone mad?"

"Quite the opposite, my love, I've come to my senses at last. You have to get over here, yes, really, right now! I think it's the only way. You won't be able to understand otherwise. I'll pay for the taxi. I promise, you'll flip out. He must have a photographic memory, you see? And in some incomprehensible way he must have picked up the secrets of perspective drawing all by himself. It's so beautiful, Hanna, so precise. It shines with a light from another world."

"What shines?"

"His traffic light. Weren't you listening? The one we passed the other evening – he's been drawing a whole series of perfect pictures of it, actually more than perfect . . ."

"More than . . ."

"Well, how can I put it? He hasn't just copied it, Hanna, not just captured it exactly, he's also added something, an artistic dimension. There's such a strange fervour in what he's done, and paradoxically enough also something mathematical, as if he even has some understanding of axonometry."

"Axo . . .?"

"Never mind! You have to come here and see," he said, and gradually she began to understand.

Out of the blue August had started to draw like a virtuoso, or so Frans claimed, and that would of course be fantastic if it were ~~~~~ ~~~~~ still not happy, and at

thrashed backwards and forwards. Now, ~~~ ~~~ with Pappa and he was a genius.

It was too much. Not that she was not happy for August. But still, it hurt, and the worst thing was: she was not as surprised as she should have been. On the contrary, it felt as if she had almost seen it coming; not that the boy would draw accurate reproductions of traffic lights, but that there was something more beneath the surface.

She had sensed it in his eyes, in that look which, when he was excited, seemed to register every little detail of his surroundings. She had sensed it in the way the boy listened to his teachers, and the nervous way he leafed through the maths books she had bought for him, and most of all she had sensed it in his numbers. There was nothing so strange as those numbers. Hour after hour he would write down series of incomprehensibly large sums, and Hanna really did try to understand them, or at least to grasp the point of it all. But however hard she tried she had not been able to work it out, and now she supposed that she had missed something important. She had been too unhappy and wrapped up in herself to fathom what was going on in her son's mind, wasn't that it?

"I don't know," she said.

"Don't know what," Frans said in irritation.

"I don't know if I can come," she said, and at the same time she heard a racket at the front door.

Lasse was coming in with his old drinking buddy Roger Winter, and that made her flinch in fear, mutter an apology to Frans and for the thousandth time dwell on the fact that she was a bad mother.

Balder stood on the chequered floor in the bedroom, the telephone in his hand, and swore. He had had the floor laid because it appealed to his sense of mathematical order, with the squares repeating themselves endlessly in the wardrobe mirrors on either side of the bed. There were days when he saw the multiplication of the squares reflected there as a teeming riddle, something with a life of its own rising up out of the schematic in the same way that thoughts and dreams arise from neurons or computer programs emerge from binary codes. But just then he was lost in quite different thoughts.

"Dear boy. What has become of your mother?" he said aloud.

August, who was sitting on the floor beside him eating a cheese and gherkin sandwich, looked up with a concentrated expression, and Balder was seized by a strange premonition that he was about to say something grown up and wise. But that was obviously idiotic. August remained as silent as ever and knew nothing about women who were neglected and had faded away. The fact that the idea had even occurred to Balder was of course due to the drawings.

84

The drawings – by now there had been three – seemed to him to be proof not only of artistic and mathematical gifts, but also of some sort of wisdom. The works seemed so mature and complex in their geometric precision that Balder could not reconcile them with August's mental limitations. Or rather, he did not want to reconcile them, because he had long ago worked out what this was about.

As the father of an autistic son Balder had long suspected that many parents hoped the notion of a savant would be their consolation prize to make up for a diagnosis of cognitive deficiencies.

years – in extreme cases within a single

Others possess encyclopaedic knowledge within a narrow field, such as bus timetables or telephone numbers. Some can calculate large sums in their heads, or remember what the weather had been like every day of their lives, or are able to tell the time to the second without looking at a watch. There are all kinds of more or less remarkable talents and, from what Balder gathered, people with these skills are called talented savants and capable of quite outstanding accomplishments given the fact that they are otherwise handicapped.

Another far less common group is where Balder hoped that August belonged: the so-called prodigious savants, individuals whose talents are sensational whichever way one looks at them. Kim Peek, for example, who was the inspiration for "Rain Man". Kim was severely mentally disabled and could not even get dressed by himself. Yet he had memorized twelve thousand books and could give a lightning-quick answer to almost any factual question. He was known as Kimputer.

Or Stephen Wiltshire, an autistic English boy who was extremely withdrawn as a child and uttered his first word when he was six – it happened to be "paper". By the age of seven Stephen was able to draw groups of buildings perfectly and in the minutest detail, having seen them for just one brief moment. He was flown above London in a helicopter and when he landed he drew the entire city in a fantastic, dizzying panorama, and with a wonderfully individual touch.

If Balder understood it all correctly, he and August must have looked at that traffic light in very different ways. Not only because the boy was plainly so much more focused, but also because Balder's brain had instantly eliminated all non-essential elements in order to concentrate on the traffic light's key message: go or stop. In all probability his perception was also clouded by his thinking about Farah Sharif, while for August the crossing must have appeared exactly as it was, in precise detail.

Afterwards he had taken the image away with him like a fine etching, and it was not until a few weeks later that he had felt the need to express it. The strangest thing of all was, he had done more than simply reproduce the traffic light and the man. He had charged them with a disquieting light, and Balder could not rid himself of the thought that August had wanted to say something more to him than: Look what I can do! For the hundredth time he stared at the drawings and it was as if a needle had gone into his heart.

It frightened him. He did not entirely understand it. But there was something about that man. His eyes were bright and hard. His jaw was tense and his lips strangely thin, almost non-existent, although that could hardly be held against him. Still, the longer he stared at him, the more frightening he looked, and all of a sudden Balder was gripped by an icy fear.

"I love you, my boy," he murmured, hardly aware of what he was saying, and possibly he repeated the sentence once or twice because the words began to sound increasingly unfamiliar to his ears.

He realized with a new sort of pain that he had never uttered them before, and once he had recovered from the first shock it occurred to him that there was something contemptible in that. Did it take an exceptional talent to make him love his own child? It would be only too typical, if so. All his life he had had an absolute obsession with achievement.

which was not innovative

him these last few months, and devote his whole attention boy.

He would become a new person.

CHAPTER 7

20.xi

Something else had happened at the magazine, something bad. But Berger did not want to give any details over the telephone. She suggested coming round to his place. Blomkvist had tried to put her off:

"You're going to freeze that beautiful bum of yours!"

Berger had paid no attention and, but for the tone in her voice, he would have been happy that she was so stubborn. Ever since he left the office he had been longing to speak to her, and maybe even pull her into the bedroom and tear all her clothes off. But something told him this was not going to happen now. She had sounded upset and mumbled, "I'm sorry," and this only made him more worried.

"I'll get a taxi right away," she said.

It was a while before she appeared, and out of boredom he went into the bathroom and looked in the mirror. He had certainly seen better days. His hair was dishevelled and needed a cut and he had bags under his eyes. That was basically Elizabeth George's fault. He swore and left the bathroom to set about cleaning up.

That was one thing at least that Berger would not be able to complain about. However long they had known each other, and however interwoven their lives, he still suffered a complex when it came to tidiness. He was a labourer's son and a bachelor, she the upper-class married woman with the perfect home in Saltsjöbaden. In any case it could do no harm for his place to look a little respectable. He filled the dishwasher, wiped the sink and put out the rubbish.

He even had time to vacuum the living room, water the flowers on the windowsill and tidy up the bookshelf and magazine rack before the doorbell rang. There was both a ring and an impatient knock. When he opened up he was horrified. Berger was frozen stiff.

She shook like a leaf, and not just because of the weather. She

her neat hairstyle

He looked down at her dark-red high-heeled

"You've got perfect snow boots on too."

"Yes. Ideal. Not to mention my decision to go without thermals this morning. Brilliant!"

"Come on in and I'll warm you up."

She fell into his arms and shook even more as he hugged her close.

"I'm sorry," she said again.

"What for?"

"For everything. For Serner. I've been a fool."

"Don't exaggerate now, Ricky."

He brushed the snowflakes from her hair and forehead and took a careful look at her cheek.

"No, no, I'll tell you everything," she said.

"But first get your clothes off and climb into a hot bath. Would you like a glass of red?"

She would, and she stayed in the bath for a long while with her glass, which he refilled two or three times. He sat on the lid of the toilet listening to her story, and despite all the ominous news there was something of a reconciliation about their conversation, as if they were steadily breaking through a wall they had lately been building up between them.

"I know you thought I was being a fool right from the start," she said. "No, don't argue, I know you too well. But you have to understand that Christer, Malin and I could see no other solution. We had recruited Emil and Sofie, and we were so proud of that. They were just about the hottest reporters around, weren't they? It was incredibly prestigious for us. It showed that *Millennium* was on the move and there was a great buzz, with really positive coverage in *Resumé* and *Dagens Media*. It was like the good old days, and personally I felt strongly about the fact that I had promised both Sofie and Emil a secure future at the magazine. 'Our finances are stable,' I said. 'We have Harriet Vanger behind us. We're going to have the money for fantastic, in-depth reporting.' You know, I really believed it too. But then . . ."

"Then the sky fell in."

"Exactly, and it wasn't just the newspaper crisis, or the collapse of the advertising market. There was also that whole situation at the Vanger Group. I'm not sure you realize what a mess it was. Sometimes I see it almost as a political coup. All those reactionary old men in the family, and women too for that matter – well, you know them better than anyone. The old racists and regressives got together and stabbed Harriet in the back. I'll never forget that call from her. I've been rolled over, she said. Crushed. Of course it was her efforts to revive and modernize the group which had annoyed them, and then her decision to appoint David Goldman to the board, the son of Rabbi Viktor Goldman. But we were also part of the picture, as you know; Andrei had just written his report on beggars in Stockholm, which we all thought was the best thing he'd ever done, and which was quoted everywhere, even abroad. But which the Vanger people—"

"Thought was lefty rubbish."

"Worse than that, Mikael – propaganda for 'lazy buggers who can't even be bothered to get themselves a job'."

"Is that what they said?"

"Something along those lines. My guess is that the story itself was irrelevant, it was just their excuse, a pretext for further undermining Harriet's role within the group. They wanted to put a stop ... ... that Henrik and Harriet had stood for."

that it was then, when it seemed as if we ... ... Levin rang."

"Someone had presumably tipped him off about what had happened."

"Without a doubt, and I don't even need to tell you that I was sceptical at first. Serner felt like the trashiest sort of tabloid. But Levin gave it the works, with his usual torrent of words, and invited me down to his big new villa in Cannes."

"What?"

"Yes, I'm sorry, I didn't tell you that either. I suppose I felt ashamed. But I was going down to the film festival in any case, to do a profile on the Iranian film director. You know, the one being persecuted because she made the documentary about nineteen-year-old Sara, who had been stoned, and I didn't think it would do any harm if Serner helped us with the travel costs. In any event, Levin and I sat up all night and talked and I remained sceptical. He was absurdly boastful and came on with all this sales talk. But eventually I began to listen to him, and do you know why?"

"He was a fantastic lay?"

"Ha, no, it was his relationship to you."

"Did he want to sleep with me, then?"

"He has boundless admiration for you."

"Bullshit."

"No, Mikael, that's where you're wrong. He loves his power and his money and his villa in Cannes. But more than that, it bugs him that he's not as cool as you. If we're talking cred, he's poor and you're stinking rich. Deep down he wants to be like you, I felt that right away, and, yes, I should have realized that that sort of envy can become dangerous. You do know what the campaign against you is all about, don't you? Your uncompromising attitude makes people feel pathetic. Your very existence reminds them just how much they've sold out, and the more you're acclaimed, the punier they themselves appear. When it's like that, the only way they can fight back is by dragging you down. The bullshit gives them back a little bit of dignity – at least that's what they imagine."

"Thanks, Erika, but I really couldn't care less about that campaign."

"I know, at least I hope that's right. But what I realized was that Levin really wanted to be in with us, and feel like one of us. He wanted some of our reputation to rub off on him and I thought that was a good incentive. If his ambition was to be cool like you, then it would be devastating for him to turn *Millennium* into a run-of-the-mill commercial Serner product. If he became known as the man who destroyed one of the most fabled magazines in Sweden, any cred he might still have would be scuppered for good. That's why I really believed him when he said that both he and the group needed a prestigious magazine, and that he only wanted to help us produce the kind of journalism we believed in. Admittedly he did want to be involved in the magazine, but I put that down to vanity, that he wanted to be able to show off and say to his yuppie friends that he was our spin doctor or something. I never thought he would dare to have a go at the magazine's soul."

"And yet that's precisely what he's doing now."

"Unfortunately, yes."

"And where does that leave your fancy psychological theory?"

"... estimated the power of opportunism. As you saw, Levin ... emplary before this campaign

magazine. ... from a journalistic inferiority ... ordinary businessmen; they despise all talk or ... things that matter. They were irritated by what they described as Levin's 'fake idealism', and in the campaign against you they saw an opportunity to put the squeeze on him."

"Dear, oh dear."

"You have no idea. At first it looked O.K. We were to adapt somewhat to the market, and, as you know, I thought some of that sounded pretty good. I have, after all, spent a fair amount of time wondering how we could reach a younger readership. I really thought that Levin and I were having a productive dialogue so I didn't worry too much about his presentation today."

"I noticed that."

"But that was before all hell broke loose."

"What are you talking about?"

"The uproar when you sabotaged his presentation."

"I didn't sabotage anything, Erika. I just left."

Berger lay in the bath, took a sip of her wine and then she smiled a wistful smile.

"When will you learn that you're Mikael Blomkvist?" she said.

"I thought I was beginning to get the hang of that."

"Apparently not, because otherwise you'd have realized that when Mikael Blomkvist walks out in the middle of a presentation about his own magazine it's a big deal, whether Mikael Blomkvist intends it to be or not."

"In that case I apologize for my sabotage."

"I'm not blaming you, not any more. Now I'm the one saying sorry, as you can see. I'm the one who's put us in this position. It probably would have gone pear-shaped anyway, whether you'd walked out or not. They were just waiting for an excuse to take a swing at us."

"What actually happened?"

"After you disappeared we all felt deflated, and Levin, whose self-esteem had taken yet another knock, no longer gave a damn about his presentation. 'There's no point,' he said. He rang his boss to report back, and he probably laid it on a bit thick. I suspect that the envy on which I had been pinning my hopes had changed into something petty and spiteful. He was back again after an hour or so and said that the group was prepared to give *Millennium* its full backing and use all its channels to market the magazine."

"You didn't like the sound of that."

"No, and I knew before he'd even said one word about it. You could tell by the look on his face. It radiated a mixture of fear and triumph and at first he couldn't find the right words. He was mostly waffling and said that the group wanted to have more insight into the business, plus content aimed at a younger readership, plus more celebrity news. But then . . ."

Berger shut her eyes, drew her hand through her wet hair, then knocked back the last of her wine.

"Yes?"

"He said that he wanted you off the editorial team."

"He *what*?"

"Of course neither he nor the group could say it straight out, still less could they afford to get headlines like 'Serner sacks Blomkvist', so Ove put it neatly by saying that he wanted you to have a freer rein and be allowed to concentrate on what you're best at: writing reportage. He suggested a strategic relocation to London and a generous stringer arrangement."

"London?"

"_____ f___ ___ of your calibre, but

"What did he do?"

"I'm almost embarrassed to tell you. Andrei stood up and said that it was the most shameful thing he'd heard in his whole life. That you were one of the best things we had in this country, a source of pride for democracy and journalism, and that the whole Serner Group should hang their heads in shame. He said that you were a great man."

"He does tend to exaggerate."

"But he's a good kid."

"He really is. What did the Serner people do then?"

"Levin was prepared for it, of course. 'You're always welcome to buy us out,' he said. 'It's just—'"

"That the price has gone up," Blomkvist completed the sentence.

"Exactly. He claimed that whichever basis you use for valuing the business would show that any price for Serner's interest should

95

be at least double what it was when the group went in, given the additional value and goodwill they've created."

"Goodwill! Have they gone mad?"

"Not at all, apparently, but they're bright, and they want to mess us about. And I wonder if they're not trying to kill two birds with one stone: pull off a good deal and get rid of a competitor by breaking us financially, all in one go."

"What the hell should we do?"

"What we're best at, Mikael: slug it out. I'll take some of my own money and we'll buy them out and fight to make this northern Europe's best magazine."

"Sure, Erika, but then what? We'll end up with a lousy financial situation which even you won't be able to do anything about."

"I know, but it'll be O.K. We've come through more difficult situations than this. You and I can waive our salaries for a while. We can manage, can't we?"

"Everything has to end some time, Erika."

"Don't say that! Ever!"

"Not even if it's true?"

"Especially not then."

"Right."

"Don't you have anything in the pipeline?" she said. "Something, anything, that will stun Sweden's media?"

Blomkvist hid his face in his hands and for some reason he thought of Pernilla, his daughter. She had said that unlike him she was going to write "for real", whatever it was that was not "real" about his writing.

"I don't think so," he said.

Berger smacked her hand hard on the bath water so that it splashed out onto his socks.

"Jesus, you must have something. There's no-one in this country who gets as many tip-offs as you do."

"Most of it's junk," he said. "But maybe . . . I was just in the process of checking something."

Berger sat up in the tub.

"What?"

"No, it's nothing," he backtracked. "It's just wishful thinking."

"In a situation like this we have to think wishfully."

"Yes, but it's just a load of smoke and nothing you can prove."

"Yet there's something inside you that believes in it, isn't there?"

that's because of one little detail which doesn't

out of the bath,

CHAPTER 8

20.xi, Evening

August was kneeling on the checked floor in the bedroom, looking at a still-life arrangement with a lit candle on a blue plate, two green apples and an orange which his father had set out for him. But nothing was happening. August stared emptily at the storm outside and Balder wondered: *Does it make sense to present the boy with a subject?*

His son only had to glance at something for it to be embedded in his mind, so why should his father of all people choose what he was supposed to draw? August must have thousands of images of his own in his head. Maybe a plate and some pieces of fruit were as wrong as could be. Once again Balder asked himself: *Was the boy trying to convey something in particular with his traffic light?* The drawing was no casual little observation. On the contrary, the stop light shone like a baleful glowering eye, and maybe – what did Balder know? – August had felt threatened by the man on that pedestrian crossing.

Balder looked at his son for the umpteenth time that day. It was shameful, wasn't it? He used to think that August was simply weird and unfathomable. Now he wondered if he and his son were not in actual fact alike. When Balder was young, the doctors did not go in so much for diagnoses. In those days, there was a far greater tendency to dismiss people as being odd. He himself had definitely been different from other children, much too serious – his facial expression never changed – and no-one in the school playground thought he was much fun. Nor did he find the other children particularly entertaining either – he sought refuge in numbers and equations and avoided talking more than he was required to.

He would probably not have been considered autistic in the same sense as August. But nowadays they probably would have stuck an Asperger's label on him. He and Hanna had believed that the early diagnosis of August would help them, yet so little had

that his son was eight, that

Rådhuset, where he was being given some prize

nothing about. He had spent a boring evening longing to get home to his computer when a beautiful woman whom he vaguely recognized – Balder's knowledge of the world of celebrity was limited – came up to him and started to talk. Balder still thought of himself as the nerd from Tappström school who got nothing but contemptuous looks from the girls. He could not understand what a woman like Hanna saw in him. At the time – as he was soon to find out – she was at the height of her career. But she seduced him and made love to him that night like no woman had done before. Then followed maybe the happiest time in his life and yet . . . the binary codes won out over love.

He worked until the marriage fell apart. Lasse Westman arrived on the scene and Hanna went downhill and probably August did as well, which should of course have made Balder wild with fury. But he knew that he too was to blame. He had bought his freedom and not bothered about his son and perhaps what was said during the custody hearing was true, that he had chosen the dream of artificial life over that of his own child. What a monumental idiot he had been.

He got out his laptop and went on Google to learn more about savant skills. He had already ordered a number of books, and in his usual way meant to teach himself everything there was to know. No damn psychologist or educationalist would be able to catch him out and tell him what August needed at this point. He would know that better than any of them and so he continued searching until his attention was caught by the story of an autistic girl called Nadia.

What happened to her was described in Lorna Selfe's book *Nadia: A Case of Extraordinary Drawing Ability in an Autistic Child* and in Oliver Sacks' *The Man Who Mistook His Wife for a Hat*. Balder read in fascination. It was a gripping story and in many ways there were parallels. Like August, Nadia had seemed perfectly healthy when she was born, and only gradually did her parents realize that something was amiss.

The girl did not start speaking. She did not look people in the eye. She disliked physical contact and did not respond to her mother's smiles or attempts at communication. She was for the most part quiet and withdrawn and compulsively tore paper into narrow strips. By the time she was six she had still not spoken a word.

Yet she could draw like Leonardo da Vinci. Already at the age of three, and out of the blue, she had begun to draw horses. Unlike other children she did not start with the entire animal, but instead with some little detail – a hoof, a rider's boot, a tail – and the strangest thing of all was that she drew fast. In a terrific hurry she put together the parts, one here, one there, until she had a perfect whole, a horse which galloped or walked. From his own efforts when he was a teenager Balder knew how exceptionally difficult it is to draw an animal in motion. However hard you try, the result is unnatural or stiff. It takes a master to tease out the lightness in the movements. Nadia was a master already at the age of three.

Her horses were like perfect stills, drawn with a light touch, and obviously not the result of any long training. Her virtuosity burst out like a breaking dam, and that fascinated her contemporaries. How was it possible for her to leapfrog centuries of development in the history of art with just a few quick hand movements? The Australian specialists Allan Snyder and John Mitchell

_____ a theory, which has

shadows fall and the differences in depth and _____ it then draws certain conclusions about shape. We are not conscious of this. But it requires an examination of the separate parts before we can register something as simple as the fact that what we see is a ball and not a circle.

It is the brain which then produces the final form and, when it does, we no longer see all the detail we first registered. We cannot see the trees for the wood, so to speak. But what struck Mitchell and Snyder was that, if only we could reproduce the original image in our minds, we would be able to see the world in an entirely new way, and perhaps even recreate it, as Nadia had done without any training whatsoever.

Nadia saw the myriad details before they had been processed, which is why she began each time with an individual part, such as a hoof or a nose, because the totality as we perceive it did not yet exist in her mind. Balder found the idea appealing, even if he saw a number of problems with the theory, or at least had a number of questions.

In many ways this was the sort of original thinking he always looked for in his research: an approach which took nothing for granted but looked beyond the obvious, down to the small details. He grew more obsessed with the subject and read on with increasing fascination until, quite suddenly, he shuddered and even cried out loud, staring at his son with a stab of anxiety. It had nothing to do with the research findings, rather with the description of Nadia's first year at school.

Nadia had been put in a school for autistic children, where the teaching was focused on getting her to talk for the first time. The girl made some progress – the words came, one by one. But there was a high price to pay. As she started to talk, her brilliance with crayons disappeared and, according to the author Lorna Selfe, it was likely that one language was being replaced by another. From having been an artistic genius, Nadia became a severely handicapped autistic girl who was able to speak a little but who had entirely lost the gift that had astounded the world. Was it worth it, just to be able to say a few words?

No, Balder wanted to shout out, possibly because he had always been prepared to do whatever it took to become a genius in his field. Anything but the ordinary! That had been his guiding principle all his life, and yet . . . he was clever enough to understand that his own elitist principles were not necessarily a good pointer to the right way forward now. Maybe a few fabulous drawings were nothing as compared to being able to ask for a glass of milk, or exchange a few words with a friend, or a father. What did he know?

Yet he refused to be faced with such a choice. He could not bear to give up the most wonderful thing that had happened in August's life. No . . . that was simply not an option. No parent should have to decide. After all, no-one could anticipate what was best for the child.

The more he thought about it, the more unreasonable it seemed, and it occurred to him that he did not believe it, or perhaps that he simply did not *want* to believe it. Nadia's was after all only one case.

He had to find out more. But just then his mobile rang. It had been ringing a lot over the last few hours. One call had been from a withheld number and another from Linus, his former assistant. He had less and less time for Linus; he was not even sure he trusted him – certainly he did not feel like talking to him now.

Yet he answered, maybe out of sheer nervousness. It was

... Security Police, and that

with uncharacteristic severity. "You're in danger

"Oh, nonsense, Gabriella! I told you, they may try to sue the shirt off my back – but that's all."

"Frans, I'm sorry, but some new information has come through, and from an extremely well-informed source at that. There does appear to be a genuine risk."

"What do you mean?" he said, distracted. With the telephone clamped between his shoulder and ear, he was skimming another article on Nadia's lost gift.

"I'm finding it hard to assess the information, I admit that, but it's worrying me, Frans. It does have to be taken seriously."

"In that case, yes. I do promise I'll be extra careful. I'll stay indoors as usual. But I'm a bit busy just now, as I was saying. Besides, I'm all but convinced that you're wrong. At Solifon—"

"Sure, sure, I could be wrong," she cut in. "That's possible. But what if I'm right, what if there's even a tiny, tiny risk that I am?"

"Well—"

"Frans, listen to me. I think you're right. Nobody at Solifon wants to do you physical harm. It's a civilized company, after all. But it seems as if someone or even more than one person in the company is in touch with a criminal organization operating out of Russia and Sweden. That's where the threat is coming from."

Balder took his eyes off the computer screen for the first time. He knew that Zigmund Eckerwald at Solifon was cooperating with a group of criminals. He had even picked up some codenames for the leader of that group, but he could not understand why they would go after him. Or could he?

"A criminal organization?" he muttered.

"Yes," Grane said. "And isn't it logical, in a way? That's more or less what you've been saying, isn't it? That once you've started stealing someone else's ideas, and made money from them, then you've already crossed the line. It's downhill from there on."

"I think what I actually said was that all you needed was a gang of lawyers. With a gang of sharp lawyers you can safely steal whatever you like. Lawyers are the hit men of our times."

"O.K., maybe so. But listen to me: I haven't yet got approval for your personal protection, so I want to move you to a secret location. I'm coming to collect you."

"What are you saying?"

"I think we have to act immediately."

"Not a chance. I and . . ."

He hesitated.

"Do you have someone else there?"

"No, no, but I can't go anywhere right now."

"Aren't you listening to what I'm saying?"

"I hear you loud and clear. But with all due respect it sounds to me as if it's mostly speculation."

"Speculation is an essential tool in assessing risk, Frans. And the person who got in touch with me . . . I suppose I shouldn't really be saying this . . . is an agent from the N.S.A. who has this particular organization under surveillance."

"The N.S.A.!" he snorted.

"I know you're sceptical of them."

"Sceptical doesn't even begin to describe it."

"O.K., O.K. But this time they're on your side, at least this agent is. She's a good person. By eavesdropping she's picked up something which could very well be a plan to eliminate you."

"Me?"

but not right now. Besides, the alarm Milton ....

I've got cameras and sensors everywhere. And you do know that I'm a stubborn bastard, don't you."

"Do you have a weapon of any kind?"

"What's got into you, Gabriella? A weapon! The most dangerous thing I own is my new cheese slicer."

"You know . . ." she said, letting the words hang.

"Yes?"

"I'm going to arrange protection for you, whether you want it or not. I doubt you'll even notice it. But since you're going to be so damned obstinate, I have another piece of advice for you."

"Tell me."

"Go public. Tell the media what you know – then, if you're lucky, there'll be no point in someone getting rid of you."

"I'll think about it."

Balder had detected a note of distraction in Grane's voice.

"O.K.?" he said.

"Wait a moment," she said. "I've got someone else on the line. I have to . . ."

She was gone, and Balder, who should have had much else to mull over, found himself thinking of only one thing: will August lose his ability to draw if I teach him to talk?

"Are you still there?" Grane asked after a short while.

"Of course."

"I'm afraid I have to go. But I promise to see to it that you get some sort of protection as rapidly as possible. I'll be in touch. Take care!"

He hung up with a sigh and thought again of Hanna, and of August and the checked floor reflected in the wardrobe doors, and of all kinds of things which seemed irrelevant just then. Almost absent-mindedly he said to himself, "They're after me."

He could see that it was not unreasonable, even though he had always refused to believe that it would actually come to violence. But what, in fact, did he know? Nothing. Besides, he could not be bothered to address it now. He continued his search for information on Nadia, and what implications this might have for his son, but that was insane. He was burying his head in the sand. Despite Grane's warning he kept surfing and soon came upon the name of a professor of neurology, an expert on savant syndrome called Charles Edelman. Instead of reading on as he normally would – Balder always preferred the written to the spoken word – he called the switchboard at the Karolinska Institute.

Then it struck him how late it was. This Edelman was unlikely to be at work still, and his home number was not on the website. But wait a moment . . . he was also the head of Ekliden, an institution for autistic children with special abilities. Balder tried calling there. The telephone rang a number of times before a woman answered and introduced herself as Nurse Lindros.

"I'm sorry to disturb you so late in the evening," Balder said.

"I'm looking for Professor Edelman. Might he possibly still be there?"

"Yes, in fact, he is. No-one is setting off for home in this dreadful weather. Who may I say is calling?"

"Frans Balder," he said, and in case it might help he added: "Professor Frans Balder."

"Just a moment," Nurse Lindros said, "I'll see if he's available."

Balder stared down at August, who was once again gripping his pencil hesitantly, and that worried him somehow, as if it were an

                        organization," he muttered again.

                                          talking to

asking ourselves if we

about the brain through the back door, as it were,

research. We were wondering—"

"I'm flattered," Balder interrupted. "But right now I have a quick question for you."

"Oh, really? Is it something to do with your research?"

"Not at all. I have an autistic son. He's eight years old and hasn't yet said a single word, but the other day we passed a traffic light on Hornsgatan and afterwards . . ."

"Yes?"

"He just sat down and drew it at lightning speed, completely perfectly. It was astonishing!"

"And you want me to come and take a look at what he's done?"

"I'd like that. But that's not why I called. The fact is that I'm worried. I've read that perhaps drawing is the way in which he interacts with the world around him, and that he might lose this ability if he learns to talk."

"I can tell that you've been reading about Nadia."

"How do you know that?"

"Because she's always mentioned in this context. But . . . may I call you Frans?"

"Of course."

"Excellent, Frans, and I'm so glad you called. I can tell you straight away that you have nothing to worry about. On the contrary – Nadia is the exception that proves the rule, no more than that. All research shows that speech development actually enhances savant abilities. It can happen, of course, that children lose those skills, but that is mostly due to other factors. They get bored, or there's a significant event in their lives. You probably read that Nadia lost her mother."

"I did."

"Maybe that was the reason, even though neither I nor anyone else can know for sure. But there's virtually no other documented case of a similar evolution, and I'm not just saying this off the top of my head, or because it happens to be my own hypothesis. There is broad consensus today to the effect that savants have everything to gain from developing their intellectual skills on all levels."

"And you're sure of that?"

"Yes, definitely."

"He's also good at numbers."

"Really?" Edelman said thoughtfully. "Why do you say that?"

"Because it is extremely rare in a savant for artistic ability to be combined with mathematical talent. These two different skills have nothing in common, and sometimes they seem even to block each other."

"But that's how it is with my son. There's a kind of geometric precision about his drawings, as if he had worked out the exact proportions."

"How fascinating. When can I see him?"

"I don't really know. For the time being I only wanted some advice."

"In that case my advice is clear: make an effort with the boy. Stimulate him. Let him develop his skills in every way."

"I . . ." Balder felt a strange pressure in his chest and found it hard to get the words out. "I want to thank you," he said. "Really thank you. Now I have to . . ."

"It's been such an honour to talk to you; it would be wonderful to be able to meet you and your son. I've developed quite a sophisticated test for savants, if I may boast a little. I could help you get

the burning candle, the yellow pencil in his hand. went across Balder's shoulders, and the tears came. Whatever else you might say about Professor Balder, he was not one to cry easily.

In fact he could not remember when it had last happened. Not when his mother died, and definitely not when watching or reading anything. He thought of himself as a block of stone. But now, in front of his son with his rows of pencils and crayons, the professor cried like a child and he just let it happen, and of course it had been Charles Edelman's words.

August would be able to learn to speak and could keep drawing, and that was overwhelming news. But Balder was not crying just because of that of course. There was also the drama at Solifon. The death threat. The secrets he was privy to and the longing for Hanna or Farah or anyone who could fill the gap in his heart.

"My little boy!" he said, so emotional he failed to notice his laptop switch itself on and show pictures from one of the surveillance cameras outside the house.

Out in the garden, in the blustering storm, there was a tall, thin man in a padded leather jacket, with a grey cap pulled down to conceal his face. Whoever it was knew that he was being filmed, and even if he seemed lean and agile there was something in his swaying walk which was reminiscent of a heavyweight boxer on his way into the ring.

Grane was sitting in her office at Säpo searching the web and the agency's records. She did not really know what she was looking for. But something unfamiliar and worrying was gnawing away at her, something vague.

Her conversation with Balder had been interrupted by Helena Kraft, chief of Säpo, who was looking for her again to discuss the same matter as before. Alona Casales at the N.S.A. wanted to continue their conversation; this time she sounded calmer, and again a little flirtatious.

"Have you managed to sort out your computers?" Grane said.

"Ha . . . yes, that was a circus, but I don't think it's anything serious. I'm sorry if I was a little cryptic last time. I don't have much of a choice. I just want to stress again that the level of threat against Professor Balder is both real and serious, even though we know nothing for certain. Did you have time to deal with it?"

"I've spoken to him. He refuses to leave his house, told me he was in the middle of something. I'm going to arrange protection."

"Fine. As you might have guessed I've done more than just quickly check you out. I'm very impressed, Miss Grane. Shouldn't someone like you be working for Goldman Sachs and earning millions?"

"Not my style."

"Mine neither. I wouldn't say no to the money, but this underpaid snooping is more my thing. Now, honey, here's the situation.

As far as my colleagues are concerned this isn't a big deal – which I happen to disagree with. And not just because I'm convinced that this group represents a threat to our national economic interests. I also think there are political implications. One of those Russian computer engineers I mentioned, a guy called Anatoli Chabarov, is also linked to Ivan Gribanov, a member of the Russian Duma. He's notorious, and a major shareholder in Gazprom."

"I understand."

"But most of it so far is just dead ends. I've spent a lot of time

. the top."

"Then what makes you think it might be a wom...

"A sort of reverence, you could say. They talk about 'Thanos' in the same way men through the ages have spoken about women they desire and revere."

"A beauty, in other words."

"Right. But maybe I'm just picking up some homoeroticism. Nothing would make me happier than if Russian gangsters and bigwigs in general were to indulge more in that department."

"Ha, true!"

"In fact I mention it only so that you'll keep an open mind if this mess ends up on your desk. You understand there are also quite a few lawyers mixed up in it. What else is new, right? Hackers steal and lawyers legitimize the theft."

"True. Balder's said to me that we're all equal before the law – if we pay the same amount."

"Yes, if you can afford a strong defence you can get away with whatever you want these days. You do know who Balder's legal opponents are, don't you? The Washington firm Dackstone & Partner."

"Sure."

"In that case you know that the firm is also used by large tech companies to sue the shit out of inventors and innovators hoping to get some modest reward for their creations."

"I discovered that when we were dealing with the lawsuits of that inventor Håkan Lans."

"Grim, wasn't it? But the interesting thing is that Dackstone crops up in one of the few conversations we've managed to track down and decrypt from this criminal network, although there the firm is simply referred to as D.P., or even D."

"So Solifon and these crooks have the same lawyers?"

"It looks like it, and that's not all. Dackstone is about to open an office in Stockholm – do you know how we found that out?"

"No," Grane said. She was beginning to feel stressed. She wanted to finish the conversation and ensure that Balder got his police protection.

"Through our surveillance of this group," Casales went on. "We know Chabarov mentions it once in passing, which suggests that there are ties to the firm. The group knew about the office opening even before it became public, and Dackstone & Partner is setting up in Stockholm together with a Swedish lawyer called Brodin. He used to be a criminal lawyer, and if you remember he was known for getting a little too cosy with his clients."

"I do remember that classic picture in the evening papers – Kenny Brodin out on the town with some gangsters, with his hands all over a call girl," Grane said.

"I saw that. I'd bet that Mr Brodin is a good place to start if you want to check out this story. Who knows? Maybe he's the link between big business and this group."

"I'll take a look at it," Grane said. "But right now I've got a number of other things to deal with. I'm sure we'll be in touch again soon."

She called the duty officer for Säpo's Personal Protection Unit, who that evening was none other than Stig Yttergren. Her heart sank. Yttergren was sixty, overweight, known to be a heavy drinker, and most of all he liked to play cards online. He was sometimes called "Officer No-Can-Do". She proceeded to explain the situation in her most authoritative tone and demanded that Professor Frans Balder in Saltsjöbaden be given a bodyguard as ~~...dly as possible.~~ As usual Yttergren responded by saying that ~~...ible at all.~~ When

~~was waiting~~

for information on Dackstone & Partner and ~~anything~~ could find linked to what Casales had been telling her – and that is when she was overcome by a sense of something horribly familiar.

But she could not put her finger on it. Before she could find what she was looking for Yttergren called back to say that no-one from Personal Protection was available. There was an unusual amount of activity for the royal family that evening, he said, some sort of public engagement with the Norwegian crown prince and princess, and the leader of the Swedish Democrats had had an ice cream thrown at his head before his guards could intervene, which meant that they had had to provide reinforcements for his late speech in Södertälje.

So Yttergren had sent out "two great guys from the regular police", Peter Blom and Dan Flinck, and Grane had to make do with that, even if their names reminded her of Kling and Klang in *Pippi Longstocking*. For a moment she had serious misgivings. Then she got angry with herself.

It was so typical of her snobbish background to judge people by their names. She might have had more cause for concern if they had a posh name like Gyllentofs or something. Then they could have been irresponsible layabouts. *I'm sure this'll be fine,* she thought.

Then she got back to work. It was going to be a long night.

CHAPTER 9

20.xi – 21.xi, Night

and the marble and all the idiotic luxuries – to be ~~...~~

happened and she just sank to the floor, breathing heavily.

Then she stood up and looked at herself in the mirror, which was not especially reassuring either. Her eyes were red. On the other hand it was not long after midnight. She must have slept for a few hours only. She took a glass from the bathroom cupboard and filled it with water. But at the same moment the details of her dream came flooding back and she crushed the glass in her hand. Blood dripped to the floor, and she swore and realized that she was unlikely to be going back to sleep.

Should she try to crack the encrypted N.S.A. file she had downloaded? No, that would be pointless, at least for now. Instead she wound a towel around her hand and took from her bookshelves a new study by Princeton physicist Julie Tammet, which described how a big star collapses into a black hole. She lay down on the sofa by the windows overlooking Slussen and Riddarfjärden.

As she began to read she felt a little better. Blood from the towel did seep onto the pages and her head would not stop hurting, but she became more and more engrossed in the book, every now and then making a note in the margin. None of it was new to her. She knew better than most that a star stays alive as a result of two opposing actions, the fusion reactions at its core forcing it outwards and the gravitational pull keeping it together. She saw it as a balancing act, a tug of war from which a victor eventually emerges, once the fuel for the reactions runs out and the explosions weaken.

Once gravity gains the upper hand, the celestial body shrinks like a punctured balloon and becomes smaller and smaller. In this way, a star can vanish into nothing. Salander liked black holes. She felt an affinity with them.

Yet, like Julie Tammet, she was not interested in black holes *per se*, but rather in the process which creates them. Salander was convinced that if only she could describe that process she would be able to draw together the two irreconcilable languages of the universe, quantum physics and the theory of relativity. But it was no doubt beyond her capabilities, just like the bloody encryption, and involuntarily she began again to think about her father.

When she was a child, that revolting specimen had raped her mother over and over again, right up until the time her mother received injuries from which she would never recover. Salander herself, then twelve, hit back with a horrific force. At the time she could have had no idea that her father was an important spy who had defected from the G.R.U., the Soviet military intelligence service, nor could she have known that a special department within the Swedish Security Police, referred to as the Section, was protecting him at any cost. Yet even then she understood that there was some mystery surrounding the man, a darkness no-one was allowed to approach in any way. That even applied to so simple a thing as his name.

Zala, or Alexander Zalachenko to be more precise. Other fathers could be reported to the social services and the police. But Zala had forces behind him which were above all that.

It was this and one other thing which for her were true black holes.

The alarm went off at 1.18 and Balder woke with a start. Was there someone in the house? He felt an inexplicable fear and reached across the bed. August was lying beside him. The boy must have _____ __ __ he whimpered with worry, as if the _____ _____ dreams. *My little*

_____ bowed. Could the alarm ____ Perhaps it was as simple as that.

He still had to check to see if that protection Gabriella Grane was organizing had arrived at last. Two men from the regular police were supposed to have been there hours ago. It was a farce. They had been delayed by the storm and by a series of conflicting orders. It was either one thing or another, and he agreed with Grane, it seemed hopelessly incompetent.

He would have to deal with that in due course. Now he had to make a call. But August was beginning to wake up, and a hysterical child banging his body against the headboard was the last thing Balder needed right now. The earplugs, it occurred to him, those old green earplugs he had bought at Frankfurt airport.

He took them from the bedside table and gently pushed them into his son's ears. Then he tucked him in and kissed him on the cheek and stroked his curly, tousled hair, straightened the collar on the boy's pyjamas and made sure that his head was resting comfortably on the pillow. Balder was frightened and should have been in a hurry, or had every reason to be. Yet he took his time and fussed over his son. Perhaps it was a sentimental moment in the midst of a crisis. Or he wanted to put off confronting whatever awaited him out there. For a moment he wished he did have a weapon. Not that he would have known how to use it.

He was a programmer, for heaven's sake, who had developed some paternal instinct in his old age, that was all. He should never have got into this mess. To hell with Solifon and the N.S.A. and all criminal gangs! But now he had to get a grip. With stealthy, uncertain steps he went into the hallway, and before doing anything else, before even looking out at the road, he turned off the alarm. The racket had set his nerves on edge and in the sudden silence which followed he stood stock still. Then his mobile rang and even though it startled him he was grateful for the distraction.

"Yes," he said.

"Hello, this is Jonas Anderberg, I'm on duty tonight at Milton Security. Is everything alright?"

"What, well . . . I think so. My alarm went off."

"I know that and, according to our instructions, when this happens you're supposed to go down to a special room in the cellar and lock the door. Are you down there?"

"Yes," he lied.

"Good, very good. Do you know what's happened?"

"No idea. The alarm woke me up. I have no clue what set it off. Could it have been the storm?"

"Unlikely . . . One moment please!"

Anderberg's voice sounded a bit unfocused.

"What is it?" Balder said nervously.

"It seems . . ."

"For God's sake, tell me what's going on."

"Sorry, just take it easy, take it easy . . . I'm going through the picture sequence from your cameras, and it does look as if . . ."

"As if what?"

"As if you've got a visitor. A man, well, you can see for yourself later, a lanky man with dark glasses and a cap has been prowling around your property. He's been there twice, as far as I can see, but as I said . . . I've only just noticed it now. I'd have to look at it more closely to be able to say more."

"What sort of person is it?"

"Well, it's hard to say."

. . . the picture sequences again.

"And what's that?"

"His walk. The man walks like a junkie – like a guy who's just taken a load of speed. There's something cocky and stilted about the way he moves, and of course that could be a sign that he's just an ordinary druggie and petty thief. On the other hand . . ."

"Yes?"

"He's done a very good job of hiding his face and then . . ."

Anderberg fell silent again.

"Keep going!"

"One moment."

"You're making me nervous, you know that?"

"Don't mean to. But you know . . ."

Balder froze. The sound of a car engine could be heard from his garage drive.

". . . you're getting a visitor."

"What should I do?"

"Stay where you are."

"O.K.," Balder said, more or less paralyzed. But he was not where Anderberg thought he was.

When the telephone rang at 1.58, Blomkvist was still awake. But his mobile was in the pocket of his jeans on the floor and he did not manage to answer it in time. In any case the call was from a withheld number, so he swore and crawled back into bed and closed his eyes.

He could really do without another sleepless night. Ever since Berger had fallen asleep a little before midnight, he had been tossing and turning and thinking about his life. Not much of it felt right, not even his relationship to Berger. He had loved her for many years, and there was every reason to think that she felt the same way about him. But it was no longer as simple as once it had been. Perhaps Blomkvist had started to feel some sympathy for Greger. Greger Beckman was Erika's husband, an artist, and he could not reasonably be accused of being grudging or small-minded. On the contrary, when Greger had realized that Erika would never get over Blomkvist or even be able to stop herself from tearing his clothes off every now and then, he had not lost his temper. He had made a deal:

"You can be with him – just so long as you always come back to me." And that's how it became.

They set up an unconventional arrangement, with Berger mostly sleeping at home with her husband in Saltsjöbaden, but sometimes here with Blomkvist at Bellmansgatan. Over the years Blomkvist had thought that it really was an ideal solution, one which many couples who lived under the dictatorship of monogamy ought to have adopted. Every time Berger said, "I love my husband more when I can also be with you," or when at some cocktail party Beckman put his arm around him in a brotherly embrace, Blomkvist had thanked his lucky stars for the arrangement.

Yet he had lately begun to have doubts, perhaps because he had had more time to think and it had occurred to him that something that is called an agreement is not necessarily always that.

On the contrary, one party might advance their self-interest under the guise of a common decision, and in the long run it often becomes clear that someone is suffering, despite assurances to the contrary. Berger's call to her husband that evening had evidently not been well received. Who knows? Maybe Beckman was also lying awake right now.

Blomkvist tried to put it out of his mind. For a little while he

. . . help much, and in the

from Malm and Eriksson, also from Andre_ Vanger in the light of the coming battle with Serner, and he answered them with more of a fighting spirit than he actually felt. After that he checked Salander's document, without expecting to find anything there. But then he lit up. She had answered. For the first time in ages she had given a sign of life:

<Balder's intelligence isn't in the least bit artificial. How's your own these days?
And what happens, Blomkvist, if we create a machine which is a little bit cleverer than we are?>

Blomkvist smiled and thought of the last time they had met, at Kaffebar on St Paulsgatan. It took a while before he noticed that her message contained two questions, the first one a friendly little jibe which perhaps regrettably contained a grain of truth. What he had written in the magazine lately had lacked intelligence and genuine newsworthiness. Like so many journalists, he had just been plugging away, occasionally trotting out clichés. But that's how it was for the moment and he was much keener to ponder Salander's second question, her riddle, not so much because in itself it interested him especially, but because he wanted to think of some clever response.

If we create a machine that is cleverer than we ourselves are, he thought, *what happens then*? He went to the kitchen, opened a bottle of Ramlösa mineral water and sat at the kitchen table. Downstairs Fru Gerner was coughing rather painfully and in the distance, amid the hubbub of the city, an ambulance wailed away in the storm. Well, he mused, then we get a machine that can do all the clever things which we ourselves can do, plus a little bit more, for example . . . He laughed out loud and understood the point of the question. A machine like that could go on to produce something more intelligent than itself in turn, and then what happens?

The same would be true of the next machine and the next one and the next one, and soon the very source of it all, man himself, would be no more interesting to the latest computer than a lab rat. There would be an explosion of intelligence beyond all control, as in the Matrix films. Blomkvist smiled and went back to his computer and wrote:

```
<If we create such a machine then we'll get
a world where not even Lisbeth is so cock-
sure.>
```

After that he sat looking out through the window, in so far as one could see anything beyond the swirling snow. Every now and then he looked through the open door at Berger, who was sleeping soundly and who knew nothing about machines more intelligent than human beings, or was not the least bit concerned about that right now.

He thought he heard his mobile give a ping, and sure enough

he had a new voicemail. That worried him, he was not really sure why. Apart from ex-girlfriends who call when they're drunk and want to have sex, you generally only get bad news at night. The voice on the message sounded harried:

My name is Frans Balder. I know it's rude to call this late. I apologize for that. But my situation has become somewhat critical, at least that's how I see it. I've just discovered that you were looking for me, which is really a strange coincidence. There are a few things I've been wanting to tell you about for some time now, I think they . . . . get in touch as soon

Balder was lying in bed, agitated and scared. . . . . . . little calmer now. The car coming up his drive had been the police guard arriving at long last. Two men in their forties, one tall and one quite short, both looking cocky and with the same short, trendy haircut. But they were perfectly polite and apologized for the delay in taking up their post.

"Milton Security and Gabriella Grane at the Security Police briefed us on the situation," one said.

They were aware that a man wearing a cap and dark glasses had been snooping around the property and that they had to be on their guard. Therefore they turned down the offer of a cup of hot tea in the kitchen. They wanted to check out the house and Balder thought that sounded perfectly professional and sensible. In other respects they did not make a very positive impression, but then he did not get an overwhelmingly negative impression either. He had put their numbers into his mobile and gone back to bed to be with August, who was sleeping, curled up, his green earplugs still in place.

But of course Balder had not been able to fall asleep again. He was listening for noises out there in the storm and eventually he sat up in bed. He had to do something, or he would go mad. He checked his mobile. He had two messages from Linus Brandell, who sounded bad-tempered and defensive all at the same time. At first Balder felt like hanging up. But then he caught a couple of things which were interesting after all. Linus had spoken to Mikael Blomkvist at *Millennium* magazine and now Blomkvist wanted to get in touch, and at that Balder began to think. Mikael Blomkvist, he muttered.

Is he to be my link with the outside world?

Balder knew very little about Swedish journalists. But he did know who Blomkvist was, and was aware of his reputation as someone who always went right to the heart of his stories, never yielding to pressure. That in itself did not necessarily make him the right man for the job – plus, somehow Balder seemed to recall hearing other less flattering things – so he called Gabriella Grane again. She knew just about everything there was to know about the media scene and had said that she would be staying up late.

"Hello," she answered right away. "I was about to get in touch. I'm just looking at that man on the C.C.T.V. We really ought to move you now, you know."

"But my God, Gabriella, the police are here – finally. They're sitting right outside the front door."

"There's no reason to suppose that the man will come through the front door."

"Why would he come at all? The man at Milton said he looked like an old junkie."

"I'm not so sure about that. He's carrying some sort of box, something technical. We should play this safe."

Balder glanced at August lying next to him.

"I'm quite happy to move tomorrow. That might help my

nerves. But I'm not going anywhere tonight – your policemen seem professional, professional enough at any rate."

"If you're going to be stubborn about this I'll see to it that Flinck and Blom make themselves conspicuous and cover the entire property."

"Fine, but that's not why I'm calling. You said I ought to go public, remember?"

"Well . . . yes . . . That's not the kind of advice you would expect from the Security Police, is it? I still think it would be a good idea, but first I'd like you to tell *us* what you know. I'm feeling a little

on your doorstep, then you know your whole year is shot, they say. Everybody here, including Helena Kraft, would advise against it in the strongest terms."

"But it's you I'm asking."

"Well, my answer is that your reasoning is sound. He's a damn fine journalist."

"Hasn't he also come in for some criticism?"

"For sure, people have been saying that he's past his prime and that his writing isn't positive or upbeat enough, or whatever. But he's an old-fashioned investigative reporter of the highest calibre. Do you have his contact details?"

"My ex-assistant gave them to me."

"Good, great. But before you get in touch with him, you must first tell us what you have. Do you promise?"

"I promise, Gabriella. Now I'm going to sleep for a few hours."

"Do that, and I'll keep in touch with Flinck and Blom and arrange a safe house for you first thing in the morning."

After he had hung up he tried again to get some rest. But it proved as impossible this time as before. The storm made him increasingly restless and worried. It felt as if something evil was travelling across the sea towards him, and he could not help listening anxiously for any unusual sounds.

It was true that he had promised Grane he would talk to her first. But he could not wait – everything he had kept bottled up for so long was throbbing to get out. He knew it was irrational; nothing could be that urgent. It was the middle of the night and, regardless of what Grane had said, he was by any reckoning safer than he had been for a long time. He had police protection and a first-rate security system. But that did not help. He was agitated, and so he got out the number Linus had given him and dialled it. But of course Blomkvist did not answer.

Why would he? It was far too late, and Balder left a voice message instead in a slightly forced, whispered voice so as not to wake August. Then he got up and put on his bedside light. On the bookshelf by the bed there was some literature which had nothing to do with his work, and both absent-minded and worried he flicked through an old novel by Stephen King, *Pet Sematary*. But that made him think even more about evil figures travelling through the night. For a long time he just stood there with the book in his hand – then he felt a stab of apprehension, which he might have dismissed as nonsense in broad daylight but which now seemed totally plausible. He had a sudden urge to speak to Farah or better still Steven Warburton in Los Angeles, who would be certain to be awake, and while imagining all sorts of unpleasant scenarios, he looked out to sea and the night and the restless clouds scudding across the sky. At that moment his mobile rang, as if it had heard his prayer. But it was neither Farah nor Warburton.

"My name is Mikael Blomkvist," the voice said. "You've been looking for me."

"That's right. I'm sorry to have called so late."

"No problem. I was awake anyway."

"Can you talk now?"

"Absolutely, I was in fact just answering a message from a person whom I think we both know. Lisbeth Salander."

"Who?"

"Sorry, maybe I've got hold of the wrong end of the stick. I thought you had hired her to go through your computers and trace

probably think it's a crazy idea.

"Sometimes I like crazy ideas."

"You wouldn't feel like coming over right now? It would mean a lot to me. I'm sitting on a story which I think is pretty explosive. I can pay for your taxi here and back."

"Thanks, but I always pick up my own tab. Tell me, why do we have to talk now, in the middle of the night?"

"Because . . ." Balder hesitated. "Because I have a feeling this is urgent, or actually it's more than a feeling. I've just been told that I'm under threat, and an hour or so ago someone was snooping around my property. I'm frightened, to be completely honest, and I want to get this information off my chest. I no longer want to be the only one in the know."

"O.K."

"O.K. what?"

"I'll come – if I can manage to get hold of a taxi."

Balder gave him the address and hung up, then called Professor Warburton in Los Angeles, and had an intense conversation with him on an encrypted line for about thirty minutes. Then he put on a pair of jeans and a black cashmere polo neck and went in search of a bottle of Amarone, in case that was the kind of thing Blomkvist might enjoy. But he got no further than the doorway before he started in fright.

He thought he had seen a movement, something flashing past, and looked anxiously towards the jetty and the sea. But it was the same desolate, storm-lashed scene as before, and he dismissed whatever it was as a figment of his imagination, a product of his nervous frame of mind, or at least he tried to. He left the bedroom and walked past the large window on his way towards the upper floor. Suddenly gripped by a new fear, he spun around again and this time he really did glimpse something over by the house next door.

A figure was racing along in the shelter of the trees, and even if Balder did not see the person for more than a matter of seconds, he could make out that it was a powerfully built man with a rucksack and dark clothes. The man ran in a crouch and something about the way he moved had a trained look to it, as if he had run like that many times before, perhaps in a distant war. It took a few moments for Balder to fumble for his mobile, and he tried to work out which of the numbers on his call list belonged to the policemen out there.

He had not put their names into his contacts, and now was uncertain. With a shaking hand he tried one which he thought was right. No-one answered, not at first. The ring tone sounded three, four, five times before a voice panted out, "Blom here, what's up?"

"I saw a man running along the line of trees by my neighbour's house. I don't know where he is now. But he could very well be up by the road near you."

"O.K., we'll check it out."

"He seemed . . ." Balder said.

"What?"

"I don't know, quick."

Dan Flinck and Peter Blom were sitting in the police car chatting about their young colleague, Anna Berzelius, and the size of her bum.

Both had recently got divorced. Their divorces had been pretty painful at first. They both had young children, wives who

had discussed all the parties in detail, especially

met, reviewing their physiques from top to bottom, and their prowess in bed. But on this occasion they had not had time to discuss Anna Berzelius in as much depth as they would have liked.

Blom's mobile rang and they both jumped, partly because he had changed his ringtone to an extreme version of "Satisfaction", but mainly of course because the night and the storm and the emptiness out here had made them edgy. Besides, Blom had his telephone in his pocket, and since his trousers were tight – his waistline had expanded as a result of all the partying – it took a while before he could get it out. When he hung up he looked worried.

"What's that about?" Flinck said.

"Balder saw a man, a quick bastard, apparently."

"Where?"

"Down by the trees next to the neighbour's house. The guy's probably on his way up towards us."

Blom and Flinck stepped out of the car. They had been outside many times over the course of this long night, but this was the first time they shivered right down to the bone. For an instant they just stood looking awkwardly to the right and the left, shocked by the cold. Then Blom – the taller of the two – took command and told Flinck to stay up by the road while he himself went down towards the water.

It was a short slope which extended along a wooden fence and a small avenue of newly planted trees. A lot of snow had fallen, it was slippery and at the bottom lay the sea. *Baggensfjärden*, Blom thought, and in fact he was surprised that the water had not frozen over, but that may have been because of the waves. Blom cursed at the storm and at this night duty which wore him out and ruined his beauty sleep. He tried to do his job all the same, not with his whole heart perhaps, but still.

He listened out for sounds and looked about him, and at first he could not pick out anything from the surroundings. It was dark. Only the light from a single lamp post shone into the property, immediately in front of the jetty, and he went down, past a garden chair which had been flung about in the storm, and in the next moment he could see Balder through the large windowpane.

Balder was standing some way inside the house, bent over a large bed, his body in a tensed position. Perhaps he was straightening the covers, it was hard to tell. He seemed busy with some small detail in the bed. Blom should not be bothering about it – he was meant to be keeping watch over the property – yet there was something in Balder's body language which fascinated him and for a second or two he lost his concentration before he was brought back to reality again.

He had a chilling feeling that someone was watching him, and he spun around, his eyes searching wildly. He saw nothing, not at first, and had just begun to calm down when he became aware of two things – a sudden movement by the shiny steel bins next to the fence, and the sound of a car up by the road. The engine stopped and a car door was opened.

Neither occurrence was noteworthy in itself. There could be an animal by the rubbish bins and cars could come or go here even late at night. Yet Blom's body stiffened completely and for a moment he just stood there, not knowing how to react. Then Flinck's voice could be heard.

"...ming!"

...watched and

did not seem the ...

himself of the apprehension that he was leaving som...

ening and unpleasant down there by the steel bins. But if his partner shouted like that, he did not have a choice, did he? And he felt secretly relieved. He had been more frightened than he cared to admit and so he hurried off and came stumbling up onto the road.

Up ahead, Flinck was chasing after an unsteady man with a broad back and clothes that were far too thin and, even though he hardly fitted the description of a "quick bastard", Blom ran after him. Soon afterwards they brought him down by the side of the ditch, right next to a couple of letterboxes and a small lantern which cast a pale light over the whole scene.

"Who the hell are you?" Flinck bellowed with surprising aggression – he had been scared too – and the man looked at them in confusion and terror.

He was not wearing a hat, he had hoarfrost in his hair and in the stubble on his chin and you could tell that he was cold and in pretty bad shape. But above all there was something extraordinarily familiar about his face.

For a few seconds Blom thought that they had arrested a known and wanted criminal and he swelled with pride.

Balder had gone back to the bedroom and tucked August in again, perhaps to hide him under the blanket if anything should happen. Then he had a completely crazy thought, prompted by the sense of foreboding he had just felt, which was accentuated by his conversation with Warburton. Probably his mind was just clouded by panic and fear.

He realized it was not a new idea but something which had been developing in his subconscious during many sleepless nights in California. So he got out his laptop, his own little supercomputer connected to a series of other machines for sufficient capacity, and opened the A.I. program to which he had dedicated his life, and then . . .

He deleted the file and all of the back-up. He barely thought it through. He was like an evil God snuffing out a life, and perhaps that was exactly what he *was* doing. Nobody knew, not even he himself, and he sat there for a little while, wondering if he would be floored by remorse and regret. It was incomprehensible, wasn't it? His life's work was gone, with just a few taps of a key.

But oddly enough it made him calmer, as if at least one aspect of his life was now protected. He got to his feet and once more looked out into the night and the storm. Then the telephone rang. It was Flinck, the second policeman.

"I just wanted to say that we apprehended the man you saw," the policeman said. "In other words, you can relax. We have the situation under control."

"Who is it?" Balder said.

"I couldn't say. He's very drunk and we have to get him to

quieten down. I just wanted to let you know. We'll get back to you."

Balder put the mobile down on the bedside table, next to his laptop, and tried to congratulate himself. Now the man was under arrest, and his research would not fall into the wrong hands. Yet he was not reassured. At first he did not understand why. Then it hit him: the man who had run along the trees had been anything but drunk.

It took a full minute or more before Blom realized that they had ~~~~~~~~~~~~~~~~~~~~~~~~~~~~~~~~~~~ rather the actor Lasse

He knew enough about Westman to be aware that man did all too often ended up in the evening papers, and you could not say that the actor was looking particularly happy. He puffed and swore as he scrambled to get to his feet and Blom tried to work out what on earth the man was doing out here in the middle of the night.

"Do you live in the area?" he said.

"I don't have to tell you a fucking thing," Westman hissed, and Blom turned to Flinck in an attempt to understand how the whole drama had begun.

But Flinck was already standing a little way off talking into his mobile, apparently with Balder. He probably wanted to show how efficient he was by passing on the news that they had seized the suspect, if indeed he was the suspect.

"Have you been snooping around Professor Balder's property?" Blom said.

"Didn't you hear what I said? I'm not telling you a fucking thing. What the hell, here I am strolling around perfectly peacefully and along comes that maniac waving his pistol. It's scandalous. Don't you know who I am?"

"I know who you are, and if we have overreacted then I apologize. I'm sure we'll have a chance to talk about it again. But right now we're in the middle of a tense situation and I demand that you tell me at once what brought you here to Professor Balder – oh no, don't you try to run away now!"

Westman was probably not trying to escape at all. He was only having trouble keeping his balance. Then he cleared his throat rather dramatically and spat right out into the air. The phlegm did not get far but flew back like a projectile and froze to ice on his cheek.

"Do you know something?" he said, wiping his face.

"No?"

"I'm not the bad guy in this story."

Blom looked nervously down towards the water and the avenue of trees and wondered yet again what he had seen there. And still he remained standing where he was, paralyzed by the absurdity of the situation.

"Well then, who is?"

"Balder."

"How so?"

"He's taken my girlfriend's son."

"Why would he have done that?"

"You shouldn't bloody well be asking me! Ask the computer genius in there! That bastard has absolutely no right to him," Westman said, and fumbled in the inside pocket of his coat.

"He doesn't have a child in the house, if that's what you think," Blom said.

"He sure as hell does."

"Really?"

"Really!"

"So you thought you'd come along here in the middle of the night, pissed as a newt, and fetch the child," Blom said, and he was about to make another crushing comment when he was interrupted by a sound, a soft clinking sound coming up from the water's edge.

"What was that?" he said.

"What was what?" answered Flinck, who was standing next to him and did not seem to have heard anything at all. It was true that the sound had not been all that loud, at least not up here.

more, and this sound was no more reassuring.

He did not know for sure, and now the car door opened and a man climbed out whom Blom, after a moment's confusion, recognized as the journalist Mikael Blomkvist, though God only knew why the hell all these celebrities had to congregate out here in the middle of the night.

CHAPTER 10

21.xi, Early Morning

Balder was standing in the bedroom next to his computer and his mobile, looking at August, who was whimpering uneasily in the bed. He wondered what the boy was dreaming. Was it about a world which he could even understand? Balder wanted to know. He felt that he wanted to start living, no longer bury himself in quantum algorithms and source codes and paranoia.

He wanted to be happy, not tormented by that constant weight in his body; he wanted instead to launch himself into something wild and magnificent, a romance even. For a few intense seconds he thought about the women who had fascinated him: Gabriella, Farah, others too.

He also thought about the woman who it turned out was called Salander. He had been spellbound by her, and as he now remembered her he saw something new in her, something both familiar and strange: she reminded him of August. That was absurd, of course. August was a small autistic boy, and while Salander was not that old either, and there may have been something boyish about her, otherwise she was his polar opposite. Dressed in black, a bit of a punk, totally uncompromising. Still it occurred to him now that her eyes had that same strange shine as August's when he had been staring at the traffic light on Hornsgatan.

Balder had encountered Salander during a lecture at the Royal

Institute of Technology in the course of a talk he was giving on technical singularity, the hypothetical state when computers become more intelligent than the human being. He had just begun by explaining the concept of singularity in terms of mathematics and physics when the door opened and a skinny girl in black strode into the lecture hall. His first thought was that it was a shame there was no other place for junkies to go. Then he wondered if the girl really was an addict. She did not seem strung out, but on the other hand she did look tired and surly, and did not appear to _____ his lecture. She just sat there slouched _____ discussion of the

concepts about, he sho...
his calculations fell apart. It was not some sort of r...
ical collapse, more a sign that his own mathematics were not up to scratch, and therefore it was sheer populism on his part to mystify singularities in black holes when it was so obvious that the main problem was the absence of a quantum mechanical method for calculating gravity.

With icy clarity – which set off a buzz in the hall – she then presented a sweeping critique of the singularity theorists he had quoted, and he was incapable of coming up with any answer other than a dismayed: "Who the hell are you?"

That was their first contact. The girl was to surprise him a few times more after that. With lightning speed or just one bright glance she immediately grasped what he was working on and, when he realized that his technology had been stolen, he had asked for her help. That had created a bond between them – they shared a secret.

Now he was standing there in the bedroom thinking of her. But his thoughts were interrupted. He was overcome by a new chilling sense of unease and he looked through the doorway towards the large window overlooking the water.

In front of it stood a tall figure in dark clothes and a tight black cap with a small lamp on his forehead. He was doing something to the window. He pulled across it with a swift and powerful movement, like an artist starting work on a fresh canvas, and before Balder had time to cry out, the entire window fell in and the figure moved towards him.

Jan Holtser usually told people that he worked on industrial security issues. In actual fact he was a former Russian special forces soldier who spent his time breaking into security systems. He had a small skilled staff and, for operations like this one, the preparations were as a rule so painstaking that the risks were not as great as one might imagine.

It's true that he was no longer a young man, but for fifty-one he kept himself in good shape with hard training and was known for his efficiency and ability to improvise. If fresh circumstances cropped up, he thought about them and took them into consideration in his planning.

His experience tended to make up for his lack of youthful vigour, and occasionally, in the limited circle within which he could talk openly, he would speak of a sort of sixth sense, an acquired instinct. He had learned over the years when to wait and when to strike, and although he had been through a bad patch a couple of years earlier and betrayed signs of weakness – humanity, his daughter would say – he now felt that he was more accomplished than ever before.

He was once more able to take pleasure in his work, that old sense of excitement. Yes, he did still dose himself with ten milligrams of Stesolid before an operation, but that was only because it enhanced his accuracy with weapons. He remained crystal clear and alert at critical moments, and most important: he always carried out the tasks he was assigned. Holtser was not someone who let people down or bailed out. That was how he thought of himself.

And yet tonight, even though his client had stressed that the job was urgent, he had considered calling it off. The bad weather was a factor. But the storm in itself would never have been enough to get him to consider cancelling. He was Russian and a soldier, and had fought in far worse conditions than these, and he hated

taller of the two, who seemed to dislike the and the black water. As he stood there staring in among the trees a little while ago, he had looked to be terrified, presumably because he had sensed Holtser's presence, but that was not something that worried Holtser. He could have slit the man's throat swiftly and soundlessly.

Still, the fact of policemen was not good news.

Their presence considerably raised the level of risk; above all it was an indication that some part of the plan had leaked out, that there was a heightened readiness. Maybe the professor had started to talk, in which case the operation would be meaningless, it might even make their situation worse. Holtser was determined not to expose his client to any unnecessary risks. He regarded that as one of his strengths. He always saw the bigger picture and, despite his profession, he was often the one who counselled caution.

He had lost count of the number of criminal gangs in his home country which had gone under because they had resorted too often to violence. Violence can command respect. Violence can silence and intimidate, and ward off risks and threats. But violence can also cause chaos and a whole chain of unwanted consequences.

All those thoughts had gone through his mind as he sat hidden behind the trees and the line of bins. For a few seconds he was resolved to abort the operation and go back to his hotel room. Yet that did not happen.

A car arrived, occupying the policemen's attention, and he spotted an opportunity, an opening. Without stopping to evaluate his motivations he fitted the elastic of the lamp over his head. He got out the diamond saw from his left-hand jacket pocket and drew his weapon, a 1911 R1 Carry with a custom-made silencer, and weighed them, one in each hand. Then, as ever, he said:

"Thy will be done, amen."

Yet he could not shake off the uncertainty. Was this right? He would have to act with lightning speed. True, he knew the house inside out and Jurij had been here twice and hacked the alarm system. Plus the policemen were hopeless amateurs. Even if he were delayed in there – say the professor did not have his computer next to his bed, as everyone had said, and they had time to come to his aid – Holtser would be able to dispose of them too without any problem. He even looked forward to it. He therefore muttered a second time:

"Thy will be done, amen."

Then he disengaged the safety on his weapon and moved rapidly to the large window overlooking the water. It may have been due to the uncertainty of the situation, but he felt an unusually strong reaction when he saw Balder standing there in the bedroom, engrossed in something, and he tried to persuade himself that everything was fine. The target was clearly visible. Yet he still felt apprehensive: Should he call the job off?

He did not. Instead he tensed the muscles in his right arm and with all his strength drew the diamond cutter across the window and pushed. The window collapsed with a disturbing crash and he rushed in and raised his weapon at Balder, who was staring hard at him, waving his hand as though in a desperate greeting. The professor began to say something confused and ceremonious which sounded like a prayer, a litany. But instead of "God" or "Jesus" Holtser heard the word "disabled". That was all he managed to catch, and in any case it did not matter. People had said all sorts of things to him.

Then he saw the weapon. The man was pointing at him. Balder raised his hand in a vain attempt to protect himself. But even though his life was on the line and fear had set its claws into him he thought only of August. Whatever else happened, even if he himself had to die, let his son be spared. He burst out:

"Don't kill my child! He's disabled, he doesn't understand anything."

Balder did not know how far he got. The whole world froze and the night and the storm seemed to bear down on him and then everything went black.

Holtser fired and as he had expected there was nothing wrong with his aim. He hit Balder twice in the head and the professor collapsed to the floor like a flapping scarecrow. There was no doubt that he was dead. Yet something did not feel right. A blustery wind swept in off the sea and brushed across Holtser's neck as if it were a cold, living being, and for a second or two he had no idea what was happening.

Everything had gone according to plan and over there was Balder's computer, just as he had been told. He should just take it and go. He needed to be efficient. Yet he stood there as if frozen to the spot and it was only after a strangely long delay that he realized why.

In the large double bed, almost completely hidden by a duvet, lay a small boy with unruly, tousled hair watching him with a glassy look. Those eyes made him uncomfortable, and that was not just because they seemed to be looking straight through him. There was more to it than that. But then again it made no difference.

He had to carry out his assignment. Nothing must be allowed to jeopardize the operation and expose them all to risk. Here was someone who was clearly a witness, especially now that he had exposed his face, and there must be no witnesses, so he pointed his weapon at the boy and looked into his glowing eyes and for the third time muttered:

"Thy will be done, amen."

Blomkvist climbed out of the taxi in a pair of black boots and a white fur coat with a broad sheepskin collar, which he had dug out of the cupboard, as well as an old fur hat that had belonged to his father.

It was then 2.40 in the morning. The Ekot news bulletin had reported a serious accident involving an articulated lorry which was now blocking the main Värmdö road. But Blomkvist and the taxi driver had seen nothing of that and had travelled together through the dark, storm-battered suburbs. Blomkvist was sick with exhaustion. All he had wanted was to stay at home and creep into bed with Erika again and go back to sleep.

But he had not felt able to say no to Balder. He could not understand why. It might have been out of some sense of duty, a feeling that he could not allow himself any easy options now that the magazine was facing a crisis, or it might have been that Balder had sounded lonely and frightened, and that Blomkvist was both sympathetic and curious. Not that he thought he was going to hear anything sensational. He was coldly expecting to be disappointed. Maybe he would find himself acting as a therapist, a night watchman in the storm. On the other hand, one never knew, and once again he thought of Salander. Salander rarely did anything

policeman in his forties, with a fading

nervous features. Further down the road was a shorter colleague of his, arguing with a drunk who was waving his arms about. More was happening out here than Blomkvist had expected.

"What's going on?" he said to the taller policeman.

He never got an answer. The policeman's mobile rang and Blomkvist overheard that the alarm system did not seem to be working properly. There was a noise coming from the lower part of the property, a crackling, unnerving sound, which instinctively he associated with the telephone call. He took a couple of steps to the right and looked down a hill which stretched all the way to a jetty and the sea and another lamp post with the same bluish light. Just then a figure came charging out of nowhere and Blomkvist realized that something was badly wrong.

*

Holtser squeezed the first pressure on the trigger and was just about to shoot the boy when the sound of a car could be heard up by the road, and he checked himself. But it was not really the car. It was because of the word "disabled" which cropped up again in his thoughts. He realized that the professor would have had every reason to lie in that last moment of his life, but as Holtser now stared at the child he wondered if it might not in fact be true.

The boy's body was too immobile, and his face radiated wonder rather than fear, as if he had no understanding of what was happening. His look was too blank and glassy to register anything properly.

Holtser recalled something he had read during his research. Balder did have a severely retarded son. Both the press and the court papers had said that the professor did not have custody of the boy. But this must surely be the boy and Holtser neither could nor needed to shoot him. It would be pointless and a breach of his own professional ethics, and this recognition came to him as a huge relief, which should have made him suspicious had he been more aware of himself at that moment.

Now he just lowered the pistol, picked up the computer and the mobile from the bedside table and stuffed them into his rucksack. Then he ran into the night along the escape route he had staked out for himself. But he did not get far. He heard a voice behind him and turned around. Up by the road stood a man who was neither of the policemen but a new figure in a fur coat and fur hat and with quite a different aura of authority. Perhaps this was why Holtser raised his pistol again. He sensed danger.

The man who charged past was athletic and dressed in black, with a headlamp on his cap, and in some way Blomkvist could not quite explain he had the feeling that the figure was part of a coordinated operation. He half expected more figures to appear out of the darkness, and that made him very uncomfortable. He called out, "Hey, you, stop!"

That was a mistake. Blomkvist understood it the instant the man's body stiffened, like that of a soldier in combat, and that was doubtless why he reacted so quickly. By the time the man drew a weapon and fired a shot as if it were the most natural thing in the world, Blomkvist had already ducked down by the corner of the house. The shot could hardly be heard, but when something smacked into Balder's letterbox there was no doubt what had happened. The taller of the policemen abruptly ended his call, but

who said anything was

"What should we do?"

"Call for reinforcements."

"But he's getting away."

"Then we'd better take a look," the taller one said, and with slow, hesitant movements, they drew their weapons and went down to the water.

A dog could be heard barking in the winter darkness, a small, bad-tempered dog, and the wind was blowing hard from the sea. The snow was whirling about and the ground was slippery. The shorter of the two policemen nearly fell over, and started flailing his arms like a clown. With a bit of luck they might avoid running into the man with the weapon. Blomkvist sensed that the figure would have no trouble at all in getting rid of those two. The quick and efficient way in which he had turned and raised his weapon suggested that he was trained for situations like this, and Blomkvist wondered what he himself should do.

He had nothing with which to defend himself. Yet he got to his feet, brushed the snow from his coat and looked down the slope again. The policemen were working their way along the water's edge towards the neighbour's house. There was no sign of the black-clad man with the gun. Blomkvist made his way down too, and as he came around to the front of the house he saw that a window had been smashed in.

There was a large gaping hole in the house and he wondered if he should summon the policemen. He never got that far. He heard something, a strange, low whimpering sound, and so he stepped through the shattered window into a corridor with a fine oak floor whose pale glow could be seen in the darkness. He walked slowly towards a doorway where the sound was coming from.

"Balder," he called out, "it's me, Mikael Blomkvist. Is everything alright?"

There was no answer. But the whimpering grew louder. He took a deep breath, walked into the room – and froze, paralyzed with shock. Afterwards he could not say what he had noticed first, or even what had frightened him most. It was not necessarily the body on the floor, despite the blood and the empty, rigid expression on its face.

It could have been the scene on the large double bed next to Balder, though it was difficult to make sense of it. There was a small child, perhaps seven, eight years old, a boy with fine features and dishevelled, dark-blond hair, wearing blue-checked pyjamas, who was banging his body against the headboard and the wall, methodically and with force. The boy's wailing did not sound like that of a crying child, more like someone trying to hurt himself as much as he could. Before Blomkvist had time to think straight he hurried over to him, but the boy was kicking wildly.

"There," Blomkvist said. "There, there," and wrapped his arms around him.

The boy twisted and turned with astonishing strength and

managed – possibly because Blomkvist did not want to hold him too tightly – to tear himself from his embrace and rush through the door out into the corridor, barefoot over the glass shards towards the shattered window, with Blomkvist racing after him shouting "No, no."

That was when he ran into the two policemen. They were standing out in the snow with expressions of total bewilderment.

CHAPTER 11

21.xi

Afterwards it was said that the police had a problem with their procedures, and that nothing had been done to cordon off the area until it was too late. The man who shot Professor Balder must have had all the time in the world to make good his escape, and the first policemen on the scene, Detectives Blom and Flinck, known rather scornfully at the station as "the Casanovas", had taken their time before raising the alarm, or at least had not done so with the necessary urgency or authority.

The forensic technicians and investigators from the Violent Crimes Division arrived only at 3.40, at the same time as a young woman who introduced herself as Gabriella Grane and who was assumed to be a relative because she was so upset. Later they came to understand that she was an analyst from Säpo, sent by the chief of that agency herself. That did not help Grane; thanks to the collective misogyny within the force, or possibly to underline the fact that she was regarded as an outsider, she was given the task of taking care of the child.

"You look as if you know how to handle this sort of thing," Erik Zetterlund said. He was the leader of the duty investigating team that night. He had watched Grane bending to examine the cuts in the boy's feet, and even though she snapped at him and declared that she had other priorities, she gave in when she looked into the boy's eyes.

August – as he was called – was paralyzed by fear and for a long time he sat on the floor at the top of the house, wrapped in a duvet, mechanically moving his hand across a red Persian carpet. Blom, who in other respects had not proved to be very enterprising, managed to find a pair of socks and put sticking plasters on the boy's feet. They noticed too that he had bruises all over his body and a split lip. According to the journalist Mikael Blomkvist – whose presence created a palpable nervousness in the house – the boy had been throwing himself against the bed and the wall down-

kind were clearly no...

when Grane simply sat beside him, a little way away, doing her own thing, and only once did he appear to be paying attention. This was when she was speaking on her mobile to Kraft and referred to the house number, 79. She did not give it much thought at the time, and soon after that she reached an agitated Hanna Balder.

Hanna wanted to have her son back at once and told Grane, to her surprise, that she should get out some jigsaw puzzles, particularly the one of the warship *Vasa*, which she said the boy's father would have had lying around somewhere. She did not describe her ex-husband as having taken the boy unlawfully, but she had no answer when asked why Westman had been out at the house demanding to have the boy back. It certainly did not seem to be concern for the child that had brought him here.

The fact of the boy's presence did, however, shed light on some of Grane's earlier questions. She now understood why Balder had been evasive about certain things, and why he had not wanted to have a guard dog. In the early morning Grane arranged for a psychologist and a doctor to take August to his mother in Vasastan, unless it turned out that he needed more urgent medical attention. Then she was struck by a different thought.

It occurred to her that the motive for murder might not have been to silence Balder. The killer could as easily have been wanting to rob him – not of something as obvious as money, but of his research. Grane had no idea what Balder had been working on during the last year of his life. Perhaps no-one knew. But it was not difficult to imagine what it might have been: most probably a development of his A.I. program, which was already regarded as revolutionary when it was stolen the first time.

His colleagues at Solifon had done everything they could to get a look at it and according to what Balder had once let slip he guarded it as a mother guards her baby, which must mean, Grane thought, that he kept it next to him while he was asleep. So she told Blom to keep an eye on August and went down to the bedroom on the ground floor where, in freezing conditions, the forensic team were working.

"Was there a computer in here?" she said.

The technicians shook their heads and Grane got out her mobile and called Kraft again.

It was soon established that Westman had disappeared. He must have left the scene amid the general turmoil, and that made Zetterlund swear and shout, the more so when it transpired that Westman was not to be found at his home either.

Zetterlund considered putting out a search bulletin, which prompted his young colleague Axel Andersson to enquire whether Westman should be treated as dangerous. Maybe Andersson was unable to tell Westman himself apart from the characters he played on screen. But to give the man his due, the situation was looking increasingly messy.

The murder was evidently no ordinary settling of scores within the family, no booze-up gone wrong, no crime committed in a fit of passion. It was a cold-blooded, well-planned assault. Matters did not improve when the chief of provincial police, Jan-Henrik Rolf, weighed in with his assessment that the killing must be treated as an attack on Swedish industrial interests. Zetterlund was finding himself at the heart of an incident of major domestic ~~_____ if he were not the brightest mind~~

~~matter of hours, was that there had not~~ people on duty during the night and his superior had chosen not to wake the National Murder Squad or any of the more experienced investigators in the Stockholm police.

Accordingly Zetterlund found himself in the midst of this confusion, feeling less and less sure of himself, and was soon shouting out his orders. To begin with he was trying to set in train an effective door-to-door enquiry. He wanted rapidly to gather as much testimony as possible, even if he was not expecting to get very much out of it. It was night-time, and dark, and there was a storm blowing. The people living nearby had most likely not seen anything at all. But you never knew. So he had himself questioned Blomkvist, though God only knew what he was doing there.

The presence of one of Sweden's best-known journalists did not make matters any easier and for a while Zetterlund imagined that Blomkvist was examining him critically with a view to writing an exposé. Probably that was just his insecurity. Blomkvist himself was shaken and throughout the interview he was unfailingly polite and keen to help. But he was not able to provide much in the way of information. It had all happened so quickly and that in itself was significant, the journalist told him.

There had been something brutal and efficient about the way in which the suspect moved, and Blomkvist said that it would not be too far-fetched to speculate that the man either was or had been a soldier, possibly even special forces. His way of spinning around to aim and fire his weapon had seemed practised. He had a lamp strapped to his tight-fitting black cap, and Blomkvist had not been able to make out any of his features.

He had been too far away, he said, and had thrown himself to the ground in the instant the figure had turned around. He should thank his lucky stars that he was still alive. He could only describe the body and the clothes, and that he did very well. According to the journalist, the man did not seem all that young, he could have been over forty. He was fit and taller than average, between 185 and 195 centimetres, powerfully built with a slim waist and broad shoulders, wearing boots and black, military-style clothes. He was carrying a rucksack and looked to have a knife strapped to his right leg.

Blomkvist thought that the man had vanished down to and along the water's edge, past the neighbouring houses, and that also matched Blom's and Flinck's accounts. The policemen had admittedly not seen the man at all. But they had heard his footsteps disappearing down along the sea and set off in vain pursuit, or so they claimed. Zetterlund had his doubts about that.

He presumed Blom and Flinck had chickened out, and had stood there in the darkness, fearful and doing nothing. In any event, that was the moment when the big mistake was made. Instead of identifying escape routes from the area and trying to cordon it off, nothing much seems to have happened. At that point

Flinck and Blom were not yet aware that someone had been killed and as soon as they knew they had had their hands full coping with a barefoot boy running hysterically out of the house. Certainly it cannot have been easy to keep a cool head. Yet they had lost precious time and, though Blomkvist exercised restraint when describing the events, it was plain to see that even he was critical. He had twice asked the policemen if they had sounded the alarm and got a nod for an answer.

Later on, when Blomkvist overheard a conversation between Flinck and the operations centre, he realized that the nod was

of bewildered failure to grasp

had not yet become involved in the investig

hand he was here, and he should at least try to avoid making a mess of things. His personal record had not been so impressive recently and this was an opportunity to put his best foot forward.

He was at the door to the living room and had just finished a call to Milton Security about the character who had been seen on the security camera earlier that night. He did not at all fit the description Mikael Blomkvist had given of the presumed murderer. He looked like a skinny old junkie, albeit one who must have possessed a high level of technical skill. Milton Security believed that the man had hacked the alarm system and put all the cameras and sensors out of action.

That certainly did not make matters any easier. It was not only the professional planning. It was the idea of committing a murder in spite of police protection and a sophisticated alarm system. How arrogant is that? Zetterlund had been about to go down to the forensic team on the ground floor, but he stayed upstairs, deeply troubled, staring into space until his gaze fastened on Balder's son. He was their key witness but incapable of speech, nor did he understand a word they said. In other words pretty much what one might expect in this shambles.

The boy was holding a small, single piece of an extremely complex puzzle. Zetterlund started towards the curved staircase leading to the ground floor – then he stopped dead. He thought back to his initial impression of the child. When he arrived on the scene, not knowing very much about what had happened, the boy had seemed the same as any other child. Zetterlund would have described him as an unusually pretty but normal-looking boy with curly hair and a shocked look in his eyes. Only later did he learn that the boy was autistic and severely handicapped. That, he thought, meant that the murderer either knew him from before or else was aware of his condition. Otherwise he would hardly have let him live and risk being identified in a witness parade, would he? Although Zetterlund did not give himself time to think this through in full, the hunch excited him and he took a few hurried paces towards the boy.

"We must question him at once," he said, in a voice that came out louder and more urgent than he had intended.

"For heaven's sake, take it easy with him," Blomkvist said.

"Don't you interfere," Zetterlund snapped. "He may have known the killer. We have to get out some pictures and show them to him. Somehow we must . . ."

The boy interrupted him by slamming the puzzle with his hand in a sudden sweeping movement. Zetterlund muttered an apology and went downstairs to join his forensic team.

Blomkvist remained there, looking at the boy. It felt as if something else was about to happen with him, perhaps a new outburst, and the last thing he wanted was for the child to hurt himself again. The boy stiffened and began to make furiously rapid circular movements over the rug with his right hand.

Then he stopped and looked up pleadingly. Though Blomkvist asked himself what that might mean, he dropped the thought when the policeman whose name he now knew to be Blom sat down with the boy and tried to get him to do the puzzle again. Blomkvist went into the kitchen to get some peace and quiet. He was exhausted and wanted to go home. But apparently he first had to look at some pictures from a surveillance camera. He had no idea when that was going to happen. It was all taking a long

Blomkvist was longing for his

story and that would raise its quality and give him

over the competition. The dramatic telephone call alone, in the middle of the night, which had got him here in the first place, would give his article an edge.

The Serner situation and the crisis at the magazine were implicit in their conversation. Berger had already planned for their temp Andrei Zander to do the preliminary research while Blomkvist got some sleep. She had said rather firmly – like someone halfway between a loving mother and an authoritative editor-in-chief – that she refused to have her star reporter dead from exhaustion before the work had even begun.

Blomkvist accepted without protest. Zander was ambitious and amicable and it would be nice to wake up and find all the spade-work done, ideally also with lists of people close to Balder whom he should be interviewing. For a little while Blomkvist welcomed the distraction of reflecting on Zander's persistent problems with women, which had been confided to him during evening sessions at the Kvarnen beer hall. Zander was young, intelligent and handsome. He ought to be a catch. But because there was something soft and needy in his character, he was time and again being dumped, and that was painful for him. Zander was an incorrigible romantic, forever dreaming about the big scoop and love with a capital L.

Blomkvist sat down at Balder's kitchen table and looked out at the darkness. In front of him, next to a matchbox, a copy of the *New Scientist* and a pad of paper with some incomprehensible equations on it, lay a beautiful but slightly ominous drawing of a street crossing. A man with watery, squinting eyes and thin lips was standing next to a traffic light. He was caught in a fleeting moment and yet you could see every wrinkle in his face and the folds in his quilted jacket and trousers. He did not look pleasant. He had a heart-shaped mole on his chin.

Yet the striking thing about the drawing was the traffic light. It shone with an eloquent, troubling glow, and was skilfully executed according to some sort of mathematical technique. You could almost see the underlying geometrical lines. Balder must have enjoyed doing drawings on the side. Blomkvist wondered, though, about the unconventional choice of subject. On the other hand, why would a person like Balder draw sunsets and ships? A traffic light was probably just as interesting to him as anything else. Blomkvist was intrigued by the fact that the drawing looked like a snapshot. Even if Balder had sat and studied the traffic light, he could hardly have asked the man to cross the street over and over again. Maybe he was imagined, or Balder had a photographic memory, just like . . . Blomkvist grew thoughtful. He picked up his mobile and for the third time called Berger.

"Are you on your way home?" she asked.

"Not yet, unfortunately. There are a couple of things I still need to look at. But I'd like you to do me a favour."

"What else am I here for?"

"Could you go to my computer and log in? You know my password, don't you?"

"I know everything about you."

"Then go into Documents and open a file called LISBETH STUFF."

"I think I have an idea where this is going."

"Oh? Here's what I'd like you to write . . ."

"Wait a second, I have to open it first. O.K., now . . . Hold on,
~~~~~ already a few things here."

~~~~~~~~~~~~~~~ the top. Are you

~~~~~~~

"Well, it's rather a lot considering that we ~~~~~
for ages. She'll probably think it's cheeky of me to ask. But I don't
think it would hurt to have her help."

"A little illegal hacking wouldn't go amiss, you mean?"

"I didn't hear that. I'll see you soon, I hope."

"I hope so."

Salander had managed to go back to sleep, and woke again at 7.30.
She was not on top form; she had a headache and she felt nauseous.
Yet she felt better than she had in the night. She bandaged her
hand, dressed, had a breakfast of two microwaved meat piroshki
and a large glass of Coca-Cola, then she stuffed some work-out
clothes into a sports bag and left the apartment. The storm had
subsided, leaving rubbish and newspapers lying all over the city.
She walked down from Mosebacke torg and along Götgatan,
muttering to herself.

She looked angry and at least two people were alarmed enough to get out of her way. But Salander was merely determined. She was not looking forward to working out, she just wanted to stick to her routine and drive the toxins out of her body. So she continued down to Hornsgatan, and just before Hornsgatspuckeln she turned into the Zero boxing club, which was down one flight of stairs in the basement. It seemed more run-down than ever that morning.

The place could have used a coat of paint and some general freshening up. It seemed as if no improvements had been made since the '70s. Posters of Ali and Foreman were still on the walls. It looked just like the day after that legendary bout in Kinshasa, possibly due to the fact that Obinze, the man in charge of the premises, had seen the fight live as a small boy and had afterwards run around in the liberating monsoon rain shouting "Ali Bomaye!" That double-time canter was not just his happiest memory, it also marked what he called the last moment of "the days of innocence".

Not long after he and his family had been forced to flee Mobutu's terror and nothing had ever been the same again. Maybe it was not so strange that he wanted to preserve that moment in history, carry it with him to this godforsaken boxing hall in the Södermalm district of Stockholm. Obinze was still constantly talking about the fight. But then he was always constantly talking about something or other.

He was tall and mighty and bald-headed, a chatterbox of epic proportions and one of many in the gym who quite fancied Salander, even if like many others he thought she was more or less crazy. Periodically she would train harder than anyone else in there and go at the punch-balls, punchbags and her sparring part-ners like a madwoman. She possessed a kind of primitive, furious energy which Obinze had seldom come across.

Once, before he got to know her, he had suggested that she take up competitive boxing. The derisive snort he got in response stopped him from asking again, though he had never understood why she trained so hard. Not that he really needed to know – one could train hard for no reason at all. It was better than drinking hard. It was better than lots of things.

Maybe it was true, as she said to him late one evening about a year ago, that she wanted to be physically prepared in case she ever ended up in difficulties again. He knew that there had been trouble before. He had read every single word about her on the net and understood what it meant to be prepared in case some shadow from the past turned up. Both his parents had been

"Doing something highly illegal."

"I can just imagine. Beating the crap out of some motorbike gang or something."

But she did not even rise to the jest. She just marched angrily in towards the changing room and he did something he knew she would hate: he stepped in front of her and looked her straight in the face.

"Your eyes are bright red."

"I've got the mother of all hangovers. Out of my way!"

"In that case I don't want to see you in here, you know that."

"Skip the crap. I want you to drive the shit out of me," she spat, and ducked past him to get changed. When she emerged wearing her outsized boxing shorts and white vest with the black skull on the chest, he saw nothing for it but to go ahead and let her have it.

He pushed her until she threw up three times in his waste-paper bin. He gave her as much grief as he could. She gave him plenty of lip back. Then she went off and changed and left the gym without even a goodbye. As so often at such moments Obinze was overcome by a feeling of emptiness. Maybe he was even a little in love. He was certainly stirred – how could one not be by a girl who boxed like that?

The last he saw of her was her calves disappearing up the stairs so he could not know that the ground swayed beneath her feet as she came out onto Hornsgatan. Salander braced herself against the wall of the building and breathed heavily. Then she set off in the direction of her apartment on Fiskargatan. Once home she drank another large glass of Coca-Cola and half a litre of juice, then she crashed onto her bed and looked at the ceiling for ten, fifteen minutes, thinking about this and that, about singularities and event horizons and certain special aspects of Schrödinger's equation, and Ed Needham.

She waited for the world to regain its usual colours before she got up and went to her computer. However reluctant she might be, she was drawn to it by a force which had not grown weaker since her childhood. But this morning she was not in the mood for any wild escapades. She hacked into Mikael Blomkvist's computer. In the next moment she froze. They had been joking about Balder and now Blomkvist wrote that he had been murdered, shot in the head.

"Jesus," she muttered and had a look at the online evening papers.

There was no explicit mention of Balder, but it was not difficult to work out that the "Swedish academic shot at his home in Saltsjöbaden" was indeed him. For the time being, the police were being tight-lipped and journalists had not managed to turn up a great deal, no doubt because they had not yet cottoned on to how big the story was. Other events from the night took precedence: the storm and the power outage right across the country and the

160

scandalous delays on the railways. There was also the odd celebrity news item which Salander could not be bothered to try to understand.

The only facts reported on the murder were that it had taken place around 3.00 in the morning and that the police were seeking witnesses in the neighbourhood, for reports of anything untoward. So far there were no suspects, but apparently witnesses had spotted unknown and suspicious persons on the property. The police were looking for more information on them. At the end of the articles it said that a press conference was going to be held .... Jan Bublanski. Salander gave

he who was asking. It was personal. She did not ...... not in the conventional way. Anger, on the other hand, yes, a cold ticking rage. And though she had a certain respect for Jan Bublanski she was not usually inclined to trust the forces of law and order.

She was used to taking matters into her own hands and she had all sorts of reasons to want to find out why Frans Balder had been murdered. Because it was no coincidence that she had sought him out and taken an interest in his situation. His enemies were most likely her enemies too.

It had begun with the old question of whether in some sense her father lived on. Alexander Zalachenko – Zala – had not only killed her mother and destroyed her childhood, he had also established and controlled a criminal network, sold drugs and arms and made a living exploiting and humiliating women. She was convinced that that sort of evil never goes away. It merely migrates into other forms. Ever since that day just over a year ago when she had woken up at dawn at Hotel Schloss Elmau in the Bavarian Alps, Salander had been pursuing her own investigation into what had become of his legacy.

For the most part his old comrades seemed to have turned into losers, depraved bandits, revolting pimps or small-time crooks. Not one of them was a villain on her father's level, and for a long time Salander remained convinced that the organization had changed and dissolved after Zalachenko's death. Yet she did not give up, and eventually she stumbled on something which pointed in a wholly unexpected direction. It was a reference to one of Zala's young acolytes, a man called Sigfrid Gruber.

Already during Zala's lifetime, Gruber was one of the more intelligent people in the network, and unlike his colleagues he had earned himself degrees in both computer science and business administration, which had apparently given him access to more exclusive circles. These days he cropped up in a couple of alleged crimes against high-tech companies: thefts of new technology, extortion, insider trading, hacker attacks.

Normally, Salander would have followed the lead no further. Not just because it seemed to have little to do with her father's old activities. Also, nothing could worry her less than a couple of rich business groups being fleeced of some of their innovations. But then everything had changed.

In a classified report from Government Communications Headquarters in Cheltenham, England, which she had got her hands on, she had come across some codenames associated with a gang Gruber seemed now to belong to. The names had set some bells ringing, and after that she had not been able to let go of the story. She put together all the information she could find about the group and kept coming across a rumour that the organization had stolen Balder's A.I. technology, and then sold it to the Russian–American games company, Truegames. Her source was unreliable – a half-open hacker site – but it was for this reason that she had turned up at the professor's lecture at the Royal Institute of Technology and given him a hard time about singularities deep within black holes. Or that was part of the reason.

PART II

THE LABYRINTHS
OF MEMORY

21 – 23.xi

Most, though not
autistic. There is also a connection between photographic
memory and synaesthesia – the condition where two or more
senses are connected, for example when numbers are seen
in colour and every series of numbers forms an image in the
mind.

* An ability to recall images, sounds or objects in memory after only
a few instants of exposure.

CHAPTER 12

21.xi

for him and he wanted to discuss the p—

meaninglessness of it all, which were often accompanied by
dreams of handing in his notice.

Bublanski certainly considered himself to be a good investigator. His record of clearing up cases was on the whole outstanding
and occasionally he was still stimulated by the job. But he was not
sure he wanted to go on investigating murders. He could learn
some new skill while there was still time. He dreamed about
teaching, helping young people to find their path and believe in
themselves, maybe because he himself suffered from bouts of the
deepest self-doubt – but he did not know which subject he would
choose. He had never specialized in one particular field, aside from
that which had become his lot in life: sudden evil death and morbid
human perversions. That was definitely not something he wanted
to teach.

It was 8.10 in the morning and he was at his bathroom mirror.

He felt puffy, worn out and bald. Absent-mindedly he picked up I.B. Singer's novel, *The Magician of Lublin*, which he had loved with such a passion that for many years he had kept it next to the lavatory in case he felt like reading it at times when his stomach was playing up. But now he only managed a few lines. The telephone rang and his mood did not improve when he recognized the number: Chief Prosecutor Richard Ekström. A call from Ekström meant not just work, but probably work with a political and media element to it. Ekström would otherwise have wriggled out of it like a snake.

"Hi, Richard, nice to hear from you," Bublanski lied. "But I'm afraid I'm busy."

"What . . .? No, no, not too busy for this, Jan. You can't miss out on this one. I heard that you'd taken the day off."

"That's right, and I'm just off to . . ." He did not want to say to his synagogue. His Jewishness was not popular in the force ". . . see my doctor," he went on.

"Are you sick?"

"Not really."

"What's that supposed to mean? Nearly sick?"

"Something like that."

"Well, in that case there's no problem. We're all nearly sick, aren't we? This is an important case, Jan. The Minister of Enterprise has been in touch, and she agrees that you should handle the investigation."

"I find it very hard to believe the minister knows who I am."

"Well, maybe not by name, and she's not supposed to be interfering anyway. But we're all agreed that we need a big player."

"Flattery no longer works with me, Richard. What's it about?" he said, and immediately regretted it. Just asking was halfway to saying yes and he could tell that Ekström accepted it as such.

"Last night Professor Frans Balder was murdered at his home in Saltsjöbaden."

168

"And who is he?"

"One of our best-known scientists, of international renown. He's a world authority on A.I. technology."

"On *what*?"

"He was working on neural networks and digital quantum processes, that sort of thing."

"I have no idea what you're talking about."

"He was trying to get computers to think, to replicate the human brain."

Replicate the human brain? Bublanski wondered what Rabbi

"It would seem that this Balder was ...

He had police protection."

"Are you saying he was killed while under police protection?"

"Well, it wasn't the most effective protection in the world. It was Flinck and Blom from the regular force."

"The Casanovas?"

"Yes. They were assigned the duty late last night at the height of the storm and the general confusion. But in their defence it has to be said that the whole situation was a total shambles. Balder was shot while our men were dealing with a drunk who had turned up at the house, out of nowhere. Unsurprisingly, the killer took advantage of that moment of inattention."

"Doesn't sound good."

"No, it looks very professional, and on top of it all the burglar alarm seems to have been hacked."

"So there were several of them?"

169

"We believe so. Furthermore, there are some tricky details."

"Which the media are going to like?"

"Which the media are going to love," Ekström said. "The lush who turned up, for example, was none other than Lasse Westman."

"The actor?"

"The same. And that's a real problem."

"Because it'll be all over the front pages?"

"Partly that, yes, but also because there's a risk we'll end up with a load of sticky divorce issues on our hands. Westman claimed he was there to bring home the eight-year-old son of his partner. Balder had the boy there with him, a boy who . . . hang on a moment . . . I want to get this right . . . who is certainly Balder's biological son, but who, according to a custody ruling, he's not competent to look after."

"Why wouldn't a professor who can get computers to behave like people be capable of looking after his own child?"

"Because previously he had shown a shocking lack of responsibility. He was a completely hopeless father, if I've understood it right. It's all rather sensitive. This little boy, who wasn't even supposed to have been at Balder's, probably witnessed the killing."

"Jesus! And what does he say?"

"Nothing."

"Is he in shock?"

"He must be, but he never says anything anyway. He's mute and apparently disabled, so he's not going to be much good to us."

"I see. So there's no suspect."

"Unless there was a reason why Westman appeared at precisely the same time as the killer entered the ground floor. You should get Westman in for questioning."

"If I decide to take on the investigation."

"As you will."

"Are you so sure of that?"

"In my view you have no choice. Besides, I've saved the best for last."

"And that is?"

"Mikael Blomkvist."

"What about him?"

"For some reason he was out there too. I think Balder had asked to see him, to tell him something."

"In the middle of the night?"

"So it would seem."

"And then he was shot?"

... and it seems the journalist

... with a private investigator on your back, one ... up in a bad light."

"Hmm, yes, maybe. We're assuming that *Millennium* have already got going with the story and right now I'm trying to find some legal justification for stopping them, or at least see to it that they're restricted in some way. I won't rule out that this case is to be regarded as a matter affecting national security."

"So we're saddled with Säpo as well?"

"No comment."

Go to hell, Bublanski thought. "Are Olofsson and the others at Industry Protection working on this?"

"No comment, as I said. When can you start?" Ekström said.

"I'll do it, but I have some conditions," Bublanski said. "I want my usual team: Modig, Svensson, Holmberg and Flod."

"Of course, O.K., but you get Hans Faste as well."

"No way!"

"Sorry, Jan, that's not negotiable. You should be grateful you get to choose all the others."

"You're the bitter end, you know that?"

"I've heard it said."

"So Faste's going to be our own little mole from Säpo?"

"Nonsense. I happen to think that all teams benefit from someone who thinks differently."

"Meaning that when the rest of us have got rid of all our prejudices and preconceived notions, we're stuck with somebody who will take us back to square one?"

"Don't be absurd."

"Faste is an idiot."

"No, Jan, he isn't. He's just . . ."

"What?"

"Conservative. He's not someone who falls for the latest feminist fads."

"Or for the earliest ones either. He may have just got his head around all that stuff about votes for women."

"Come on, Jan, get a grip. Faste is an extremely reliable and loyal investigator, and I won't listen to any more of this. Any other requests?"

How about you go take a running jump? Bublanski thought. "I need to go to my doctor's appointment, and in the meantime I want Modig to lead the investigation," he said.

"Is that really such a wise idea?"

"It's a damned wise idea," he growled.

"O.K., O.K., I'll see to it that Zetterlund hands over to her," Ekström said with a wince.

Ekström was now far from sure he should have agreed to take on this investigation.

Alona Casales rarely worked nights. She had managed to avoid them for a decade and justified her stance on the grounds that her rheumatism forced her from time to time to take strong cortisone tablets, which not only turned her face into the shape of a full moon, but also raised her blood pressure. She needed her sleep and her routine. Yet here she was, at 3.10 in the morning.

She had driven from her home in Laurel, Maryland, in a light rain, past the sign saying "N.S.A. NEXT RIGHT – STAFF ONLY", past the barriers and the electric fence, towards the black, cube-like main building in Fort Meade. She left her car in the sprawling parking area alongside the pale-blue golf-ball-like radome with ⸻ ⸻ ⸻ her way through the security

bawling out a young man whose face ⸻ pretty weird guy, Casales thought, just like all those young genius hackers Needham had surrounded himself with. The kid was skinny and anaemic-looking with a hairstyle from hell, and had strangely rounded shoulders which shook with some sort of spasm. Maybe he was frightened. He shuddered every now and then, and it did not help matters that Needham was kicking at his chair leg. The young man looked as if he were waiting for a slap, a clip across the ear. But then something unexpected happened.

Needham calmed down and ruffled the boy's hair like a loving father. That was not like him. He did not go in for demonstrative affection. He was a cowboy who would never do anything as dubious as hug another man. But perhaps he was now so desperate that he was prepared to give normal humanity a go. Ed's zip was undone and he had spilled coffee or Coca-Cola on his shirt. His face was an unhealthy flushed colour, his voice hoarse and rough from shouting. Casales thought that no-one of his age and weight should be pushing himself so hard.

Although only half a day had gone by, it looked as if Needham and his boys had been living there for a week. There were coffee cups and fast-food remnants and discarded caps and college jerseys everywhere, and a rank stench of sweat and tension in the air. The team was clearly in the process of turning the whole world upside down in their efforts to trace the hacker. She called out to them in a hearty tone:

"Go for it, guys! . . . Fix the bastard!"

She did not really mean it. Secretly she thought the breach was amusing. Many of these programmers seemed to think they could do whatever liked, as if they had carte blanche, and it might actually do them some good to see that the other side could hit back. Here in the Puzzle Palace their shortcomings only showed when they were confronted with something dire, as was happening now. She had been woken by a call saying that the Swedish professor had been murdered at his home outside Stockholm, and even though that in itself was not a big deal for the N.S.A. – not yet, at any rate – it did mean something to Casales.

The killing showed that she had read the signs right, and now she had to see if she could move forward one more step. She logged in and opened the diagrammatic overview of the organization she had been tracking. The evasive Thanos sat right at the top, but there were also names of real people like the member of the Russian Duma Ivan Gribanov, and the German, Gruber.

She did not understand why the N.S.A. gave such low priority to the matter, and why her superiors kept suggesting that other, more mainstream law-enforcement agencies should be taking care of it. They could not rule out the possibility that the network had state backing, or links to Russian state intelligence, and that it was all to do with the trade war between East and West. Even though the evidence was sparse and ambiguous, there were indications that western technology was being stolen and ending up in Russian hands.

But it was difficult to get a clear view of this tangled web or even to know whether any crime had been committed – perhaps it was purely by chance that a similar technology had been developed somewhere else. These days, industrial theft was an altogether nebulous concept. Assets were being borrowed all the time, sometimes as a part of creative exchanges, sometimes just dressed up to seem legitimate.

Large businesses, bolstered by threatening lawyers, regularly _____ _____ companies, and nobody

terms, and Casales took a solemn vow ____ in trying to unseat Thanos. She did not get far. In fact she only managed to stretch her arms and massage her neck before she heard puffing and panting behind her.

Needham looked dreadful. His back must have given out on him too. Her own neck felt better just looking at him.

"Ed, to what do I owe this honour?"

"I'm thinking you and I are working on the same problem."

"Park your butt, old man."

"You know, from my limited perspective . . ."

"Don't knock yourself, Ed."

"I'm not knocking myself at all. It's no secret I couldn't care less who's high or low, who thinks this and who thinks that. I focus on my own stuff. I protect our systems, and the only thing that really impresses me is when people are good at their jobs."

"You'd hire the Devil himself if he was any good in I.T."

"I can respect just about any enemy, if he knows what he's doing. Does that make sense to you?"

"It does."

"As I'm sure you've heard, a rootkit's been used to access our server and install a R.A.T., and that program, Alona, is like pure music. So compact and beautifully written."

"You've met a worthy opponent."

"Without a doubt, and my guys feel the same way. They're putting on this outraged patriotic act or whatever the hell it is we're supposed to do. But actually they want nothing more than to meet that hacker and pit their skills against his, and for a while I thought: O.K., get over it! Maybe the damage isn't so great after all. This is just one genius hacker who wants to show off, and maybe there's a silver lining. I mean, we've already learned a lot about our vulnerability chasing after this clown. But then I began to wonder if maybe I was being conned – maybe the whole performance on my mail server was just a smokescreen, hiding something altogether different."

"Such as?"

"Such as a search for certain pieces of information."

"Now I'm curious."

"You should be. We've identified which areas the hacker was checking out and basically it's all related to the same thing, the network you've been working on, Alona. They call themselves the Spiders, don't they?"

"The Spider Society, to be precise. But I think it's some kind of joke."

"The hacker was looking for information on that group and their connections to Solifon and that made me think, maybe he's with them and wants to find out how much we know about them."

"That sounds possible. They know how to hack."

"But then I changed my mind."

"Why?"

"Because it looks like the hacker also wanted to show us something. You know, he got himself superuser status which gave him access to documents maybe even you haven't seen, highly classified stuff. But actually the file he uploaded is so heavily encrypted that neither he nor we have the slightest chance of reading it unless the fucker who wrote it gives us the private keys. Anyway . . . ."

"What?"

"The hacker revealed through our own system that we cooperate with Solifon too, the same way the Spiders do. Did you

off the job completely."

"That would be outrageous."

"Relax, there's a loophole. And that's why I dragged my sorry ass all the way over to your desk. Start working for me instead."

"What do you mean?"

"This goddamn hacker knows things about the Spiders, and if we can crack his identity we'll both get a break and then you'll be able to see your investigation through."

"I see what you're saying."

"So it's a yes?"

"It's a sort of," she said. "I want to focus on finding out who shot Frans Balder."

"And you'll keep me informed?"

"O.K."

"Good."

"Tell me," she said, "if this hacker is so clever, won't he have covered his tracks?"

"No need to worry about that. No matter how smart he's been, we'll find him and we'll flay him alive."

"What happened to all that respect for your opponent?"

"It's still there, my friend. But we'll crush him all the same and lock him up for life. No fucker breaks into my system."

CHAPTER 13

21.xi

Ramlösa, swallowed two Alvedon, took out to write a summary of what had happened. He did not get far before the telephone started ringing.

The news was out: "Star reporter Mikael Blomkvist and T.V. star Lasse Westman" had found themselves at the centre of a "mysterious" murder drama, mysterious because no-one was able to work out why Westman and Blomkvist of all people, together or separately, had been on the scene when a Swedish professor was shot in the head. The questions seemed to be insinuating something sinister and that was why Blomkvist quite candidly said that he had gone there, despite the lateness of the hour, because Balder had asked to speak to him urgently.

"I was there because of my job."

He was being more defensive than he needed to be. He wanted to provide an explanation for the accusations out there, although that might prompt more reporters to dig into the story. Apart from that he said "No comment", and if that was not the ideal response it was at least straightforward and unambiguous. After that he turned off his mobile, put his father's old fur coat back on again and set out in the direction of Götgatan.

So much was going on at the office that it reminded him of the old days. All over the place, in every corner, there were colleagues sitting and working with concentration. Berger was bound to have made one or two impassioned speeches and everybody must have been aware of the significance of the moment. The deadline was just ten days away. There was also the threat from Ove Levin and Serner hanging over them and the whole team seemed up for the fight. They all jumped to their feet when they saw him and asked to hear about Balder and the night, and his reaction to the Norwegians' proposal. But he wanted to follow their good example.

"Later, later," he said, and went to Andrei Zander's desk.

Zander was twenty-six years old, the youngest person in the office. He had done his time as an intern at the magazine and had stayed on, sometimes as a temp, as now, and sometimes as a freelancer. It pained Blomkvist that they had not been able to give him a permanent job, especially since they had hired Emil Grandén and Sofie Melker. He would have preferred to take on Zander. But Zander had not yet made a name for himself, and he still had a lot to learn.

He was a superb team player, and that was good for the magazine, but not necessarily good for him. Not in this cynical business. The boy was not conceited enough, although he had every reason to be. He looked like a young Antonio Banderas, and was quicker on the uptake than most. But he did not go to any lengths to promote himself. He just wanted to be a part of it all and produce good journalism – he thought the world of *Millennium*. Blomkvist suddenly felt that he loved everyone who loved *Millennium*. One fine day he would do something big for young Zander.

"Hi, Andrei," he said. "How are things?"

"Not bad. Busy."

"I expected nothing less. What have you managed to dig up?"

"Quite a bit. It's on your desk, and I've also written a summary. But can I give you some advice?"

"Good advice is exactly what I need."

"In that case go straight to Zinkens väg, to see Farah Sharif."

"Who?"

"A seriously gorgeous professor of computer science. She's ... the whole day off."

... right now is an attrac-

an ideal p...

"Have you checked her out otherwise."

"Sure, and we can't altogether rule out the possibility that she has an agenda of her own. But she was close to Balder. They were at university together and have co-authored a couple of scientific papers. There are also a few society-page photos which show the two of them together. She's a big name in her field."

"O.K., I'll go. Will you let her know I'm on my way?"

"I will," Zander said, and gave Blomkvist the address. So Blomkvist left the office almost immediately, just as he had the previous day, and began to leaf through the research material as he was walking down towards Hornsgatan. Two or three times he bumped into people, but he was concentrating so hard that he scarcely apologized, and when at last he raised his head, his feet had not taken him as far as Farah Sharif's place.

He had stopped off at Mellqvist's coffee bar and so he drank two double espressos standing up. Not just to get rid of his tiredness. He thought a jolt of caffeine might help with his headache, but afterwards he wondered if it had been the right cure. As he left the coffee shop he felt worse than when he had arrived, but that was because of all the morons who had read about the night's dramatic events and were making idiotic remarks. They say that young people want nothing more than to become celebrities. He ought to explain to them that it is not worth aspiring to. It just drives you nuts, especially if you haven't slept and you've seen things that no human being should have to see.

Blomkvist went up Hornsgatan, past McDonald's and the Co-op, cut across to Ringvägen, and as he glanced to the right he stiffened, as if he had seen something significant. But what? It was just a street crossing with a high traffic-accident rate and vast volumes of exhaust fumes, nothing more. Then it came to him.

It was the very traffic light Balder had drawn with his mathematical precision, and so once again Blomkvist puzzled over the choice of subject matter. It was not in any way an unusual crossing; it was run down and banal. Maybe that was the point.

The work of art is in the eye of the beholder, and even that conveyed no more than that Balder had been here, and had maybe sat on a bench somewhere studying the traffic light. Blomkvist went on past Zinkensdamm sports centre and turned right onto Zinkens väg.

Detective Sergeant Sonja Modig had been running around all morning. Now she was in her office and looked briefly at a framed photograph on her desk. It showed her six-year-old son Axel on the football pitch after scoring a goal. Modig was a single parent and had a hell of a time organizing her life. She was expecting to have a hellish time at work in the next few days too. There was a knock on the door. It was Bublanski at last, and she was supposed to be handing over responsibility for the investigation. Not that

Officer Bubble looked as if he wanted to take responsibility for anything at all.

He was looking unusually dashing in a jacket and tie and a freshly ironed blue shirt. He had combed his hair over his bald patch. There was a dreamy and absent look on his face, as if murder investigations were the last thing on his mind.

"What did the doctor say?" she asked.

"The doctor said that what matters is not that we believe in God; God is not small-minded. What matters is for us to under-
̶t̶ ̶life̶ is serious and rich. We should appreciate it and also
̶ ̶ ̶ ̶ ̶ ̶ ̶ ̶ ̶ ̶W̶h̶ ̶ ̶v̶e̶r̶ finds a balance

chocolate ̶ ̶ ̶
nail the guy who shot Professor Balder ̶t̶h̶e̶n̶ ̶ ̶ ̶
the world a little better."

"Swiss orange chocolate and a solution to this murder sounds like a decent start."

Modig broke off a piece of chocolate and gave it to Bublanski, who chewed it with a certain reverence.

"Exquisite," he said.

"Isn't it?"

"Just think if life could be like that sometimes," he said, pointing at the photograph of the jubilant Axel on her desk.

"What do you mean?"

"If joy could express itself with the same force as pain," he said.

"Yes, just imagine."

"How are things with Balder's son?" he said.

"Hard to tell," she said. "He's with his mother now. A psychologist has assessed him."

"And what have we got to go on?"

"Not much yet, unfortunately. We've found out what the murder weapon was. A Remington 1911 R1 Carry, bought recently. We're going follow it up, but I feel sure we're not going to be able to trace it. We have the images from the surveillance cameras, which we're analyzing. But whatever angle we look at we still can't see the man's face, and we can't spot any distinguishing features either – no birthmarks, nothing, only a wristwatch which is just about visible in one sequence. It looks expensive. The guy's clothes are black. His cap is grey without any branding. Jerker tells me he moves like an old junkie. In one picture he's holding a small black box, presumably some kind of computer or G.S.M. station. He probably used it to hack the alarm system."

"I'd heard that. How *do* you hack a burglar alarm?"

"Jerker has looked into that too and it isn't easy, especially not an alarm of this specification, but it can be done. The system was connected to the net and to the mobile network and sent a feed of information to Milton Security over at Slussen. It's not impossible that the guy recorded a frequency from the alarm with his box and managed to hack it that way. Or else he'd bumped into Balder when he was out walking and stole some information electronically from the professor's N.F.C."

"What's an N.F.C.?"

"Near Field Communication, a function on Balder's mobile which he used to activate the alarm."

"It was simpler in the days when burglars had crowbars," Bublanski said. "Any cars in the area?"

"A dark-coloured vehicle was parked a hundred metres away by the side of the road with the engine running on and off, but the only person to have seen it is an old lady by the name of Birgitta Roos; she has no idea what make it was. Maybe a Volvo, according to her. Or like the one her son has. Her son has a B.M.W."

"Oh, wonderful."

"Yes, so the investigation is looking a bit bleak," Modig said. "The killers had the advantage of the night and the weather. They could move around the area undisturbed, and apart from what Mikael Blomkvist told us we've only got one sighting. It's from a thirteen-year-old, Ivan Grede. A slightly odd, skinny figure who had leukaemia when he was small and who has decorated his room entirely in a Japanese style. He has a precocious way of expressing himself. Young Ivan went for a pee in the middle of the night and from the bathroom window he saw a tall man by the water's edge. The man was looking out over the water and making the sign of

aggressive and religious at

walk into the water and drown himself.

monial about the situation, he said, and something aggressive."

"But there was no suicide."

"No, the man jogged on in the direction of Balder's house. He had a rucksack, and dark clothes, possibly camouflage trousers. He was powerful and athletic and reminded Ivan of his old toys, he said, his ninja warriors."

"That doesn't sound good either."

"Not good at all. Presumably this was the man who shot at Blomkvist."

"And Blomkvist didn't see his face?"

"No, he threw himself to the ground when the man turned and shot at him. It all happened very quickly. But according to Blomkvist the man looked as if he had military training and that fits with Ivan Grede's observations. I have to agree: the speed and efficiency of the operation point in that direction."

"Have you got to the bottom of why Blomkvist was there?"

"Oh, definitely. If anything was done properly last night, it was the interviews with him. Have a look at this." Modig handed over a transcript. "Blomkvist had been in touch with one of Balder's former assistants who claimed that the professor had been targeted by a data breach and had his technology stolen. The story interested Blomkvist. But Balder had been living as a recluse and had virtually no contact with the outside world. All the shopping and errands were done by a housekeeper called . . . just a second . . . Fru Rask, Lottie Rask, who incidentally had strict instructions not to say a word about the son living in the house. I'll come to that in a moment. Then last night I'm guessing that Balder was worried and wanted to get some anxiety off his chest. Don't forget, he had just been told that he was subject to a serious threat. Plus his burglar alarm had gone off and two policemen were guarding the house. Perhaps he suspected that his days were numbered. No way of knowing. In any case he called Mikael Blomkvist in the middle of the night and said he wanted to tell him something."

"In the olden days in situations like that you would call a priest."

"So now you call a journalist. Well, it's pure speculation. We only know what Balder said on Blomkvist's voicemail. Apart from that we have no idea what he was planning to tell him. Blomkvist says he doesn't know either, and I believe him. But I seem to be pretty much the only one who does. Ekström, who's being a massive nuisance, by the way, is convinced Blomkvist is holding back things which he plans to publish in his magazine. I find that very hard to believe. Blomkvist is a tricky bugger, we all know that. But he isn't someone who will knowingly, deliberately sabotage a police investigation."

"Definitely not."

"Ekström is coming on strong and saying that Blomkvist should be arrested for perjury and obstruction and God knows what else."

"That's not going to help."

"No, and bearing in mind what Blomkvist is capable of I think we're better off staying on good terms with him."

"I suppose we'll have to talk to him again."

"I agree."

"And this thing with Lasse Westman?"

"We've just spoken to him, and it's not an edifying story. Westman had been to every bar in town – Konstnärsbaren, Teatergrillen, Café Opera, Riche, you get the idea – and was ranting and raving about Balder and the boy for hours on end. He drove his friends crazy. The more Westman drank and the more money

was concerned for the boy. But in that Westman has a conviction for assault."

"No, I didn't."

"He had a relationship some years ago with some fashion blogger, Renata Kapusinski. He beat the crap out of her. I think he even bit her rather badly in the cheek. Also, Balder had intended to report him. He never sent in the paperwork – perhaps because of the legal position he found himself in – but it clearly suggests that he suspected Westman of being violent towards his son as well."

"What are you saying?"

"Balder had noticed unexplained bruises on the boy's body – and in this he's backed up by a psychologist from the Centre for Autism. So it was . . ."

". . . probably not love and concern which drove Westman out to Saltsjöbaden."

"More likely it was money. After Balder took back his son, he had stopped or at least reduced the child support he had agreed to pay."

"Westman didn't try to report him for that?"

"He probably didn't dare to, in the circumstances."

"What else does the custody ruling say?" Bublanski said, after a pause.

"That Balder was a useless father."

"Was he?"

"He certainly wasn't evil, like Westman. But there'd been an incident. After the divorce, Balder had his son every other weekend, and at that time he was living in an apartment in Östermalm with books from floor to ceiling. One of those weekends, when August was six, he was in the sitting room – with Balder glued to his computer in the next room as usual. We don't know exactly what happened. But there was a small stepladder propped against one of the bookshelves. August climbed it and probably took hold of some of the books higher up and fell and broke his elbow. He knocked himself unconscious, but Balder didn't hear anything. He just kept working and only after several hours did he discover August lying on the floor next to those books, moaning. At that he became hysterical and drove the boy to A. & E."

"And he lost custody altogether?"

"Not only that. He was declared emotionally immature and incapable of taking care of his child. He was not to be allowed to be alone with August. But frankly, I don't think much of that ruling."

"Why not?"

"Because it was an uncontested hearing. The ex-wife's lawyer went at it hammer and tongs, while Balder grovelled and said he was useless and irresponsible and unfit to live and God knows what else. What the tribunal wrote was malicious and tendentious, to my mind. To the effect that Balder had never been able to connect with other people and had always sought refuge with machines. Now that I've had time to look into his life a little, I'm not that impressed by how it was dealt with. His guilt-laden tirades and self-criticism were taken as gospel by the tribunal. At any rate Balder was extremely cooperative. As I said, he agreed to pay a large amount of child support, forty thousand a month, I believe, plus a one-off payment of nine hundred thousand kronor for unforeseen expenses. Not long after that he took himself off to America."

"But then he came back."

Westman had failed to live up to their responsibilities when it came to his schooling. It had been agreed that August would be taught at home, but the special-needs teachers seem to have been played off against each other. Probably the money for his education was misappropriated and fake teachers' names used, all sorts of stuff like that. But that's an altogether different story which somebody will have to look into at some point."

"You were talking about the woman from the Centre for Autism."

"That's right. She smelled a rat and called Hanna and Westman and was informed that everything was fine. But she had a feeling that wasn't true. So against normal practice she made an unannounced home visit and, when they finally let her in, she could tell that the boy was not doing well, that his development had stagnated. She also saw those bruises. So she rang Balder in San

Francisco, had a long conversation with him and soon after that he moved back and took his son with him to his new house in Saltsjöbaden, disregarding the custody order."

"How did he manage that, seeing as Westman was so keen to get the child support?"

"Good question. According to Westman, Balder more or less kidnapped the boy. But Hanna has a different version of the story. She says that Frans turned up and seemed to have changed, so she let him take August. She even thought he would be better off with his father."

"And Westman?"

"According to her, Westman was drunk and had just landed a big part in a new T.V. production, and was feeling cocky and over-confident. So he agreed to it. However much he may have gone on about the boy's welfare, I think he was glad to be rid of him."

"But then?"

"Then he regretted it, and on top of everything else he was sacked from the series because he couldn't stay sober. He suddenly wanted to have August back, or not so much him, of course . . ."

"The child support."

"Exactly, and that was confirmed by his drinking pals. When Westman's credit card was rejected during the course of yesterday evening, he really started ranting and raving about the boy. He bummed five hundred kronor off a young woman in the bar to pay for a taxi to Saltsjöbaden in the middle of the night."

Bublanski was lost in his thoughts for a while and gazed once again at the photograph of Modig's son.

"What a mess," he said.

"Right."

"Under normal circumstances we would be close to solving this one. We'd find our motive somewhere in that custody battle. But these guys who hack alarm systems and look like ninja warriors, they don't fit the picture."

190

"No."

"There's something else I'm wondering about."

"What's that?"

"If August can't read, then what was he doing climbing up to reach those books?"

Blomkvist was sitting opposite Farah Sharif at her kitchen table with a cup of tea, looking out at Tantolunden park. Even though he knew it was a sign of weakness, he wished he did not have a ~~story~~ to write. He wished he could just sit there without having

tional way surely but with a regal ~~bearing~~

her.

"Tell me, what was he like," Blomkvist said.

"Frans?"

"Yes."

"A paradox."

"In what way?"

"In all sorts of ways. But mainly because he worked so hard on the one thing which worried him more than anything else. Maybe a bit like Oppenheimer at Los Alamos. He was engrossed in something he believed could be our ruin."

"Now you've lost me."

"Frans wanted to replicate biological evolution on a digital level. He was working on self-teaching algorithms – the idea is they can enhance themselves through trial and error. He also contributed to the development of quantum computers, as people call them, which Google, Solifon and the N.S.A. are working on. His objective was to achieve A.G.I., or Artificial General Intelligence."

"And what is that?"

"It's when something has the intelligence of a human being, but the speed and precision of a computer. If a thing like that could be created, it would give us enormous advantages within numerous fields."

"No doubt about it."

"There is an extraordinary amount of research going on in this area, and even though most scientists aren't specifically aiming for A.G.I., competition is driving us in that direction. Nobody can afford *not* to create applications which are as intelligent as possible. Nobody can afford to put the brake on development. Just think of what we have achieved so far. Just think back to what you had in your mobile five years ago compared to what's in there today."

"True."

"Before he became so secretive, Frans told me he estimated that we could get to A.G.I. within thirty or forty years. That may sound ambitious, but for my part I wonder if he wasn't being too conservative. The capacity of computers doubles every eighteen months, and the human brain is bad at grasping that kind of exponential growth. It's like the grain of rice on the chessboard, you know? You put one grain of rice on the first square, two on the second, four on the third, eight on the fourth."

"And soon the grains of rice have flooded the world."

"The pace of growth goes on increasing and in the end it escapes our control. The interesting thing isn't actually when we reach A.G.I., but what happens after that. Just a few days after we've reached A.G.I., we'll have A.S.I. – Artificial Super-Intelligence – used to describe something more intelligent than we are. After that it'll just get quicker and quicker. Computers will start enhancing themselves at an accelerating pace, perhaps by a factor of ten, and become a hundred, a thousand, ten thousand times cleverer than we are. What happens then?"

"I dread to think."

"Quite. Intelligence in itself is not predictable. We don't know where human intelligence will take us. We know even less what will happen with a super-intelligence."

"In the worst case we'll be no more interesting to the computer than little white mice," Blomkvist said, thinking of what he had written to Salander.

"_____ ? We share __ per cent of our D.N.A. with

"I mean, how do you think a computer ____

up to find itself captured and controlled by primitive little creatures like us. Why would it put up with that?" she said. "Why on earth should it show us any consideration, still less let us dig around in its entrails in order to shut down the process? We risk being confronted by an explosion of intelligence, a technological singularity, as Verner Vinge put it. Everything that happens after that lies beyond our event horizon."

"So the very instant we create a super-intelligence we lose control, is that right?"

"The risk is that everything we know about the world will cease to be relevant, and it'll be the end of human existence."

"You *are* joking."

"I know it sounds crazy, but it's a very real question. There are thousands of people all over the world working to prevent a development like this. Many are optimists, or even foresee some kind of utopia. There's talk of friendly A.S.I., super-intelligences which are programmed from the start to do nothing but help us. The idea is something along the lines of what Asimov envisioned in his book *I, Robot*: built-in laws which forbid the machines to harm us. The writer and innovator Kurzweil has visions of a wonderful world in which nanotechnology allows us to integrate ourselves with computers, and share our future with them. But there are no guarantees. Laws can be repealed. The intent of initial programming can be changed and it's fatally easy to make anthropomorphic mistakes: to ascribe human characteristics to machines and misunderstand what drives them inherently. Frans was obsessed with these questions and, as I said, he was of two minds. He both longed for intelligent computers and he also worried about them."

"He couldn't help but build his monsters."

"A bit like that, though that's putting it drastically."

"How far had he got?"

"Further, I think, than anyone could imagine, and that may have been yet another reason why he was so secretive about his work at Solifon. He was afraid his program would end up in the wrong hands. He was even afraid the program would come into contact with the Internet and merge with it. He called it August, after his son."

"And where is it now?"

"He never went anywhere without it. It must have been right by the bed when he was shot. But the terrible thing is that the police say there was no computer there."

"I didn't see one either. But then my focus was elsewhere."

"It must have been dreadful."

"Perhaps you heard that I also saw the man who killed him," Blomkvist said. "He was carrying a rucksack."

"That doesn't sound good. But with a bit of luck the computer will turn up somewhere in the house."

"Let's hope so. Do you have any idea who stole his technology the first time around?"

"Yes, I do, as a matter of fact."

"That interests me a lot."

"I can see that. But the sad thing is that I have some personal responsibility for this mess. Frans was working himself to death, you see, and I was worried he would burn out. That was about the time he had lost custody of August."

"When was that?"

"Two years ago. He was utterly worn out. He wasn't sleeping, ～～～～～～～self, yet he was incapable of

"His technology was stolen.

"He had clear proof of that when the application from Truegames was submitted to the U.S. Patent Office in August last year. Every unique aspect of his technology had been duplicated and written down there – it was obvious. At first they all suspected their computers had been hacked, but I was sceptical from the start – I knew how sophisticated Frans' encryption was. But since there was no other plausible explanation, that was the initial assumption, and for a while maybe Frans believed it himself. It was nonsense of course."

"What are you saying?" Blomkvist burst out. "Surely the data breach was confirmed by experts."

"Yes, by some idiot show-off at the N.D.R.E. But that was just Frans' way of protecting his boys, or it could have been more than that. I suspect he also wanted to play detective, although heaven knows how he could be so stupid. You see . . ." Farah took a deep breath, "I learned all this only a few weeks ago. Frans and little August were here for dinner and I sensed at once that he had something important to tell me. It was hanging in the air. After a couple of glasses he asked me to put away my mobile and began to speak in a whisper. I have to admit that at first I was simply irritated. He was going on again about his young hacker genius."

"Hacker genius?" Blomkvist said, trying to sound neutral.

"A girl he spoke about so much that it was doing my head in. I won't bore you with the full story, but she'd turned up out of the blue at one of his lectures and practically lectured *him* on the concept of singularity. She impressed Frans, and he started to open up to her – it's understandable. A mega-nerd like Frans can't have found all that many people he could talk to at his own level, and when he realized that the girl was also a hacker he asked her to take a look at their computers. At the time they had all the equipment at the home of a guy called Linus Brandell, one of the assistants."

All Blomkvist said was, "Linus Brandell."

"Yes," Farah said. "The girl came round to his place in Östermalm and just threw him out. Then she got to work on the computers. She couldn't find any sign of a breach, but she didn't leave it at that. She had a list of Frans' assistants and hacked them all from Linus' computer. It didn't take long for her to realize that one of them had sold him out to none other than Solifon."

"And who was it?"

"Frans didn't want to tell me, even though I pressed him. But the girl apparently called him directly from Linus' apartment. Frans was in San Francisco at the time, and you can imagine: betrayed by one of his own! I was expecting him to report the guy right away and raise hell. But he had a better idea. He asked the girl to pretend they really had been hacked."

"Why would he do that?"

"He didn't want any traces of evidence to be tidied away. He wanted to understand more about what had happened. I suppose it makes sense – for one of the world's leading software businesses to steal and exploit his technology was obviously far more serious than if some good-for-nothing, unprincipled shit of a student had done the same. Because Solifon isn't just one of the most respected research groups in the U.S.A., they had also been trying to recruit Frans for years. He was livid. 'Those bastards were trying to seduce me, and they stole from me at the same time,' he growled."

"Let me be sure I've got this right." Blomkvist said. "You're _____ _____ to find out why and how

ined his computers. She gave him the spe____ that enabled him to dig into the mess. In the end it turned out to be much more difficult than he expected, and people started getting very suspicious. It wasn't long before he became fantastically unpopular, so he kept more and more to himself. But he did find something."

"What?"

"This is where it all gets sensitive. I really shouldn't be telling you."

"Yet here we are."

"Yet here we are. Not only because I've always had the utmost respect for your journalism. It occurred to me this morning that it may not have been a coincidence that Frans rang you last night rather than Säpo's Industry Protection Group, whom he had also been in touch with. I think he was beginning to suspect a leak there. It may have been no more than paranoia – Frans displayed a variety of symptoms of persecution mania – but it was you he called, and now I hope that I can fulfil his wish."

"I hope you can."

"At Solifon there's a department called 'Y'," Farah said. "Google X is the model, the department where they work on 'moonshots', as they call them, wild and far-fetched ideas, like looking for eternal life or connecting search engines to brain neurons. If any place will achieve A.G.I. or A.S.I., that's probably it. Frans was assigned to 'Y'. But that wasn't as smart as it may have sounded."

"And why not?"

"Because he had found out from his hacker girl that there was a secret group of business intelligence analysts at 'Y', headed up by a character called Zigmund Eckerwald, also known as Zeke."

"And who is that?"

"The very person who had been communicating with Frans' treacherous assistant."

"So Eckerwald was the thief."

"A thief of the highest order. On the face of it, the work carried out by Eckerwald's group was perfectly legitimate. They compiled information on leading scientists and promising research projects. Every large high-tech firm has a similar operation. They want to know what's going on and who they should be recruiting. But Frans understood that the group went beyond that. They stole – through hacker attacks, espionage, moles and bribery."

"But then why didn't he report them?"

"It was tricky to prove. They were careful, to be sure. But in the end Frans went to the owner, Nicolas Grant. Grant was horrified and apparently organized an internal investigation. But the investigation found nothing, either because Eckerwald had got rid of the evidence or because the investigation was just for show. It left Frans in a tight spot. Everyone turned on him. Eckerwald must have been behind it, and I'm sure he had no trouble getting the others to join in. Frans was already perceived as paranoid and became progressively isolated and frozen out. I can picture it. How he would sit there and become more and more awkward and contrary, and refuse to say a word to anyone."

"So he had no concrete evidence, you think?"

"Well, he did at least have the proof the hacker girl had given him: that Eckerwald had stolen Frans' technology and sold it on."

"And he knew that for sure?"

"Without a shadow of a doubt. Besides, he had realized that Eckerwald's group was not working alone. It had backing from ~~~~~~~~~~ intelligence services

~~~~~ said, ~~~~~
'Thanos'."

"Thanos?"

"That's right. He said that this individual was greatly feared. But he didn't want to say more than that. He needed life insurance, he claimed, for when the lawyers came after him."

"You said you didn't know which of his assistants sold him out. But you must have given it a great deal of thought," Blomkvist said.

"I have, and sometimes, I don't know . . . I wonder if it wasn't all of them."

"Why do you say that?"

"When they started working for Frans, they were young, ambitious and gifted. By the time they finished, they were fed up with life and full of anxieties. Maybe Frans worked them too hard. Or maybe there's something else tormenting them."

"Do you have all their names?"

"I do. They're my boys – unfortunately, I'd have to say. First there's Linus Brandell, I've already mentioned him. He's twenty-four now, and just drifts around playing computer games and drinking too much. For a while he had a good job as a games developer at Crossfire. But he lost it when he started calling in sick and accusing his colleagues of spying on him. Then there's Arvid Wrange, maybe you've heard of him. He was a promising chess player once upon a time. His father pushed him in a pretty inhuman way and in the end Arvid had enough and came to study with me. I'd hoped that he would have completed his Ph.D. long ago. But instead he props up the bars around Stureplan and seems rootless. He came into his own for a while when he was with Frans. But there was also a lot of silly competition among the boys. Arvid and Basim, the third guy, came to hate each other – at least Arvid hated Basim. Basim Malik probably doesn't do hate. He's a sensitive, exceedingly smart boy who was taken on by Solifon Nordic a year ago. But he ran out of steam pretty quickly. Right now he's being treated for depression at Ersta hospital and it so happens that his mother, whom I know vaguely, rang me this morning to tell me that he's under sedation. When he found out what had happened to Frans, he tried to slash his wrists. It's devastating, but at the same time I do wonder: was it just grief? Or was it also guilt?"

"How is he now?"

"He's not in any danger from a physical point of view. And then there's Niklas Lagerstedt, and he . . . well, what can I say about him? He's not like the others, at least not on the surface. He wouldn't drink himself into oblivion or even think of harming himself. He's a young man with moral objections to most things, including violent computer games and porn. He's a member of the Mission Covenant Church. His wife is a paediatrician and they have a young son called Jesper. On top of all that he's a consultant with the National Criminal Police, responsible for the computer system coming into service in the new year, which means he's had to go through security clearance. But who knows how thorough it was."

"Why do you say that?"

"Because behind that respectable facade he's a nasty piece of work. I happen to know that he's embezzled parts of his father-in-law's and his wife's fortune. He's a hypocrite."

"Have the boys been questioned?"

"Säpo have talked to them, but nothing came of it. At that time _____ thought that Frans was the victim of a data breach."

_____ _____ again now."

_____ _____

ask?"

"I saw a fantastic drawing at his home, of a traffic light up here on the intersection of Hornsgatan and Ringvägen. It was flawless, a sort of snapshot in the dark."

"How strange. Frans wasn't usually in this part of town."

"There's something about that drawing that won't let go of me," Blomkvist said, and he realized to his surprise that Farah had taken hold of his hand. He stroked her hair. Then he stood up with a feeling that he was onto something. He said goodbye and went out onto the street.

On the way back up Zinkens väg he called Berger and asked her to type another question in LISBETH STUFF.

CHAPTER 14

21.xi

Ove Levin was sitting in his office with a view over Slussen and Riddarfjärden, not doing much at all except Googling himself in the hope of coming across something to cheer him up. What he found himself reading was that he was sleazy and flabby and that he had betrayed his ideals. All that in a blog written by a slip of a girl at the Institute for Media Studies at Stockholm University. It made him so furious that he even forgot to write her name in the little black book he kept, of people who would never get a job in the Serner Group.

He could not be bothered to burden his brain with idiots who had no idea what it takes and would only ever write underpaid articles in obscure cultural magazines. Rather than wallow in destructive thoughts, he went into his online account and checked his portfolio. That helped a bit, at least to begin with. It was a good day on the markets. The Nasdaq and the Dow Jones had both gone up last night and the Stockholmsindex was 1.1 per cent higher too. The dollar, to which he was rather too exposed, had risen, and according to the update of a few seconds ago his portfolio was worth 12,161,389 kronor.

Not bad for a man who had once covered house fires and knife fights for the morning edition of *Expressen*. Twelve million, plus the apartment in Villastaden and the villa in Cannes. They could post whatever they wanted on their blogs. He was well provided for, and he checked the value of his portfolio again. 12,149,101. Jesus Christ, was it dropping? 12,131,737. He grimaced. There was no reason why the market should be falling, was there? The employment figures had been good, after all. He took the tumble in value almost personally and could not help thinking of *Millennium*, however insignificant it might be in the bigger picture. He found himself getting worked up again and reluctantly he remembered the openly hostile look on Erika Berger's beautiful face at the meeting yesterday afternoon. Things had not improved this morning.

who wasn't even going to keep his jo

if Ove Levin and Serner Media had anything to do with it. Instead they said: why Frans Balder, of all people?

Why on earth did he have to be murdered right under Blomkvist's nose? Wasn't that just typical? So infuriating. Even if those useless journalists out there hadn't realized it yet, Levin knew that Balder was a big name. Not long ago Serner's own newspaper, *Business Daily*, had produced a special supplement on Swedish scientific research which had given him a price tag: four billion kronor, though God knows how they got to that figure. Balder was a star, no doubt about it. Most importantly, he was a Garbo. He never gave interviews, and that made him all the more sought after.

How many requests had Balder received from Serner's own journalists after all? As many as he had refused or, for that matter, simply not bothered to answer. Many of Levin's colleagues out there thought Balder was sitting on a fantastic story. He couldn't bear the idea that, so the newspaper reports said, Balder had wanted to talk to Blomkvist in the middle of the night. Could Blomkvist really have a scoop on top of everything else? That would be disastrous. Once more, almost obsessively, Levin went onto the *Aftonbladet* site and was met with the headline:

WHAT DID TOP SWEDISH SCIENTIST HAVE TO SAY TO MIKAEL BLOMKVIST?

MYSTERY CALL JUST BEFORE THE MURDER

The article was illustrated by a double-column photograph of Mikael Blomkvist which did not show any flab at all. Those bastard editors had gone and chosen the most flattering photograph they could find, and that made him angrier still. *I have to do something about this*, he thought. But what? How could he put a stop to Blomkvist without barging in like some old East German censor and making everything worse? He looked out towards Riddarfjärden and an idea came to him. *Borg*, he thought. *My enemy's enemy can be my best friend*.

"Sanna," he shouted.

"Yes, Ove?"

Sanna Lind was his young secretary.

"Book a lunch at once with William Borg at Sturehof. If he says he has something else on, tell him this is more important. He can even have a raise," he said, and thought: why not? If he's prepared to help me in this mess then it's only fair he gets something out of it.

Hanna Balder was standing in the living room at Torsgatan looking in despair at August, who had yet again dug out paper and crayons.

She had been told that she had to discourage him, and she did not like doing it. Not that she questioned the psychologist's advice and expertise, but she had her doubts. August had seen his father murdered and if he wanted to draw, why stop him? Even if it did not seem be doing him much good.

His body trembled when he started drawing and his eyes shone with an intense, tormented light. The pattern of squares spreading out and multiplying in mirrors was a strange theme, given what had happened. But what did she know? Maybe it was the same as ~~with his series~~ of numbers. Even though she did not understand ~~something~~ to him, and

~~decided~~

But suddenly the boy's back stiffened ~~like~~ could not help thinking back to what the psychologist had said. She took a hesitant step forward and looked down at the paper. She gave a start, and felt very uncomfortable. At first she could not make sense of it.

She saw the same pattern of squares repeating themselves in two surrounding mirrors and it was extremely skilfully done. But there was something else there as well, a shadow which grew out of the squares, like a demon, a phantom, and it frightened the living daylights out of her. She started to think of films about children who become possessed. She snatched the drawing from the boy and crumpled it up without fully understanding why. Then she shut her eyes and expected to hear that heart-rending toneless cry again.

But she heard no cry, just a muttering which sounded almost like words – impossible because the boy did not speak. Instead

Hanna prepared herself for a violent outburst, with August thrashing back and forth over the living-room floor. But there was no attack either, only a calm and composed determination as August took hold of a new piece of paper and started to draw the same squares again. Hanna had no choice but to carry him to his room. Afterwards she would describe what happened as pure horror.

August kicked and screamed and lashed out, and Hanna only just managed to keep hold of him. For a long time she lay in the bed with her arms knotted around him, wishing that she could go to pieces herself. She briefly considered waking Lasse and asking him to give August one of those tranquilizing suppositories they now had, but then discarded that idea. Lasse would be bound to be in a foul mood and she hated to give a child tranquilizers, however much Valium she took herself. There had to be some other way.

She was falling apart, desperately considering one option after the other. She thought of her mother in Katrineholm, of her agent Mia, of the nice woman who rang last night, Gabriella Grane, and then of the psychologist again, Einar Fors-something, who had brought August to her. She had not particularly liked him. On the other hand he had offered to look after August for a while, and this was all his fault in the first place.

He was the one who said August should not draw, so he should be sorting out this mess. In the end she let go of her son and dug out the psychologist's card to call him. August immediately made a break for the living room to start drawing his damn squares again.

Einar Forsberg did not have a great deal of experience. He was forty-eight years old and with his deep-set blue eyes, brand-new Dior glasses and brown corduroy jacket he could easily be taken for an intellectual. But anyone who had ever disagreed with him would know that there was something stiff and dogmatic about his way of thinking and he often concealed his lack of knowledge behind dogma and cocksure pronouncements.

It had only been two years since he qualified as a psychologist. Before that he was a gym teacher from Tyresö, and if you had asked his old pupils about him they would all have roared: "Silence, cattle! Be quiet, oh my beasts!" Forsberg had loved to shout those words, only half joking, when he wanted order in the classroom, and even though he had hardly been anyone's favourite teacher he had kept his boys in line. It was this ability which ~~had~~ put his skills to better use elsewhere.

long-term work. Children would come ~~with~~ ences at home and the psychologists were far too busy trying to manage breakdowns and aggressive behaviour to be able to devote themselves to resolving underlying causes. Even so, Forsberg thought he was doing some good, especially when he used his old classroom authority to quieten hysterical children, or when he handled crisis situations out in the field.

He liked to work with policemen and he loved the tension in the air after dramatic events. He had been excited and expectant as he drove out to the house in Saltsjöbaden in the course of his night duty. There was a touch of Hollywood about the situation, he thought. A Swedish scientist had been murdered, his eight-year-old son had been at the house, and he, Forsberg, had been sent to try to get the boy to open up. He straightened his hair and his glasses several times in the rear-view mirror.

He wanted to make a stylish impression, but once he arrived

he was not much of a success. He could not make the boy out. Still, he felt acknowledged and important. The detectives asked him how they should go about questioning the child and – even though he did not have a clue – his answer was received with respect. That gave his ego a little boost and he did his best to be helpful. He found out that the boy suffered from infantile autism and had never spoken or been receptive to the world around him.

"There's nothing we can do for the time being," he said. "His mental faculties are too weak. As a psychologist I have to put his need for care first." The policemen listened to him with serious expressions and let him drive the boy home to his mother – who was another little bonus in the whole story.

She was the actress Hanna Balder. He had had the hots for her ever since he saw her in "The Mutineers" and he remembered her hips and her long legs, and even though she was now a bit older she was still attractive. Besides, her current partner was clearly a bastard. Forsberg did his best to appear knowledgeable and charming in a low-key way; within moments he got an opportunity to be authoritative, and that made him proud.

With a wild expression on his face the son began to draw black and white blocks, or squares, and Forsberg pronounced that this was unhealthy. It was precisely the kind of destructive compulsive behaviour that autistic children slip into, and he insisted that August stop immediately. This was not received with as much gratitude as he had hoped for. Still, it had made him feel decisive and manly, and while he was at it he almost paid Hanna a compliment for her performance in "The Mutineers". But then he decided that it was probably not the right time. Maybe that had been a mistake.

Now it was 1.00 in the afternoon, and he was back home at his terraced house in Vällingby. He was in the bathroom with his electric toothbrush, feeling exhausted, when his mobile rang. At first he was irritated – but then he smiled. It was none other than Hanna Balder.

"Forsberg," he answered in an urbane voice.

"Hello," she said. "August, August . . ."

She sounded desperate and angry.

"Tell me, what's the problem?"

"All he wants to do is draw his chessboard squares. But you're saying he isn't allowed to."

"No, no, it's compulsive. But please, just stay calm."

". . . . . to stay calm?"

"Wouldn't that be letting him down . . ."

"On the contrary, you're just taking account of his needs. I'll see to it personally that you can visit us as often as you like."

"Maybe that's the best solution."

"I'm sure of it."

"Will you come right away?"

"I'll be with you as soon as I can," he said. First he had to smarten himself up a bit. Then he added: "Did I tell you that I loved you in 'The Mutineers'?"

It was no surprise to Levin that William Borg was already at the table at Sturehof, nor that he ordered the most expensive items on the menu, sole *meunière* and a glass of Pouilly-Fumé. Journalists generally made the most of it when he invited them to lunch. But it did surprise – and annoy – him that Borg had taken the initiative, as if he were the one with the money and the power. Why had he mentioned that raise? He should have kept Borg on tenterhooks, let him sit there and sweat instead.

"A little bird whispered in my ear that you're having difficulties with *Millennium*," Borg said, and Levin thought, *I'd give my right arm to wipe that self-righteous smirk off his face*.

"You've been misinformed," he said stiffly.

"Really?"

"We have the situation under control."

"How so, if you don't mind my asking?"

"If the editorial team is disposed to accept change and is ready to recognize the problems it has, we'll back them."

"And if not . . ."

"We'll pull out, and *Millennium* will be unlikely to stay afloat for more than a few months, which would of course be a great shame. But that's what the market looks like at the moment. Better magazines than *Millennium* have gone under. It's been only a modest investment for us and we can manage without it."

"Skip the bullshit, Ove. I know that this is a matter of pride for you."

"It's just business."

"I'd heard that you wanted to get Mikael Blomkvist off the editorial team."

"We've been thinking of transferring him to London."

"Isn't that a bit harsh, considering what he's done for the magazine?"

"We've made him a very generous offer," Levin said, feeling that he was being unnecessarily defensive and predictable.

He had almost forgotten the purpose of the lunch.

"Personally I don't blame you," Borg said. "You can ship him off to China, for all I care. I'm just wondering if it isn't going to be a bit tricky for you if Blomkvist makes a grand comeback with this Frans Balder story."

"Why would that happen? He's lost his sting. You of all people have pointed that out – and with considerable success, if I may say so," Levin said with an attempt at sarcasm.

"Well, yes, but I did get a little help."

"Not from me, you didn't; of that you can be sure. I hated that column. Thought it was badly written and tendentious. The one who kicked off the campaign against him was Thorvald Serner, you know that."

"But you can't be altogether unhappy about the way things are going right now?"

"Listen to me, William. I have the greatest respect for Mikael

Levin feel better right away.

"That's how it is. We should be grateful to Blomkvist for the revelations he's given us, and I wish him all the best, I really do. But unfortunately it's not my job to get nostalgic and look back to the good old days. I have to concede that you have a point in suggesting that the man has got out of step with the times, and that he could get in the way of our plans to relaunch *Millennium*."

"True, true."

"So for that reason it would be good if there weren't too many headlines about him right now."

"Positive headlines, you mean?"

"Maybe so, yes," Levin said. "That's another reason I invited you to lunch."

"Grateful for that, of course. And I do think I have something to offer. I had a call this morning from my old squash buddy," Borg said, clearly trying to regain his earlier self-confidence.

"And who's that?"

"Richard Ekström, the chief prosecutor. He's in charge of the preliminary investigation into the Balder killing. And he's not a member of the Blomkvist fan club."

"After that Zalachenko business, right?"

"Exactly. Blomkvist scuppered his entire strategy on that case and now he's worried that he's sabotaging this investigation as well."

"In what way?"

"Blomkvist isn't saying everything he knows. He spoke to Balder just before the murder and came face to face with the killer. Even so, he had surprisingly little to say for himself during the interviews. Ekström suspects he's saving the juiciest bits for his article."

"Interesting."

"Isn't it? We're talking about a man who was ridiculed in the media and is now so desperate for a scoop that he's prepared to let someone get away with murder. An old star reporter willing to cast social responsibility to the winds when his magazine finds itself in a financial crisis. And who has just learned that Serner Media wants to kick him off the editorial team. Hardly surprising that he's gone a step or two too far."

"I see your point. Is it anything you'd like to write about?"

"I don't think that would be productive, to be honest. Too many people know that Blomkvist and I have it in for each other. You'd be better off leaking to a news reporter and then supporting the story on your editorial pages. You'll get some good quotes from Ekström."

Levin was looking out onto Stureplan, where he spotted a beautiful woman in a bright red coat, with long strawberry-blonde hair. For the first time that day he gave a big smile.

"Maybe that isn't such a bad idea," he added, ordering some wine for himself too.

*

212

Blomkvist came walking down Hornsgatan towards Mariatorget. Further away, by Maria Magdalena kyrka, there was a white van with an ugly dent in its front wing, and next to it two men were waving their arms around and shouting at each other. But although the scene had attracted a crowd of onlookers, Blomkvist hardly noticed it.

He was thinking about how Balder's son had sat on the floor of the large house in Saltsjöbaden, reaching out over the Persian rug. The boy's hand had stains on the back of it and on the fingers, possibly ink from felt tips or pens, and that movement he was ~~making had looked as if he were drawing something complicated~~

~~seen him throwing himself against~~ understood that there was something exceptional about him. Now, as he cut across Mariatorget, a strange thought occurred to him and would not let him go. Up by Götgatsbacken he came to a stop.

He must at the very least follow it up, so he got out his mobile and looked up Hanna Balder. The number was unlisted, and unlikely to be one which he would find in *Millennium*'s contacts. He thought of Freja Granliden, a society reporter at *Expressen* whose columns could not be said to enhance the prestige of the profession. She wrote about divorce, romance and royalty, but she had a quick brain and a good line in repartee, and whenever they met they had a good time together. He rang her number, but it was engaged of course.

These days, reporters on the evening papers were forever on the telephone, under such deadline pressure that they never left their desks to take a look at what real life was like. But he got her in the end and was not in the least surprised that she let out a little yelp of delight.

"Mikael," she said, "what an honour! Are you finally going to give me a scoop? I've been waiting for so long."

"Sorry. This time *you* have to help *me*. I need an address and a phone number."

"What do I get in return? Maybe a wicked quote about what you got up to last night."

"I could give you some career advice."

"And what might that be?"

"Stop writing crap."

"Right, and then who's going to keep track of all the telephone numbers the classy reporters need? Who are you looking for?"

"Hanna Balder."

"I can imagine why. Did you meet her drunken boyfriend out there?"

"Don't you start fishing now. Do you know where she lives?"

"Torsgatan 40."

"You know it just like that?"

"I have a brilliant memory for trivia. If you hang on, I'll give you the phone number and the front-door code as well."

"That's really kind."

"But you know . . ."

"Yes?"

"You're not the only one looking for her. Our own bloodhounds are on the trail too, and from what I hear she hasn't answered her telephone all day."

"Wise woman."

Afterwards Blomkvist stood in the street, unsure what to do. Chasing down unhappy mothers in competition with crime reporters from the evening papers was not quite what he had hoped his day would bring. But he hailed a taxi and was driven off in the direction of Vasastan.

Hanna Balder had accompanied August and Forsberg to Oden's Medical Centre for Children and Adolescents, opposite Observatorielunden on Sveavägen. The medical centre consisted of two apartments which had been knocked together, but even though the furnishings and the courtyard had a private and sheltered feel to them, there was nonetheless something institutional about it all. Probably that had less to do with the long corridors and closed _____ ____ _____ressions on the faces of the

children. But it felt too late to be having

way home she consoled herself with the thought that it would only be for a short time. Maybe she would pick up August as soon as this evening?

Then she thought about Lasse and his bouts of drunkenness and she told herself yet again that she needed to leave him and get a grip on her life. As she walked out of the lift at her apartment she gave a start. An attractive man was sitting there on the landing, writing in a notebook. As he got to his feet and greeted her she saw that it was Mikael Blomkvist. She was terrified, so guilt-ridden, that she supposed he was going to write some kind of exposé. That was absurd. He just gave an embarrassed smile and twice apologized for disturbing her. She could not help but feel a huge sense of relief. She had admired him for a long time.

"I have no comment to make," she said, in a voice which actually suggested the opposite.

"I'm not after a quote either," he said. She remembered hearing that he and Lasse had arrived together – or at least at the same time – at Frans' house the previous night, although she could not imagine what the two of them might have in common.

"Are you looking for Lasse?" she said.

"I'd like to hear about August's drawings," he replied, and at that she felt a stab of panic.

Yet she allowed him in. It was probably careless of her. Lasse had gone off to cure his hangover in some local dive and could be back any time. He would go crazy if he found a journalist in their home. But Blomkvist had not only worried Hanna, he had also made her curious. How on earth did he know about the drawings? She invited him to sit on the grey sofa in the living room while she went to the kitchen to get some tea and biscuits. When she came back with a tray he said:

"I wouldn't be bothering you if it wasn't absolutely necessary."

"You're not bothering me," she said.

"You see, I met August last night, and I haven't been able to stop thinking about him."

"Oh?"

"I didn't understand it then," he said, "but I had the feeling he was trying to tell us something. Now I'm convinced he wanted to draw. He was making these determined movements with his hand over the floor."

"He's become obsessed with drawing."

"So he went on doing that here at home?"

"And how! He started the minute we got here. He was manic, and what he drew was amazing, but his face became flushed and he was breathing heavily, so the psychologist said he had to stop. It was compulsive and destructive, was his opinion."

"What did he draw?"

"Nothing special really. I'd guess it was inspired by his puzzles.

But it was very cleverly done, with shadows and perspective and everything."

"But what was it?"

"Squares."

"What kind of squares?"

"Chessboard squares, I think you would call them," she said. Maybe she was imagining things, but she detected a trace of excitement in Blomkvist's eyes.

"Only chess squares?" he said. "Nothing more?"

"Mirrors too," she said. "Chessboard squares reflected in

"Oh my God!"

"What's the matter?"

"Because . . ."

A wave of shame washed over her.

"Because the last thing I saw before I snatched the drawing away from him was a menacing shadow emerging out of those squares," she said.

"Do you have the drawing here?"

"No, or rather yes."

"Yes?"

"I'm afraid I threw it away. But it will still be in the bin."

Blomkvist had coffee grounds and yoghurt all over his hands as he pulled a crumpled piece of paper out of the rubbish and smoothed it out on the draining board. He brushed it off with the back of his hand and looked at it in the glare of the kitchen lights.

The drawing was not finished, not by any means, and it consisted mostly of chessboard squares, just as Hanna had said, seen from above or from the side. Unless you had been in Balder's bedroom, it would not be obvious that the squares represented a floor, but Blomkvist immediately recognized the mirrors on the wardrobe to the right of the bed. He also recognized the darkness, that special darkness that had met him in the course of the night.

He felt transported back to the moment when he had walked in through the broken window – apart from one small important detail. The room he had entered had been almost dark, whereas the drawing showed a thin source of light falling diagonally from above, extending out over the squares. It gave contours to a shadow which was not distinct or meaningful, but which felt eerie, perhaps for that very reason.

The shadow was stretching out an arm and Blomkvist, who saw the drawing in a very different light to Hanna, had no trouble interpreting what that signified. The figure meant to kill. Above the chessboard squares and the shadow there was a face which had not yet materialized.

"Where is August now?" he said. "Is he sleeping?"

"No. He . . . I've left him with someone else for a while. I couldn't handle him, to be honest."

"Where is he?"

"At Oden's Medical Centre for Children and Adolescents. On Sveavägen."

"Who knows that he's there?"

"No-one."

"Just you and the staff?"

Hanna nodded.

"Then it has to stay that way. Will you excuse me for a moment?"

Blomkvist took out his mobile and called Bublanski. In his mind he had already drafted yet another question for LISBETH STUFF.

*

Bublanski felt frustrated: the investigation was going nowhere. Neither Balder's Blackphone nor his laptop had been found, so they had not been able to map his contacts with the outside world, despite having had detailed discussions with the service provider.

For the time being they had little more than smokescreens and clichés to go on, Bublanski thought: a ninja warrior had materialized swiftly and effectively and then vanished into the darkness. In fact the attack had something far too perfect about it, as if it had been carried out by a person free of all the usual human failings and contradictions which as a rule feature in a murder. This

a savant," Blomkvist said.

"A what?"

"A boy who may be severely mentally disabled but nonetheless has a special gift. He draws like a master, with a remarkable mathematical sharpness. Did someone show you the drawings of the traffic light which had been lying on the kitchen table in Saltsjöbaden?"

"Yes, briefly. Are you saying it wasn't Balder who drew them?"

"It was the boy."

"They looked like astonishingly mature pieces of work."

"But they were drawn by August. This morning he sat down and drew the chessboard squares on the floor in his father's bedroom, and he didn't stop at that. He sketched a shaft of light and a shadow. My theory is that it's the killer's shadow and the light from his headlamp, but of course one couldn't yet say for certain. The boy was interrupted in his work."

"Are you pulling my leg?"

"This is hardly the moment."

"How do you know all this?'

"I'm at the home of the boy's mother, Hanna Balder, and I'm looking at the drawing. The boy is no longer here. He's at . . ." The journalist hesitated. "I don't want to say more than that over the telephone."

"You say that the boy was interrupted in the middle of his drawing?"

"His mother stopped him on a psychologist's advice."

"How could one do something like that?"

"He probably didn't realize what the drawings represented, he just saw them as something compulsive. I suggest you send some people over right away. You've got your witness."

"We'll be there as soon as we can be."

Bublanski ended the call and went to share Blomkvist's news with the team, though soon after he wondered whether this had been wise.

CHAPTER 15

21.xi

word, and only now that ~~~~~

absolved of her promise.

Now she was going to proceed on her own terms. But it was not all that easy. Arvid Wrange had not been at home, and instead of calling him she wanted to come down on his life like a bolt of lightning and so had been out searching for him, her hoodie pulled over her head. Wrange lived the life of a drone. But as with so many other drones, he had a routine, and Salander had been able to find a number of signposts through the trail of pictures he posted on Instagram and Facebook: Riche on Birger Jarlsgatan and the Teatergrillen on Nybrogatan, the Raucher Chess Club and Café Ritorno on Odengatan and a number of others, including a shooting club on Fridhelmsgatan, plus the addresses of two girl-friends.

Wrange had changed since the last time she had him on her radar. Not only had he got rid of his nerdy look. His morals were also at an ebb. Salander was not big on psychological theory, but she could see for herself that his first major transgression had led to a succession of others. Wrange was no longer an ambitious student, eager to learn. Now he was addicted to porn and bought sex online, violent sex. Two of the women had afterwards threatened to report him.

The man had a fair amount of money. He also had a load of problems. As recently as that morning he had Googled "witness protection Sweden", which was careless of him. Even though he was no longer in contact with Solifon, at least not from his computer, *they* were probably still keeping an eye on *him*. It would be unprofessional not to. Maybe he was beginning to crack up beneath the new urbane exterior, and that served Salander's purpose. When she once again rang the chess club – chess being the only apparent connection with his former life – she was pleasantly surprised to hear that Wrange had just arrived there.

So now she walked down the small flight of steps on Hälsingegatan and along a corridor to some shabby premises where a motley crowd of mostly older men were sitting hunched over their chessboards. The atmosphere was somnolent, and nobody seemed even to notice her let alone question her presence. They were all busy with their games, and the only sound was the click of the chess clocks and the occasional swear word. There were framed photographs of Kasparov, Magnus Carlsen and Bobby Fischer on the walls and even one of a pimply, teenaged Arvid Wrange playing the chess star Judit Polgár.

A different, older version of him was sitting at a table further in and to the right, and he seemed to be trying out some new opening. Next to him were a couple of shopping bags. He was wearing a yellow lambswool sweater with a clean and ironed white shirt and a pair of shiny English shoes, a little too stylish for the surroundings. Salander approached him with careful, hesitant steps and asked if he would like a game. He responded by looking her up and down, then he said, "O.K."

"Nice of you," she replied like a well-mannered young girl, and sat down. She opened with E4, he answered with B5, the Polish gambit, and then she closed her eyes and let him play on.

Wrange tried to concentrate on the game, but he was not managing too well. Fortunately this punk girl was going to be easy pickings. She wasn't bad, as it turned out – she probably played a lot – but what good was that? He toyed with her a little, and she was bound

Who knows? Maybe he could even get her to

hard to convince himself that

did the goddamn professor expect when he treated him as if he didn't exist? But of course it wouldn't look good that Wrange had sold him down the river. He consoled himself with the thought that an idiot like Balder must have made thousands of enemies, but deep down he knew: the one event was linked to the other, and that scared him to death.

Ever since Balder had started working at Solifon, Wrange had been afraid that the drama would take a frightening new turn, and here he was now, wishing that it would all just go away. That must have been why he went into town this morning on a compulsive spree to buy a load of designer clothes, and had ended up here at the chess club. Chess still managed to distract him, and the fact was that he was feeling better already. He felt like he was in control and smart enough to keep on fooling them all. Look at how he was playing.

This girl was not half bad. In fact there was something unorthodox and creative in her play, and she would probably be able teach most people in here a thing or two. It was just that he, Arvid Wrange, was crushing her. His play was so brilliant and sophisticated that she had not even noticed he was on the brink of trapping her queen. Stealthily he moved his pieces forward and snapped hers up without sacrificing more than a knight. In a flirty, casual tone bound to impress her he said, "Sorry, baby. Your queen is down."

But he got nothing in return, no smile, not a word, nothing. The girl upped the tempo, as if she wanted to put a quick end to her humiliation, and why not? He'd be happy to keep the process short and take her out for two or three drinks before he pulled her. Maybe he would not be very nice to her in bed. The chances were that she would still thank him afterwards. A miserable cunt like her would be unlikely to have had a fuck for a long time and would be totally unused to guys like him, cool guys who played at this level. He decided to show off a bit and explain some higher chess theory. But he never got the chance. Something on the board did not feel quite right. His game began to run into some sort of resistance he could not understand. For a while he persuaded himself that it was only his imagination, perhaps the result of a few careless moves. If only he concentrated he would be able to put things right, and so he mobilized his killer instinct.

But it only got worse.

He felt trapped – however hard he tried to regain the initiative she hit back – and in the end he had no choice but to acknowledge that the balance of power had shifted, and shifted irreversibly. How crazy was that? He had taken her queen, but instead of building on that advantage he had landed in a fatally weak position. Surely she had not deliberately sacrificed her queen so early in the game? That would be impossible – the sort of thing you read about in books, it didn't happen in your local chess club in

Vasastan, and it definitely wasn't something that pierced punk chicks with attitude problems did, especially not to great players like him. Yet there was no escape.

In four or five moves he would be beaten and so he saw no alternative but to knock over his king with his index finger and mumble congratulations. Even though he would have liked to serve up some excuses, something told him that that would make matters worse. He had a sneaking feeling that his defeat was not just down to bad luck, and almost against his will he began to feel frightened again. Who the hell *was* she?

and now she no longer seemed

"Nobody special.

"So we haven't met before?"

"Not exactly."

"But nearly, is that it?"

"We've met in your nightmares, Arvid."

"Is this some kind of joke?"

"Not really."

"What do you mean?"

"What do you think I mean?"

"How should I know?"

He could not understand why he was so scared.

"Frans Balder was murdered last night," she said in a monotone.

"Well . . . yes . . . I read that," he stammered.

"Terrible, isn't it?"

"Awful."

"Especially for you, right?"

"Why especially for me?"

"Because you betrayed him, Arvid. Because you gave him the kiss of Judas."

His body froze. "That's bullshit," he spat out.

"As a matter of fact it's not. I hacked your computer, cracked your encryption and saw very clearly that you sold on his technology to Solifon. And you know what?"

He was finding it hard to breathe.

"I'm sure you woke up this morning and wondered if his death was your fault. I can help you there: it *was* your fault. If you hadn't been so greedy and bitter and pathetic, Frans Balder would be alive now. I should warn you that's making me pretty fucking angry, Arvid. I'm going to hurt you badly. First of all by making you suffer the same sort of treatment you inflict on the women you find online."

"Are you insane?"

"Probably, yes," she said. "Empathy-deficit disorder. Excessive violence. Something along those lines."

She gripped his hand with a force which scared him out of his wits.

"Arvid, do you know what I'm doing right now? Do you know why I seem a bit distracted?"

"No."

"I'm sitting here trying to decide what to do with you. I'm thinking in terms of suffering of biblical proportions. That's why I'm a bit distracted."

"What do you want?"

"I want revenge – haven't I made that clear?"

"You're talking crap."

"Definitely not, and I think you know it too. But there is a way out."

"What do I have to do?"

He could not understand why he said it. *What do I have to do?* It was an admission, a capitulation, and he considered taking it back, putting pressure on her instead, to see if she had any proof or if she was bluffing. But he could not bring himself to do it. Only later did he realize that it was not just the threats she tossed out or the uncanny strength of her hands.

It was the game of chess, the queen sacrifice. He was in shock, and something in his subconscious told him that a woman who plays like that must also know his secrets.

"... do I have to do?" he said again.

... and you're going to tell

had plucked ...

"Let's not exaggerate," said Modig, ... next to him. She was right. It was not much more than some chess squares on a piece of paper, after all, and as Mikael Blomkvist had pointed out over the telephone there was something strangely mathematical about the work, as if the boy were more interested in the geometry than in the threatening shadow above. But Bublanski was excited all the same. He had been told over and over how mentally impaired the Balder boy was, how little he would be able to help them. Now the boy had produced a drawing which gave Bublanski more hope than anything else in the investigation. It strengthened his long-held conviction that one must never underestimate anyone or cling to preconceived ideas.

They had no way of being sure that what August was illustrating here was the moment of the murder. The shadow could, at least in theory, be associated with some other occasion, and there was no guarantee that the boy had seen the killer's face or that he

227

would be able to draw it. And yet deep down that was what Bublanski believed. Not just because the drawing, even in its present state, was masterful. He had studied the other drawings too, in which you could see, beyond the street crossing and the traffic light, a shabby man with thin lips who had been caught red-handed jaywalking, if you looked at it purely from a law-enforcement point of view. He was crossing the street on a red, and Amanda Flod, another officer on the team, had recognized him straight away as the out-of-work actor Roger Winter, who had convictions for drink-driving and assault.

The photographic precision of August's eye ought to be a dream for any murder investigator. But Bublanski did realize that it would be unprofessional to set his hopes too high. Maybe the murderer had been masked at the time of the killing or his face had already faded from the child's memory. There were many possible scenarios and Bublanski cast a glum look in the direction of Modig.

"Maybe this is just wishful thinking on my part," he said.

"For a man who's beginning to doubt the existence of God, you seem to have no problem hoping for miracles."

"Well, maybe."

"But it's worth getting to the bottom of. I agree with that," Modig said.

"Good, in that case let's see the boy."

Bublanski went out of the kitchen and nodded at Hanna Balder, who was sunk in the living-room sofa, fumbling with some tablets.

Lisbeth Salander and Arvid Wrange came out into Vasaparken arm in arm, like a pair of old friends out for a stroll. Appearances can be deceptive: Wrange was terrified as Salander steered them towards a park bench. The wind was getting up again and the temperature creeping down – it was hardly a day for feeding the pigeons – and Wrange was cold. But Salander decided that the bench would do and forced him to sit down, holding his arm in a vice-like grip.

"Right," she said. "Let's make this quick."

"Will you keep my name out of it?"

"I'm promising nothing, Arvid. But your chances of being able to go back to your miserable life will increase significantly if you tell me every detail of what happened."

"O.K.," he said. "Do you know Darknet?"

"I know it," she said.

~~. D—knet like Lisbeth Salander. Darknet was the~~

But Darknet was not in itself

better than anyone. These days, when spy agencies and the big software companies follow every step we take online, even honest people can need a hiding place. Darknet was also a hub for dissidents, whistle-blowers and informants. Opposition forces could protest on Darknet out of reach of their government, and Salander had used it for her own more discreet investigations and attacks. She knew its sites and search engines and its old-fashioned workings far away from the known, visible net.

"Did you put Balder's technology up for sale on Darknet?" she said.

"No, I was just casting about. I was pissed off. You know, Frans hardly even said hello to me. He treated me like dirt, and he didn't really care about that technology of his either. It had the potential to make all of us rich, but he only wanted to play and experiment with it like a little kid. One evening when I'd had a few drinks I just chucked out a question on a geek site: 'Who can pay good money for some revolutionary A.I. technology?'

"And did you get an answer?"

"It took a while. I had time to forget that I'd even asked. But in the end someone calling himself Bogey wrote back with some pretty well-informed questions. At first my answers were ridiculously unguarded, but soon I realized what a mess I'd got myself into, and I became terrified that Bogey would steal the technology."

"Without you getting anything for it."

"It was a dangerous game. To be able to sell Frans' technology I had to tell people about it. But if I said too much then I would already have lost it. Bogey flattered me rotten – in the end he knew exactly where we were and what sort of software we were working on."

"He meant to hack you."

"Presumably. He somehow managed to get hold of my name, and that floored me. I became totally paranoid and announced that I wanted to pull out. But by then it was too late. Not that Bogey threatened me, at least not directly. He just went on and on about how he and I were going to do great things together and earn masses of money. In the end I agreed to meet him in Stockholm at a Chinese boat restaurant on Söder Mälarstrand. It was a windy day, I remember, and I stood there freezing. I waited more than half an hour, and afterwards I wondered if he had been checking me out in some way."

"But then he showed up?"

"Yes. At first I didn't believe it was him. He looked like a junkie, or a beggar, and if I hadn't seen that Patek Philippe watch on his wrist I probably would have tossed him twenty kronor. He had amateur tattoos and dodgy-looking scars on his arms, which he waved about as he walked. He was wearing this awful-looking trench coat and he seemed to have been more or less living on the streets. The strangest thing of all was that he was proud of it. It was only the watch and the hand-made shoes which showed that he had at some point managed to lift himself out of the gutter. Other than that, he seemed keen to stick to his roots. Later on, when I'd given him everything and we were celebrating our deal over a few bottles of wine, I asked about his background."

"I hope for your sake that he gave you some details."

"If you want to track him down, I have to warn you . . ."

"I don't want advice, Arvid. I want facts."

"Fine. He was careful," he said. "But I still got a few things. He ... He grew up in a big city in Russia,

away and lived on the street. He stole, ... wells to get a little warmth, got drunk on cheap vodka, sniffed glue and was abused and beaten. But he also discovered one thing."

"What?"

"That he had talent. He was an expert at breaking and entering, which became his first source of pride, his first identity. He was capable of doing in just a few seconds what took others hours. Before that he had been a homeless brat, everyone had despised him and spat at him. Now he was the boy who could get himself in wherever he wanted. It became an obsession. All day long he dreamed of being some sort of Houdini in reverse – he didn't want to break out, he wanted to break in. He practised for ten, twelve, fourteen hours a day, and in the end he was a legend on the streets – or so he said. He started to carry out bigger operations, using computers he stole and reconfigured to hack in everywhere. He made a heap of money which he blew on drugs, and often he was robbed or taken advantage of. He could be clear as a bell when he was on one of his jobs, but afterwards he would lie around in a narcotic haze and someone would walk all over him. He was a genius and a total idiot at the same time, he said. But one day everything changed. He was saved, raised up out of his hell."

"How?"

"He had been asleep in some dump of a place that was due to be pulled down, and when he opened his eyes and looked around in the yellowish light there was an angel standing before him."

"An angel?"

"That's what he said, an angel, and maybe it was partly the contrast with everything else in there, the syringes, the left-over food, the cockroaches. He said she was the most beautiful woman he had ever seen. He could scarcely look at her, and he got this idea that he was going to die. It was an ominous, solemn feeling. But the woman explained, as if it were the most natural thing in the world, that she would make him rich and happy. If I've understood it right, she kept her promise. She gave him new teeth, got him into rehab. She arranged for him to train as a computer engineer."

"So ever since he's been hacking computers and stealing for this woman and her network."

"That's right. He became a new person, or maybe not completely new – in many ways he's still the same old thief and bum. But he no longer takes drugs, he says, and he spends all his free time keeping up to date with new technology. He finds a lot on Darknet and he claims to be stinking rich."

"And the woman – did he say anything more about her?"

"No, he was extremely careful about that. He spoke in such evasive and respectful terms that I wondered for a while if she wasn't a fantasy or hallucination. But I reckon she really does exist. I could sense sheer physical fear when he was talking about her – he said that he would rather die than let her down, and then he showed me a Russian patriarchal cross made of gold, which she had given him. One of those crosses, you know, which has a slanted beam down by the foot, one end pointing up and the other down. He told me this was a reference to the Gospel according to St Luke and the two thieves who were hanged next to Jesus on the cross. The one thief believes in Jesus and goes to heaven. The other mocks him and is thrust down into hell."

"That's what awaits you if you fail her."

"That's about it, yes."

"So she sees herself as Jesus?"

"In this context the cross probably has almost nothing to do with Christianity. It's the message she wants to pass on."

Truegames."

"Yes, but I don't get it . . . not when I think of it now."

"What don't you get?"

"How could you know all this?"

"Because you were dumb enough to send an email to Eckerwald at Solifon, don't you remember?"

"But I wrote nothing to suggest that I'd sold the technology. I was very careful about that."

"What you said was enough for me," she said. She got to her feet, and it was as if his entire being collapsed.

"Wait, what's going to happen now? Will you keep me out of this?"

"You can always hope," she said, and walked off towards Odenplan with purposeful steps.

*

233

Bublanski's mobile rang as he was on his way down to the front entrance on Torsgatan. It was Professor Edelman. Bublanski had been trying to reach him ever since he realized that the boy was a savant. Bublanski had found out online that two Swedish authorities were regularly quoted on this subject: Lena Ek at Lund University and Charles Edelman at the Karolinska Institute. But he had not been able to get hold of either, so he had postponed the search and gone off to see Hanna Balder. Now Edelman was ringing back, and he sounded shaken. He was in Budapest, he said, at a conference on heightened memory capacity. He had just arrived there and seen the news about the murder a moment ago, on C.N.N.

"Otherwise I would have got in touch right away," he said.

"What do you mean?"

"Professor Balder rang me yesterday evening."

That made Bublanski jump. "What did he want?"

"He wanted to talk about his son and his son's talent."

"Did you know each other?"

"Not in the slightest. He contacted me because he was worried about his boy, and I was stunned to hear from him."

"Why?"

"Because it was Frans Balder. He's a household name to us neurologists. We tend to say he's like us in wanting to understand the brain. The only difference is that he also wants to build one."

"I've heard something about that."

"I'd been told that he was an introverted and difficult man. A bit like a machine himself, people sometimes used to joke: nothing but logic circuits. But with me he was incredibly emotional, and it shocked me, to be honest. It was . . . I don't know, as if you were to hear your toughest policeman cry. I remember thinking that something must have happened, something other than what we were talking about."

"That sounds right. He had finally accepted that he was under a serious threat," Bublanski said.

"But he also had reason to be excited. His son's drawings were apparently exceptionally good, and that's not common at all at that age, not even with savants, and especially not in combination with proficiency in mathematics."

"Mathematics?"

"Yes indeed. From what Balder said his son had mathematical skills too. I could spend a long time talking about that."

"What do you mean?"

the same time maybe not

"True, Chief Inspector. So what can I do for you?"

Bublanski thought through everything that had happened in Saltsjöbaden and it struck him that it would do no harm to be cautious.

"All I can say is that we need your help and expert knowledge as a matter of urgency."

"The boy was a witness to the murder, was he not?"

"Yes."

"And you want me to try to get him to draw what he saw?"

"I'd prefer not to comment."

Professor Edelman was standing in the lobby of the Hotel Boscolo in Budapest, a conference centre not far from the glittering Danube. The place looked like an opera house, with magnificent high ceilings, old-fashioned cupolas and pillars. He had been looking forward to the week here, the dinners and the presentations. Yet he was agitated and ran his fingers through his hair.

"Unfortunately I'm not in a position to help you. I have to give an important lecture tomorrow morning," he had said to Bublanski, and that was true.

He had been preparing the talk for some weeks and he was going to take a controversial line with several eminent memory experts. He recommended an associate professor, Martin Wolgers, to Bublanski.

But as soon as he hung up and exchanged looks with Lena Ek – Lena had paused next to him, holding a sandwich – he began to have regrets. He even began to envy young Martin Wolgers, who was not yet thirty-five, always looked far too good in photographs, and on top of it all was beginning to make a name for himself.

It was true that Edelman did not fully understand what had happened. The police inspector had been cryptic and was probably worried that someone might be listening in on the call. Yet the professor still managed to grasp the bigger picture. The boy was good at drawing and was witness to a murder. That could mean only one thing, and the longer Edelman thought about it the more he fretted. He would be giving many more important lectures in his life, but he would never get another chance to play a part in a murder investigation at this level. However he looked at the assignment he had so casually passed on to Wolgers, it was bound to be much more interesting than anything he might be involved in here in Budapest. Who knows? It could even make him some sort of celebrity.

He visualised the headline: PROMINENT NEUROLOGIST HELPS POLICE SOLVE MURDER, or better still: EDEL-MAN'S RESEARCH LEADS TO BREAKTHROUGH IN MURDER HUNT. How could he have been so stupid as to turn it down? He took out his mobile and called Chief Inspector Bublanski.

*

Bublanski and Modig had managed to park not far from the Stockholm Public Library and had just crossed the street. Once again the weather was dreadful, and Bublanski's hands were freezing.

"Did he change his mind?" Modig said.

"Yes. He's going to shelve his lecture."

"When can he be here?"

"He's looking into it. Tomorrow morning at the latest."

They were on their way to Oden's Medical Centre on Sveavägen to meet the director, Torkel Lindén. The meeting was

————————————————ments for August

ising start.

Lindén turned out not to be the hefty figure Bublanski had expected. He was hardly more than 150 centimetres tall and had short, possibly dyed black hair and pinched lips. He wore black jeans, a black polo-necked sweater and a small cross on a ribbon around his neck. There was something ecclesiastical about him, and his hostility was genuine.

He had a haughty look and Bublanski became aware of his own Jewishness – which tended to happen whenever he encountered this sort of malevolence and air of moral superiority. Lindén wanted to show that he was better, because he put the boy's physical well-being first rather than offering him up for police purposes. Bublanski saw no choice but to be as amiable as possible.

"Pleased to meet you," he said.

"Is that so?" Lindén said.

"Oh yes, and it's kind of you to see us at such short notice. We really wouldn't come barging in like this if we didn't think this matter was of the utmost importance."

"I imagine you want to interview the boy in some way."

"Not exactly," Bublanski said, not quite so amiably. "I have to emphasize first of all that what I'm saying now must remain strictly between us. It's a question of security."

"Confidentiality is a given for us. We have no loose lips here," Lindén said, in such a way as to imply that it was the opposite with the police.

"My only concern is for the boy's safety," Bublanski said sharply.

"So that's your priority?"

"As a matter of fact, yes," the policeman said with even greater severity. "And that is why nothing of what I'm about to tell you must be passed on in any way – least of all by email or by telephone. Can we sit somewhere private?"

Sonja Modig did not think much of the place. But then she was probably affected by the crying. Somewhere nearby a little girl was sobbing relentlessly. They were sitting in a room which smelled of detergent and also of something else, maybe a lingering trace of incense. A cross hung on the wall and there was a worn teddy bear lying on the floor. There was not much else to make the place cosy or attractive, and since Bublanski, usually so good-natured, was about to lose his temper, she took matters into her own hands and gave a calm, factual account of what had taken place.

"We are given to understand," she said, "that your colleague, Einar Forsberg, said that August should not be allowed to draw."

"That was his professional judgement and I agree with it. It doesn't do the boy any good," Lindén said.

"Well, I don't see how anything could do him much good under these circumstances. He probably saw his father being killed."

"But we don't want to make things any worse, do we?"

"True. But the drawing August was not allowed to finish could lead to a breakthrough in the investigation and therefore I'm afraid we must insist. You can of course ensure there are people present with the necessary expertise."

"I still have to say no."

Modig could hardly believe her ears.

"With all due respect for your work," Lindén went on doggedly, "here at Oden's we help vulnerable children. That's our job and our calling. We're not an extension of the police force. That's how it is, and we're proud of it. For as long as the children are here, they should feel confident that we put their interests first."

over there, for that matter.

to express ourselves? You and I can talk or write, or even go out and get a lawyer. August doesn't have those means of communication. But he can draw, and he seems to want to tell us something. Shouldn't we let him give form to something which must be tormenting him?"

"In our judgement—"

"No," she cut him off. "Don't tell us about your judgement. We're in contact with the person who knows more than anyone else in this country about this particular condition. His name is Charles Edelman, he's a professor of neurology and he's on his way here from Hungary to meet the boy."

"We can of course listen to him," Lindén said reluctantly.

"Not just listen. We let him decide."

"I promise to engage in a constructive dialogue, between experts."

"Fine. What's August doing now?"

"He's sleeping. He was exhausted when he came to us."

Modig could tell that nothing good would come of it were she to suggest that the boy be woken up.

"In that case we'll come back tomorrow morning with Professor Edelman, and I am sure we will all be able to work together on this matter."

CHAPTER 16

21.xi – 22.xi

into broader domestic policy implications.

Superintendent Mårten Nielsen was formally leading the team and had recently returned from a year of study at the University of Maryland in the U.S. He was undoubtedly intelligent and well informed, but too right-wing for Grane's tastes. It was rare to find a well-educated Swede who was also a wholehearted supporter of the American Republican Party – he even expressed some sympathy for the Tea Party movement. He was passionate about military history and lectured at the Military Academy. Although still young – thirty-nine – he was believed to have extensive international contacts.

He often had trouble, however, asserting himself in the group, and in practice the real leader was Ragnar Olofsson, who was older and cockier and could silence Nielsen with one peevish little sigh or a displeased wrinkle above his bushy eyebrows. Nor was

Nielsen's life made any easier by the fact that Detective Inspector Lars Åke Grankvist was also on the team.

Before joining the Security Service, Grankvist had been a semi-legendary investigator in the Swedish police's National Murder Squad, at least in the sense that he was said to be able to drink anybody else under the table and to manage, with a sort of boisterous charm, to keep a lover in every town. It was not an easy team in which to hold one's own, and Grane kept an ever lower profile as the afternoon wore on. But this was due less to the men and their macho rivalry than to a growing sense of uncertainty.

Sometimes she wondered if she knew even less now than before. She realized, for example, that there was little or no proof to support the theory of the suspected data breach. All they had was a statement from Stefan Molde at the N.D.R.E., and not even he had been sure of what he was saying. In her view his analysis was more or less rubbish. Balder seemed to have relied primarily on the female hacker he had turned to for help, the woman not even named in the investigation, but whom his assistant, Linus Brandell, had described in such vivid terms. It was likely that Balder had been withholding a lot from Grane before he left for America.

For example, was it a coincidence that he had found a job at Solifon?

The uncertainty gnawed at her and she was indignant that no help was coming from Fort Meade. She could not get hold of Alona Casales, and the N.S.A. was once again a closed door, and so she in turn was no longer passing on any news. Just like Nielsen and Grankvist, she found herself overshadowed by Olofsson. He kept getting information from his source at the Violent Crimes Division and immediately passing it on to Helena Kraft.

Grane did not like it, and in vain she had pointed out that this traffic not only increased the risk of a leak but also seemed to be costing them their independence. Instead of searching their own channels, they were all too slavishly relying on the information which flowed in from Bublanski's team.

"We're like people cheating in an exam, waiting for someone to whisper the answer instead of thinking for ourselves," she had said to the whole team, and this had not made her popular.

Now she was alone in her office, determined to move ahead on her own, trying to see the bigger picture. It might get her nowhere, but on the other hand it would do no harm. She heard steps outside in the corridor, the click-clack of determined high heels which Grane by now recognized only too well. It was Kraft, who came ⋯⋯⋯⋯⋯⋯⋯⋯⋯ in her dark hair pulled into a tight bun.

"Sounds sensible.

"Do you know what Erich Maria Remarque said?"

"That it's not much fun in the trenches, or something."

"Ha, no, that it's always the wrong people who have the guilty conscience. Those who are really responsible for suffering in the world couldn't care less. It's the ones fighting for good who are consumed by remorse. You've got nothing to be ashamed of, Gabriella. You did what you could."

"I'm not so sure about that. But thanks anyway."

"Have you heard about Balder's son?"

"Just very quickly from Ragnar."

"At 10.00 tomorrow morning Chief Inspector Bublanski, Detective Sergeant Modig and a Professor Edelman will be seeing the boy at Oden's Medical Centre for Children and Adolescents, on Sveavägen. They're going to try and get him to draw some more."

"I'll keep my fingers crossed. But I'm not too happy to know about it."

"Relax, leave the paranoia to me. The only ones who know about this are people who can keep their traps shut."

"I suppose you're right."

"I want to show you something. There are photographs of the man who hacked Balder's burglar alarm."

"I've seen them already. I've even studied them in detail."

"Have you?" Kraft said, handing over an enlarged and blurred picture of a wrist.

"What about it?"

"Take another look. What do you see?"

Grane looked and saw two things: the luxury watch she had noted before and, beneath it, barely distinguishable between the glove and the jacket cuff, a couple of lines which looked like amateur tattoos.

"Contrasts," she said. "Some cheap tattoos and a very expensive watch."

"More than that," Kraft said. "That's a 1951 Patek Philippe, model 2499, first series, or just possibly second series."

"Means nothing to me."

"It's one of the finest wristwatches in the world. A few years ago a watch like this sold at auction at Christie's in Geneva for just over two million dollars."

"Are you kidding?"

"No, and it wasn't just anyone who bought it. It was Jan van der Waal, a lawyer at Dackstone & Partner. He bid for it on behalf of a client."

"Dackstone & Partner? Don't they represent Solifon?"

"Correct. We don't know whether the watch in the surveillance image is the one that was sold in Geneva, and we haven't been able to find out who that client was. But it's a start, Gabriella. A scrawny type who looks like a junkie and who wears a watch of this calibre – that should narrow the field."

"Does Bublanski know this?"

"It was his technical expert Jerker Holmberg who discovered it. Now I want you and your analytical brain to take it further. Go home, get some sleep and get started on it in the morning."

The man who called himself Jan Holtser was sitting at home in his apartment on Högbergsgatan in Helsinki, not far from Esplanaden park, looking through an album of photographs of ~~~~~~~~ Olga ~~~~~ was now twenty-two and studying medi-

before embarking on a ~~~~~ p~~~~~
commitment to the "weak and vulnerable".

It was pure pinko left-wing lunacy, in Holtser's opinion, not at all in keeping with Olga's character. He saw it as her attempt to stake out her independence. Behind all the talk about beggars and the sick he thought she was still quite like him. Once upon a time Olga had been a promising 100-metre runner. She was 186 centimetres tall, muscular and explosive, and in the old days she had loved watching action films and listening to him reminisce about the war in Chechnya. Everyone at school had known better than to pick a fight with her. She hit back, like a warrior. Olga was definitely not cut out to minister to the sick and degenerate.

Yet she claimed to want to work for Médecins Sans Frontières or go off to Calcutta like some Mother Teresa. Holtser could not bear the thought. The world belongs to the strong, he felt. But he loved his daughter, however daft some of her ideas, and tomorrow she was coming home for the first time in six months for a few days' leave. He solemnly resolved that he would be a better listener this time, and not pontificate about Stalin and great leaders and everything that she hated.

He would instead try to bring them closer again. He was certain that she needed him. At least he was pretty sure that he needed her. It was 8.00 in the evening and he went into the kitchen and pressed three oranges and poured Smirnoff into a glass. It was his third Screwdriver of the day. Once he had finished a job he could put away six or seven of them, and maybe he would do that now. He was tired, weighed down by all the responsibility laid on his shoulders, and he needed to relax. For a few minutes he stood with his drink in his hand and dreamed about a different sort of life. But the man who called himself Jan Holtser had set his hopes too high.

The tranquillity came to an abrupt end as Bogdanov rang on his secure mobile. At first Holtser hoped that Bogdanov just wanted to chat, to release some of the excitement that came with every assignment. But his colleague was calling about a very specific matter and sounded less than happy.

"I've spoken to T.," he said. Holtser felt a number of things all at once, jealousy perhaps most of all.

Why did Kira ring Bogdanov and not him? Even if it was Bogdanov who brought in the big money, and was rewarded accordingly, Holtser had always been convinced that he was the one closer to Kira. But Holtser was also worried. Had something gone wrong after all?

"Is there a problem?" he said.

"The job isn't finished."

"Where are you?"

"In town."

"Come on up in that case and explain what the hell you mean."

"I've booked a table at Postres."

"I don't feel like going to some posh restaurant. Get yourself over here."

"I haven't eaten."

"I'll fry something up."

"Sounds good. We've got a long night ahead of us."

Holtser did not want another long night. Still less did he feel like telling his daughter that he would not be at home the next day. But he had no choice. He knew as surely as he knew that he loved Olga: you could not say no to Kira.

and needy when it suited, but also indomitable, hard and cold as ice, and sometimes plain evil. Nobody brought out the sadist in him like she did.

She may not have been intelligent in the conventional sense, and many pointed that out to try to take her down a peg or two. But the same people were still stupefied in her presence. Kira played them like a violin and could reduce even the toughest of men to blushing and giggling schoolchildren.

It was 9.00 and Bogdanov was sitting next to him shovelling in the lamb chop Holtser had prepared. Oddly enough his table manners were almost passable. That may have been Kira's influence. In many ways Bogdanov had become quite civilized – and then again not. However he tried to put on airs, he could never entirely rid himself of the appearance of the petty thief and speed addict. He had been off drugs for ages and was a computer engineer with university qualifications, but still looked ravaged by street life.

"Where's your bling watch?" Holtser said. "Are you in the doghouse?"

"We both are."

"It's that bad?"

"Maybe not."

"The job isn't finished, you said?"

"No, it's that boy."

"Which boy?" Holtser pretended not to understand.

"The one you so nobly spared."

"What about him? He's a retard, you know."

"Maybe so, but he can draw."

"What do you mean, draw?"

"He's a savant."

"A *what*?"

"You should try reading something other than your fucking gun magazines for once."

"What are you talking about?"

"It's someone who's autistic or handicapped in some other way, but who has a special gift. This boy may not be able to talk or think like a normal person, but he has a photographic memory. The police think the little bastard is going to be able to draw your face, and then they're going to run it through their facial-recognition software, and then you're screwed, aren't you? You must be there somewhere in Interpol's records?"

"Yes, but Kira can't expect us to—"

"That's exactly what she expects. We have to fix the boy."

A wave of emotion and confusion washed over Holtser and once again he saw before him that empty, glassy look from the double bed which had made him feel so uncomfortable.

"The hell I will," he said, without really believing it.

"I know you've got problems with children. I don't like it either. But we can't avoid this one. Besides, you should be grateful. Kira could just as easily have sacrificed you."

"I suppose so."

"Then it's settled. I've got the plane tickets in my pocket. We'll take the first flight in the morning to Arlanda, at 6.30, and then we're going to some place on Sveavägen called Oden's Medical Centre for Children and Adolescents."

"So the boy's in a clinic."

"Yes, and that's why we need to do some planning. Let me just finish eating."

curve factorization and set about cracking the file she had downloaded from the N.S.A.

But however hard she tried, she could not manage it. She had not really been expecting to do so. It was a sophisticated encryption, named after the originators Rivest, Shamir and Adleman. R.S.A. has two keys – one public, one secret – and is based on Euler's *phi* function and Fermat's little theorem, but above all on the simple fact that it is easy to multiply two large prime numbers. A calculator will give you the answer in the blink of an eye. Yet it is all but impossible to work backwards and, on the basis of the answer, calculate the prime numbers you started out with. Computers are not yet efficient at prime-number factorization, something which had exasperated Lisbeth Salander and the world's intelligence organizations many times in the past.

For about a year now Salander had been thinking that E.C.M., the Elliptic Curve Method, would be more promising than previous algorithms, and she had spent long nights writing her own factorization program. But now, in the early hours of the morning, she realized it would need more refinement to have even the slightest chance of success. After three hours of work, she took a break and went to the kitchen, drank some orange juice straight from the carton and ate two microwaved piroshki.

Back at her desk she hacked into Blomkvist's computer to see if he had come up with anything new. He had posted two more questions for her and she realized at once: he wasn't so hopeless after all.

<Which of Frans Balder's assistants betrayed him?> he wrote. And that was a reasonable question.

But she did not answer. She could not care less about Arvid Wrange. And she had made progress and worked out who the hollow-eyed junkie was, the man Wrange had been in touch with, who had called himself Bogey. Trinity in Hacker Republic remembered somebody with that same handle from a number of sites some years previously. That did not necessarily mean anything – Bogey was not the most original alias. But Salander had traced the posts and thought she could be onto something – especially when he carelessly dropped that he was a computer engineer from Moscow University.

Salander was unable to find out when he graduated, or any other dates for that matter, but she got hold of a couple of nerdy details about how Bogey was hooked on fine watches and crazy for the Arsène Lupin films from the '70s, about the gentleman thief of that name.

Then Salander posted questions on every conceivable website for former and current students at Moscow University, asking if anybody knew a scrawny, hollow-eyed ex-junkie who had been a street urchin and master thief and loved Arsène Lupin films. It was not long before she got a reply.

"That sounds like Jurij Bogdanov," wrote someone who introduced herself as Galina.

According to this Galina, Bogdanov was a legend at the university. Not just because he had hacked into all the lecturers' computers and had dirt on every one of them. He was always asking people: will you bet me one hundred roubles I can't break into that house over there?

Many who did not know him thought this was easy money. But Jurij could pick any door lock, and if for some reason he failed he would shin up the facade or the walls instead. He was known for ˌ ˌ ˌ ˌ ˌ ˌ ˌ He was said once to have kicked a dog

university – at least according ˌ ˌ

Jurij Bogdanov was now thirty-four years old. He had left Russia and lived in Berlin on Budapester Strasse, not far from the Michelin-starred restaurant Hugo's. He ran a white-hat computer security business – Outcast Security – with seven employees and a turnover in the last financial year of twenty-two million euros. It was ironic – yet somehow entirely logical – that his front was a company which protected industrial groups from people like himself. He had not had any criminal convictions since he took his exams in 2009 and managed a wide network of contacts – one of the members of his board of directors was Ivan Gribanov, member of the Russian Duma and a major shareholder in the oil company Gazprom – but she could find nothing to get her further.

Blomkvist's second question was:

```
<Oden's Medical Centre on Sveavägen: is it
safe? (Delete this as soon as you read it)>
```

He did not explain why he was interested in the place. But she knew that Blomkvist was not someone who threw questions out at random. Nor did he make a habit of being unclear.

If he was being cryptic, then he had a reason to be: the information must be sensitive. There was evidently something significant about this medical centre. Salander soon discovered that it had attracted a number of complaints – children had been forgotten or ignored and had been able to self-harm. Oden's was managed privately by its director, Torkel Lindén, and his company Care Me and, if one was to believe past employees, Lindén's word was law. The profit margin was always high because nothing was bought unless absolutely necessary.

Lindén himself was a former star gymnast, among other things a one-time Swedish high-bar champion. Nowadays he was a passionate hunter and member of a Christian congregation that took an uncompromising line on homosexuality. Salander went onto the websites of the Swedish Association for Hunting and Wildlife Management and the Friends of Christ to see what kinds of activities were going on there. Then she sent Lindén two fake but enticing emails which looked as if they had come from the organizations, attaching PDF files with sophisticated malware which would open automatically if Lindén clicked on the messages.

By 8.23 she had got onto the server and immediately confirmed her suspicions. August Balder had been admitted to the clinic the previous afternoon. In the medical file, underneath a description of the circumstances which had resulted in his admittance, it said:

Infantile autism, severe mental impairment. Restless. Severely traumatized by death of father. Constant observation required. Difficult to handle. Brought jigsaw puzzles. Not allowed to draw! Observed to be compulsive and destructive. Diagnosis by psychologist Forsberg, confirmed by T.L.

And the following had been added underneath, clearly somewhat later:

> Professor Charles Edelman, Chief Inspector Bublanski and Detective Sergeant Modig will visit A. Balder at 10.00 on Wednesday, November 22. T.L. will be present. Drawing under supervision.

Further down still it said:

> Change of venue. A. Balder to be taken by T.L. and Professor
> _____ ____ Hanna Balder on Torsgatan, Bublanski and

of witness statement in the

Bublanski and Sonja Modig be interested in the boy's drawing, and why else would Blomkvist have been so cautious in framing his question?

None of this must be allowed to get out. No killer must be able to find out that the boy might be able to draw a picture of him. Salander decided to see for herself how careful Lindén had been in his correspondence. Luckily he had not written anything more about the boy's drawing ability. He had on the other hand received an email from Edelman at 23.10 last night, copied to Modig and Bublanski. That email was clearly the reason why the meeting place had been changed. Edelman wrote:

> <Hi Torkel, How good of you to see me at your medical centre. I really appreciate it. But I'm afraid I have to be a bit awkward. I think we stand the best chance of getting

```
a good result if we arrange for the boy to
draw in an environment where he feels
secure. That's not in any way to criticize
your medical centre. I've heard a lot of
good things about it.>
```
The hell you have, Salander thought, and read on:
```
<Therefore I'd like us to move the boy to
his mother, Hanna Balder, on Torsgatan,
tomorrow morning. The reason being that it
is recognized in literature on the subject
that the presence of the mother has a posi-
tive effect on children with savant skills.
If you and the boy wait outside the entrance
on Sveavägen at 9.15, then I can pick you
up as I go by. That would give us the
opportunity for a bit of a chat between
colleagues.
Best regards
Charles Edelman>
```
Bublanski and Modig had replied at 7.01 and 7.14 respectively. There was good reason, they wrote, to rely on Edelman's expertise and follow his advice. Lindén had just now, at 7.57, confirmed that he and the boy would wait for Charles Edelman outside the entrance on Sveavägen. Salander sat for a while, lost in thought. Then she went to the kitchen and picked up a few old biscuits from the larder, and looked out towards Slussen and Riddarfjärden. *So*, she thought, *the venue for the meeting has been changed.*

Instead of doing his drawing at the medical centre, the boy would be driven home to his mother. The presence of the mother has a positive effect, Edelman wrote. There was something about that phrase Salander did not like. It felt old-fashioned, didn't it? And the introduction itself was not much better: "The reason being that it is recognized in literature on the subject . . ."

It was stilted. Although it was true that many academics could not write to save their lives, and she knew nothing about the way in which this professor normally expressed himself, would one of the world's leading neurologists really feel the need to lean on what is recognized in the literature? Wouldn't he be more self-assured?

Salander went to her computer and skimmed through some of Edelman's papers on the net; she may have found the odd little touch of vanity, even in the most factual passages, but there was nothing clumsy or psychologically naive in what he had written. ~~.......~~ ~~........ sharp.~~ So she went back to the

~~transmit messages from any address~~

In other words, the email from Edelman was a fake, and the copies to Bublanski and Modig were no more than a smokescreen. She hardly even needed to check; she already knew what had happened: the police's replies and the approval of the altered arrangements were also a bluff. It didn't just mean that someone was pretending to be Edelman. There also had to be a leak, and above all, somebody wanted the boy outside on the street on Sveavägen.

Somebody wanted him defenceless in the street so that . . . what? They could kidnap or get rid of him? Salander looked at her watch; it was already 8.55. In just twenty minutes Torkel Lindén and August Balder would be outside waiting for someone who was not Professor Edelman, and who had anything but good intentions towards them.

What should she do? Call the police? That was never her first choice. She was especially reluctant when there was a risk of leaks. Instead, she went onto Oden's website and got hold of Lindén's office number. But she only made it as far as the switchboard. Lindén was in a meeting. So she found his mobile. After ending up in his voicemail, she swore out loud, and sent him both a text and an email telling him not to go out into the street with the boy, not under any circumstances. She signed herself "Wasp" for lack of any better idea.

Then she threw on her leather jacket and rushed out. But she turned, ran back into the apartment and packed her laptop with the encrypted file and her pistol, a Beretta 92, into a black sports bag before hurrying out again. She wondered if she should take her car, the B.M.W. M6 Convertible gathering dust in the garage. But she decided a taxi would be quicker. She soon regretted it. When a taxi finally appeared, it was clear that rush-hour had not subsided.

Traffic inched forward and Centralbron was almost at a standstill. Had there been an accident? Everything went slowly, everything but the time, which flew. Soon it was 9.05, then 9.10. She was in a tearing hurry and in the worst case it was already too late. Most likely Lindén and the boy went out onto the street ahead of time and the killer, or whoever it was, had already struck.

She dialled Lindén's number again. This time the call went through, but there was no answer, so she swore again and thought of Mikael Blomkvist. She had not actually spoken to him in ages. But now she called him and he answered, sounding irritated. Only when he realized who it was did he brighten up:

"Lisbeth, is that you?"

"Shut up and listen," she said.

Blomkvist was in the *Millennium* offices on Götgatan, in a foul mood. It was not just because he had had another bad night. It was T.T. Usually a serious and decent news agency, T.T. had put out a bulletin claiming that Mikael Blomkvist was sabotaging the murder enquiry by withholding crucial information, which he intended to publish first in *Millennium*.

Allegedly his aim was to save the magazine from financial disaster and rebuild his own "ruined reputation". Blomkvist had known that the story was in the offing. He had had a long conversation with its author, Harald Wallin, the evening before. But he could not have imagined such a devastating result.

It was made up of idiotic insinuations and unsubstantiated accusations, but Wallin had nonetheless managed to produce ~~~~~~~~~~~~~~~~~~~~ ~lmost objective, almost credible. The

story like this one, not only ~~~~ ~~~~ ~~~ body else to jump on the bandwagon, it just about requires them to take a tougher line. It explained why Blomkvist woke up to the online papers saying

BLOMKVIST SABOTAGES MURDER INVESTIGATION

and

BLOMKVIST ATTEMPTS TO SAVE MAGAZINE.
MURDERER RUNS FREE.

The print media were good enough to put quotation marks around the headlines. But the overall impression was nevertheless that a new truth was being served up with the breakfast coffee. A columnist by the name of Gustav Lund, who claimed to be fed up with all the hypocrisy, began his piece by writing: "Mikael Blomkvist, who has always thought of himself as a cut above the rest, has now been unmasked as the biggest cynic of us all."

"Let's hope they don't start waving subpoenas at us," said Malm, designer and part-owner of the magazine, as he stood next to Blomkvist, nervously chewing gum.

"Let's hope they don't call in the Marines," Blomkvist said.

"What?"

"It was meant to be a joke."

"Oh, O.K. But I don't like the tone," Malm said.

"Nobody likes it. But the best we can do is grit our teeth and get on with business as usual."

"Your phone's buzzing."

"It's always buzzing."

"How about answering it, before they come up with anything worse?"

"Yes, yes," Blomkvist muttered.

It was a girl. He thought he recognized the voice but, caught off guard, he could not at first place it.

"Who's that?" he said.

"Salander," she said, and at that he gave a big smile.

"Lisbeth, is that you?"

"Shut up and listen," she said. And so he did.

The traffic had eased and Salander and the taxi driver, a young man called Ahmed who told her he had seen the Iraq war at close quarters and lost his mother and two brothers in terrorist attacks, had emerged onto Sveavägen and passed the Stockholm Concert Hall on their left. Salander, who was a terrible passenger, sent off yet another text message to Lindén and tried to call some other member of staff at Oden's, anybody who could run out and warn him. No reply. She swore aloud, hoping that Blomkvist would do better.

"Is it panic stations?" Ahmed said from the driver's seat.

When Salander replied, "Yes," Ahmed shot the red light and got a fleeting smile out of her.

After that she focused on every metre they covered. Away to the left she caught a glimpse of the School of Economics and the Public Library – there was not far to go now. She scanned for the street numbers on the right-hand side, and at last saw the address. Thankfully there was no-one lying dead on the pavement. Salander pulled out some hundred-kronor notes for Ahmed. It was an ordinary, dreary November day, no more than that, and people were ~~on their way to work. But wait~~ She looked over towards the

~~anything from her oblique angle.~~

It opened slowly, as if the person about to come out was hesitant or found the door heavy, and all of a sudden Salander shouted to Ahmed to stop. She jumped out of the moving car, just as the man across the street raised his right hand and aimed a pistol with a telescopic sight at the door sliding slowly open.

CHAPTER 17

22.xi

The man who called himself Jan Holtser was not happy with the situation. The place was wide open and it was the wrong time of day. The street was too busy, and although he had done his best to cover his face, he was uncomfortable in daylight, and so near the park. More than ever he felt that he hated killing children.

But that's the way it was and he had to accept that the situation was of his own making.

He had underestimated the boy and now he had to correct his mistake. He must not let wishful thinking or his own demons get in the way. He would keep his mind on the job, be the professional he always was and above all not think about Olga, still less recall that glassy stare which had confronted him in Balder's bedroom.

He had to concentrate now on the doorway across the street and on his Remington pistol which he was keeping under his windbreaker. But why wasn't anything happening? His mouth felt dry. The wind was biting. There was snow lying in the street and on the pavement and people were hurrying back and forth to work. He tightened his grip on the pistol and glanced at his watch.

It was 9.16, and then 9.17. But still no-one emerged from the doorway across the road and he cursed: was something wrong?

All he had to go on was Bogdanov's word, but that was assurance enough. The man was a wizard with computers and last night he had sat engrossed in his work, sending off fake emails and getting the language right with the help of his contacts in Sweden. Holtser had taken care of the rest: studying pictures of the place, selecting the weapon and above all organizing the getaway car – a rental which Dennis Wilton of the Svavelsjö Motorcycle Club had fixed for them under a false name and which was now standing ready three blocks away, with Bogdanov at the wheel.

immediately behind him and

side of the street. Holtser cross

always did and started to take up the pressure on the trigger of his weapon. But what was happening?

The door did not open. The man hesitated and looked down at his mobile. *Get a move on*, Holtser thought. *At last, here we go . . .* slowly, slowly the door was pushed open and they were on their way out, and Holtser raised his pistol, aiming at the boy's face through the telescopic sight, and saw once more those glassy eyes. Suddenly he felt an unexpected, violent rush of excitement. Suddenly he did want to kill the boy. Suddenly he wanted to snuff out that frightening look, once and for all. But then something happened.

A young woman came running out of nowhere and threw herself over the boy as Holtser fired and hit the target. At least he hit something, and he shot again and again. But the boy and the woman had rolled behind a car, quick as lightning. Holtser caught his breath and looked right and left. Then he raced across the street, commando-style.

This time he was not going to fail.

Lindén had never been on satisfactory terms with his telephones. His wife, Saga, leaped with anticipation at every call, hoping that it would bring a new job or a new offer; he just felt uncomfortable whenever his mobile rang.

It was because of all the complaints. He and the medical centre were always taking abuse. In his view that was all part of their business – Oden's was an emergency centre and so inevitably emotions tended to run high. But he also knew on some level that the complaints were justified. He may have driven his cost-cutting too far. Occasionally he just ran away, went out to the woods and let the others get on with it. On the other hand, he did from time to time get recognition, most recently from no less a person than Professor Edelman.

The professor had irritated him at first. He did not like it when outsiders meddled in the way the clinic managed their procedures. But he felt more conciliatory since he had been praised in that email this morning. Who knows? He might even get the professor to support the idea of the boy staying on at Oden's for a while. That might add some spark to his life, although he could not quite understand why. As a rule he tended to keep himself apart from the children.

There was something enigmatic about this August Balder which intrigued him. From the very first he had been aggravated by the police and their demands. He wanted August to himself and hoped perhaps to be associated with some of the mystique surrounding the boy – or at least be able to understand what those endless rows of numbers meant, the ones he had written on that comic in the playroom. But it was far from easy. The boy seemed to shun any form of contact and now he was refusing to come out to the street.

He was being hopelessly contrary, and Lindén was forced to drag him by his elbow.

"Come on, come *on*," he muttered.

Then his mobile buzzed. Somebody was determined to get hold of him.

He did not answer. Probably it was some trivial nonsense, yet another complaint. But as he reached the door, he decided to check his messages. There were several texts from a withheld number, and they were saying something strange, presumably some kind of a joke: they told him not go outside. He was under no circum-stances to go into the street.

Obviously he was in danger, and he looked across the street in terror, and there saw a tall, powerful man running towards him across Sveavägen. What the hell did he have in his hand? Was that a pistol?

Without a thought for August, Lindén turned to go back through the door and for a second or two he thought he was going to make it to safety. But he never did.

Salander's reaction had been instinctive as she launched herself on top of the boy. She had hurt herself when she hit the pavement, or at least there was pain in her shoulder and chest. But she had no time to take stock. She took hold of the child and hid behind a car and they lay there breathing heavily while shots were fired. After that it became disturbingly quiet, and when Salander peered under the car she could see the sturdy legs of their attacker racing across the street. It crossed her mind to grab the Beretta from her sports bag and return fire, but she realized she would not have time. On the other hand . . . a large Volvo came crawling past, so she jumped to her feet and in one confused rush lifted the boy and ran towards the car. She wrenched open the back door and threw herself in with him.

"Drive!" she yelled, as she saw blood spreading onto the seat.

Jacob Charro was twenty-two and the proud owner of a Volvo XC60 which he had bought on credit with his father as guarantor. He was on his way to Uppsala to have lunch with his uncle and aunt and cousins, and he was looking forward to it. He was dying to tell them that he'd got a place on Syrian F.C.'s first team.

The radio was playing Avicii's "Wake Me Up" and he was drumming his fingers on the steering wheel as he drove past the Concert Hall and the School of Economics. Something was going on further down the street. People were running in all directions. A man was shouting and the cars in front of him were driving erratically, so he slowed down. If there had been an accident, he might be able to help. Charro was always dreaming of being a hero.

But this time he got a fright. The man to the left of him ran through the traffic across the road, looking like a soldier on an offensive. There was something brutal in his movements and Charro was about to floor the accelerator when he heard his rear door being yanked open. Someone had thrown themselves in and he started shouting. He had no idea what. Maybe it was not even in Swedish. But the person – it was a girl with a child – yelled back:

"Drive!"

He hesitated for a second. Who *were* these people? Maybe they meant to rob him, or steal the car. He could not think straight, the whole situation was crazy. Then he had no choice but to act. His rear window was shattered because someone was shooting at them, so he accelerated wildly and with a pounding heart drove through a red at the intersection with Odengatan.

"What's all this about?" he shouted. "What's going on?"

"Shut it!" the girl snapped back. In the rear-view mirror he could see her examining the small boy who had large terrified eyes, checking him over with practised movements, like a hospital nurse. Then he noticed for the first time that there was not just broken glass all over the back seat. There was blood too.

"Has he been shot?"

"I don't know. Just keep driving. Go left there . . . Now!"

"O.K., O.K.," he said, terrified now, and he took a hard left up

in the mirror. Black hair and a ────────

for a moment he felt that as far as she was concerned he simply did not exist. But then she muttered something which sounded almost cheerful.

"Good news?" he asked.

She did not answer. Instead she pulled off her leather jacket, took hold of her white T-shirt and then . . . Jesus! She ripped it apart with a sudden jerk and was sitting there naked from the waist up, not wearing a bra or anything, and he glanced in bewilderment at her breasts which stood straight out, and above all at the blood that ran over them like a rivulet, down towards her stomach and the waistband of her jeans.

The girl had been hit somewhere below the shoulder, not far above her heart, and was bleeding heavily. Using the T-shirt for a bandage, she wound it tightly to staunch the flow of blood and put her leather jacket back on. She looked ridiculously pleased with herself, especially since some of the blood had splashed onto her cheek and forehead, like war paint.

"So the good news is that you got shot and not the boy?" he said.

"Something like that," she said.

"Should I take you to the Karolinska hospital?"

"No."

Salander had found both the entry and exit holes. The bullet must have gone straight through the front of her shoulder, which was bleeding profusely – she could feel her heart pounding all the way up to her temples. But she did not think any artery had been severed, or at least so she hoped. She looked back. The attacker must have had a getaway car somewhere close by, but nobody seemed to be following them. With any luck they had managed to escape fast enough.

She quickly looked down at the boy – August – who was sitting with his hands crossed over his chest, rocking backwards and forwards. It struck Salander that she ought to do something, so she brushed the glass fragments from the boy's hair and legs, and that made him sit still for a moment. Salander was not sure that was a good sign. The look in his eyes was rigid and blank. She nodded at him and tried to look as if she had the situation under control. She was feeling sick and dizzy and the T-shirt she had wound around her shoulder was by now soaked in blood. She was afraid that she might be losing consciousness and tried to come up with some sort of plan. One thing was crystal clear: the police were not an option. They had led the boy right into the path of the assailant and were plainly not on top of the situation. So what should she do?

She could not stay in this car. It had been seen at the shooting and the shattered rear window was bound to attract attention. She should get the man to drive her home to Fiskargatan. Then she could take her B.M.W., registered to Irene Nesser, if only she had the strength to drive it.

"Head towards Västerbron!" she ordered.

"O.K., O.K.," said the man driving.

"Do you have anything to drink?"

"A bottle of whisky – I was going to give it to my uncle."

"Pass it back here," she said, and was handed a bottle of Grant's, which she opened with difficulty.

She tore off her makeshift bandage and poured whisky onto ...bullet wound. She took one, two, three big mouthfuls, and ... ...dawned on her that that

"I need something else to bandage my ...

"O.K., but—"

"No buts."

"If you want me to help you, you could at least tell me why you were being shot at. Are you criminals?"

"I'm trying to protect the boy, it's that simple. Those bastards were after him."

"Why?"

"None of your business."

"So he's not your son."

"I don't even know him."

"So why are you helping him?"

Salander hesitated.

"We have the same enemies," she said. At that the young man pulled off his V-necked pullover – with a certain amount of reluctance and difficulty – as he steered the car with his other hand.

Then he unbuttoned his shirt, took it off and handed it back to Salander, who wound it gingerly around her shoulder. August, who was worryingly immobile now, looked down at his skinny legs with a frozen expression, and once again Salander asked herself what she ought to be doing.

They could hide out at her place on Fiskargatan. Blomkvist was the only person who knew the address, and the apartment could not be traced through her name on any public register. But it was still a risk. There had been a time when she was known up and down the country as a complete lunatic, and this enemy was certainly skilled at digging up information.

Someone on Sveavägen might have recognized her; the police might already be turning everything upside down to find her. She needed a new hiding place, not linked to any of her identities, and so she needed help. But from whom? Holger?

Her former guardian, Holger Palmgren, had almost recovered from his stroke and was living in a two-room apartment on Liljeholmstorget. Holger was the only person who really knew her. He was loyal to a fault and would do everything in his power to help. But he was elderly and anxious and she did not want to drag him into this if she could help it.

There was Blomkvist of course, and in fact there was nothing wrong with him. Still, she was reluctant to contact him again – perhaps *precisely* because there was nothing wrong with him. He was such a damn good person. But what the hell . . . you could hardly hold that against him, or at least not too much. She called his mobile. He picked up after just one ring, sounding alarmed.

"It's such a relief to hear your voice! What the hell has happened?"

"I can't tell you now."

"It looks like one of you's been shot. There's blood here."

"The boy's O.K."

"And you?"

"I'm O.K."

"You've been shot."

"You'll have to wait, Blomkvist."

She looked out at the town and saw that they were close to Västerbron already. She turned to the driver:

"Pull up there, by the bus stop."

"Are you getting out?"

"*You're* getting out. You're going to give me your mobile and wait outside while I talk. Is that clear?"

He glanced at her, terrified, then passed back his mobile, turned the car and got out. Salander continued her conversation.

app and also the ~~~~~~~~ line of communication."

"Right."

"If you're as much of an idiot as I think you are, whoever helps you do it has to remain anonymous. I don't want any weak links."

"Of course."

"And then . . ."

"Yes?"

"Only use it in an emergency. All other communication should be through a special link on your computer. You or the person who isn't an idiot needs to go into www.pgpi.org and download an encryption program for your emails. I want you to do that right now, then I want you to find a safe hiding place for the boy and me – somewhere not connected to you or *Millennium* – and let me have the address in an encrypted email."

"It's not your job to keep the boy safe, Lisbeth."

"I don't trust the police."

"Then we'll have to find someone else you *do* trust. The boy is autistic, he has special needs. I don't think you should be responsible for him, especially not if you're wounded . . ."

"Are you going to keep talking crap or do you want to help me?"

"Help you of course."

"Good. Check LISBETH STUFF in five minutes. I'll give you more information there. Then delete it."

"Lisbeth, listen to me, you need to get to a hospital. You need to be fixed up. I can tell by your voice . . ."

She hung up, waved the young man back in from the bus stop, got out her laptop and through her mobile hacked into Blomkvist's computer. She wrote out instructions on how to download and install the encryption program.

She then told the man to drive her to Mosebacke torg. It was a risk, but she had no choice. The city was beginning to look more and more blurred.

Blomkvist swore under his breath. He was standing on Sveavägen, not far from the body of Torkel Lindén and the cordon which the police who had been first on the scene were putting in place. Ever since Salander's original call he had been engaged in a frenzy of activity. He had thrown himself into a taxi to get here and had done everything he could during the trip to stop the boy and the director from walking out onto the street.

The only other member of staff he had managed to get hold of at Oden's Medical Centre was Birgitta Lindgren, who had rushed into the hallway only to see her colleague fall against the door with a fatal bullet wound to his head. When Blomkvist arrived ten minutes later she was beside herself, but she and another woman by the name of Ulrika Franzén, who had been on her way to the offices of Albert Bonniers the publishers further up the street, had

still been able to give Blomkvist a pretty coherent account of what
had happened.

Which was why Blomkvist knew, even before his mobile rang
again, that Salander had saved August Balder's life. She and the
boy were now in some car with a driver who had no reason to be
enthusiastic about helping them, having been shot at. Blomkvist
had seen the blood on the pavement and in the street and, even
though the call reassured him somewhat, he was still extremely
concerned. Salander had sounded in a bad way and yet – no
~~~~~~~ she had been as pig-headed as ever.

~~~~~~~~~~~~~~~~~~~ determined to hide the

prosecutor.

But this was Salander after all, and ~~ ~~~~~
would damn well help her, even if Berger threw a fit. He took a
deep breath and pulled out his mobile. But a familiar voice was
calling out behind him. It was Jan Bublanski. Bublanski came
running along the pavement looking as if he were close to physical
collapse, and with him were Detective Sergeant Modig and a tall,
athletic man in his fifties, presumably the professor Salander had
mentioned.

"Where's the boy?" Bublanski panted.

"He was whisked away in a big red Volvo, somebody rescued
him."

"Who?"

"I'll tell you what I know," Blomkvist said, not sure what he
would or should say. "But first I have to make a call."

"Oh no, first you're going to talk to us. We have to send out a
nationwide alert."

"Talk to that lady over there. Her name is Ulrika Franzén. She knows more than I do. She saw it happen, she's even got some sort of description of the assailant. I arrived after it happened."

"And the man who saved the boy?"

"The *woman* who saved him. Fru Franzén has a description of her as well. But just give me a minute here . . ."

"How did you know something was going to happen in the first place," Modig spat, with unexpected anger. "They said on the radio that you had called the emergency services before any shots were fired."

"I had a tip-off."

"From whom?"

Blomkvist took another deep breath and looked Modig straight in the eye, unmoveable as ever.

"Whatever may have been written in today's papers, I hope you realize that I want to cooperate with you in every way I can."

"I've always trusted you, Mikael. But I'm beginning to have my doubts," Modig said.

"O.K., I understand that. But you have to understand that *I* don't trust *you* either. There's been a serious leak – you've grasped that much, haven't you? Otherwise this wouldn't have happened," he said, pointing at the prone body inside the cordon.

"That's true, and it's absolutely terrible," Bublanski said.

"I'm going to make my call now," Blomkvist said, and he walked up the street so he could talk undisturbed.

But he never made any call. He realised that the time had come to get serious about security, so he walked back and informed Bublanski and Modig that he had to go to his office immediately, but he was at their disposal whenever they needed him. At that moment, to her own surprise, Modig took hold of his arm.

"First you have to tell us how you knew that something was going to happen," she said firmly.

"I'm afraid I have to invoke my right to protect my sources," Blomkvist answered with a pained smile.

Then he waved down a taxi and took off for the office, deep in thought. *Millennium* usually used Tech Source, a consultancy firm with a team of young women who gave the magazine quick and efficient help whenever they had more complex I.T. issues. But he did not want to bring them in now. Nor did he feel like turning to Christer Malm, even though he knew more about I.T. than anyone on the editorial team. Instead he thought of Zander, who was already involved in the story and was also great with

Blomkvist decided to ask for his help, and promised

Blomkvist – all the years as,

woodwork again, spewing their bile on Twitter and online forums and in emails. This time the racist mob had joined in, because *Millennium* had been in the forefront of the battles against xenophobia and racism for many years.

The worst part was surely that this hate campaign made it so much more difficult for everyone to do their jobs. All of a sudden people were less inclined to share information with the magazine. On top of that there was a rumour that Chief Prosecutor Ekström was planning to issue a search warrant for the magazine's offices. Berger did not really believe it. That kind of warrant was a serious matter, given the right to source protection.

But she did agree with Malm that the present toxic atmosphere would give even lawyers ludicrous ideas about how they should act. She was standing there thinking about how to retaliate when Blomkvist stepped into the offices. To her surprise, he did not

273

want to talk to her. Instead he went straight to Zander and ushered him into her room.

After a while she followed. She found the young man looking tense. She heard Blomkvist mention "P.G.P." She had been on an I.T. security course so she knew what that meant, and she saw Zander making notes before, without so much as a glance in her direction, he made a beeline for Blomkvist's laptop in the open-plan office.

"What was all that about?" she said.

Blomkvist told her in a whisper. She could barely take it in, and he had to repeat himself.

"So you want me to find a hiding place for them?"

"Sorry to drag you into this, Erika," he said. "But I don't know anyone who has as many friends with summer houses as you do."

"I don't know, Mikael. I really don't know."

"We can't let them down. Salander has been shot. The situation is desperate."

"If she's been shot, she should go to a hospital."

"She won't. She wants to protect the boy at all costs."

"To give him the calm he needs to draw the murderer."

"Yes."

"It's too great a responsibility, Mikael, too great a risk. If something happens, the fallout would destroy the magazine. Witness protection is not our job. This is something for the police – just think of all the questions that will be thrown up by those drawings, both for the investigation and on a psychological level. There has to be another solution."

"Maybe – if we were dealing with someone other than Lisbeth Salander."

"You know what? I get really pissed off with the way you always defend her."

"I'm only trying to be realistic. The authorities have let the

274

Balder boy down and put his life in danger – I know that infuriates Salander."

"So we just have to go along with it, is that it?"

"We don't have a choice. She's out there somewhere, hopping mad, and has nowhere to go."

"Take them to Sandhamn then."

"There's too much of a connection between Lisbeth and me. If it comes out that it's her, they would search my addresses straight away."

"O.K. then."

come up with a single name.

"I'm racking my brains," she said.

"Well, do it quickly, then give the address and directions to Andrei. He knows what to do."

Berger needed some air and so she went down into Götgatan and walked in the direction of Medborgarplatsen, running through one name after another in her mind. But not one of them felt right. There was too much at stake, and everyone she thought of was in some way not right or had some drawback or even if not she was reluctant to expose them to the risk or put them to the trouble by asking, perhaps because she herself was so upset by the situation. On the other hand . . . here was a small boy and people were trying to kill him and she had promised. She had to come up with something.

A police siren wailed in the distance and she looked over towards the park and the Tunnelbana station and at the mosque on the hill. A young man went by, surreptitiously shuffling some papers, and then suddenly – Gabriella Grane. At first the name surprised her. Grane was not a close friend and she worked at a place where it was unwise to flout any laws. Grane would risk losing her job if she so much as thought about this, and yet . . . Berger could not get it out of her head.

It was not just that Grane was an exceptionally good and responsible person. A memory also kept intruding. It was from last summer, in the early hours of the morning or maybe even at daybreak after a crayfish party out at Grane's summer house on Ingarö island, when the two had been sitting in a garden swing on the terrace looking down at the water through a gap in the trees.

"This is where I'd run to if the hyenas were after me," Berger had said, without really knowing what she meant. She had been feeling tired and vulnerable at work, and there was something about that house which she thought would make it an ideal place of refuge.

It stood on a rock promontory with steep, smooth sides, and the surrounding trees and elevation shielded it from onlookers. She remembered Grane saying, "If the hyenas come after you, you're welcome to be here, Erika."

Maybe it was asking too much, but she decided to give it a try. She went back to the office to call from the encrypted Redphone app which Zander had by then installed for her too.

CHAPTER 18

22.xi

"I have a . . ." Berger said.

But Grane had already hung up – this was no time for personal calls. She walked into the meeting room wearing an expression that suggested she meant to start a minor war. Crucial information had been leaked and now a second person was dead and one more apparently seriously wounded. She had never felt more like telling the whole lot of them to go to hell. They had been so eager to get hold of new information that they had lost their heads. For half a minute she did not hear one word her colleagues were saying. She just sat there, seething. But then she pricked up her ears.

Someone was saying that Blomkvist, the journalist, had called the emergency services before shots were fired on Sveavägen. That was strange, and now Erika Berger had called, and she was not the type to make casual calls, and certainly not during working hours. She might have had something important or even critical to say. Grane got up and made an excuse.

"Gabriella, you need to listen to this," Kraft said in an unusually sharp tone.

"I have to make a call," she replied, and suddenly she was not in the least interested in what the head of the Security Police thought of her.

"What sort of call?"

"A call," she said, and left them to go into her office.

Berger at once asked Grane to call her instead on the Samsung. The minute she had her friend on the line again, she could tell that something was going on. There was none of the usual friendly enthusiasm in her voice. On the contrary, Grane sounded worried and tense, as if she knew from the start that the conversation was important.

"Hi," she said simply. "I'm still really pushed. But is this about August Balder?"

Berger felt acutely uncomfortable. "How did you know?"

"I'm on the investigation and I've just heard that Mikael Blomkvist was tipped off about what was going to happen on Sveavägen."

"You've already heard that?"

"Yes, and now of course we're eager to know how that came about."

"Sorry. I can't tell you that."

"O.K. Understood. But why did you call?"

Berger closed her eyes. How could she have been such an idiot?

"I'm so sorry. I'll have to ask somebody else," she said. "You have a conflict of interest."

"I'm happy to take on almost any conflict of interest, Erika. But I can't stand the thought of your withholding information. This investigation means more to me than you can imagine."

"Really?"

"Yes, it does. I knew that Balder was under serious threat, but still I couldn't prevent the murder, and I'm going to have to live with that for the rest of my life. So, please, don't hide anything from me."

"I'm going to have to, Gabriella. I'm sorry. I don't want you to get into trouble because of us."

"I saw Mikael in Saltsjöbaden the night before last, the night of the murder."

"He didn't mention that."

"It wouldn't have made sense for me to identify myself."

"O.K.," Grane said, obviously disapp...
call never happened. Good luck now."

"Thanks," Berger said, and went back to searching through her contacts.

Grane went back to the meeting room, her mind whirling. What was it that Erika had wanted? She did not fully understand and yet she had a vague idea. As she came back into the room the conversation died and everyone looked at her.

"What was that about?" Kraft said.

"Something private."

"That you had to deal with now?"

"That I had to deal with. How far had you got?"

"We were talking about what happened on Sveavägen," said Ragnar Olofsson, the head of division, "but as I was saying, we don't yet have enough information. The situation is chaotic, and it looks as if we're losing our source in Bublanski's group. The detective inspector seems to have become paranoid."

"You can't blame him," Grane said.

"Well . . . perhaps not. We've talked about that too. We'll leave no stone unturned until we know how the attacker worked out that the boy was at the medical centre and that he was going to go out by the front door when he did. No effort will be spared, I need hardly say. But I must emphasize that a leak did not necessarily come from within the police. The information was quite widely known – at the medical centre of course, by the mother and her unreliable partner Lasse Westman, and in the offices of *Millennium*. And we can't rule out hacker attacks. I'll come back to that. If I might continue with my report?"

"Please."

"We've been discussing how Mikael Blomkvist comes into this, and this is where we're worried. How could he know about a shooting before it happens? In my opinion, he's got some source close to the criminals themselves, and I see no reason for us to tiptoe around his efforts to protect those sources. We have to find out where he got his information from."

"The more so since he seems desperate and will do anything for a scoop," Superintendent Mårten Nielsen said.

"It would appear that Mårten has some excellent sources too. He reads the evening papers," Grane said acidly.

"Not the evening papers, sweetie. T.T. – a source which even we at Säpo regard as fairly reliable."

"That was absurd and defamatory, and you know it as well as I do," Grane said.

"I had no idea you were so besotted with Blomkvist."

"Idiot!"

"Stop this at once!" Kraft said. "This is ridiculous behaviour! Carry on, Ragnar. What do we know about what happened?"

"The first people on the scene were two regular police officers,

Erik Sandström and Tord Landgren," Olofsson said. "My information comes from them. They were there on the dot of 9.24, and by then it was all over. Torkel Lindén was dead, shot in the back of the head, and the boy, well, we don't know. According to witnesses, he was hit too. We have blood in the street. But nothing is confirmed. The boy was driven away in a red Volvo – we do at least have parts of the registration number plus the model of the vehicle. We'll get the name of its owner very shortly."

Grane noticed that Kraft was writing everything down, just as she had done at their earlier meetings.

"............?" she said.

"What makes you say that? ....

"There were professionals on both sides. The assailant seems to have been standing and watching the door from a low green wall on the other side of Sveavägen, in front of the park. There's a lot to suggest that this is the man who shot Frans Balder. Not that anyone has seen his face clearly; it's possible he was wearing some sort of mask. But he seems to have moved with the same exceptional efficiency and speed. And in the opposite camp there was this woman."

"What do we know about her?"

"Not much. She was wearing a black leather jacket, we think, and dark jeans. She was young with black hair and piercings – a punk, according to one witness – also short, but fierce. She appeared out of nowhere, throwing herself over the boy and shielding him. The witnesses all agree that she was not some ordinary member of the public. She seemed to have training, or had at least found herself in similar situations before. Then there's the car – we have conflicting reports. One witness says it just happened to be driving by, and the woman and the boy threw themselves in more or less while it was moving. Others – especially those guys from the School of Economics – think the car was part of the operation. Either way, we have a kidnapping on our hands."

"It doesn't make sense. This woman saved the boy only to abscond with him?" Grane said.

"That's what it looks like. Otherwise we would have heard from her by now, wouldn't we?"

"How did she get to Sveavägen?"

"We don't know yet. But a witness, a former editor-in-chief of a trade-union paper, says the woman looked somehow familiar," Olofsson said.

He went on to say something else, but by then Grane had stopped listening. She was thinking, *Zalachenko's daughter – it has to be Zalachenko's daughter*, knowing full well how unfair it was to call her that. The daughter had nothing to do with the father. On the contrary, she had hated him.

But Grane had known her by that name ever since, years earlier, she had read everything she could lay her hands on about the Zalachenko affair. While Olofsson went on speculating, she began to feel the pieces were falling into place. Already the day before she had identified some commonalities between Zalachenko's old network and the group which called itself the Spiders, but had dismissed them. She had believed there was a limit to how far thuggish criminals could develop their skills; it seemed entirely unreasonable to suppose that they could go from seedy-looking biker types in their leather waistcoats to cutting-edge hackers. Yet the thought had occurred to her. Grane had even wondered if the girl who helped Linus Brandell trace the break-in on Balder's computers might have been Zalachenko's daughter. There was a Säpo file on the woman, with a note that said "Hacker?

Computer savvy?", and even though it seemed prompted by the surprisingly favourable reference she had received for her work at Milton Security, it was clear from the document that she had devoted a great deal of time to research into her father's criminal organization.

Most striking of all was that there was a known connection between the woman and Mikael Blomkvist. It was unclear what exactly that connection was; Grane did not for one moment believe the malicious rumours that it was a blackmail situation or something to do with sado-masochistic sex, but the connection was there. Both Blomkvist and the woman – who matched the

She was about to present her theory when she noticed something which made her hesitate.

It was nothing so remarkable, not at all. It was just that Kraft was once again meticulously writing down what Olofsson had said. It was probably good to have a senior boss who was so committed, but there was something rather too zealous about that scratching pen, and it made Grane wonder if a senior boss, whose job it was to see the bigger picture, should be so preoccupied with every tiny detail. Without really knowing why, she began to feel very uneasy.

It may have been because she herself was busy pointing a finger at someone on flimsy grounds, but also Kraft seemed to blush at that moment perhaps because she realized that she was being observed, and looked away in embarrassment. Grane decided not to finish the sentence she had begun.

"Or rather . . ."

"Yes, Gabriella?"

"Oh, nothing," she said, feeling a sudden need to get away, and even though she knew that it would not look good, she left the meeting room once more and went to the toilet.

Later she would remember how she stared at herself in the mirror and tried to understand what she had seen. Had Kraft really blushed, and if so, what did that mean? Maybe nothing, she decided, absolutely nothing, and, even if it was indeed shame or guilt that Grane had read in her face, it could have been about almost anything. It occurred to her that she did not know her boss all that well. But she knew enough to be sure that she would not send a child to his death for financial or any other gain, no, that was out of the question.

Grane had simply become paranoid, a typically suspicious spy who saw moles everywhere, even in her own reflection. "Idiot," she muttered, and smiled at herself despondently, as if to dismiss the idea and come back down to earth. But that didn't solve anything. In that instant she thought she saw a new kind of truth in her own eyes.

She suspected that she was quite like Helena Kraft in that she was capable and ambitious and wanted to get a pat on the back from her superiors. That was not necessarily always a good thing, though. With that tendency, if you operate in an unhealthy culture you risk becoming just as unhealthy yourself and – who knows – perhaps it is the will to please that leads people to crime just as often as evil or greed.

People want to fit in and do well, and so they do indescribably stupid things. Is that what had happened here? If nothing else then Hans Faste – because surely he was Säpo's source in Bublanski's group – had been leaking to them because that was what he was expected to do and because he wanted to score points with Säpo. Olofsson had seen to it that Kraft was kept informed of every little detail; she was his boss and he wanted to be in her good books and then . . . well, maybe Kraft in turn had passed on some information because she wanted to be seen to be doing a good job. But, if so, by whom? The head of the national police, the government, foreign intelligence, in that case most likely American or English, who perhaps then . . .

Grane did not take this train of thought any further. She asked herself again if she was letting her imagination run away with her but, even if she was, she still could not trust her team. She wanted to be good at her job, but not necessarily by doing her duty to Säpo.

~~~~~ ~~~~~ ~~~~~ ~~ ~~ ~~fe. Instead of Kraft's face

had argued her case so well that ~~Berger~~
That is no doubt the disadvantage of having intelligent friends: they see straight through you.

Not only had Grane worked out what Berger wanted to talk to her about, she had also persuaded her that she felt a moral responsibility and would never reveal the hiding place, however much that might appear to conflict with her professional duty. She said she had a debt to repay and insisted on helping. She was going to courier over the keys to her summer house on Ingarö and arrange for directions to be sent over the encrypted link which Andrei Zander had set up.

Further up Götgatan a beggar collapsed, scattering two carrier bags full of plastic bottles across the pavement. Berger hurried over but the man, who was soon on his feet again, declined her help so she gave him a sad smile and went back up to the *Millennium* offices.

Blomkvist was looking upset and exhausted. His hair was standing on end and his shirt hung outside his trousers. She had not seen him looking so worn out in a long time. Yet when his eyes shone like that, there was no stopping him. It meant he had entered into that absolute concentration from which he would not emerge until he had got to the heart of the story.

"Have you found a hiding place?" he said.

She nodded.

"It might be best if you say nothing more. We have to keep this to as small a circle of people as possible."

"That sounds sensible. But let's hope it's a short-term solution. I don't like the idea of Lisbeth Salander being responsible for the boy."

"Who knows? Maybe they'll be good for each other."

"What did you tell the police?"

"Almost nothing."

"Not a good time to be keeping things under wraps."

"Not really, no."

"Maybe Salander is prepared to make a statement, so you can get some peace and quiet."

"I don't want to put any pressure on her. She's in bad shape. Can you get Zander to ask her if we can send a doctor out there?"

"I will. But you know . . ."

"What?"

"I'm actually coming round to the idea that she's doing the right thing," Berger said.

"Why do you say that, all of a sudden?"

"Because I too have my sources. Police headquarters isn't a secure place right now," she said, and walked over to Zander with a determined stride.

CHAPTER 19

22.xi, Evening

Inevitably there were corrupt and dep~~~~~ ~~~~~
But to deliver a small, mentally disabled boy into the hands of a
cold-blooded murderer was beyond the pale, and he refused to
believe that anyone in the force would be capable of that. Perhaps
the information had seeped out by some other route. Their telephones might be tapped or they had been hacked, although he
could not think that notes about August's abilities had been
written in any computer. He had been trying to reach the Säpo
head, Helena Kraft, to discuss the matter. He had stressed that it
was important, but she had not returned his call.

The Swedish Trade Council and the Ministry of Enterprise had
been onto him, which was worrisome. Even if it was not said in
so many words, their main concern was not for the boy or the
shooting on Sveavägen, but rather for the research programme
which Frans Balder had been working on, which appeared to have
been stolen on the night of his murder.

Several of the most skilled computer technicians in the force and three I.T. experts from Linköping University and the Royal Institute of Technology had been to the house in Saltsjöbaden, but they had found no trace of this research, either on his computers or among the papers which he had left behind.

"So now, on top of everything else, we have an Artificial Intelligence on the loose," Bublanski muttered to himself. He was reminded of an old riddle his mischievous cousin Samuel liked to put to his friends in synagogue. It was a paradox: if God is indeed omnipotent, is he then capable of creating something more intelligent than himself? The riddle was considered disrespectful, he recalled, even blasphemous. It had that evasive quality which meant that, however you answered, you were wrong. There was a knock at the door, and Bublanski was brought back to the questions at hand. It was Modig, ceremoniously handing over another piece of Swiss orange chocolate.

"Thank you," he said. "Have you got anything new?"

"We think we know how the killers got Lindén and the boy out of the building. They sent fake emails from our and Professor Edelman's addresses and arranged a pick-up on the street."

"Is that possible?"

"Yes, and it's not even very difficult."

"Terrifying."

"True, but that still doesn't explain how they knew to access the Oden's Medical Centre computer, or how they found out that Edelman was involved."

"I suppose we'd better have our own computers checked out," Bublanski said gloomily.

"Already in hand."

"Is this how it was meant to be, that we won't dare to write or say anything for fear of being overheard?"

"I don't know. I hope not. Meanwhile we have a Jacob Charro out there waiting to be interviewed."

"Who's he?"

"A footballer, plays for Syrian F.C. And he's the man who drove the woman and August Balder away from Sveavägen."

A muscular young man with short dark hair and high cheekbones was sitting in the interview room. He was wearing a mustard-coloured V-neck pullover without a shirt and seemed at once agitated and a little proud.

Modig opened with: "18.35 on November 22. Interview with witness Jacob Charro, twenty-two years old, resident in Norborg. Tell us what happened this morning."

"Were you able to see what he looked like?"

"Not really, but since then it's struck me that there was something unnatural about his face."

"What do you mean?"

"Like it wasn't his real face. He was wearing sunglasses which must have been secured around his ears, but his cheeks, it looked as if he had something in his mouth, I don't know. Then there was his moustache and eyebrows, and the colour of his skin."

"Do you think he was wearing a mask?"

"Something like that. But I didn't have time to think too much about it. Before I knew it the rear door of the car was yanked open and then . . . what can I say? It was one of those moments when everything happens all at once – the whole world comes down onto your head. Suddenly there were strangers in my car and the rear windscreen shattered. I was in shock."

"What did you do?"

"I accelerated like crazy. The girl who jumped in was shouting at me to drive, and I was so scared I hardly knew what I was doing. I just followed orders."

"Orders?"

"That's how it seemed. I reckoned we were being chased, and I didn't see any other way out. I kept swerving and that, just like the girl told me to, and besides . . ."

"Go on."

"There was something about her voice. It was so cold and intense, I found myself hanging on to it, as if it were the only thing that was in control in all the mayhem."

"You said you thought you recognized the woman?"

"Yes, but not at the time, definitely not. I was scared to death and was busy concentrating on all the weird things that were happening. There was blood all over the place back there."

"Coming from the boy or the woman?"

"I wasn't sure at first, and neither of them seemed to know either. But then I heard her say something like 'Yes!', like something good had happened."

"What was that about?"

"The girl realized she was the one bleeding and not the boy, and that really struck me. It was like, 'Hurray, I've been shot,' and I tell you, it wasn't some little graze. However she tried to bandage it, she couldn't staunch the blood. It just kept oozing out, and the girl kept getting paler and paler. She must have felt like shit."

"And still she was happy that it wasn't the boy who'd been hit."

"Exactly. Like a mother."

"But she wasn't the child's mother."

"No. They didn't even know each other, she said, and that became more and more obvious. She didn't have a clue about children."

"On the whole," Modig said, "how did you think she treated the boy?"

"Not sure how to answer that, to be honest. I wouldn't say she had the world's best social skills. She treated me like a damn servant, but even so . . ."

"Yes?"

"I reckon she was a good person. I wouldn't have wanted her to be my babysitter, if you see what I mean. But she was O.K."

"So you reckon the child is safe with her?"

"She's obviously fucking crazy. But the little boy . . . he's called August, right?"

"That's correct."

August with her life, if it comes to it. That was

She didn't say more than

down my details. She was going to pay for the damage to the car, she said, plus a little extra."

"Did she look as though she had money?"

"Going by her appearance alone, I'd say she lived in a dump. But the way she behaved . . . I don't know. It wouldn't surprise me if she was loaded. You could tell that she was used to getting her own way."

"What happened then?"

"She told the boy to get out of the car."

"And did he?"

"He just rocked backwards and forwards and didn't move. But then her tone hardened. She said it was a matter of life and death or something like that, and he tottered out of the car with his arms stiff, as if he was sleepwalking."

"Did you see where they went?"

"Only that it was to the left – towards Slussen. But the girl . . ."

"Yes?"

"Well, she was obviously feeling like shit. She was weaving about and seemed on the point of collapse."

"Doesn't sound good. And the boy?"

"Probably wasn't in great shape either. He was looking really odd. The whole time in the car I worried he was going to have some sort of fit. But when he got out he seemed to have come to terms with the situation. In any case he kept asking, 'Where?' over and over. 'Where?'"

Modig and Bublanski looked at each other.

"Are you sure about that?" Modig said.

"Why shouldn't I be?"

"Well, you might have thought you heard him saying that because he had a questioning look on his face."

"Why would I have thought that?"

"Because the boy's mother says he doesn't speak at all, has never said a single word," Modig said.

"Are you joking?"

"No, and it would be odd for him to suddenly start speaking under these very circumstances."

"I heard what I heard."

"O.K., and what did the woman answer?"

"'Away', I think. 'Away from here.' Something like that. Then she almost collapsed, like I said. And she told me to drive off."

"And you did?"

"Like a bat out of hell."

"And then you realized who you'd had in your car?"

"I'd already worked out that the boy was the son of that genius who'd been murdered. But the girl . . . she vaguely reminded me of someone. I was shaking like a leaf and in the end I couldn't drive any more. I stopped on Ringvägen, by Skanstull, got myself a beer at Clarion Hotel and tried to calm down. And that's when it hit me. It was the girl who was wanted for murder a few years ago, but then the charges were dropped, and it came out that she'd been through some terrible things in a mental hospital when she was a child. I remember it well – the father of a friend of mine had been tortured in Syria, and he was having more or less the same stuff done to him at the time, electroshock therapy and that sort of shit, because he couldn't deal with his memories. It was like he was being tortured all over again."

"Are you sure about that?"

"That he was tortured?"

~~~~~~~ Salander."

~~~

That same tattoo was mentioned in articles."

Berger arrived at Grane's summer house with several shopping bags filled with food, crayons and paper, a couple of difficult puzzles and a few other things. But there was no sign of August or Salander. Salander had not responded, either on her Redphone app or on the encrypted link. Berger was sick with anxiety.

Whichever way she looked at it, this did not bode well. Admittedly Salander was not known for needless communication or reassurance, but it was she who had asked for a safe house. Also she had responsibility for a child, and if she was not answering their calls under those circumstances, she must be in a bad way.

Berger cursed aloud and walked out onto the terrace where she and Grane had been sitting and talking about escaping from the world. That was only a few months ago, but it felt like an age.

There was no table now, no chairs, no bottles, no hubbub behind them, only snow, branches and debris flung there by the storm. It was as if life itself had abandoned the place. Somehow the memory of that crayfish party increased the sense of desolation, as if the festivities were draped like a ghost over its walls.

Berger went back into the kitchen and put some microwaveable food into the refrigerator: meatballs, packets of spaghetti with meat sauce, sausage stroganoff, fish pie, potato cakes and a whole lot of even worse junk food Blomkvist had advised her to buy: Billys Pan Pizza, piroshki, chips, Coca-Cola, a bottle of Tullamore Dew, a carton of cigarettes, three bags of crisps, three bars of chocolate and some sticks of fresh liquorice. She set out drawing paper, crayons, pencils, an eraser and a ruler and compass on the large round table. On the top sheet of paper she drew a sun and a flower and wrote the word *WELCOME* in four warm colours.

The house was close to Ingarö beach, but you could not see it from there. It lay high up on the rock promontory, concealed behind pine trees. It consisted of four rooms. The kitchen with glass doors onto the terrace was the largest and also the heart of the house. In addition to the round table there was an old rocking chair and two worn, sagging sofas which nonetheless managed to look inviting thanks to a pair of red tartan rugs. It was a cosy home.

It was also a good safe house. Berger left the door open, put the keys in the top drawer of the hall closet, as agreed, and made her way back down the flight of wooden steps flanking the steep, smooth rock slope – the only way to the house for anyone arriving by car.

The sky was dark and turbulent, the wind blowing hard again. Her spirits were low and did not improve during the drive home. Her thoughts turned to Hanna Balder. Berger had not exactly been a member of the fan club – Hanna often played the parts of women who were both sexy and dim-witted, whom all men thought they could seduce, and Berger was disgusted by the film industry's devotion to that type of character. But none of that was true any longer and Berger regretted that she had been so ungracious at the time. She had been too hard on the woman; it was much too easy to criticize when a pretty girl gets a big break early in her career.

Nowadays, on the rare occasions Hanna Balder appeared in a major production, her eyes tended to reflect a restrained sorrow, which gave depth to the parts she played, and – what did Berger

may have been genuine. She had been through some

hours. Since morning,

had come

mother's immediate circle. Lasse Westman

trusted, seemed to be staying in the house all day to avoid the journalists camped outside. They were in a bind, and Berger did not like it. She hoped *Millennium* would still be able to tell the story with dignity and depth, without the magazine or anyone else coming to harm. She had no doubt that Blomkvist would be up to it, given the way he looked right now. Besides, he had Zander to help him.

Berger had a soft spot for Zander. Not long ago, over dinner at her and Greger's home in Saltsjöbaden, he had told them his life story, which had only increased her sympathy.

When Zander was eleven he lost both his parents in a bomb blast in Sarajevo. After that he came to live in Tensta outside Stockholm with an aunt who altogether failed to notice either his intellectual disposition or the psychological wounds he bore. He had not been there when his parents were killed, but his body

295

reacted still as if he were suffering from post-traumatic stress. To this day he detested loud noises and sudden movements. He hated seeing unattended bags in public places, and loathed violence with a passion Berger had never encountered in anyone else.

As a child he sought refuge in his own worlds. He immersed himself in fantasy literature, read poetry and biographies, adored Sylvia Plath, Borges and Tolkien and learned everything there was to know about computers. He dreamed of writing heart-rending novels about love and human tragedy, and was an incurable romantic who hoped that great passion would heal his wounds. He was not in the least bit interested in the outside world. One evening in his late teens, however, he attended a public lecture given by Mikael Blomkvist at the Institute for Media Studies at Stockholm University. It changed his life.

Blomkvist's fervour inspired him to bear witness to a world which was bleeding with injustice, intolerance and petty corruption. He started to imagine himself writing articles critical of society instead of tear-jerking romances. Not long after that he knocked on *Millennium*'s door and asked if there was anything they would let him do – make coffee, proofread, run errands. Berger, who had seen the fire in his eyes right from the start, assigned him some minor editorial tasks: public notices, research and brief portraits. But most of all she told him to study, and he did so with the same energy he put into everything else. He read political science, mass-media communications, finance and international conflict resolution, and at the same time he helped out on temporary assignments at *Millennium*.

He wanted to become a heavyweight investigative journalist, like Blomkvist. But unlike so many other investigative journalists he was no tough guy. He remained a romantic. Blomkvist and Berger had both spent time trying to sort out his relationship problems. He was too open and transparent. Too good, as Blomkvist would often say.

But Berger believed that Zander was in the process of shedding that youthful vulnerability. She had been seeing the change in his journalism. That ferocious ambition to reach out and touch people, which had made his writing heavy-handed at first, had been replaced by a more effective, matter-of-fact style. She knew he would pull out all the stops now that he had been given the chance to help Blomkvist with the Balder story. The plan was for Blomkvist to write the big, central narrative, and for Zander to help with the research as well as writing some explanatory side-

Berger thought they made a great team.

walked into the offices and

him of – withhold information.

He was in many ways a model, law-abiding citizen. But if there was anyone who could get him to cross the line, it was Lisbeth Salander. Blomkvist would rather dishonour himself than betray her, which is why he kept repeating to the police: "I assert my right to protect my sources." No wonder he was unhappy and worried about the consequences. But, like Berger, he had far greater fears for Salander and the boy than for their own situation.

"How's it going?" she asked, after watching him for a while.

"What? . . . Well . . . O.K. How was it out there?"

"I made up the beds and put food in the fridge."

"Good. And the neighbours didn't see you?"

"There wasn't a soul there."

"Why are they taking so long?" he said.

"I just don't know, but I'm worried sick."

"Let's hope they're resting at Lisbeth's."

"Let's hope so. What else did you find out?"

"Quite a bit. But . . ." Blomkvist trailed off.

"Yes?'

"It's just that . . . it feels as if I'm being thrown back in time, going back to places I've been to before."

"You'll have to explain better," she said.

"I will . . ." Blomkvist glanced at his computer screen. "But first I have to keep on digging. Let's speak later," he said, and so she left him and got her things to drive home, although she would be ready to stay with him at a second's notice.

CHAPTER 20

23.xi

Comidential...

a result. A small boy's life is in danger. In spite of immense efforts we still don't know how this happened. The leak could have been at our end, or at Säpo, or at Oden's Medical Centre, or in the group around Professor Edelman, or from the boy's mother and her partner, Lasse Westman. We know nothing for certain, and therefore we have to be *extremely* circumspect, paranoid even."

"We may also have been hacked or phonetapped," Modig said. "We seem to be dealing with criminals whose command of new technologies is far beyond anything we've seen before."

"Very true," Bublanski said. "We need to take precautions at every level, not say anything significant relating to this investigation – or to any other – over the telephone, no matter how highly our superiors rate our new mobile-phone system."

"They think it's great because it cost so much to install," Holmberg said.

"Maybe we should also be reflecting a little on our own role," Bublanski said, ignoring him. "I was just talking to a gifted young analyst at Säpo, Gabriella Grane – you may have heard of her. She pointed out that the concept of loyalty is not as straightforward as one might think for us policemen. We have many different loyalties, don't we? There's the obvious one, to the law. There's a loyalty to the public, and to one's colleagues, but also to our bosses, and to ourselves and our careers. Sometimes, as all of you know, these interests end up competing with each other. We might choose to protect a colleague at work and thereby fail in our duty to the public, or we might be given orders from higher up, as Hans Faste was, and then that conflicts with the loyalty he should have had to us. But from now on – and I'm deadly serious – there's only one loyalty I want to hear of, and that is to the investigation itself. We're going to catch the murderers and we're going to make sure that no-one else falls victim to them. Agreed? Even if the prime minister himself or the head of the C.I.A. calls and goes on about patriotism and major career opportunities, you still won't utter a peep, will you?"

"No," they said, as one.

"Excellent. As we all know, the person who intervened on Sveavägen was none other than Lisbeth Salander, and we're doing everything in our power to find out where she is."

"Which is why we've got to release her name to the media!" Svensson called out, somewhat heatedly. "We need help from the public."

"We don't all agree on this, so I'd like to raise the question again. Let's remember that in the past Lisbeth Salander has had some very shabby treatment, from us and from the media . . ."

"At this point that doesn't matter," Svensson said.

"And it's conceivable that people recognized her on Sveavägen and her name will come out at any moment anyway, in which case this would no longer be an issue. But before that happens, bear in mind that she saved the boy's life."

"No doubt about that," Svensson said. "But then she more or less kidnapped him."

"Our information suggests that she was determined to protect the boy at all costs," Modig said. "Salander's experience of public institutions has been anything but positive – her entire childhood was marred by the injustices inflicted on her by Swedish offi-cialdom. If she suspects, as we do, that there's a leak inside the police force, then there's no chance she's going to contact us. Fact."

"That's irrelevant," Svensson insisted.

"Maybe," Modig said. "Jan and I share your view that the most _____ _____ it's in the interests of the inves-

risk. But that still leaves a number _____ _____ ethical thing to do? And I have to say, even if there's been a leak here we cannot accept that Salander should keep the boy hidden away. He's a crucial part of the investigation and, leak or no leak, we're better at protecting a child than an emotionally disturbed young woman could ever be."

"Absolutely. Of course," Bublanski muttered.

"And even if this isn't a kidnapping in the ordinary sense – yes, even if it's been carried out with the best of intentions – the poten-tial harm to the child could be just as great. Psychologically it must be hugely damaging for him to be, as it were, on the run after everything he's been through."

"True," Bublanski said. "But the question still remains: how do we deal with the information we have?"

"There I agree with Curt. We have to release her name and photograph right away. It could produce invaluable leads."

"Probably," Bublanski said. "But it could at the same time help the killers. We have to assume that they haven't given up looking for the boy. Quite the opposite in fact. And since we have no idea what the connection is between the boy and Salander, we don't know what sort of clues her name would provide them with. I'm not persuaded that we would be protecting the boy by giving the media these details."

"But neither do we know if we're protecting him by holding them back," Holmberg said. "There are too many pieces of the puzzle missing for us to draw any conclusions. Is Salander doing this for someone else, for example? Or does she have her own agenda for the child, apart from to protect him?"

"And how could she have known that Torkel Lindén and the boy would come out onto Sveavägen at that exact moment?" Svensson said.

"Maybe she just happened to be there."

"Doesn't seem likely."

"The truth is often unlikely," Bublanski said. "That's the nature of truth. But I agree, it doesn't feel like a coincidence in this case, not under the circumstances."

"What about the fact that Mikael Blomkvist also knew something was going to happen?" Amanda Flod said.

"There's some sort of connection between Blomkvist and Salander," Holmberg said.

"True."

"Blomkvist knew that the boy was at Oden's Medical Centre, didn't he?"

"The mother told him," Bublanski said. "As you might imagine, she's feeling quite desperate now. I've just had a long conversation with her. But there was no reason on earth why Blomkvist should have known that Lindén and the boy would be tricked into going out onto the street."

"Could he have had access to a computer at Oden's?" Flod said pensively.

"I can't imagine Mikael Blomkvist getting involved in hacking," Modig said.

"But what about Salander?" Holmberg said. "What do we actually know about her? We have a massive file on the girl. Yet the last time we had anything to do with her, she surprised us on every count. Maybe appearances are just as deceptive this time around."

"I agree," Svensson said. "We have far too many question

And that's exactly why

We ha...

name and picture and then look carefully

come in," Holmberg said with authority. He seemed to have the backing of the whole group, and at that Bublanski closed his eyes and reflected that he loved them all. He felt a greater affinity with his team than he did for his own brothers and sisters, or even his parents. But right now he felt compelled to disagree with them.

"We'll do everything we can to try to find them. But for the time being we will not release the name and picture. That would only make the situation more fraught, and I don't want to risk giving the killers any leads at all."

"And you feel guilty," Holmberg said, without warmth.

"I feel very guilty," Bublanski said, thinking of his rabbi.

Blomkvist was so worried about the boy and Salander that he hardly slept. Time and again he had tried to reach Salander via the Redphone app, but she had not answered. He had not heard a word from her since yesterday afternoon. Now he was sitting in the office, trying to immerse himself in his work and figure out what it was that had escaped him. For some time already he had had a sense – impossible to put his finger on – that there was a key piece missing, something which could shed light on the whole story. Perhaps he was fooling himself. Maybe it was just wishful thinking, a need to see a grand design. The last message from Salander on the encrypted link was:

```
<Jurij Bogdanov. Check him out. He's the one
who sold Balder's technology to Eckerwald at
Solifon.>
```

There were some images of Bogdanov on the net. They showed him wearing pinstriped suits which fit perfectly but still managed to look wrong on him, as if he had stolen them on the way to the photographer's. Bogdanov had long, lank hair, a pockmarked face and large rings under his eyes and you could just about make out some amateurish tattoos beneath his shirt cuffs. His look was dark, intense and piercing. He was tall, but he cannot have weighed more than sixty kilos.

He looked like an old jailbird, but, most striking, there was something about his body language which Blomkvist recognized from the images on the surveillance cameras at Balder's place. The man gave the same tattered, rough-edged impression.

There were also interviews he had given as a businessman in Berlin in which he vouchsafed that he had been born more or less on the streets. "I was doomed to end up dead in an alleyway with a needle stuck in my arm. But I managed to pull myself out of the muck. I'm intelligent and I'm one hell of a fighter," he said. There was nothing in the details of his life to contradict these claims, save for the suspicion that he may not have been raised exclusively through his own efforts. There were clues to suggest he had been given a helping hand by powerful people who had spotted his talent. In a German technology magazine, a security chief at the Horst credit institution was quoted as saying, "Bogdanov has magic in his eyes. He can detect vulnerabilities in security systems like no-one else. He's a genius."

So Bogdanov was a star hacker, although the official version had him acting only as a "white hat", someone who served the good, legal side, who helped companies identify flaws in their I.T. security in exchange for decent compensation. There was nothing in the least suspicious about his company, Outcast Security. The board members were all respectable, well-educated people. But Blomkvist did not leave it at that. He and Zander scrutinized every

There were rumours that he had been convicted of grievous bodily harm and procuring. He had been married twice – both wives were dead, and Blomkvist had not been able to find a cause of death in either case. But the most interesting discovery he made was that the man had served as a substitute board member of a company – minor and long-since defunct – by the name of Bodin Construction & Export, which had dealt in "sales of construction materials".

The owner of the company had been Karl Axel Bodin, the alias of Alexander Zalachenko, a name that revived memories of the evil conspiracy which became the subject of *Millennium*'s greatest scoop. Zalachenko who was Salander's father, and her dark shadow, the black heart behind her throbbing determination to exact revenge.

Was it a coincidence that his name had cropped up? Blomkvist knew better than anyone that if you dig deep enough into a story, you will always find links. Life is constantly treating us to illusory connections. It was just that, when it came to Lisbeth Salander, he stopped believing in coincidence.

If she broke a surgeon's fingers or delved into the theft of some advanced A.I. technology, you could be sure that she had not only thought it through to the last particle, she would also have a reason. Salander was not one to forget an injustice. She retaliated and she righted wrongs. Could her involvement in this story be connected to her own background? It was by no means inconceivable.

Blomkvist looked up from his computer and glanced at Zander. Zander nodded back at him. The faint smell of something cooking was coming from the kitchen. Thudding rock music could be heard from Götgatan. Outside the storm was howling, and the sky was still dark and wild. Blomkvist went into the encrypted link out of habit, not expecting to find anything. But then his face lit up. He even let out a small whoop of joy.

It said:

<OK now. We'll be going to the safe house shortly.>

He wrote:

<Great news. Drive carefully.>

Then he could not resist adding:

<Who are we actually after?>

She answered at once:

<You'll soon work it out, smartarse!>

"O.K." was an exaggeration. Salander was better, but still in bad shape. For half of yesterday, in her apartment, she had been barely conscious and only managed with the greatest difficulty to drag herself out of bed to see that August had something to eat and drink and make sure he had pencils, crayons and paper. But as she approached him now she could see even from a distance that he had drawn nothing.

There was paper scattered all over the coffee table in front of him, but no drawings. Instead she saw rows of scribbles. More absent-mindedly than out of curiosity she tried to make out what they were – he had written numbers, endless series of numbers, and even if at first they made no sense to her, she was intrigued. Suddenly she gave a whistle.

"Oh my God," she muttered.

They were staggeringly large numbers which formed a familiar pattern alongside the numbers next to them. As she looked through the papers and came across the simple sequence 641, 647, _____ ____ _____ _____ any doubt: they were sexy prime

kneeling by the coffee table, as ___ __ ___ to go on writing his numbers. It occurred to her that she had read something about savants and prime numbers, but she put it out of her mind. She was far too unwell for any kind of advanced thinking. Instead she went into the bathroom and took two more Vibramycin antibiotics which had been lying around in her apartment for years.

She packed her pistol and her computer, a few changes of clothes and to be on the safe side she put on a wig and a pair of dark glasses. When she was ready she asked the boy to get up. He did not respond, just held his pencil in a tight grip. For a moment she stood in front of him, stumped. Then she said sternly, "Get up!" and he did.

They put on their outer layers, took the lift down to the garage and set off for the safe house on Ingarö. Her left shoulder was tightly strapped and it ached, so she steered with her right hand.

The top of her chest was hurting, she had a fever and had to stop a couple of times at the side of the road to rest. When finally they got to the beach and the jetty by Stora Barnvik on Ingarö, and followed the directions to climb the wooden steps up the slope to the house, she collapsed exhausted on the first bed she saw. She was shivering and freezing cold.

Soon after, breathing laboriously, she got up and sat at the kitchen table with her laptop, and tried once more to crack the file she had downloaded from the N.S.A. But she did not even come close. August sat next to her, looking stiffly at the pile of paper and crayons Berger had left for him, no longer interested in prime numbers, still less in drawing pictures. Perhaps he was in shock.

The man who called himself Jan Holtser was sitting in a room at the Clarion Hotel Arlanda, talking on the telephone with his daughter. As he had expected, she did not believe him.

"Are you scared of me?" she said. "Are you afraid I'm going to cross-examine you?"

"No, Olga, absolutely not," he said. "It's just that . . ."

He could not find the words. He knew Olga could tell he was hiding something, and ended the conversation sooner than he wanted to. Bogdanov was sitting next to him on the hotel bed, swearing. He had been through Balder's computer at least a hundred times and found "fuck all", as he put it. "Not a single fucking thing!"

"I stole a computer with nothing on it," Holtser said.

"Right."

"So what was the professor using it for?"

"For something very important, clearly. I can see that a large file, presumably connected to other computers, was deleted recently. But I can't recover it. He knew his stuff, that guy."

"Useless," Holtser said.

"Completely fucking useless."

"And the Blackphone?"

"There are a couple of calls I haven't been able to trace, presumably from the Swedish security services or the N.D.R.E. But there's something bothering me much more."

"What's that?"

"A long conversation the professor had just before you stormed in – he was talking to someone at the M.I.R.I., Machine Intelligence Research Institute."

"What's the problem with that?"

⋯ was having some sort of crisis.

"That would be bad.

Bogdanov nodded and Holtser swore quietly. Nothing had gone as planned and neither of them was used to failing. But here were two major mistakes in a row, and all because of a child, a retarded child.

That was bad enough. But the worst of it was that Kira was on her way, and it sounded like she had lost it. Neither of them was used to that either. On the contrary, they had grown accustomed to her cool elegance, the air of invincibility it gave their operations. Now she was furious, completely off the wall, screaming at them that they were useless, incompetent cretins. It was not so much that those shots might have missed Balder's son. It was because of the woman who had appeared out of nowhere and rescued the boy. That woman sent Kira around the bend.

When Holtser had begun to describe her – the little he had seen – Kira bombarded him with questions. Whatever answer he gave seemed to be wrong, or at least sent her berserk, yelling that they should have killed her and that this was typical of them, brainless, useless. Neither of them could make sense of her violent reaction – they had never heard her yell like that before.

In fact there was a lot they did not know about her. Holtser would never forget his evening with her in a suite at Hotel d'Angleterre in Copenhagen – they had had sex for the third or fourth time, and later they had been lying in bed drinking champagne and chatting about his wars and his murders, as they so often did. While stroking her arm he had discovered three scars side by side on her wrist.

"How did you get those, gorgeous?" he had said, and got a look of pure loathing in return.

He had never been allowed to sleep with her again. He took it to be a punishment for having asked. Kira looked after the group and gave them a lot of money. But neither he nor Bogdanov, nor anyone else in the group, was allowed to ask about her past. That was one of the unspoken rules and none of them would ever dream of trying. For better or for worse she was their benefactor, mostly for better, they thought, and they went along with her whims, living in constant uncertainty as to whether she would be affectionate or cold, or even give them a brutal, stinging slap.

Bogdanov closed the computer and took a swallow of his drink. They were trying to limit their drinking, so that Kira would not use that against them. But it was nearly impossible. The frustration and adrenalin drove them to it. Holtser fingered his mobile nervously.

"Didn't Olga believe you?" Bogdanov said.

"Not a word. Soon she'll see a child's drawing of me on every billboard."

"I don't buy that drawing thing. Probably just wishful thinking on the part of the police."

"So we're supposed to kill a child for no reason?"

"It wouldn't surprise me. Shouldn't Kira be here by now?"

"Any time now."

"Who do you think it was?"

"Who?"

"The girl who appeared from nowhere."

"No idea," Holtser said. "Not sure Kira knows either. But she's worried about something."

"We'll probably end up having to kill them both."

"That might be the least of it."

. . . not feeling well. That was obvious. Red patches flared

and forth across the . . .

and a line there, followed by some small circles, buttons, Salander thought, then a hand, details of a chin, an unbuttoned shirt front. It began to go more quickly and the tension in the boy's back and shoulders subsided – as if a wound had burst open and begun to heal.

There was a searing, tortured look in his eyes, and every now and then he shivered. But there was no doubt that something within him had eased. He picked up some new crayons and started to draw an oak-coloured floor, on which appeared pieces of a puzzle that seemed to represent a glittering town at night-time. It was clear even from the unfinished drawing that it would be anything but a pleasant one.

The hand and the unbuttoned shirt front became part of a large man with a protruding belly. He was standing, bent like a jack-knife, beating a small person on the floor, a person who was not in the drawing for the simple reason that he was observing the scene, and on the receiving end of the blows.

It was an ugly scene, no doubt about that. But even though the picture revealed an assailant, it did not seem to have anything to do with the murder. Right in the middle, at the epicentre of the drawing, a furious, sweaty face appeared, every foul and bitter furrow captured with precision. Salander recognized it. She rarely watched T.V. or went to the cinema, but she knew it was the face of the actor Lasse Westman, the partner of August's mother. She leaned forward to the boy and said, with a holy, quivering rage:

"We'll never let him do that to you again. Never."

CHAPTER 21

23.xi

Even the most ~~~~~~

raise all hell if anyone tried to mess with him. Ingram did not like scenes, still less humiliation, and that was what awaited him if he picked a fight with Needham.

While Needham was brash and explosive, Ingram was a refined upper-class boy with spindly legs and an affected manner. Ingram was a serious power player and had influence where it mattered, be it in Washington or in the world of business. As a member of the N.S.A. management, he ranked just below Admiral Charles O'Connor. He might be quick to smile and adept at handing out compliments, but his smile never reached his eyes.

He had leverage over people and was in charge, among other things, of "monitoring strategic technologies" – more cynically known as industrial espionage, that part of the N.S.A. which gives the American tech industry a helping hand in global competition. He was feared as few others were.

But now as he stood in front of Needham in his fancy suit, his body seemed to shrink. Even from thirty metres away, Casales knew exactly what was about to happen: Needham was on the brink of exploding. His pale, exhausted face was going red. Without waiting he got to his feet, his back crooked and bent, his belly sticking out, and he roared in a furious voice, "You sleazy bastard!"

No-one but Needham could call Jonny Ingram a "sleazy bastard", and Casales loved him for it.

August started on a new drawing.

He sketched a few lines. He was pressing so hard on the paper that the black crayon broke and, just like the last time, he drew rapidly, one detail here and another one there, disparate bits which ultimately came together and formed a whole. It was the same room, but there was a different puzzle on the floor, easier to make out: it represented a red sports car racing by a sea of shouting spectators in a stand. Above the puzzle not one but two men could be seen standing.

One of them was Westman again. This time he was wearing a T-shirt and shorts and he had bloodshot, squinting eyes. He looked unsteady and drunk, but no less furious. He was drooling. Yet he was not the more frightening figure in the drawing. That was the other man, whose watery eyes shone with pure sadism. He too was unshaven and drunk, and he had thin, almost non-existent lips. He seemed to be kicking August, although again the boy could not be seen in the picture, his very absence making him extremely present.

"Who's the other one?" Salander said.

August said nothing. But his shoulders shook, and his legs twisted into a knot under the table.

"Who's the other one?" Salander said again, in a more forceful tone, and August wrote on the drawing in a shaky, childish hand:

ROGER

Roger – the name meant nothing to Salander.

A couple of hours later in Fort Meade, once his hacker boys had cleaned up after themselves and shuffled off, Needham walked over to Casales. The odd thing was, he no longer looked at all angry or upset. He was radiant with defiance and carrying a notebook. One of his braces had slipped off his shoulder.

"Hey, bud," she said. "Tell me, what's going on?"

"I got some vacation time." he said. "I'm off to Stockholm."

leaks. Then the whole thing gets swept under the carpet."

"How the hell can he lay down something like that?"

"They don't want to awaken any sleeping dogs, he says, and run the risk of anyone finding out about the attack. It would be devastating if it ever got out. Just think of all the malicious glee, and all the people whose heads would roll, starting with yours truly."

"He threatened *you*?"

"Did he ever! Went on about how I would be humiliated publicly, even sued."

"You don't seem worried."

"I'm going to break him."

"How? Our glamour boy has powerful connections everywhere, you know that."

"I have a few of my own. Besides, Ingram isn't the only one with dirt on people. That damn hacker was gracious enough to link and match our computer files and show us some of our own dirty laundry."

"That's a bit ironic, isn't it?"

"It takes a crook to know one. At first the data didn't look all that spectacular, not compared to the other stuff we're doing. But when we started to get into it . . ."

"Yes?"

"It turned out to be dynamite."

"In what way?"

"Ingram's closest colleagues not only *collect* trade secrets to help our own major companies. Sometimes they also *sell* the information for a lot of money. And that money, Alona, doesn't always find its way into the coffers of the organization . . ."

"But into their own pockets."

"Exactly. I already have enough evidence on that to put two of our top industrial-espionage executives behind bars."

"Jesus."

"Unfortunately it's less straightforward with Ingram. I'm convinced he's the brains behind the whole thing. Otherwise all of this doesn't add up. But I don't have a smoking gun, not yet, which makes the whole operation risky. There's always a chance – though I wouldn't bet on it – that the file the hacker downloaded has something specific on him. But it's impossible to crack – a goddamn R.S.A. encryption."

"So what are you going to do?"

"Tighten the net. Show the world that our very own co-workers are in cahoots with criminal organizations."

"Like the Spiders."

"Like the Spiders. And plenty of other bad guys. It wouldn't surprise me if they were involved in the killing of your professor in Stockholm. They had a clear interest in seeing him dead."

"You've got to be joking."

"I'm completely serious. Your professor knew things that could have blown up in their faces."

"Holy shit. And you're off to Stockholm like some private detective to investigate it all?"

"Not like a private detective, Alona. I'm going to be official, and while I'm there I'm going to give our hacker such a pummelling she won't be able to stand."

"Wait, Ed. Did I hear you say she?"

"You'd better believe it. Our hacker's a she!"

that it was loaded. She went onto the P.G.P. link. Andrei Zander was asking how they were, and she gave a short reply.

Outside, the storm was shaking the trees and bushes. She helped herself to some whiskey and a piece of chocolate, then went out onto the terrace and from there to the rock slope where she carefully reconnoitred the terrain, noticing a small cleft partway down. She counted her steps and memorized the lie of the land.

By the time she got back, August had made another drawing of Westman and the Roger person. She supposed he needed to get it out of his system. But still he had not drawn anything from the night of the murder. Perhaps the experience was blocked in his mind.

Salander was overcome by a feeling of time running away from them and she cast a worried look at August. For a minute or so she focused on the mind-boggling numbers he had put down on paper next to the new drawing. She studied their structure until suddenly she spotted a sequence which did not fit in with the others.

It was relatively short: 2305843008139952128. She got it immediately. It was not a prime number, it was – and here her spirits lifted – a number which, according to a perfect harmony, is made up of the sum of all its positive divisors. It was, in other words, a perfect number, just as 6 is because it can be divided by 3, 2 and 1 and 3 + 2 + 1 happen to add up to 6. She smiled. And then she had an exhilarating thought.

"Now you're going to have to explain yourself," Casales said.

"I will," Needham said. "But first, even though I trust you, I need you to give me a solemn promise that you won't say any of this to anybody."

"I promise, you jerk."

"Good. Here's the story: after I yelled at Ingram, mostly for the sake of appearances, I told him he was right. I even pretended to be grateful to him for putting a stop to our investigation. We wouldn't have gotten any further anyway, I said, and it was partly true. From a purely technical point of view we were out of options. We'd done everything and then some, but it was pointless. The hacker put red herrings all over the place and kept leading us into new mazes and labyrinths. One of my guys said that even if we got to the end, against all odds, we wouldn't believe we'd made it. We'd just kid ourselves that it was a new trap. We were prepared for just about anything from this hacker, anything but flaws and weaknesses. So if we kept going the usual way we'd had it."

"You don't tend to go the usual way."

"No, I prefer the roundabout way. The truth is, we hadn't given up at all. We'd been talking to our hacker contacts out there and our friends in the software companies. We did advanced searches, surveillance and our own computer breaches. You see, when an attack is as complex as this one, you can always be sure there's been some research up front. Certain specific questions have been asked. Certain specific sites have been visited and inevitably some of that becomes known to us. But there was one factor above all that played into our hands, Alona: the hacker's skill. It was so incredible that it limited the number of suspects. Like a criminal suddenly running a hundred metres in 9.7 seconds at a crime scene – you'd be pretty sure the guy is a certain Mr Bolt or one of his close rivals, right?"

"So it's at that level?"

like shooting in the dark – like calling out into the dead of night. Nobody knew anything, or they claimed they didn't. A few names were mentioned, but none of them felt right. For a while we chased down some Russian, a Jurij Bogdanov – an ex-druggie and thief who apparently can hack into anything he damn well likes. The security companies were already trying to recruit him when he was living on the street in St Petersburg, hot-wiring cars, weighing in at forty kilos of skin and bone. Even the people from the police and intelligence services wanted him on their side. They lost that battle, needless to say. These days Bogdanov looks clean and successful and has ballooned to sixty kilos of skin and bone, but we're pretty sure he's one of the crooks in your organization, Alona. That was another reason he interested us. There had to be a connection to the Spiders, because of the searches that got carried out, but then . . ."

"You couldn't understand why one of their own would be giving us new leads and associations?"

"Exactly, and so we looked further. After a while another outfit cropped up in the conversations."

"Which one?"

"They call themselves Hacker Republic. They have a big reputation out there. A bunch of talents at the top of their game and rigorous about their encryptions. And for good reason. We're constantly trying to infiltrate these groups, and we're not the only ones. We don't just want to find out what they're up to, we also want to recruit their people. These days there's big competition for the sharpest hackers."

"Now that we've all become criminals."

"Ha, yes, maybe. Whatever, Hacker Republic has major talent. Lots of the guys we talked to backed that up. And it wasn't just that. There were also rumours that they had something big going on, and then a hacker with the handle Bob the Dog, who we think is linked to the gang, was running searches and asking questions about one of our guys, Richard Fuller. Do you know him?"

"No."

"A manic-depressive self-righteous prick who's been bugging me for a while. The archetypal security risk, who gets arrogant and sloppy when he's in a manic phase. He's just the kind of person a bunch of hackers *should* be targeting, and you'd need classified information to know that. His mental-health issues aren't exactly common knowledge – his own mother hardly knows. But I'm pretty confident that in the end they didn't get in via Fuller. We've examined every file he's received recently and there's nothing there. We've scrutinized him from top to bottom. But I bet Fuller was part of Hacker Republic's original plan and then they changed strategy. I can't claim to have any hard evidence against them, not at all, but my gut feeling is still that these guys are behind the break-in."

"You said the hacker was a girl."

"Right. Once we'd homed in on this group we found out as much as possible about them. It wasn't easy to separate rumour from myth from fact. But one thing came up so often that in the end I saw no reason to question it."

"And what's that?"

"Hacker Republic's big star is someone who uses the alias Wasp."

"Wasp?"

"I won't bore you with technical details, but Wasp is something of a legend in certain circles, one of the reasons being her ability

"Without a doubt. So we started to search everything we could find about this Wasp, to try to crack the handle. No-one was particularly surprised when that didn't work. This person wouldn't leave openings. But you know what I did then?" Needham said proudly.

"Tell me."

"I looked up what the word stood for."

"Beyond its literal meaning, you mean?"

"Right, but not because I or anyone else thought it would get us anywhere. Like I said, if you can't get there on the main road, you take the side roads; you never know what you might find. It turns out Wasp could mean all sorts of things. Wasp stands for Women Airforce Service Pilots, is a comedy by Aristophanes, a famous short film from 1915, a satirical magazine from nineteenth-century San Francisco and there's also of course White Anglo-Saxon

Protestant, plus a whole lot more. But those references are all a little too sophisticated for a hacker genius; they don't go with the culture. But you know what did fit? The superhero in Marvel Comics: Wasp is one of the founding members of the Avengers."

"Like the movie?"

"Exactly, with Thor, Iron Man, Captain America. In the original comics she was even their leader for a while. I have to say, Wasp is a pretty badass superhero, kind of rock and roll, a rebel who wears black and yellow with insect's wings and short black hair. She's got attitude, the underdog who hits back and can grow or shrink. All the sources we've been talking to think that's the Wasp we're looking for. It doesn't necessarily mean the person behind the handle is some Marvel Comics geek. That handle has been around for a while, so maybe it's a childhood thing that stuck, or an attempt at irony. Like the fact that I named my cat Peter Pan even though I never liked that self-righteous asshole who doesn't want to grow up. Anyway . . ."

"Anyway?"

"I couldn't help noticing that this criminal network our Wasp was looking into also uses names from Marvel Comics. They sometimes call themselves the Spider Society, right?"

"Yes, but I think that's just a game, as I see it, thumbing their noses at those of us who monitor them."

"Sure, I get that, but even jokes can give you leads, or cover up something serious. Do you know what the Spider Society in the Marvel Comics does?"

"No."

"They wage war against the 'Sisterhood of the Wasp'."

"O.K., fine, it's an interesting detail, but I don't understand how that could be your lead."

"Just wait. Will you come downstairs with me to my car? I have to head to the airport quite soon."

*

It was not late, but Blomkvist knew that he could not keep going much longer. He had to go home and get a few hours' sleep and then start working again tonight or tomorrow morning. It might help too if he had a few beers on the way. The lack of sleep was pounding in his forehead and he needed to chase away a few memories and fears. Perhaps he could get Zander to join him. He looked over at his colleague.

Zander had youth and energy to spare. He was banging away at his keyboard as if he had just started work for the day, and every now and then he flicked excitedly through his notes. Yet he had been in the office since 5.00 in the morning. It was now 5.45 in

"I'll take that as a yes," Blomkvist said. "How about Folksoperan?"

Folksoperan was a bar and restaurant on Hornsgatan, not far away, which attracted journalists and the arty crowd.

"It's just that . . ."

"Just that what?"

"I've got this portrait to do, of an art dealer working at Bukowski's who got onto a train at Malmö Central and was never seen again. Erika thought it would fit into the mix," Zander said.

"Jesus, the things she makes you do, that woman."

"I honestly don't mind. But I'm having trouble pulling it together. It feels so messy and contrived."

"Do you want me to have a look at it?"

"I'd love that, but let me do some more work on it first. I would die of embarrassment if you saw it in its present state."

"In that case deal with it later. But come on now, Andrei, let's go and at least get something to eat. You can come back and work afterwards if you must," Blomkvist said. He looked over at Zander.

That memory would stay with him for a long time. Zander was wearing a brown checked jacket and a white shirt buttoned up all the way. He looked like a film star, at any rate even more like a young Antonio Banderas than usual.

"I think I'd better stay and keep plugging away," he said. "I have something in the fridge which I can microwave."

Blomkvist wondered if he should pull rank, order him to come out and have a beer. Instead he said:

"O.K., we'll see each other in the morning. How are they doing out there meanwhile? No drawing of the murderer yet?"

"Seems not."

"We'll have to find another solution tomorrow. Take care," Blomkvist said, getting up and putting on his overcoat.

Salander remembered something she had read about savants a long time ago in *Science* magazine. It was an article by Enrico Bombieri, an expert in number theory, referring to an episode in Oliver Sacks' *The Man Who Mistook His Wife for a Hat* in which a pair of autistic and mentally disabled twins recite staggeringly high prime numbers to each other, as if they could see them before their eyes in some sort of inner mathematical landscape.

What these twins were able to do and what Salander now wanted to achieve were two different things. But there was still a similarity, she thought, and decided to try, however sceptical she might be. So she brought up the encrypted N.S.A. file and her program for elliptic-curve factorization. Then she turned to August. He responded by rocking back and forth.

"Prime numbers. You like prime numbers," she said.

August did not look at her, or stop his rocking.

"I like them too. And there's one thing I'm particularly interested in just now. It's called factorization. Do you know what that is?"

August stared at the table as he continued rocking and did not look as if he understood anything at all.

"Prime-number factorization is when we rewrite a number as the product of prime numbers. By product in this context I mean the result of a multiplication. Do you follow me?"

August's expression did not change, and Salander wondered if she should just shut up.

"According to the fundamental principles of arithmetic, every

often impossible

prime numbers. A really bad person has used this to code a secret message. Do you understand? It's a bit like mixing a drink: easy to do but harder to unmix again."

August neither nodded nor said a word. But at least his body was no longer rocking.

"Shall we see if you're any good at prime-number factorization, August? Shall we?"

August did not budge.

"I'll take that as a yes. Shall we start with the number 456?"

August's eyes were bright but distant, and Salander had the feeling that this idea of hers really was absurd.

It was cold and windy and there were few people out. But Blomkvist thought the cold was doing him good – he was perking up a bit. He thought of his daughter Pernilla and what she said about writing "for real", and of Salander of course, and the boy. What were they doing right now?

On the way up towards Hornsgatspuckeln he stared for a while at a painting hanging in a gallery window which showed cheerful, carefree people at a cocktail party. At that moment it felt, perhaps wrongly, as if it had been ages since he had last stood like that, drink in hand and without a care in the world. Briefly he longed to be somewhere far away. Then he shivered, suddenly struck by the feeling that he was being followed. Perhaps it was a consequence of everything he had been through in the last few days. He turned round, but the only person near him was an enchantingly beautiful woman in a bright red coat with flowing dark-blonde hair. She smiled at him a little uncertainly. He gave her a tentative smile back and was about to continue on his way. Yet his gaze lingered, as if he were expecting the woman to turn at any moment into something more run of the mill.

Instead she became more dazzling with each passing second, almost like royalty, a star who had accidentally wandered in among ordinary people, a gorgeous spread in a fashion magazine. The fact was that right then, in that first moment of astonishment, Blomkvist would not have been able to describe her, or provide even one single detail about her appearance.

"Can I help you?" he said.

"No, no," she said, apparently shy, and there was no getting away from it: her hesitancy was beguiling. She was not a woman you would have thought to be shy. She looked as if she might own the world.

"Well then, have a nice evening," he said, and turned again, but he heard her nervously clear her throat.

"Aren't you Mikael Blomkvist?" she said, even more uncertain now, looking down at the cobbles in the street.

"Yes, I am," he said, and smiled politely, as he would have done for anybody.

"Well, I just want to say that I've always admired you," she said, raising her head and gazing into his eyes with a long look.

"I'm flattered. But it's been a long time since I wrote anything decent. Who are you?"

"My name is Rebecka Mattson," she said. "I've been living in Switzerland."

"And now you're home for a visit?"

"Only for a short time, unfortunately. I miss Sweden. I even miss November in Stockholm. But I guess that's how it is when you're homesick, isn't it?"

blue cashmere shawl,

Rebecka Mattson did not look like your typical *Millennium* reader. But there was no reason to be prejudiced, even against rich expatriate Swedes.

"Do you work there?" he said.

"I'm a widow."

"I see."

"Sometimes I get so bored. Were you going somewhere?"

"I was thinking of having a drink and a bite to eat," he said, at once regretting his reply. It was too inviting, too predictable. But it was at least true.

"May I keep you company?" she asked.

"That would be nice," he said, sounding unsure. Then she touched his hand – unintentionally, at least that is what he wanted to believe. She still seemed bashful. They walked slowly up Hornsgatspuckeln, past a row of galleries.

"How nice to be strolling here with you," she said.

"It's a bit unexpected."

"So true. It's not what I was thinking when I woke up this morning."

"What were you thinking?"

"That the day would be as dreary as ever."

"I don't know if I'll be such good company," he said. "I'm pretty much immersed in a story."

"Are you working too hard?"

"Maybe so."

"Then you need a little break," she said, giving him a bewitching smile, filled with longing or some sort of promise. At that moment he thought she seemed familiar, as if he had seen that smile before, but in another form, distorted somehow.

"Have we met before?" he said.

"I don't think so. Except that I've seen you a thousand times in pictures, and on T.V."

"So you've never lived in Stockholm?"

"When I was a little girl."

"Where did you live then?"

She pointed vaguely up Hornsgatan.

"Those were good times," she said. "Our father took care of us. I often think about him. I miss him."

"Is he no longer alive?"

"He died much too young."

"I'm sorry."

"Thank you. Where are we headed?"

"Well," he said, "there's a pub just up Bellmansgatan, the Bishops Arms. I know the owner. It's quite a nice place."

"I'm sure . . ."

Once again she had that diffident, shy look on her face, and once again her hand happened to brush against his fingers – this time he wasn't so sure it was accidental.

"Perhaps it isn't fancy enough?"

"Oh, I'm sure it's fine," she said apologetically. "It's just that people tend to stare at me. I've come across so many bastards in pubs."

"I can believe that."

"Wouldn't you . . .?"

"What?"

She looked down at the ground again and blushed. At first he thought he was seeing things. Surely adults don't blush like that? But Rebecka Mattson from Switzerland, who looked like seven
red like a little schoolgirl.

for a second he thought
happen after all, as if he were about to embark on an adventure.

But his uncertainty would not abate. At first he could not understand why. He did not normally have a problem with this kind of situation – he had more success than most when it came to women flirting with him. This particular encounter had developed very quickly, but he was not unused to that either. So it was something about the woman herself, wasn't it?

Not only was she young and exceptionally beautiful and should have had better things to do than chase after burned-out, middle-aged journalists. It was something in her expression, and in the way she switched between bold and shy, and the physical contact. Everything he had at first found spontaneous increasingly seemed to him to be affected.

"How lovely, and I won't stay long. I don't want to spoil your story," she said.

"I'll take full responsibility for any spoiled stories," he said, and tried to smile back.

It was a forced smile and in that instant he caught a strange twitch in her eyes, a sudden icy chill which in a second turned into its very opposite, full of affection and warmth, like an acting exercise. He became more convinced that there was something wrong. But he had no idea what, and did not want his suspicions to show, at least not yet. What was going on? He wanted to understand.

They continued on up Bellmansgatan – not that he was thinking of taking her back to his place any longer, but he needed time to figure her out. He looked at her again. She really was gorgeous. Yet it occurred to him that it was not her beauty which had first captivated him. It was something else, something more elusive. Just then he saw Rebecka Mattson as a riddle to which he ought to have the answer.

"A nice part of town, this," she said.

"It's not bad." He looked up towards the Bishops Arms.

Diagonally across from the pub, just a bit higher up by the crossroads with Tavastgatan, a scrawny, lanky man in a black cap was standing under a streetlight studying a map. A tourist. He had a brown suitcase in his other hand and white sneakers and a black leather jacket with its fur collar turned up, and under normal circumstances Blomkvist would not have given him a second glance.

But now he observed that the man's movements were nervous and unnatural. Perhaps Blomkvist was suspicious to begin with, but the distracted way he was handling the map seemed more and more contrived. Now he raised his head and stared straight at Blomkvist and the woman, studying them for a brief second. Then he looked down at his map again, seeming ill at ease, almost trying to hide his face under the cap. The bowed, almost timid head reminded Blomkvist of something, and again he looked into his companion's dark eyes.

His look was persistent and intense. She gazed at him with affection, but he did not reciprocate; instead he scrutinized her. Then her expression froze. Only in that moment did Blomkvist smile.

He smiled because suddenly the penny had dropped.

CHAPTER 22

23.xi, Evening

Salander got up from the table. She did not want to pester August any longer. The boy was under enough pressure as it was and her idea had been crazy from the start.

One always expects too much of these poor savants, and what August had done was already impressive. She went out onto the terrace again and gingerly felt the area around the bullet wound, which was still aching. She heard a sound behind her, a hasty scratching on paper, so she turned and went back inside. When she saw what August had written, she smiled:

$$2^3 \times 3 \times 19$$

She sat down and said, without looking at him this time, "O.K.! I'm impressed. But let's make this a little harder. Have a go at 18,206,927."

August was hunched over the table and Salander thought it might have been unkind to throw an eight-digit figure at him right away. But if they were to stand any chance of getting what she needed they would need to go much higher than that. She was not surprised to see August begin to sway nervously back and forth. But after a few seconds he leaned forward and wrote on his paper: 9419 × 1933.

"Good. How about 971,230,541?"

August wrote: 983 × 991 × 997.

"That's great," Salander said, and on they went.

Outside the black, cube-like office building in Fort Meade with its reflective glass walls, not far from the big radome with its dish aerials, Casales and Needham were standing in the packed car park. Needham was twirling his car keys and looking beyond the electric fence in the direction of the surrounding woods. He should be on his way to the airport, he said, he was late already. But Casales did not want to let him leave. She had her hand on his

"That's insane."

"A psychologist would have fun with it."

"This kind of fixation must run deep."

"I get the feeling it's real hatred," he said.

"You will look after yourself over there, won't you?"

"Don't forget I used to be in a gang."

"That's a long time ago, Ed, and many kilos ago too."

"It's not a question of weight. What is it they say? You can take the boy out of the ghetto . . ."

"Yes, yes."

"You can never get rid of it. Besides, I'll have help from the N.D.R.E. in Stockholm. They're itching as much as I am to put that hacker out of action once and for all."

"What if Ingram finds out?"

"That wouldn't be good. But, as you can imagine, I've been

preparing the ground a bit. Even exchanged a word or two with O'Connor."

"I figured as much. Is there anything I can do for you?"

"Yep."

"Shoot."

"Ingram's crew seems to have had full insight into the Swedish police investigation."

"They've been eavesdropping on the police?"

"Either that or they have a source, maybe an ambitious soul at Säpo. If I put you together with two of my best hackers, you could do some digging."

"Sounds risky."

"O.K., forget it."

"That wasn't a no."

"Thanks, Alona. I'll send info."

"Have a good trip," she said, as Needham smiled defiantly and got into his car.

Looking back, Blomkvist could not explain how he had worked it out. It might have been something in the Mattson woman's face, something unknown and yet familiar. The perfect harmony of that face might have reminded him of its very opposite, and that together with other hunches and misgivings gave him the answer. True, he was not yet absolutely sure of it. But he had no doubt that something was very wrong.

The man now walking off with his map and brown suitcase was the very figure he had seen on the security camera in Saltsjöbaden, and that coincidence was too improbable not to be of some significance, so Blomkvist stood there for a few seconds and thought. Then he turned to the woman who called herself Rebecka Mattson and tried to sound confident:

"Your friend is heading off."

"My friend?" she said, genuinely surprised. "What friend?"

"Him up there," he said, pointing at the man's skeletal back as he sauntered gawkily down Tavastgatan.

"Are you joking? I don't know anyone in Stockholm."

"What do you want from me?"

"I just want to get to know you, Mikael," she said, fingering her blouse, as if she might undo a button.

"Stop that!" he said roughly, and was about to lose his temper when she looked at him with such vulnerable, piteous eyes that he was thrown. For a moment he thought he had made a mistake.

"Are you cross with me?" she said, hurt.

had no time to stop her ....

and walked away up the hill on high heels, so resolutely self-assured that he wondered if he should stop her and fire some probing questions. But he could not imagine that anything would come of it. Instead he decided to tail her.

It was crazy, but he saw no alternative, so he let her disappear over the brow of the hill and then set off in pursuit. He hurried up to the crossroads, sure that she could not have gone far. But there was no sign of her, or of the man either. It was as if the city had swallowed them up. The street was empty, apart from a black B.M.W. backing into a parking space some way down the street, and a man with a goatee wearing an old-fashioned Afghan coat who came walking in his direction on the opposite pavement.

Where had they gone? There were no side streets for them to slip into, no alleys. Had they ducked into a doorway? He walked on down towards Torkel Knutssonsgatan, looking left and right.

Nothing. He passed what had been Samir's Cauldron, once a favourite local of his and Berger's; now called Tabbouli, it served Lebanese food. They might have stepped inside.

But he could not see how she would have had time to get there; he had been hot on her heels. Where the hell was she? Were she and the man standing somewhere nearby, watching him? Twice he spun around, certain that they were right behind him, and once he gave a start because of an icy feeling that someone was looking at him through a telescopic sight.

When eventually he gave up and wandered home it felt as though he had escaped a great danger. He had no idea how close to the truth that feeling was, yet his heart was beating fiercely and his throat was dry. He was not easily scared, but tonight he had been badly frightened by an empty street.

The only thing he did understand was who he needed to speak to. He had to get hold of Holger Palmgren, Salander's old guardian. But first he would do his civic duty. If the man he had seen was the person from Balder's security camera, and there was even a minimal chance that he could be found, the police had to be informed. So he rang Bublanski.

It was not at all easy to convince the chief inspector. It had not been easy to convince himself. But he still had some residual credibility to fall back on, however many liberties he had taken with the truth of late. Bublanski said that he would send out a unit.

"Why would he be in your part of town?"

"I have no idea, but it wouldn't hurt to see if you can find him, would it?"

"I suppose not."

"The best of luck to you in that case."

"It's damn unsatisfactory that the Balder boy is still out there somewhere," Bublanski said reproachfully.

"And it's damn unsatisfactory that there was a leak in your unit," Blomkvist said.

"We've identified *our* leak."

"You have? That's fantastic."

"It's not all that fantastic, I'm afraid. We believe there may have been several leaks, most of which did minimal damage except maybe for the last."

"Then you'll have to make sure you put a stop to it."

"We're doing all we can, but we're beginning to suspect . . ." And then he paused.

"What?"

"Nothing."

"O.K., you don't have to tell me."

Blomkvist crossed over Ringvägen and went down into the Tunnelbana. He took the red line towards Norsborg and got off at Liljeholmen, where for about a year Holger Palmgren had been living in a small, modern apartment. Palmgren had sounded alarmed when he heard Blomkvist's voice on the telephone. But as soon as he had been assured that Salander was in one piece – Blomkvist hoped he wasn't wrong about this – he made him feel welcome.

Palmgren was a lawyer, long retired, who had been Salander's guardian for many years, ever since the girl was thirteen and had been locked up in St Stefan's psychiatric clinic in Uppsala. He was elderly and not in the best of health, having suffered two strokes. For some time now he had been using a Zimmer frame, and had trouble getting around even so. The left side of his face drooped and his left hand no longer functioned. But his mind was clear and his long-term memory was outstanding – especially on Salander.

No-one knew Lisbeth Salander as he did. Palmgren had succeeded where all the psychiatrists and psychologists had failed, or perhaps had not wanted to succeed. After a childhood from hell, when the girl had lost faith in all adults and in all authority, Palmgren had won her confidence and persuaded her to open up. Blomkvist saw it as a minor miracle. Salander was every therapist's nightmare, but she had told Palmgren about the most painful parts of her childhood. That was why Blomkvist now keyed in the front-door code at Liljeholmstorget 96, took the lift to the fifth floor and rang the doorbell.

"My dear old friend," Holger said in the doorway, "it's so wonderful to see you. But you're looking pale."

"I haven't been sleeping well."

"Not surprising, when people are shooting at you. I read about it in the paper. A dreadful story."

"Appalling."

"Have there been any developments?"

"I'll tell you all about it," Blomkvist said, sitting on a yellow sofa with its back to the balcony, waiting for Palmgren to settle with difficulty into a wheelchair next to him.

Blomkvist ran through the story in broad outline. When he came to the point of his sudden inspiration, or suspicion, on the cobblestones in Bellmansgatan, he was interrupted:

"What are you saying?"

"I think it was Camilla."

Palmgren looked stunned. "*That* Camilla?"

"The very same."

"Jesus," Palmgren said. "What happened?"

"She vanished. But afterwards I felt as if my brain were on fire."

"I can well understand. I was sure Camilla had disappeared off the face of the earth."

"And I had almost forgotten that there were two of them."

"There were two of them alright, very much so: twin sisters who loathed each other."

"I remember that," Blomkvist said. "But I need to be reminded of as much as you can tell me, to fill the gaps in the story as I know it. I've been asking myself why on earth Salander got involved in this story. Why would she, the superhacker, take an interest in a simple data breach?"

"Well, you know the background, don't you? The mother, Agneta Salander, was a cashier at Konsum Zinken and lived with

ndagatan. They might have had quite a

time and his visits

assaulted and raped Agneta while the girls sat in the next room and heard everything. One day Lisbeth found her mother unconscious on the floor."

"And that was the first time she took revenge?"

"The second time. The first was when she stabbed Zalachenko several times in the shoulder."

"But now she firebombed his car."

"Yes. Zalachenko burned like a torch. Lisbeth was committed to St Stefan's psychiatric clinic."

"And her mother was admitted to Äppelviken nursing home."

"For Lisbeth that was the most painful part of the story. Her mother was then twenty-nine, and she was never herself again. She survived at the nursing home for fourteen years, with severe brain injuries and suffering a great deal of pain. Often she could not communicate at all. Lisbeth went to see her as frequently as she could, and I know she dreamed that her mother would one day recover so they could talk again and look after each other. But it never happened. That if anything is the darkest corner of Lisbeth's life. She saw her mother wither away and eventually die."

"It's terrible. But I've never understood Camilla's part in the story."

"That's more complicated, and in some ways I think one has to forgive the girl. After all, she too was only a child, and before she was even aware of it she became a pawn in the game."

"In what way?"

"They chose opposite camps in the battle, you could say. It's true that the girls are fraternal twins and not alike in appearance, but they also have completely different temperaments. Lisbeth was born first, Camilla twenty minutes later. She was apparently a joy to behold, even when she was tiny. While Lisbeth was an angry creature, Camilla had everyone exclaiming, 'Oh, what a sweet girl!' and it can't have been a coincidence that Zalachenko showed more forbearance towards her from the start. I say forbearance because obviously it was never a question of anything kinder in those first years. Since Agneta was no more than a whore to him, it followed that her children were bastards with no claim on his affections, little wretches who just got in the way. And yet . . ."

"Yes?"

"And yet even Zalachenko noticed that one of the children was beautiful. Sometimes Lisbeth would say there was a genetic defect in her family and, even though it's doubtful that her claim would stand up to medical scrutiny, it cannot be denied that Zala fathered some exceptional children. You came across their half-brother, Ronald Niedermann, didn't you? He was blond, enormous and had congenital analgesia, the inability to feel pain, so was therefore an ideal hit man and murderer, while Camilla . . . well, in her case the genetic abnormality was quite simply that she was astoundingly, ridiculously lovely to look at, and that just got worse as she grew older. I say worse because I'm pretty sure that it was a misfortune. The effect may have been exaggerated by the fact that her twin sister always looked sour. Grown-ups were liable to frown when they saw her. But then they would notice Camilla, and light up and go soft in the head. Can you imagine what an effect that must have had on her?"

"It must have been tough to get passed over."

"I wasn't thinking of Lisbeth, and I don't remember seeing any evidence that she resented the situation. If it had just been a ques-

her beam again. Camilla learned early on to exploit that. She became expert at it, a mistress of manipulation. She had large, expressive doe eyes."

"She still does."

"Lisbeth told me how Camilla would sit for hours in front of the mirror, practising her look. Her eyes were a fantastic weapon. They could both bewitch you and freeze you out, make children and adults alike feel special one day and rejected the next. It was an evil gift and, as you might guess, she soon became very popular at school. Everyone wanted to be with her and she took advantage of it in every conceivable way. She made sure that her classmates gave her small presents daily: marbles, sweets, small change, pearls, brooches. And those who didn't, or generally didn't behave as she wanted, she wouldn't even look at the next day. Anyone who had ever found themselves basking in her radiance knew how painful that was. Her classmates did everything they could to be in her good graces. They fawned over her. With one exception, of course."

"Her sister."

"That's right, and so Camilla turned them against Lisbeth. She got some fierce bullying going – they pushed Lisbeth's head into the toilet and called her a freak and a weirdo and all sorts of names. This went on until one day they found out who they were picking on. But that's another story, and one you're familiar with."

"Lisbeth doesn't turn the other cheek."

"No indeed. But the interesting thing in this story from a psychological point of view is that Camilla learned how to dominate and manipulate her surroundings from an early age. She worked out how to control everybody, apart from two significant people in her life, Lisbeth and her father, and that exasperated her. She put a vast amount of energy into winning those fights as well, and she needed totally different strategies for each of them. She could never win Lisbeth over, and pretty soon I think she gave up. In her eyes, Lisbeth was simply strange, just a surly, stroppy girl. Her father, on the other hand . . ."

"He was evil through and through."

"He was evil, but he was also the family's centre of gravity. He was the one around whom everything revolved, even if he was rarely there. He was the absent father. In a normal family such a figure can take on a quasi-mystical status for a child, but in this case it was much more than that."

"In what way?"

"I suppose I mean that Camilla and Zalachenko were an unfortunate combination. Although Camilla hardly understood it herself, she was only interested in one thing, even then: power. And her father, well, you can say many things about him, but he was not short of power. Plenty of people can testify to that, not least that wretched lot at Säpo. No matter how firmly they tried to put their foot down, they still ended up huddled like a flock of frightened sheep when they came eyeball to eyeball with him. There was an ugly, imposing self-assurance about Zalachenko which was merely amplified by the fact that he was untouchable. It made no difference how many times he was reported to the social welfare agency – the Security Police always protected him. This is what persuaded Lisbeth to take matters into her own hands. But for Camilla, things were completely different."

"She wanted to be like him."

"Yes, I think so. Her father was her ideal – she wanted the same

even as a little girl she often said that she despised weak people.

"She despised her mother too, do you think?"

"Unfortunately I think you're right. Lisbeth once told me something which I've never been able to forget."

"What's that?"

"I've never told anyone."

"Isn't it about time then?"

"Well, maybe, but in that case I need a strong drink. How about a good brandy?"

"That wouldn't be such a bad idea. But you stay right where you are, I'll get some glasses and the bottle," Blomkvist said, going to the mahogany drinks cabinet in the corner by the kitchen door.

He was digging around among the bottles when his iPhone rang. It was Zander, or at least his name was on the display. But when Blomkvist answered no-one was there; it must have been a

CHAPTER 23

23.xi, Evening

what was happening. Her mind

realized she was not going to get any further by this route either. It was hardly surprising – how could August succeed where super-computers had failed? Her expectations had been absurdly high from the start and what he had achieved was impressive enough. But still she felt disappointed.

She went out into the darkness to survey the barren, untamed landscape around her. Below the steep rock slope lay the beach and a snow-covered field with a deserted dance pavilion.

On a lovely summer's day the place was probably teeming with people. Now it was empty. The boats had been pulled up on land and there was not a sign of life; no lights were shining in the houses on the other side of the water. Salander liked it. At least she liked it as a hiding place at the end of November.

If someone arrived by car she was unlikely to pick up the sound of the engine. The only possible place to park was down by the beach, and to get to the house you had to climb up the wooden steps over the steep rock slope. Under the cover of darkness, someone might be able to sneak up on them. But she would sleep tonight. She needed it. Her wound was still giving her pain – maybe that was why she had got her hopes up about August, against the odds. But when she went back into the house, she realized that there was something else besides.

"Normally Lisbeth isn't someone who bothers about the weather or what's going on beyond her immediate focus," Palmgren said. "She blocks out everything she considers unimportant. But on this occasion she did mention that the sun was shining on Lundagatan and in Skinnarviksparken. She could hear children laughing. On the other side of the windowpane people were happy – perhaps that was what she was trying to say. She wanted to point out the contrast. Ordinary people were having ice cream and playing with kites and balls. Camilla and Lisbeth sat locked in their bedroom and could hear their father assaulting their mother. I believe this was just before Lisbeth took her revenge on Zalachenko, but I'm not sure about the sequence of events. There were many rapes, and they followed the same pattern. Zala would appear in the afternoon or evening, very drunk. Sometimes he would ruffle Camilla's hair and say things like, 'How can such a pretty girl have such a loathsome sister?' Then he would lock his daughters into their room and settle down in the kitchen to have more to drink. He drank his vodka neat, and often he would sit quietly at first, smacking his lips like a hungry animal. Then he would mumble something like, 'And how's my little whore today?' – sounding almost affectionate. But Agneta would do something wrong, or rather Zalachenko would decide that she had done something wrong, and then the first blow came, usually a slap followed by, 'I thought my little whore was going to behave herself today.' Then he would shove her into the bedroom and beat her. After a while slaps would turn to punches. Lisbeth could tell from the sounds. She could tell exactly what sort of blows they were, and even where they landed. She felt it as clearly as if she herself were the victim of this savagery. After the punches came the kicks. Zala kicked and shoved her mother against the wall and shouted 'bitch' and 'tramp' and 'whore', and that aroused him. He was turned on by her suffering. Only when Agneta was black and blue and bleeding did he rape her, and when he climaxed he would yell even fouler insults. Then it would be quiet for a while. All that could be heard was Agneta's choked sobbing and Zala's own heavy breathing. Then he would get up

"The girls' bedroom was quite small. However hard they tried to get away from each other, the beds were still close and, while the abuse went on, each one usually sat on her own mattress, facing the other. They hardly ever said anything, and usually avoided eye contact. On this day Lisbeth was staring through the window at Lundagatan – that's probably why she talked about the sunlight and the children out there. But then she looked at her sister, and that's when she saw it."

"She saw what?"

"Camilla's right hand, beating against her mattress. It could have been a sign of nervous or compulsive behaviour. That's what Lisbeth thought at first. But then she noticed that the hand was beating in time to the blows from the bedroom, and at that she looked up at Camilla's face. Her sister's eyes were glowing with excitement, and the eeriest thing was: Camilla looked just like

347

Zala himself and she was smiling. She was suppressing a smirk, and in that instant Lisbeth realized that Camilla was not only trying to ingratiate herself with her father. She was also right behind his violence. She was cheering him on."

"That's sick."

"But that's how it was. Do you know what Lisbeth did? She remained perfectly calm. She sat down next to Camilla and took her hand almost tenderly. Perhaps Camilla thought her sister was looking for some comfort or closeness. Stranger things have happened. Then Lisbeth rolled up her sister's shirt sleeve and dug her fingernails into Camilla's wrist – down to the bone – gouging open a terrible wound. Blood streamed onto the bed. Lisbeth dragged Camilla to the floor and swore she would kill both her and her father if the beatings and the rapes did not stop."

"Jesus!"

"You can imagine the hatred between the sisters. Both Agneta and the social services were so worried that something even more serious would happen that they were kept apart. For a while they arranged a home elsewhere for Camilla. But sooner or later they would have clashed again. In the end, as you know, things did not turn out like that. I believe the sisters only saw each other once after Lisbeth was locked up – several years later, when a disaster was narrowly averted – but I know none of the details. I haven't heard anything of Camilla for a long time now. The last people to have had contact with her are the foster family with whom she lived in Uppsala, people called Dahlgren. I can get you the number. But ever since Camilla was eighteen or nineteen and she packed a bag and left the country she hasn't been heard from. That's why I was astonished when you said that you had met her. Not even Lisbeth, with her famous ability to track people down, has been able to find her."

"So she *has* tried?"

"Oh yes. As far as I know, the last time was when her father's estate was to be apportioned."

"I had no idea."

"Lisbeth mentioned it in passing. She didn't want a single penny from that will – to her it was blood money – but she could tell that there was something strange about it. There were assets of four million kronor: the farm in Gosseberga, some securities and also a run-down industrial site in Norrtälje, a cottage somewhere, and various other bits and pieces. Not insignificant by any means, and yet . . ."

". . . worth much more."

his death was torture to her.

"Camilla had obviously concealed her new identity well."

"I assume so."

"Do you have any reason to think Camilla might have taken over her father's trafficking business?"

"Maybe, maybe not. She may have struck out into something altogether different."

"Such as?"

Palmgren closed his eyes and took a long sip of his brandy.

"I can't be sure of this, Mikael. But when you told me about Professor Balder, I had a thought. Do you have any idea why Lisbeth is so good with computers? Do you know how it all started?"

"I have no idea."

"Then I'll tell you. I wonder if the key to your story doesn't lie there."

*

When Salander came in from the terrace and saw August huddled in a stiff and unnatural position by the round table, she realized that the boy reminded her of herself as a child.

That is exactly how she had felt at Lundagatan, until one day it became clear to her that she had to grow up far too soon, to take revenge on her father. It was a burden no child should have to bear. But it had at least been the beginning of a real life, a more dignified life. No bastard should be allowed to do what Zalachenko had done with impunity. She went to August and said solemnly, as if giving an important order, "You're going to go to bed now. When you wake up I want you to do the drawing that will nail your father's killer. Do you get that?" The boy nodded and shuffled into his bedroom while Salander opened her laptop and started to look for information about Lasse Westman and his circle of friends.

"I don't think Zalachenko himself was much use with computers," Palmgren said. "He wasn't of that generation. But perhaps his dirty business grew to such a scale that he had to use a computer program to keep his accounts, and to keep them away from his accomplices. One day he came to Lundagatan with an I.B.M. machine which he installed on the desk next to the window. Nobody in the family had seen a computer before. Zalachenko promised that if anyone so much as touched the machine he would flay them alive. For all I know that was telling, from a purely psychological point of view. It increased the temptation."

"Forbidden fruit."

"Lisbeth was around eleven at the time. It was before she tore into Camilla's right arm, and before she went for her father with knives and petrol bombs. You could say it was just before she became the Lisbeth we know today. She lacked stimulation. She had no friends to speak of, partly because Camilla had made sure that nobody came anywhere near her at school, but partly because she really was different. I don't know if she realized it herself yet. Her teachers and those around her didn't. But she was an extremely gifted child. Her talent alone set her apart. School was deadly boring for her. Everything was obvious and easy. She needed only to take a quick look at things to understand them, and during lessons she sat there daydreaming. I do believe, however, that by then she had managed to find some things in her free time which interested her – advanced maths books, that sort of thing. But basically she was bored stiff. She spent a lot of time reading her Marvel comics, which were way below her intellectual level but

~~~~~~~~~ ther therapeutic function."

of reading material. Perhaps

white view of the world, helped her to gain some clarity.

"You mean that she understood she had to grow up and become a superhero herself."

"In some way, maybe, in her own little world. At the time she didn't know that Zalachenko had been a Soviet spy, and that his secrets had given him a unique position in Swedish society. She can have had no idea either that there was a special section within Säpo which protected him. But like Camilla she sensed that her father had some sort of immunity. One day a man in a grey overcoat appeared at the apartment and hinted that their father must come to no harm. Lisbeth realized early on that there was no point in reporting Zalachenko to the police or the social services. That would only result in yet another man in a grey overcoat turning up on their doorstep.

"Powerlessness, Mikael, can be a devastating force, and before

Lisbeth was old enough to do something about it she needed a place of strength, a refuge. She found that in the world of super-heroes. I know better than most how important literature can be, whether it's comic books or fine old novels, and I know that Lisbeth grew particularly attached to a young heroine called Janet van Dyne."

"Van Dyne?"

"That's right, a girl whose father was a rich scientist. The father is murdered – by aliens, if I remember right – and in order to take her revenge Janet van Dyne gets in touch with one of her father's old colleagues, and in his laboratory acquires superpowers. She becomes the Wasp, someone you can't push around, either liter-ally or figuratively."

"I didn't know that. So that's where she gets her handle from?"

"Not just the handle. I knew nothing about all that sort of stuff, obviously – I was an old dinosaur who got the Phantom mixed up with Mandrake the Magician – but the first time I saw a picture of the Wasp, it gave me a start. There was so much of Lisbeth in her. There still is, in a way. I think she picked up a lot of her style from that character. I don't want to make too much of it, but I do know she thought a great deal about the transfor-mation Janet van Dyne underwent when she became the Wasp. Somehow she understood that she herself had to undergo the same drastic metamorphosis: from child and victim to someone who could fight back against a highly trained and ruthless intel-ligence agent.

"Thoughts like these occupied her day and night and so the Wasp became an important figure for her during her period of transition, a source of inspiration. And Camilla found out about it. That girl had an uncanny ability to nose out other people's weaknesses – she used her tentacles to feel for their sensitive points and would then strike exactly there. So she came to make fun of the Wasp in whichever way she could. She even found out who her Marvel enemies were and began to call herself by their names, Thanos and all the others."

"Did you say Thanos?" Blomkvist said, suddenly alert.

"I think that's what he was called, a destroyer who once fell in love with Death itself. Death had appeared to him in the shape of a woman, and after that he wanted to prove himself worthy of her, or something like that. Camilla became a fan of his so as to provoke Lisbeth. She even called her gang of friends the Spider Society – in one of the comics that group are the sworn enemies of the Sisterhood of the Wasp."

"Really?" Blomkvist said, his mind racing.

feeling that he had lit upon something important.

"I don't know," Palmgren said. "They're grown women now, but we mustn't forget that those were decisive times in their lives, when everything changed. Looking back, it's perfectly possible that small details could turn out to be of fateful significance. It wasn't just that Lisbeth lost a mother and was then locked up. Camilla's existence too was smashed to pieces. She lost her home, and the father she admired suffered severe burns. As you know, after the petrol bomb Zalachenko was never himself again. Camilla was put in a foster home miles from the world whose undisputed leading light she had been. It must have been bitterly hurtful for her too. I don't for one second doubt that she's hated Lisbeth with a murderous fury ever since."

"It certainly looks like it," Blomkvist said.

Palmgren took another sip of brandy. "The sisters were already effectively in a state of out-and-out war, and somehow I think they both knew that everything was about to blow up to change their lives for ever. I think they were even preparing for it."

"But in different ways."

"Oh yes. Lisbeth had a brilliant mind, and infernal plans and strategies were constantly ticking away in her head. But she was alone. Camilla was not so bright, not in the conventional sense – she never had a head for studies, and was incapable of understanding abstract reasoning – but she knew how to manipulate people to do her bidding, so, unlike Lisbeth, she was never alone. If Camilla ever discovered that Lisbeth was good at something which could be a threat to her, she never tried to acquire the same skill, for the simple reason she knew she couldn't compete with her sister."

"So what did she do instead?"

"Instead she would track down somebody – or better still more than one person – who could do whatever it was, and strike back with their help. She always had minions. But forgive me, I'm getting ahead of myself."

"Yes, tell me what happened with Zalachenko's computer?"

"Lisbeth was short of stimulation, as I said. And she would lie awake at night, worrying about her mother. Agneta bled badly after the rapes, but wouldn't go to a doctor. She probably felt ashamed. Periodically she sank into deep depressions and no longer had the strength to go to work or look after the girls. Camilla despised her even more. 'Mamma is weak,' she'd say. As I told you, in her world, to be weak was worse than anything else. Lisbeth, on the other hand, saw a person she loved – the only person she had ever loved – fall victim to a dreadful injustice. She was a child in so many ways, but she was also becoming convinced that she was the only person in the world who could save her mother from being beaten to death. So she got up in the middle of one night – carefully, of course, so as not to wake Camilla – and saw the computer on the desk by the window overlooking Lundagatan.

"At that time she didn't even know how to switch on a computer. But she worked it out. The computer seemed to be whispering to her: 'Unlock my secrets.' She didn't get far, not at first. A password was needed. Since her father was known as Zala, she tried that, and Zala666 and similar combinations, and everything else she could think of. But nothing worked. I believe this went on for two or three nights, and if she slept at all then it was at school or at home in the afternoon.

"Then one night she remembered something her father had

describe it as a moment which changed her for ever. She thrived once she overcame that barrier. She explored what was intended to stay hidden."

"And Zalachenko never knew of this?"

"It seems not, and she understood nothing at first. It was all in Russian. There were various lists, and some numbers – accounts of the revenues from his trafficking operations. To this day I have no idea how much she worked out then and how much she found out later. She came to understand that her mother was not the only one made to suffer by her father. He was destroying other women's lives too, and that made her wild with rage. That is what turned her into the Lisbeth we know today, the one who hates men who . . ."

". . . hate women."

"Precisely. But it also made her stronger. She saw that there

355

was no turning back – she had to stop her father. She went on with her searches on other computers, including at school, where she would sneak into the staffroom, and sometimes she pretended to be sleeping over with the friends she didn't have while in fact she stayed overnight at school and sat at the computers until morning. She started to learn everything about hacking and programming, and I imagine that it was the same as when other child prodigies discover their niche – she was in thrall. She felt that she was born for this. Many of her contacts in the digital world began to take an interest in her even then, the way the older generation has always engaged with younger talents, whether to encourage or crush them. Many people out there were irritated by her unorthodox ways, her completely new approach. But others were impressed, and she made friends, including Plague – you know about him. She got her first real friends by way of the computer and above all, for the first time in her life, she felt free. She could fly through cyberspace, just like the Wasp. There was nothing to tie her down."

"Did Camilla realize how accomplished she'd become?"

"She certainly had her suspicions. I don't know, I really don't want to speculate, but sometimes I think of Camilla as Lisbeth's dark side, her shadow figure."

"The evil twin."

"A bit, though I don't like to call people evil, especially not young women. If you want to dig into it yourself I suggest you get in touch with Margareta Dahlgren, Camilla's foster mother after the havoc at Lundagatan. Margareta lives in Stockholm now, in Solna, I think. She's a widow and has had a desperately sad life."

"In what way?"

"Well, that may also be of interest. Her husband Kjell, a computer programmer at Ericsson, hanged himself a short time before Camilla left them. A year later their nineteen-year-old daughter also committed suicide by jumping from a Finland ferry

– at least that's what the inquest concluded. The girl had emotional problems – she struggled with her self-esteem – but Margareta never believed that version, and she even hired a private detective. Margareta is obsessed by Camilla, and to be honest I've always had a bit of a problem with her, I'm embarrassed to say. Margareta got in touch with me straight after you published your Zalachenko story. As you know, that's when I had just been discharged from the rehabilitation clinic. I was mentally and physically at the end of my tether and Margareta talked endlessly. She was fixated. The sight of her number on my telephone display would exhaust me, and I went to some efforts to avoid her. But now when I think

stood up and embraced Palmgren.

Out on Liljeholmstorget the storm tore into him again. He pulled his coat close around him and thought of Salander and her sister, and for some reason also of Andrei Zander.

He decided to call him to find out how he was getting on with his story on the art dealer. But Zander never picked up.

CHAPTER 24

23.xi, Evening

Zander had called Blomkvist because he had changed his mind. Of course he wanted to go out for a beer. How could he not have taken him up on the offer? Blomkvist was his idol and the very reason he had gone in for journalism. But once he dialled the number he felt embarrassed and hung up. Maybe Blomkvist had found something better to do. Zander did not like disturbing people unnecessarily, and least of all Blomkvist.

Instead he worked on. But however hard he tried, he got nowhere. The words just would not come out right and after about an hour he decided to take a walk, and so he tidied his desk and checked once again that he had deleted every word on the encrypted link. Then he said goodbye to Emil Grandén, the only other person left in the office.

Grandén was thirty-six and had worked at both T.V.4's "Cold Facts" and *Svenska Morgon-Posten*. Last year he had been awarded the Stora Journalist prize for Investigative Reporter of the Year. But Zander thought – even though he tried not to – that Grandén was conceited and overbearing, at least towards a young temp like him.

"Going out for a bit," Zander said.

Grandén looked at him as if there was something he had forgotten to say. Then he uttered in a bored tone, "O.K."

Zander felt miserable. It may only have been Grandén's arrogant attitude, but it was more likely because of the article about the art dealer. Why was he finding it so difficult? Presumably because all he wanted to do was help Blomkvist with the Balder story. Everything else felt secondary. But he was also spineless, wasn't he? Why had he not let Blomkvist take a look at what he had written?

No-one could raise the level of a story like Blomkvist could, with just a few light pen strokes or deletions. Never mind. Tomorrow he would see the story with fresh eyes and then Blomkvist could read it, however bad it might be. Zander closed

to run away ...

human being in danger, and so he rushed down the stairs yelling, "Stop, let her go!"

At first that seemed like a fatal mistake – the hollow-eyed man pulled out a knife and muttered some threat in English. Zander's legs nearly gave way, yet he managed to muster the last remnants of his courage and spat back, like something from a B-movie, "Hey, get lost! If you don't, you'll regret it." After a few seconds of posturing, the man took off with his tail between his legs. Zander and the woman were left alone in the stairwell, and that too was like a scene from a film.

At first the woman was shaken and shy. She spoke so softly that Zander had to lean in close to hear what she was saying, and it took a while before he understood what had happened. The woman had been living in a marriage from hell, she said, and even though she was now divorced and living with a protected identity her ex-husband had managed to track her down and send some stooge to harass her.

"That's the second time that foul man has thrown himself at me today," she said.

"Why were you up here?"

"I tried to get away and ran in, but it didn't help. I can't thank you enough."

"It was nothing."

"I'm so fed up with nasty men," she said.

"I'm a nice man," he said, perhaps a little too quickly, and that made him feel pathetic. He was not in the least bit surprised that the woman did not answer but looked down at the stairs in embarrassment.

He felt ashamed of such a cheap reply. But then, just as he thought he had been rejected, she raised her head and gave him a careful smile.

"I think you really might be. My name's Linda."

"I'm Andrei."

"Nice to meet you, Andrei, and thank you again."

"Thank you too."

"What for?"

"For . . ."

He didn't finish his sentence. He could feel his heart beating, his mouth was dry. He looked down the staircase.

"Yes, Andrei?" she said.

"Would you like me to walk you home?"

He regretted saying that too.

He was afraid it would be misinterpreted. But instead she gave him another of her enchanting, hesitant smiles, and said that she would feel safe with him by her side, so they went out into the street and down towards Slussen. She told him how she had been living more or less locked up in a big house in Djursholm. He said that he understood – he had written a series of articles on violence against women.

"Are you a journalist?" she said.

"I work at *Millennium*."

"Wow," she said. "Is that for real? I'm a huge fan of that magazine."

"It's done a lot of good things," he said shyly.

"It really has," she said. "A while ago I read a wonderful article about an Iraqi who had been wounded in the war and got sacked from his job as a cleaner at some restaurant in the city. He was left completely destitute. Today he's the owner of a whole chain

Millennium...

Blomkvist, and Zander did not object to that. But secretly he dreamed of recognition for himself too, and now this beautiful Linda had praised him without even meaning to.

It made him so happy and proud that he plucked up the courage to suggest a drink at Papagallo, since they were just passing. To his delight she said, "What a good idea!" so they went into the restaurant, Zander's heart pounding. He tried to avoid looking into her eyes.

Those eyes had knocked him off his feet and he could not believe this was really happening. They sat down at a table not far from the bar and Linda tentatively put out her hand. As he took it he smiled and mumbled something, hardly aware of what he was saying.

He looked down at his mobile – Grandén was calling. To his

own surprise he ignored it and turned off his ringer. For once the magazine would have to wait. He just wanted to gaze into Linda's face, to drown in it. She was so beautiful that it felt like a punch to the stomach, yet she seemed so fragile, like a wounded bird.

"I can't imagine why anyone would want to hurt you," he said.

"It happens all the time."

Perhaps he could understand it after all. A woman like her probably attracted psychopaths. No-one else would dare ask her out. Most men would just shrivel up and feel inferior.

"It's so nice to be sitting here with you," he said.

"It's so nice to be sitting here with *you*," she retorted, gently stroking his hand. They each ordered a glass of red wine and started to talk, they had so much to say, and he didn't notice his mobile vibrating in his pocket, not once but twice, which is how he came to ignore a call from Blomkvist for the first time in his life.

Soon afterwards she took his hand and led him out into the night. He did not ask where they were going. He was prepared to follow her anywhere. She was the most wonderful creature he had ever met, and from time to time she gave him a smile that made every paving stone, every breath, sound out a promise that something wonderful and overwhelming was happening. *You live an entire life for the sake of a walk like this*, he thought, barely noticing the cold and the city around him.

He was intoxicated by her company and what might await him. But maybe – he wasn't sure – there was a hint of suspicion too. At first he dismissed these thoughts, his usual scepticism at any form of happiness. And yet he could not help asking himself: *Is this too good to be true?*

He studied Linda with a new focus, and noticed that not everything about her was attractive. As they walked past Katarinahissen he even thought he noticed something hard in her eyes. He looked anxiously down at the choppy waters. "Where are we going?"

"I have a friend with a small apartment in Mårten Trotzigs gränd," she said. "She lets me use it sometimes. We could have another drink there." That made him smile as if it were the most wonderful idea he had ever heard.

Yet he felt more and more confused. Not long ago he had been looking after her, and now she had taken the initiative. When a quick glance at his mobile told him that Blomkvist had rung twice, he felt he had to call back immediately. Come what may, he could

... magazine down.

... I'm in

not want to be...

and the statue of Evert Taube. The troubadour was standing there immobile, holding a sheet of music in his right hand, looking up at the sky in dark glasses. Should he suggest that they meet the following day?

"Maybe—" he started.

He got no further, because she pulled him to her and kissed him with a force which emptied his mind. Then she stepped up the pace again. She held his hand and pulled him to the left into Västerlånggatan, then right into a dark alley. Was that someone behind them? No, no, the footsteps and voices he could hear came from further away. It was just him and Linda, wasn't it? They passed a window with a red frame and black shutters and came to a grey door which Linda had some trouble opening. The key was shaking in her hand and he wondered at that. Was she still afraid of her ex-husband and his goon?

They climbed a dark stone stairway. Their footsteps echoed and there was a faint smell of something rotten. On one of the steps past the third floor he saw a playing card, the queen of spades, and he did not like that, but he could not understand why, it was probably some silly superstition. He tried to ignore it, and think about how great it was that they had met. Linda was breathing heavily. Her right hand was clenched. A man's laughter could be heard in the alley. Not laughing at him, surely? He was just agitated. But it felt as if they were climbing and climbing and not getting anywhere. Could the house really be so tall? No, here they were. The friend lived in the attic apartment.

The name on the door was Orlov and again Linda took out her bunch of keys. This time her hand was not shaking.

Blomkvist was sitting in an apartment with old-fashioned furniture on Prostvägen in Solna, next to a large churchyard. Just as Palmgren had anticipated, Margareta Dahlgren agreed to see him at once, and even though she had sounded manic over the telephone she turned out to be an elegant lady in her sixties. She was wearing a fashionable fawn jumper and neatly pressed black trousers. Perhaps she had had time to dress up for him. She was in high-heeled shoes and had it not been for her restless eyes he would have thought her to be a woman at peace with herself, despite everything.

"You want to hear about Camilla," she said.

"Especially about her life more recently – if you know anything about it," he said.

"I remember when she came to us," she said, as if she had not been listening. "My husband Kjell thought we could make a contribution to society at the same time as adding to our little family. We had only one child, you see, our poor Moa. She was fourteen then, and quite lonely. We thought it would do her good if we took in a foster daughter of roughly the same age."

"Did you know what had happened in the Salander family?"

"We didn't have all the details, but we knew that it had been awful and traumatic and the mother was sick and the father had suffered serious burns. We were deeply moved and were expecting to meet a girl who had fallen apart, someone who would need an incredible amount of care and affection. But do you know what arrived?"

"Tell me."

"The most adorable girl we'd ever seen. It wasn't just that she was pretty. My goodness, you should have heard her talk. She was so wise and mature, and she told such heart-rending stories about

whole family lit up, as if something glamorous had come into our lives and made everything bigger and more beautiful, and we blossomed. And Moa blossomed most of all. She began to take care of her appearance, and quite soon she became more popular at school. There was nothing I wouldn't have done for Camilla right then. And Kjell, my husband, what can I say? He was a new person. He was smiling and laughing all the time, and we began to make love again, if you'll forgive my being so frank. Perhaps I should have started to worry even then. But it felt like everything had finally fallen into place for our family. For a while we were all happy, as everybody is who meets Camilla. They're happy to start with. Then . . . after some time with her you don't want to live any more."

"Is it as bad as that?"

"It's horrific."

"So what happened?"

"A poison began to spread among us. Camilla slowly took control of our family. Looking back, it's impossible to say when the party ended and the nightmare began. It had happened so gradually and imperceptibly that we woke up one day and realized everything was ruined: our trust, our sense of security, the very foundations of our life together. Moa's self-confidence plummeted. She lay awake at night weeping, saying she was ugly and horrible and didn't deserve to live. Only later did we find out that her savings account had been cleaned out. I still don't know how that happened. But I'm convinced Camilla blackmailed her. Blackmail came as naturally to her as breathing. She collected compromising information on people. For a long time I thought she was keeping a diary, but actually it was a catalogue of all the dirt she'd collected about people close to her. And Kjell . . . the bastard . . . you know, I believed him when he said that he'd started having problems sleeping and needed to use the bed in the basement guest room. But that was an excuse to be with Camilla. Starting when she was sixteen, she would sneak in there at night and have perverted sex with him. I say perverted because I got wind of what was going on when I asked about the cuts on Kjell's chest. He didn't say anything then, of course. Just gave me some unconvincing explanation and somehow I managed to suppress my suspicions. But do you know what they did? In the end Kjell came clean: Camilla tied him up and cut him with a knife. He said she enjoyed it. Sometimes I even hoped it was true, strange though that may sound, but I hoped that she got something out of it and didn't only want to torture him, to destroy his life."

"Did she blackmail him too?"

"Oh yes, but I don't have the full story. He was so humiliated by Camilla that he wasn't willing to tell me the truth, even when all was lost. Kjell had been the rock in our family. If we lost our way while out driving, if there was a flood, if any of us fell ill, he was the calm, sensible one. 'It'll all be alright,' he would say in his wonderful voice – I still fantasize about it. But after a few years with Camilla in the house he was a wreck. Hardly dared to cross the road, looked a hundred times to make sure it was safe. And he lost all motivation at work, he just sat with his head hanging. One of his closest colleagues, Mats Hedlund, rang and told me in confidence that an inquiry had been set up to investigate whether Kjell had been selling company secrets. It sounded crazy. Kjell was the most honest man I've ever known. Plus if he'd sold anything, where was the money? We had less than ever. His bank account was stripped bare, same with our joint account."

You want to know what happened to Camilla. But there was no end to the misery. Moa started cutting herself and practically stopped eating. One day she asked me if I thought she was scum. 'My God, darling,' I replied, 'how can you say something like that?' Then she told me it was Camilla. That Camilla had claimed every single person who had ever met Moa thought she was repulsive. I sought all the help I could: psychologists, doctors, wise friends, Prozac. But to no avail. One gloriously beautiful spring day, when the rest of Sweden was celebrating some ridiculous triumph in the Eurovision Song Contest, Moa jumped from a ferry, and my life ended with hers – that's how it felt. I no longer had the will to live and spent a long time in hospital being treated for depression. But then . . . I don't know . . . somehow the paralysis and grief turned to rage, and I felt that I needed to understand. What had actually happened to our family? What sort of evil had seeped in? I started to make enquiries about Camilla, not because I wanted to see her again, not under any circumstances. But I wanted to understand her, the same way a parent of a murder victim wants to understand the murderer."

"What did you discover?"

"Nothing to begin with. She had covered her tracks – it was like chasing a shadow, a phantom. I don't know how many tens of thousands of kronor I spent on private detectives and other unreliable people who promised to help me. I was getting nowhere, and it was driving me crazy. I became fixated. I hardly slept, and none of my friends could bear to be with me any more. It was a terrible time. People thought I was being obsessive and stubborn, maybe they still do – I don't know what Holger Palmgren told you. But then . . ."

"Go on."

"Your story on Zalachenko was published. Naturally the name meant nothing to me, but I started to put two and two together. I read about his Swedish identity, Karl Axel Bodin, and about his connection with Svavelsjö Motorcycle Club, and then I remembered all the dreadful evenings towards the end, after Camilla had turned her back on us. At the time I was often woken up by the noise of motorbikes, and I could see those leather waistcoats with that awful emblem from my bedroom window. It didn't surprise me that she mixed with those sorts of people. I no longer had any illusions about her. But I had no idea that this was the world she came from – and that she was expecting to take over her father's business interests."

"And did she?"

"Oh yes. In her own dirty world she fought for the rights of women – at least for her own rights – and I know that it meant a lot to many of the girls in the club, most of all to Kajsa Falk."

"Who was she?"

"A sassy, lovely-looking girl, her boyfriend was one of the

leaders. She spent a lot of time at our home during that last year, and I remember liking her. She had big blue eyes with a slight squint, and a compassionate, vulnerable side behind her tough exterior. After reading your story I looked her up again. She didn't say a word about Camilla, though she was by no means unpleasant. I noticed that her style had changed: the biker girl had become a businesswoman. But she didn't talk about it. I thought I'd hit another dead end."

"But it wasn't?"

"No. About a year ago Kajsa looked me up of her own accord, _____ _____ _____ changed again. There was nothing reserved _____ _____ _____ Not

majority of the assets _____ _____ _____ Berlin, and some to Camilla. She inherited part of the _____ business you wrote about in your report, and that made my heart bleed. I doubt Camilla cared about those women, or felt any sort of compassion for them. But still, she didn't want to have anything to do with those activities. She said to Kajsa that only losers bother with that sort of filth. She had a completely different, modern vision of what the organization should be doing, and after hard negotiation she got one of her half-brothers to buy her out. Then she disappeared to Moscow with her capital and some of the employees who wanted to follow her, Kajsa Falk among them."

"Do you know what sort of business she was setting up?"

"Kajsa never got enough of an insight to understand it, but we had our suspicions. I think it was to do with those trade secrets at Ericsson. By now I'm almost certain Camilla really did get Kjell to steal and sell on something valuable, presumably by black-mailing him. I've also found out that in her first years with us she asked some computer geeks at school to hack into my computer. According to Kajsa, she was more or less obsessed with hacking. Not that she learned anything about it herself, not at all, but she was forever talking about the money one could make by accessing bank accounts and hacking servers and stealing information. She must have developed a business along those lines."

"That sounds very possible."

"It was probably at a very high level. Camilla would never settle for anything less. According to Kajsa, she soon found her way into influential circles in Moscow, and among other things became the mistress of some rich, powerful member of the Duma, and with him she began to forge connections with a strange crew of top engineers and criminals. She wound them round her little finger, and she knew exactly where the weak point in the domestic economy was."

"And what was that?"

"The fact that Russia is little more than a petrol station with a flag on top. They export oil and natural gas, but manufacture nothing worth mentioning. Russia needs advanced technology."

"She wanted to give them that?"

"That, at least, is what she pretended. But obviously she had her own agenda. I know that Kajsa was impressed by the way she built alliances with people and got herself political protection. She probably would have been loyal to Camilla for ever if she hadn't become scared."

"What was she scared of?"

"Kajsa got to know a former elite soldier – a major, I believe – and just lost her bearings. According to confidential information that Camilla had access to via her lover, the man had carried out a few shady operations for the Russian government. Among other things he had killed a well-known journalist, I presume you've heard of her, Irina Azarova. She'd taken a line against the government in various reports and books."

"Oh yes, truly a heroine. A horrible story."

"Absolutely. Something went wrong in the planning. Azarova was supposed to meet a critic of the regime in an apartment on a backstreet in a suburb south-east of Moscow, and according to the plan the major was supposed to shoot her as she came out. But no-one knew that the journalist's sister had developed pneumonia, and Irina had to look after two nieces aged eight and ten. As she and the girls walked out of the front entrance the major shot all three of them in the face. After that he fell into disgrace

evicted from his apartment. From Camilla's perspective that was a perfect set-up: a ruthless person whom she could use, and who found himself in a vulnerable situation."

"So she got him on board."

"Yes, they met. Kajsa was there too, and the strange thing was that she immediately took a liking to this man. He wasn't at all what she'd been expecting, nothing like the people she knew at Svavelsjö M.C., who were also killers. The man was very fit, very strong, and had a brutal look about him, but he was also cultivated and polite, she said, somehow vulnerable and sensitive. Kajsa could tell that he felt really terrible about shooting those children. He was a murderer, a man whose speciality had been torture during the war in Chechnya, but he still had his moral boundaries, she said, and that's why she was so upset when Camilla got her claws into him – almost literally. She dragged her nails across his

371

chest and hissed like a cat, 'I want you to kill for me.' Her words were charged with sexual tension, and with the skill of the devil she awakened the man's sadism. The more gruesome his descriptions of his murders, the more excited she became. I'm not sure I understood it all, but it scared Kajsa to death. Not the murderer himself, but Camilla. Her beauty and allure managed to bring out the predator in him."

"You never reported this to the police?"

"I asked Kajsa over and over. I told her she needed protection. She said she already had it and she forbade me to talk to the police. I was stupid enough to listen to her. After her death I told the investigators what I'd heard, but I doubt they believed me – presumably not. It was nothing but hearsay about a man without a name in another country. Camilla was nowhere to be found in any records, and I never discovered anything about her new identity. And certainly poor Kajsa's murder is still unsolved."

"I do understand how painful this must still be," Blomkvist said.

"You do?"

"I think so," he said, and was about to rest a sympathetic hand on her arm.

He was brought up short by his mobile buzzing in his pocket. He hoped it was Zander. But it was Stefan Molde. It took Blomkvist a few seconds to identify him as the person at the N.D.R.E. who had been in touch with Linus Brandell.

"What's this about?" he said.

"A meeting with a senior civil servant who's on his way to Sweden. He wants to see you as early as possible tomorrow morning at the Grand Hôtel."

Blomkvist made an apologetic gesture in Fru Dahlgren's direction.

"I have a tight schedule," he said, "So if I'm to meet anybody, at the very least I want a name and an explanation."

"The man's name is Edwin Needham, and it's about someone using the handle Wasp, who is suspected of serious crimes."

Blomkvist felt a wave of panic. "O.K.," he said. "What time?"

"Five o'clock tomorrow morning would work."

"You've got to be joking!"

"Regrettably there's nothing to joke about in all this. I suggest that you're punctual. Mr Needham will see you in his room. You'll have to leave your mobile at reception, and you'll be searched."

Blomkvist got to his feet and took his leave of Margareta Dahlgren.

PART III

ASYMMETRIC PROBLEMS

24.xi – 3.xii

numbers have become secrecy's best friends.

CHAPTER 25

24.xi, Early Morning

biology who was said these days to have distanced himself altogether from Roger.

Salander wrote down Roger Winter's address and then hacked into the supercomputer N.S.F. M.R.I. She also opened the program with which she was trying to construct a dynamic system for finding the elliptic curves which were most likely to do the job, and with as few iterations as possible. But whatever she tried, she was unable to get any closer to a solution. The N.S.A. file remained impenetrable. In the end she went and looked in on August. She swore. The boy was awake, sitting up in bed writing something on a piece of paper, and as she came closer she could see that he was doing more prime-number factorizations.

"It's no good. It's not getting us anywhere," she muttered, and when August began to rock to and fro hysterically once again she told him to pull himself together and go back to sleep.

It was late and she decided that she too should rest for a while. She took the bed next to his, but it was impossible to sleep. August tossed and turned and whimpered, and in the end Salander decided to say something, to try to settle him. The best she could think of was, "Do you know about elliptic curves?"

Of course she got no answer. That did not deter her from giving as simple and clear an explanation as she could.

"Do you get it?" she said.

August did not reply.

"O.K., then," she went on. "Take the number 3,034,267, for example. I know you can easily find its prime-number factors. But it can also be done using elliptic curves. Let's for example take curve $y^2 = x^3 - x + 4$ and point P = (1.2) on that curve."

She wrote the equation on a piece of paper on the bedside table. But August did not seem to be following at all. She thought about those autistic twins she had read up on. They had some mysterious way of identifying large prime numbers, yet could not solve the simplest equations. Perhaps August was like that too. Perhaps he was more of a calculating machine than a genuine mathematical talent, and in any case it didn't matter right now. Her bullet wound was aching again and she needed some sleep. She needed to drive out all her old childhood demons, which had come to life again because of the boy.

It was past midnight by the time Blomkvist got home and, even though he was exhausted and had to get up at the crack of dawn, he sat down at his computer and Googled Edwin Needham. There were quite a few Edwin Needhams in the world, including a successful rugby player who had made an extraordinary comeback having had leukaemia.

There was one Edwin Needham who seemed to be an expert on water purification, and another who was good at getting himself into society photographs and looking daft. But none of them seemed right for someone who could have been involved in cracking Wasp's identity and accusing her of criminal activity. There was an Edwin Needham who was a computer engineer with a Ph.D. from M.I.T., and that was at least the right line of business, but not even he seemed to fit. He was now a senior executive at Safeline, a leading business in computer virus protection, and that company would certainly have an interest in hackers. But the statements made by this Ed, as he was known, were all about market share and new products. Nothing he said rated higher than the usual clichéd sales talk, not even when he got the chance to talk about his leisure pursuits: bowling and fly fishing. He loved

the whole point. He read through the material again and this time it struck him as something concocted, a facade. Slowly but surely he came to the opposite conclusion: this was the man. You could smell the intelligence services a mile off, couldn't you? It felt like N.S.A. or C.I.A. Once again he looked at the photograph with the salmon, and this time he thought he saw something very different.

He saw a tough guy putting on an act. There was something unwavering about the way he stood and his mocking grin into the camera, at least that is what Blomkvist imagined, and again he thought of Salander. He wondered if he ought to tell her about this meeting. But there was no reason to worry her now, especially since he did not actually know anything, so instead he decided to go to bed. He needed to sleep for a few hours and have a clear head when he met Needham in the morning. As he slowly brushed his teeth and undressed and climbed into bed, he realized he was more tired than he could have imagined and fell asleep in no time. He dreamed that he was being dragged under and almost drowned in the river Needham had been standing in. Afterwards he had a vague image of himself crawling along the riverbed surrounded by flopping, thrashing salmon. But he cannot have slept for long. He woke with a start and the growing conviction that he had overlooked something. His mobile was lying on the bedside table and his thoughts turned to Zander. The young man must have been on his mind all along.

Linda had double-locked the door. There was nothing odd about that – a woman in her situation had to take all possible precautions. It still made Zander feel uncomfortable, but he put that down to the apartment, or so he tried to convince himself. It was not at all what he had been expecting. Could this really be the home of one of her girlfriends?

The bed was broad but not especially long, and both the headboard and the footboard were made of shiny steel latticework. The bedspread was black, which made him think of a bier, and he disliked the pictures on the walls – mostly framed photographs of men with weapons. There was a sterile, chilly feel to the whole place.

On the other hand he was probably just nervous and exaggerating everything, or looking for an excuse to get away. A man always wants to escape the thing he loves – hadn't Oscar Wilde said something like that? He looked at Linda. Never before had he seen such an extraordinarily beautiful woman, and now she was coming towards him in her tight blue dress which accentuated her figure. As if she had been reading his mind she said, "Would you rather go home, Andrei?"

"I do have quite a lot on my plate."

"I understand," she said, kissing him. "Then you must of course go and get on with your work."

"Maybe that would be best," he muttered as she pressed herself against him, kissing him with such force that he had no defence.

He responded to her kiss and put his hands on her hips, and she gave him a shove. She pushed him so hard that he staggered and fell backwards onto the bed, and for a moment he was scared. But then he looked at her. She was smiling as tenderly now as before and he thought: this was nothing more than a bit of rough play. She really wanted him, didn't she? She wanted to make love with him there and then, and he let her straddle his body, unbutton his shirt, and draw her fingernails over his stomach while her eyes

"Close your eyes and lie absolutely still," she said.

He obeyed and could hear her fiddling with something, he was not sure what. Then heard a click and felt metal around his wrists, and realized he had been handcuffed. He was about to protest, he did not really go in for that sort of thing, but it all happened so fast. With lightning speed, as if she had done it many times, she locked his hands to the headboard. Then she bound his feet with rope and pulled tight.

"Gently," he said.

"Don't worry," but then she gave him a look he did not like and said something in a solemn voice. He must have misheard. "*What?*" he said.

"I'm going to cut you with a knife, Andrei," she said, and fixed a broad piece of tape across his mouth.

*

381

Blomkvist was trying to tell himself not to worry. Why would anything have happened to Zander? No-one – apart from Berger and himself – knew that he was involved in protecting the whereabouts of Salander and the boy. They had been extremely careful with that piece of information, more careful than with any other part of the story. And yet . . . why had there been no word from him?

Zander was not someone who ignored his mobile. On the contrary, he normally picked up on the first ring whenever Blomkvist called. But now there was no way of getting hold of him, and that was strange, wasn't it? Or maybe . . . again Blomkvist tried to convince himself that Zander was busy working and had lost track of time, or in the worst case had dropped his mobile. That was probably all it was. But still . . . after all these years Camilla had appeared out of nowhere. Something must be going on, and what was it Bublanski had said?

"We live in a world in which paranoia is a requirement."

Blomkvist reached for the telephone on the bedside table and called Zander again. He got no answer this time either, so decided to wake their new staff member, Emil Grandén, who lived near Zander in the Röda bergen area of Vasastan. Grandén sounded less than enthusiastic but promised to go over to Zander's right away to see if he was there. Twenty minutes later he rang back. He had been banging on Zander's door for a while, he said, and he definitely wasn't at home.

Blomkvist got dressed and left his apartment, hurrying through a deserted and storm-lashed Södermalm district up to the magazine offices on Götgatan. With any luck, he thought, Zander would be lying asleep on the sofa. It would not be the first time he had nodded off at work and not heard the telephone. That would be the simple explanation. But Blomkvist felt more and more uneasy. When he opened the door and turned off the alarm he shivered, as if expecting to find a scene of devastation, but after a search of the premises he found no trace of anything untoward. All the information on his encrypted email program had been carefully deleted, just as they had agreed. It all looked as it should, but there was no Zander lying on the office sofa, which was looking as shabby and empty as ever. For a short while Blomkvist sat there, lost in thought. Then he rang Grandén again.

"Emil," he said, "I'm sorry to harass you like this in the middle of the night. But this whole story has made me paranoid."

"I can understand that."

"I couldn't help hearing that you sounded a bit stressed when I was talking about Andrei. Is there anything you haven't told

at the other end of the line become laboured. There had been a terrible mistake.

"Out with it, Emil, and fast," he said.

"So . . ."

"Yes?"

"I had a call from a Lina Robertsson at the Data Inspection Authority. She said that you'd spoken and she agreed to raise the level of security on your computer, given the circumstances. Apparently the recommendations she'd given you were wrong and she was worried the protection would be insufficient. She said she wanted to get hold of the person who'd arranged the encryption for you asap."

"And what did you say?"

"That I knew nothing about it, except that I'd seen Andrei doing something at your computer."

"So you said she should get in touch with Andrei."

"I happened to be out at the time and told her that Andrei was probably still in the office. She could ring him there, I said. That was all."

"Jesus, Emil."

"But she sounded really—"

"I don't care how she sounded. I just hope you told Andrei about the call."

"Maybe not right away. I'm pretty snowed under at the moment, like all of us."

"But you told him later."

"Well, he left the office before I got a chance to say anything."

"So you called him instead."

"Absolutely, several times. But . . ."

"Yes?"

"He didn't answer."

"O.K.," Blomkvist said, his voice ice cold.

He hung up and dialled Bublanski's number. He had to try twice before the chief inspector came to the telephone. Blomkvist had no choice but to tell him the whole story – without discussing Salander and August's location.

Then he called Berger.

Salander had fallen asleep, but she was still ready for action. She was still in her clothes, with her leather jacket and her boots on. She kept waking up, either because of the howling storm or because August was moaning, even in his sleep. But each time she dropped off again, or at least dozed, and had short, strangely realistic dreams.

Now she was dreaming about her father beating her mother, and even then she could feel that old, fierce rage from her childhood. She felt it so keenly that it woke her up again. It was 3.45 and those scraps of paper on which she and August had written their numbers were still lying on the bedside table. Outside, snow was falling. But the storm seemed to have calmed and nothing unusual could be heard, just the wind howling and rustling through the trees.

Yet she felt uneasy, and at first she thought it was the dream lying like a fine mesh over the room. Then she shuddered. The bed next to her was empty – August was gone. She shot out of bed without making a sound, grabbed her Beretta from the bag on the floor and crept into the large room next to the terrace.

The next moment she breathed a sigh of relief. August was sitting at the table, busy with something. Without wanting to

and the bandage and inspected the bullet wound. It didn't look good, and she still felt weak. She swallowed another couple of antibiotic pills and tried to rest. She might even have gone back to sleep for a few moments. She was aware of a vague sensation that she had seen both Zala and Camilla in her dream, and the next second she became aware of a presence, though she had no idea what. A bird flapped its wings outside. She could hear August's laboured breathing in the kitchen. She was just about to get up when a scream pierced the air.

By the time Blomkvist left the office in the early morning hours to take a taxi to the Grand Hôtel, he still had no news of Zander. He tried again to persuade himself that he had been overreacting, that any moment now his colleague would be calling from some friend's place. But the worry would not go away. He was vaguely aware that it had started snowing again, and that a woman's shoe had been left lying on the pavement. He took out his Samsung and called Salander on the Redphone app.

Salander did not pick up, and that did not make him any calmer. He tried once more and sent a text from the Threema app: <Camilla's after you. Leave now!> Then he caught sight of a taxi coming down from Hökens gata and noticed the driver give a start when he saw him. At that moment Blomkvist looked dangerously determined. It did not help that he failed to respond to the driver's attempts to chat. He just sat back in the darkness, his eyes bright with worry.

Stockholm was more or less deserted. The storm had abated but there were still white-crested waves on the water. Blomkvist looked across to the Grand Hôtel on the other side and wondered if he should forget about the meeting with Mr Needham and drive straight out to Salander instead, or at least arrange for a police car to go there. No, he couldn't do that without warning her. Another leak would be disastrous. He opened the Threema app again and tapped in:

<Shall I get help?>

No answer. Of course there was no answer. He paid the fare and climbed out of the taxi, lost in thought. By the time he was pushing through the revolving doors of the hotel it was 4.20 in the morning – he was forty minutes early. He had never been forty minutes early for anything. But he was burning inside and, before going to the reception desk to hand in his mobiles, he called Berger. He told her to try to get hold of Salander and to keep in touch with the police.

"If you hear anything, call the Grand Hôtel and ask for Mr Needham's room."

"And who's he?"

"Someone who wants to meet me."

"At this time?"

*

Needham was in room 654. The door opened and there stood a man reeking of sweat and rage. There was about as much resemblance to the figure in the fishing photograph as there would be between a hungover dictator and his stylized statue. Needham had a drink in his hand and looked grim, dishevelled and a little bit like a bulldog.

"Mr Needham," Blomkvist said.

"Ed," Needham said. "I'm sorry to haul you over here at this ungodly hour, but it's urgent."

"So it would seem," Blomkvist said drily.

"D̶o̶ ̶y̶o̶u̶ ̶h̶a̶v̶e̶ any idea what I want to talk to you about?"

taste in my mouth . . .

sion, aren't you?"

Blomkvist gave a forced smile. "Can we just get to the point?" he said.

"Just relax. I'll be crystal clear. I assume you know where I work."

"Not exactly," he said truthfully.

"In Puzzle Palace, SIG.INT. City. I work for the world's spittoon."

"The N.S.A."

"Damn right. Do you have any idea how fucking insane you have to be to mess with us, Mikael Blomkvist? Do you?"

"I have a pretty good idea," he said.

"And do you know where I think your girlfriend really belongs?"

"No."

"She belongs behind bars. For life!"

Blomkvist gave what he hoped was a calm, composed little smile. But in fact his mind was spinning. Did Salander hack the N.S.A.? The mere thought terrified him. Not only was she in hiding, with killers on the hunt for her. Was she also going to have the entire U.S. intelligence shock troops descend on her? It sounded . . . well, how did it sound? It sounded totally off the wall.

One of Salander's abiding characteristics was that she never did anything without first carefully analyzing the potential consequences. She did not follow impulses or whims and therefore he could not imagine she would take such an idiotic risk if there was the slightest chance of being found out. Sometimes she put herself in danger, that was true, but there was always a balance between costs and benefits. He refused to believe that she had got herself into the N.S.A.'s systems, only to allow herself to be outwitted by the splenetic bulldog standing in front of him.

"I think you're jumping to conclusions," he said.

"Dream on, dude. But you heard me use the word 'really' just then. Some word, hey? Can be used in all sorts of ways. I don't really drink in the mornings, and yet here I am with a glass in my hand, ha ha! What I'm trying to say is that you might be able to save your girlfriend's skin if you promise to help me with one or two things."

"I'm listening," he said.

"Peachy. Let me begin by asking for a guarantee that you'll not quote me as your source."

Blomkvist looked at him in surprise. He had not expected that.

"Are you some kind of whistleblower?"

"God help me, no. I'm a loyal old bloodhound."

"But you're not acting officially on behalf of the N.S.A."

"You could say that right now I have my own agenda. Sort of doing my own thing. Well, how about it?"

"I won't quote you."

"Great. I also want to make sure we agree that what I'm going to tell you now will stay between us. You might be wondering why the hell I'm telling a fantastic story to an investigative journalist, only to have him keep his trap shut."

"Good question."

"I have my reasons. And I trust you – don't ask me why. I'm betting that you want to protect your girlfriend, and you think the real story is elsewhere. Maybe I'll even help you with that, if you're prepared to cooperate."

"That remains to be seen," Blomkvist said stiffly.

"Well, a few days ago we had a data breach on our intranet, our NSANet. You know about that, don't you?"

cables and that's also where we have our big databases and store classified analyses and reports – from Moray-rated documents, the least sensitive, all the way up to Umbra Ultra Top Secret, which even the President of the United States isn't allowed to see. The system is run out of Texas, which by the way is idiotic. But it's still my baby. Let me tell you, Mikael, I worked my ass off to create it. Hammered away at it day and night so that no fucker could misuse it, never mind hack it. Every single little anomaly sets alarm bells ringing, plus there's a whole staff of independent experts monitoring the system. These days you can't do a goddamn thing on the web without leaving footprints. At least that's the theory. Everything is logged and analyzed. You shouldn't be able to touch a single key without it triggering a notification. But . . ."

"Somebody did."

"Yes, and maybe I could have made my peace with it. There are always weak spots, we can always do better. Weak spots keep us on our toes. But it wasn't just the fact that she managed to get in. It was how she did it. She forced our server and created an advanced bridge, and got into the intranet via one of our systems administrators. That alone was a damn masterpiece. But that wasn't all, not by a long chalk: then the bitch turned herself into a ghost user."

"A what?"

"A ghost. She flew around in there without anyone noticing."

"And your alarm bells didn't go off?"

"That damn genius introduced a Trojan unlike anything else we knew, because otherwise our system would have identified it right away. The malware then kept upgrading her status. She got more and more access and soaked up highly classified passwords and codes and started to link and match records and databases, and suddenly – bingo!"

"Bingo what?"

"She found what she was looking for, and then she stopped wanting to be invisible – now she wanted to show us what she'd found, and only then did my alarm bells go off: exactly when she wanted them to."

"And what did she find?"

"She found our hypocrisy, Mikael, our double-dealing, and that's why I'm sitting here with you and not on my fat ass in Maryland, sending the Marines after her. She was like a thief breaking into a house just to point out that it was already full of stolen goods, and the minute we found that out she became truly dangerous – so dangerous that some of our senior people wanted to let her off."

"But not you."

"Not me. I wanted to tie her to a lamp post and flay her alive. But I had no choice except to give up my pursuit, and that, Mikael, seriously pissed me off. I may look calm now, but you should have seen me . . . Jesus!"

"You were hopping mad."

"Damn right I was, and that's why I've had you come here at this godforsaken hour. I need to get hold of Wasp before she flees the country."

"Why would she run?"

"Because she's gone from one crazy thing to the next, hasn't she?"

"I don't know."

"I think you do."

"And what makes you think she's your hacker in the first

been given

Swede muttered a confused apology and ran out of the room. But Needham would not let him get away that easily, and so he grabbed his coat and chased after him.

Blomkvist was racing down the corridor like a sprinter. Needham did not know what was going on, but if it had something to do with the Wasp/Balder story, he wanted to be there. He had some trouble keeping up – the journalist was in too much of a hurry to wait for the lift and instead hurtled down the stairs. By the time Needham reached the ground floor, panting, Blomkvist had already retrieved his mobiles and was engrossed in another conversation while he ran on towards the revolving doors and out into the street.

"What's happening?" Needham said as the journalist ended his call and was trying to hail a taxi on the street.

"Problems!" Blomkvist said.

"I can drive you."

"Like hell you can. You've been drinking."

"At least we can take my car."

Blomkvist slowed his pace and turned to Needham.

"What is it you want?"

"I want us to help each other."

"You'll have to catch your hacker on your own."

"I no longer have the authority to catch anybody."

"O.K., so where's the car?"

As they ran to Needham's rental car parked over by the Nationalmuseum, Blomkvist hurriedly explained that they were heading out to the Stockholm archipelago, towards Ingarö. He would get directions on the way and was not planning to observe any speed limits.

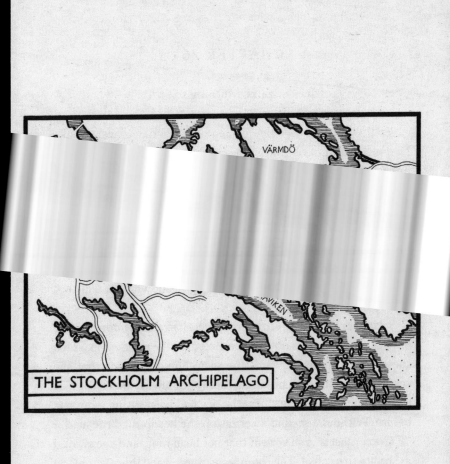

THE STOCKHOLM ARCHIPELAGO

CHAPTER 26

24.xi, Morning

August screamed, and in the same instant Salander heard footsteps, rapid footsteps along the side of the house. She grabbed her pistol and jumped to her feet. She felt terrible, but ignored it.

As she rushed over to the doorway she saw a large man appear on the terrace. For a moment she thought she had a split-second advantage, but the figure did not stop to open the glass doors. He charged straight through them with his weapon drawn and shot at the boy.

Salander returned fire, or perhaps she had already done so, she did not know. She was not even conscious of the moment in which she started running towards the man. She only knew that she crashed into him with numbing force and now lay on top of him right by the round table where the boy had been sitting moments before. Without a second's hesitation she headbutted the man.

The contact was so violent that her head rang, and she swayed as she got to her feet. The room was spinning and there was blood on her shirt. Had she been hit again? She had no time to think. Where was August? No-one at the table, only pencils and drawings, crayons, prime-number calculations. Where the hell was he? She heard a whimpering by the refrigerator and, yes, there he was, sitting and shaking, his knees drawn up to his chest. He must have had time to throw himself to the floor.

Salander was about to rush over to him when she heard new, worrying sounds from outside, voices and branches snapping. Others were approaching, there was no time to lose. They had to be away from here. In a blinding flash she visualized the surrounding terrain and raced over to August. "Come on!" she said. August did not budge. Salander picked him up in one swift movement, her face twisted in pain. Every movement hurt. But they had to get away and August must have understood that too because he wriggled out of her grasp. So she sprang over to the table, grabbed her computer and August's coat, and made for the

the floor who raised himself groggily and

the others would be here an

still . . . the drawing was also a weapon, and the cause of all the madness. She left August with her computer on the rock ledge she had identified the night before. She then launched herself back up the slope and into the house and looked on the table. At first she could not see it. Drawings of that bastard Westman were everywhere, and rows of prime numbers.

But there – there it was, and above the chess squares and the mirrors there was now a pale figure with a sharply defined scar on his forehead, which Salander by now recognized only too well. It was the same man who was lying on the floor in front of her, moaning. She whipped out her mobile, took a photograph and sent it to Bublanski and Modig. She had even scribbled a line at the top of the paper. But a second later she realized that was a mistake.

They were surrounded.

*

Salander had sent the same word to his Samsung as she had to Berger: <CRISIS>. It hardly left room for misunderstanding, not coming from Salander. However Blomkvist looked at it, it could only mean that she and August had been discovered, and at worst they were under attack even now. He floored the accelerator as he passed Stadsgårdskajen and emerged onto the Värmdö road.

He was driving a brand-new Audi A8, with Needham sitting next to him. Needham looked grim, and every now and then tapped something into his mobile. Blomkvist was not sure why he had allowed him to come along – maybe he wanted to discover what the man had on Salander, or no, there was something else as well. Maybe Needham could even be useful. In any case he could hardly make the situation any worse. The police had by now been alerted, but he doubted they would able to assemble a unit quickly enough – especially as they were sceptical about the lack of information. Berger had been the focal point, trying to keep them all in contact with each other, and she was the only one who knew the way. He needed all the help he could get.

He was approaching Danviksbron. Needham said something, he did not hear what. His thoughts were elsewhere. He thought of Zander – what had they done to him? Why the hell had he not come out for a beer? Blomkvist tried his number again. He tried calling Salander too. But nobody answered.

"Do you want me to tell you what we have on your hacker?" Needham said.

"Yes . . . why not?"

But they did not get anywhere this time either. Blomkvist's mobile rang. Bublanski.

"I hope you realize that you and I are going to have a lot to talk about later, and you can count on there being legal consequences."

"I hear you."

"But for now I'm calling to give you some information. We

396

know that Lisbeth Salander was alive at 4.22. Was that before or after she texted you?"

"Before, it must have been before."

"O.K."

"How can you be so specific about the time?"

"She sent us something extremely interesting. A drawing. I have to say, Mikael, it exceeded our hopes."

"So she got the boy to draw."

"Oh yes. I have no idea what technical issues might arise in terms of admissibility of evidence, if any, or what objections a clever defence lawyer might raise. But as far as I'm concerned

"When will you be at the scene?"

"As soon as possible . . . hold on a second!"

Blomkvist could hear another telephone ringing in the background, and for a minute or so Bublanski was gone on another call. When he returned, he said briefly:

"We've had reports of gunfire out there. It doesn't sound good."

Blomkvist took a deep breath. "Any news on Andrei?" he said.

"We've traced his mobile signal to a base station in Gamla Stan, but no further. We've had no signal at all for a while now, as if the mobile has been smashed or just stopped working."

Blomkvist drove even faster; fortunately the roads were empty at that hour. At first he said very little to Needham, just a brief account of what was going on, but in the end he could not hold back. He needed something else to think about.

"So what is it you think you've found out?"

"About Wasp? For a long time, zip. We were convinced that we'd reached the end of the line," Needham said. "We'd left no stone unturned, and still got nowhere. In a way it made sense."

"How so?"

"A hacker capable of a breach like that should also be able to cover all tracks. I realized pretty soon we wouldn't get anywhere by conventional means. So I skipped all the forensic bullshit and went straight for the big question: who had the chops to pull this off? That question was our best hope. There's hardly anyone out there with that level of ability. In that sense, you could say that the hacker's skill worked against them. Plus, we had analyzed the rootkit itself, and that . . ." Needham looked down at his mobile.

"Yes?"

"It had artistic qualities. Personal style, you might say. Now we just had to find its author, and so we started to send posts to the hacker community, and very soon there was one name, one handle, which came up time after time. Can you guess which one?"

"Maybe."

"It was Wasp. Sure, there were other names, but Wasp stood out. I ended up hearing so much mythical bullshit about this person that I was dying to crack their identity, and we went right back in time. We read every word Wasp had written online, studied every operation that had Wasp's signature on it. Soon we were certain that Wasp was a woman, and we guessed that she was Swedish. Several of the early posts were written in Swedish, which isn't much to go on. But since there was a Swedish connection in the organization she was tracking, and Frans Balder was Swedish, it was at least a good place to start. I got in touch with the N.D.R.E., and they searched their records, and then in fact . . ."

"What?"

"They had a breakthrough. Many years earlier they'd investigated a hacker operation that used that very handle, Wasp. It was so long ago that Wasp wasn't yet even particularly good at encryption."

"What happened?"

"Wasp had been looking for data on individuals who'd defected from other countries' intelligence services, and that was enough to trigger the N.D.R.E.'s warning system. Their investigation led them to a psychiatric clinic for children in Uppsala, to a computer belonging to the head physician there, a man named Teleborian. Apparently he'd done some work for the Swedish Security Police, so he was above suspicion. Instead the N.D.R.E. concentrated on some mental-health nurses who were targeted because they were

who are crazy good. It was obvious to me that we should look at every child in the clinic at the time. I had three of my guys investigate each one of them, inside and out, and do you know what we found? One of the children was the daughter of former spy and arch-villain Zalachenko, who was known to our colleagues at the C.I.A., and then everything got really interesting. As you probably know, there are some overlaps between the network the hacker was investigating and Zalachenko's old crime syndicate."

"That doesn't necessarily mean it was Wasp who hacked you."

"Of course not. But we took a closer look at this girl, and what can I say? She has an interesting background, doesn't she? A lot of information about her in the public record has been mysteriously deleted, but we still found more than enough and . . . I don't know, I may be wrong, but I get the feeling we're on the right track. Mikael, you don't know shit about me. But I know what it's like for a kid to see extreme violence at close quarters. And I know what it's like when society doesn't lift a finger to punish the guilty party. It hurts like hell, and I'm not at all surprised that most children who experience it go under. They turn into destructive bastards themselves."

"Yes, unfortunately."

"But just a few grow to be as strong as bears, Mikael, and they stand up and fight back. Wasp was one of those, wasn't she?"

Blomkvist nodded pensively and pressed down on the accelerator a little more.

"They locked her up and kept trying to break her. But she kept coming back, and do you know what I think?"

"No."

"She got stronger each time. She became positively lethal. She hasn't forgotten a single thing that happened. It's all etched into her, isn't it? And maybe that's at the bottom of this whole goddamn mess."

"What is it you want?" Blomkvist said bluntly.

"I want what Wasp wants. I want to set some things right."

"Plus get your hands on the hacker."

"I want to meet her and give her a piece of my mind and plug every last damn hole in our security. But above all I want to get my own back on certain people who wouldn't let me finish my job because Wasp exposed them. I have reason to believe you're going to help me with that."

"Why so?"

"Because you're a fine reporter. Fine reporters don't want dirty secrets to go on being dirty secrets."

"And Wasp?"

"Wasp is going to get a chance to do her worst. You're going to help me with that too."

"Or else?"

"Or else I'll find a way of putting her inside, and making her life hell again, I swear."

"But for now all you want to do is talk to her?"

"No fucker is going to be allowed to hack into my system again, so I need to understand exactly how she did it. I want you to give her that message. I'm prepared to let your girlfriend go free if she'll sit down with me and explain."

"I'll tell her. Let's just hope . . ."

"That she's still alive," Needham said. They turned left at high speed in the direction of Ingaröstrand.

only seen . . .

Blomkvist looked like a problem. He looked like a man who could not be fooled or broken so easily.

With the younger journalist it was different. He looked like the archetypal weakling, yet nothing could have been further from the truth. Zander had resisted for longer than anyone Holtser had ever tortured. Despite excruciating pain he had refused to break. His eyes shone with a grim determination which seemed buttressed by a higher principle, and at one point Holtser thought they would have to give up, that Zander would rather endure any suffering than talk. It was not until Kira solemnly promised that both Berger and Blomkvist from *Millennium* would be made to suffer as well that Zander finally caved in.

By then it was 3.30 in the morning. Holtser knew that he would always remember the moment. Snow was falling on the skylights. The young man's face was dried out and hollow-eyed. Blood had splashed up from his chest and flecked his mouth and cheeks. His lips, which for a long time had been covered with tape, were split and oozing. He was a wreck, but still you could tell that he was a beautiful young man.

Holtser thought of Olga – how would she have felt about him? Wasn't this journalist just the kind of educated man she liked, someone who fights injustice, takes the side of beggars and outcasts? He thought about that, and about other things in his own life. After that he made the sign of the cross, the Russian cross, where one way leads to heaven and the other to hell, and then he glanced over at Kira. She was lovelier than ever.

Her eyes burned with light. She was sitting on a stool by the bed wearing an elegant blue dress – which had largely escaped the bloodstains – and said something in Swedish to Zander, something which sounded soft and tender. Then she took him by the hand. He gripped hers in return. He had nowhere else to turn for comfort. The wind howled outside in the alley. Kira nodded and smiled at Holtser. Snowflakes fell on the window ledge.

Afterwards they were sitting together in a Land Rover on the way out to Ingarö. Holtser felt empty, and was not happy with the way things were going. But there was no getting away from the fact that his own mistake had led them there, so he sat quietly, listening to Kira. She was strangely excited and spoke with searing hatred of the woman they were about to confront. Holtser did not think it was a good sign, and if he could have brought himself to do so he would have urged her to turn back and get the hell out of the country.

But he said nothing as the snow fell and they drove on in the darkness. Kira's sparkling, cold eyes frightened him, but he pushed away the thought. He had to give her credit at least – she had been amazingly quick to put two and two together.

Not only had she worked out who had hurtled in to save the boy on Sveavägen. She had also guessed who would know where the boy and the woman had disappeared to, and the person she came up with was none other than Mikael Blomkvist. They were baffled by her reasoning. Why would a reputable Swedish journalist harbour a person who appeared from nowhere and abducted a child from a crime scene? But the more they examined the theory, the more it held together. Not only did the woman – whose name was Lisbeth Salander – have close ties to the reporter, but something also happened at the *Millennium* offices.

and the boy disappeared from Sveavägen.

That in itself was no guarantee that the journalist knew where they now were. But as time went on there were more indications that the theory might be right, and in any case Kira did not seem to need cast-iron evidence. She wanted to go for Blomkvist. Or, if not him, then someone else at the magazine. More than anything she was obsessive in her determination to track down the woman and the child.

Maybe Holtser could not understand the subtleties of Kira's motives. But it was for his benefit that they were going to do away with the boy. Kira chose to take significant risks for Holtser, and he was grateful, he really was, even though now in the car he felt uneasy.

He tried to draw strength from thinking about Olga. Whatever happened, she must not wake up and see a drawing of her father on all the front pages. He tried to reassure himself that the hardest part was behind them. Assuming Zander had given them the right location, the job should be straightforward. They were three heavily armed men, four if you counted Bogdanov, who spent most of the time staring at his computer as usual.

The team consisted of Holtser, Bogdanov, Orlov and Dennis Wilton, a gangster who had been a member of Svavelsjö M.C. but who now worked for Kira. Four men against one woman who was probably asleep, and was also protecting a child. It shouldn't be a problem, not at all. But Kira was almost manic:

"Don't underestimate Salander!"

She said it so many times that even Bogdanov, who always agreed with everything she said, began to get irritated. Of course Holtser had seen how fit and fast and fearless the woman had been on Sveavägen. But the way Kira described her, she must be some kind of superwoman. It was ridiculous. Holtser had never met a woman who could remotely be a match for him – or even for Orlov – in combat. Still, he promised to be careful. First he would go up and check out the terrain and prepare a strategy. They would not be drawn into a trap. He stressed this many times over, and when finally they arrived at an inlet next to a rocky slope and a jetty, he took command. He told the others to get ready in the shelter of the car while he went ahead to identify the house.

Holtser liked early mornings. He liked the silence and the feeling of transition in the air. Now he was leaning forward as he walked, and listening. It was reassuringly dark – no lights were on. He left the jetty behind him and came to a wooden fence with a rickety gate, right next to an overgrown prickly bush. He opened the gate and started to climb up the steep wooden steps holding the handrail on the right, and soon he was able to make out the house above.

It lay hidden behind pine trees and aspens and was only a dark outline, with a terrace on the south side. On the terrace were some glass doors which they would have no trouble breaking through. At first sight he saw no serious difficulty. He was moving almost soundlessly and for a moment he considered finishing off the job himself. Maybe it was even his moral responsibility, and it should be no more difficult than other jobs he had done. On the contrary.

There were no policemen this time, no guards, nor any sign of an alarm system. True, he did not have his assault rifle with him, but then there was no need for it. The rifle was excessive, the result

position he could not see into it. He kept still, now less and less sure of himself. Could it be the wrong house?

He resolved to get closer and peer in, and then . . . he was transfixed in the darkness. He was being observed. Those eyes which once before had looked at him were now staring glassily in his direction. That was when he should have reacted. He should have sprinted around to the terrace, gone straight in and shot the boy. But again he hesitated. He could not bring himself to draw his weapon. Faced with that look, he was lost.

The boy let out a shrill scream which seemed to set the window vibrating, and only then did Holtser tear himself out of his paralysis and race up onto the terrace. Without a moment's reflection he hurtled straight through the glass doors and fired with what he thought was great precision, but he never found out whether he hit his target.

An explosive shadow-like figure came at him with such speed that he hardly had time to brace himself. He knew that he fired another shot and that someone shot back. In the next instant he slammed onto the floor with his full weight, a young woman tumbling over him with a rage in her eyes that was beyond anything he had ever seen. He reacted instinctively and tried to shoot again. But the woman was like a wild animal. She threw her head back and . . . Crack!

When he came to he had a taste of blood in his mouth and his pullover was sticky and wet. He must have been hit. Just then the boy and the woman passed him, and he tried to grab hold of the boy's leg. At least he thought he did. But suddenly he was gasping for breath.

He no longer understood what was going on. Except that he was beaten, but by whom? By a woman? That insight became a part of his pain as he lay on the floor amidst glass and his own blood, breathing heavily, his eyes shut. He hoped it would be over soon. When he opened his eyes again he was surprised to see the woman still there. Had she not just left? No, she was standing by the table, he could see her thin boyish legs. He tried his utmost to get up. He looked for his weapon, and at the same time heard voices through the broken window, and then he moved once more to attack the woman.

But before he could do anything the woman exploded into motion and stormed out. From the terrace she threw herself headlong into the trees. Shots resounded in the dark and he muttered to himself, "Kill the bastards." But it was all he could do to get to his feet and he cast a dull glance at the table in front of him.

There was a mass of crayons and paper which he looked at without really taking it all in. Then it was as if a claw had taken hold of his heart. He saw an evil demon with a pale face raising his hand to kill. It took a second or so for him to realize that the demon was himself, and he shuddered.

Yet he could not take his eyes off the image. Only then did he notice something scribbled at the top:

Mailed to police 4.22.

CHAPTER 27

24.xi, Morning

When Aram Barzani of the Rapid Response Unit made his way into Gabriella Grane's house at 4.52 he saw a large man dressed in black spreadeagled on the floor next to the round table.

He approached cautiously. The house seemed to have been abandoned. But he was not taking any risks. There were recent reports of a fierce gunfight up at the house and he could hear the excited voices of his colleagues outside on the steep rock slope.

"Here!" they shouted. "Here!"

Barzani did not understand what was going on, and for a moment he hesitated. Should he go to them? He decided to see first what condition the man on the floor was in. There was broken glass and blood all around, and the table was strewn with torn-up pieces of paper and crushed crayons. The man on the ground was crossing himself feebly. He was mumbling something. Probably a prayer. It sounded Russian; Barzani caught the word "Olga". He told the man that a medical team was on its way.

"They were sisters," the man said in English.

But it sounded so confused that Barzani attached no importance to it. Instead he searched through the man's clothes, made sure that he was unarmed, and thought he had probably been shot in the stomach. His pullover was soaked in blood, and he looked alarmingly pale. Barzani asked what had happened. He got no reply, not at first. Then the man gasped out another strange sentence.

"My soul was captured in a drawing," he said, and seemed to be about to lose consciousness.

Aram stayed for a few minutes to watch him, but when he heard from the ambulance crew he left the man and went down to the rocky slope. He wanted to discover what his colleagues had been shouting about. The snow was still falling and it was icy underfoot. Down by the water voices could be heard and the sound of more cars arriving. It was still dark and hard to see and there were many uneven rocks and straggly pines. The landscape was dramatic and

nine now. They were crazy about football – did nothing else, talked about nothing else. Björn and Anders. He and Dilvan had given them Swedish names because they had thought it would make their lives easier. What kind of people come out here to kill a child? He was gripped by a sudden fury. But in the next moment he breathed a sigh of relief.

There was no boy there, but two men lying on the ground, apparently both shot in the stomach. One of them – a brutal-looking type with pockmarked skin and a stubby boxer's nose – tried to get up, but was easily pushed down again. His face betrayed his humiliation and his right hand was shaking with pain or rage. The other man, who was wearing a leather jacket and had his hair in a ponytail, seemed in worse shape. He lay still and stared in shock at the dark sky.

"No sign of the child?" Barzani said.

"Nothing," his colleague Klas Lang said.

"And the woman?"

"No sign."

Barzani was not sure if this was good news and he asked a few more questions. But no-one knew what had happened. The only certainty was that two automatic weapons, Barrett REC7s, had been found thirty or forty metres away, close to the jetty. They were assumed to belong to the men, but when asked how they had ended up there, the man with the pockmarked face spat out an incomprehensible answer.

Barzani and his colleagues spent the next fifteen minutes combing the terrain. All they could find were further signs of combat. More and more people began to arrive on the scene: ambulance crew, Detective Sergeant Modig, two or three crime scene technicians, a succession of regular policemen and the journalist Mikael Blomkvist, who was accompanied by a massive American with a crew cut who immediately commanded everyone's respect. At 5.25 they were informed that a witness was waiting to be interviewed down by the seashore and parking area. The man wanted to be addressed as K.G. He was actually called Karl-Gustav Matzon. He had fairly recently bought a new-build on the other side of the water. According to Lang, he needed to be taken with a pinch of salt: "The old boy has a very vivid imagination."

Modig and Holmberg were standing in the parking area, trying to make sense of what had happened. The picture so far was fragmented and they were hoping that the witness K.G. Matzon would bring a measure of clarity to the night.

But when they saw him coming towards them along the shoreline, that seemed less and less likely. K.G. Matzon was resplendent in a Tyrolean hat, green checked trousers and a red Canada Goose jacket and he was sporting an absurd twirly moustache. He looked as if he were trying to be funny.

"K.G. Matzon?" Modig said.

"The very same," he said, and without any prompting – maybe he realized that his credibility needed a boost – he explained that he ran True Crimes, a publishing house which produced books on notable crimes.

"Excellent. But right now we'd like a factual account – not some sales pitch for a forthcoming book," Modig said, to be on the safe side. Matzon said that, of course, he understood.

He was after all a "respectable person". He had woken up at a ridiculous hour, he said, and lain there listening to "the silence _____ " But just before 4.30 he heard something which he _____ dressed

as if a war had _____

"You heard more shots?"

"There were cracks of gunfire from the promontory on the other side of the inlet and I stared across, stunned, and then . . . did I mention I was a birdwatcher?"

"No, you didn't."

"Well, it's made my eyesight very good, you see. I've got eagle eyes. I'm used to pinpointing tiny details far off, and I'm sure that's why I noticed a small dot on the rock ledge up there, do you see it? The edge of it sort of cuts into the rock slope like a pocket."

Modig looked up at the slope and nodded.

"At first I couldn't tell what it was," Matzon continued. "But then I realized it was a child – a boy, I think. He was sitting up there in a crouch and trembling, at least that's how it seemed to me, and then suddenly . . . my God, I'll never forget it."

"What?"

"Someone came racing down from above, a woman, and she leaped into the air and landed so violently on the rock ledge that she all but fell off it, and after that they sat there together, she and the boy, and just waited, and waited for the inevitable, and then . . ."

"Yes?"

"Two men appeared holding assault rifles and shot and shot, and as I'm sure you can imagine, I just threw myself to the ground. I was scared I'd get hit. But I couldn't help looking up at them all the same. You see, from where I was the boy and the girl were clearly visible. But they were invisible to the men standing at the top, at least for the moment. It was obvious to me that it was only a matter of time before they were discovered and there was no escape. As soon as they left the rock ledge the men would see them and kill them. It was a hopeless situation."

"But we've found neither the boy nor the woman up there," Modig said.

"That's just it! The men got closer and closer – they only needed to lean forward to see the woman and the child. In the end they could probably have heard them breathing. But then . . ."

"Yes?'

"You're not going to believe this. That man from the Rapid Response Unit definitely didn't."

"Well, go ahead and tell me, and we can worry later about whether it's believable."

"When the men stopped to listen, maybe they sensed they were very close, the woman leaped to her feet and shot them. Bang, bang! Then she rushed forward and threw their weapons away. It was like an action film, and after that she ran, or rather rolled, almost fell down the slope with the boy to a B.M.W. standing here in the parking area. Just before they got into the car I saw that the woman was holding something – it looked like a computer bag."

"Did they drive away in the B.M.W.?"

"At a fearful speed. I have no idea where they went."

"Of course not."

"But that's not all."

"What do you mean?"

"There was another car there – a Range Rover, I think, black, a new model."

"And what happened to that one?"

"I was busy ringing the emergency services, but just as I was about to hang up I saw two more people coming down from the wooden steps over there, a tall thin man and a woman. I didn't get a good look at them from that distance. But I can still tell you

just nodded as if he thought he deserved it. Then he got behind the wheel and they were gone."

Modig noted everything down, realizing that she had to get out a nationwide search bulletin for both the Range Rover and the B.M.W. without delay.

Gabriella Grane was drinking a cappuccino in her kitchen on Villagatan and thinking that she was holding it together, all things considered. But she was probably in shock.

Helena Kraft wanted to see her at 8.00 in the office at Säpo. Grane guessed that she wouldn't just get the sack. There would be judicial consequences too, which would pretty much ruin her prospects of finding another job. At thirty-three, her career was over.

And that was by no means the worst of it. She had known that she was flouting the law and had taken a conscious risk. But she had done it because she believed it was the best way to protect Frans Balder's son. Now, after the shoot-out at her summer place, no-one seemed to know where the boy was. He might be injured, or even dead. Grane was racked by the most devastating feelings of guilt: first the father and now the son.

She got up and looked at the clock. It was 7.15 and she needed to get going to give herself time to clean out her desk before the meeting with Kraft. She made up her mind to behave with dignity, to not make any excuses or beg to be allowed to stay. Her Blackphone rang, but she couldn't be bothered to answer. Instead she put on her boots and her Prada coat and an extravagant red scarf. If she was going under, she might just as well go with a bit of panache. She stood in front of the hall mirror and touched up her make-up, wryly giving herself the victory sign, as Nixon had when he resigned. Then her Blackphone rang again and this time she answered reluctantly. It was Casales at the N.S.A.

"I've just heard," she said.

Of course she had.

"How are you feeling?"

"What do you think?"

"Like the worst person in the whole world?"

"Pretty much."

"Who'll never get another job?"

"Spot on, Alona."

"In that case, let me tell you, you've nothing to be ashamed of. You did the right thing."

"Are you trying to be funny?"

"Doesn't seem like the moment for jokes, sweetheart. You have a mole on your team."

Gabriella took a deep breath. "Who is it?"

"Nielsen."

Gabriella froze. "Do you have proof?"

"Oh yes, I'll send it all over in a few minutes."

"Why would Nielsen betray us?"

"I guess he didn't see it as a betrayal."

"What on earth did he see it as if not betrayal?"

"Collaborating with Big Brother maybe, doing his duty by the leading nation in the free world? What do I know?"

"So he gave you information."

"He helped us to help ourselves, actually. He gave us information about your server and your encryption. It's not as outrageous as it sounds. Let's face it, we listen in on everything from the neighbours' gossip to the prime minister's telephone calls."

"But it went wrong."

"Sometimes things go wrong, no matter how careful you are."

"Thanks, Alona, it's nice of you to say so. But if anything has happened to August Balder, I will never forgive myself."

"Gabriella, the boy is O.K. He's cruising around in a car somewhere with Miss Salander, in case someone's still chasing them."

Grane could not take it in. "What do you mean?"

"That he's unhurt, babe, and that thanks to him his father's murderer has been caught and identified."

"You're saying August is alive?"

"That's right."

"How do you know?"

"Let's just say I have a very well-placed source."

"Alona . . ."

"Yes?"

"If what you say is true, you've given me back my life."

After hanging up, Grane rang Kraft and insisted that Mårten Nielsen be present at their meeting. Reluctantly, Kraft agreed.

It was 7.30 in the morning when Needham and Blomkvist made their way down the steps from Grane's summer house to the Audi in the parking area by the beach. Snow lay over the landscape and neither of them said a word. At 5.30 Blomkvist had got a text message from Salander, as brisk and to the point as ever.

<August unhurt. We'll keep our heads down a while longer.>

Again Salander had not mentioned her own state of health. But it was an incredible relief to hear about the boy. Afterwards Blomkvist had been questioned at length by Modig and Holmberg and he told them every detail of what he and the magazine had been doing over the past few days. They were not friendly or well disposed towards him, yet he got the feeling that somehow they understood. Now, an hour later, he was walking past the jetty. Up the slope a deer scampered into the forest. Blomkvist settled into the driving seat and waited for Needham, who came loping along in his wake. The American's back was giving him trouble.

On the way to Brunn they found themselves in traffic. For several minutes nothing moved and Blomkvist thought of Zander, who was constantly on his mind. They had still not had any sign of life from him.

"Can you get something noisy on the radio?" Needham said.

Blomkvist tuned into 107.1 and got James Brown belting out what a sex machine he was.

"Give me your phones," Needham said.

He stacked them next to the speakers at the back of the car. He clearly meant to talk about something sensitive, and Blomkvist had nothing against that – he had to write his story and needed all the facts he could get. But he also knew better than most that there's no such thing as a leak without an agenda. Although Blomkvist felt a certain affinity with Needham and even appreciated his grumpy charm, he did not trust him for one second.

"Let's hear it," he said.

"You could put it this way," Needham began. "We know that in business and industry there's always someone taking advantage of inside information."

"Agreed."

"For a while we were pretty much spared that in the world of intelligence, for the simple reason that we guarded different kinds of secrets. The dynamite was elsewhere. But since the end of the

was seen as criminal or unethical decades ago is now standard operating procedure. We haven't been much better at the N.S.A., in fact maybe we're even . . ."

"The worst?"

"Just take it easy, let me finish," Needham said. "I'd say we have a certain moral code. But we're a large organization with tens of thousands of employees and inevitably there are rotten apples – even one or two very highly placed rotten apples I was thinking of handing you."

"Out of the kindness of your heart, of course," Blomkvist said with a touch of sarcasm.

"O.K., maybe not entirely. But listen. When senior management at our place crosses the line and gets into criminal activities, what do you think happens?"

"Nothing very nice."

"As you know, there's a corrupt unit at Solifon, headed up by a man called Zigmund Eckerwald, whose job it is to find out what the competing tech companies are up to. They not only steal the technology but also sell what they steal. That's bad for Solifon and maybe even for the whole Nasdaq."

"And for you too."

"That's right. It turns out that our two most senior executives in industrial espionage – their names are Jacob Barclay and Brian Abbot – get help from Eckerwald and his gang. In exchange the N.S.A. helps Eckerwald with large-scale communications monitoring. Solifon identifies where the big innovations are happening, and our idiots pluck out the drawings and the technical details."

"I assume the money this brings in doesn't always end up in the state coffers."

"It's worse than that, buddy. If you do this sort of thing as a state employee, you make yourself very vulnerable, especially because Eckerwald and his gang are also helping major criminals. To be fair, at first they probably didn't know their clients were major criminals."

"But that's what they were?"

"Damn right. And they took advantage too. I could only dream of recruiting hackers at their level of expertise, and the very essence of their business is to exploit information, so you can imagine: once they realized what our guys at the N.S.A. were up to, they knew they were sitting on a goldmine."

"So they were in a position to blackmail."

"Talk about having the upper hand. Our guys haven't just been stealing from large corporations. They've also plundered small family businesses and solo entrepreneurs who are struggling to survive. It wouldn't look too good if everything came out. So as a result the N.S.A. is forced to help not just Eckerwald and Solifon, but also the criminals."

"You mean the Spiders?"

"You got it. Maybe for a while everyone stays happy. It's big business and the money's rolling in. But then a little genius pops up in the middle of the action, a certain Professor Balder, and he's just as good at ferreting around as he is at doing everything else. So he finds out about this scheme, or at least part of it. Then of course everyone's scared shitless and decides that something has to be done. I'm not entirely clear on how these decisions got made. I'm guessing our guys hoped legal threats would be enough. But when you're in bed with a bunch of criminals . . . The Spiders prefer violence, so they draw our guys into the plan at a late stage, just to bind them in even more tightly."

another thing I've been wondering about," Blomkvist said.

"Shoot."

"You mentioned two guys, Barclay and Abbot. Are you sure it stops with them? Who's their boss?"

"I can't give you his name unfortunately. It's classified."

"I suppose I'll have to live with that."

"You will," Needham said inflexibly. At that moment Blomkvist noticed that traffic was starting to flow again.

CHAPTER 28

24.xi, Afternoon

Professor Edelman was standing in the car park at the Karolinska Institute wondering what in heaven's name he had let himself in for. He was embarking on an arrangement which would mean his having to cancel a whole series of meetings, lectures and conferences.

Even so he felt strangely elated. He had been entranced not just by the boy but also by the young woman who looked as if she had come straight from a street brawl, but who drove a brand new B.M.W. and spoke with chilling authority. He had barely been aware of what he was doing when he said, "Yes, sure, why not?" to her questions, although it was obviously both foolish and rash. The only grain of independence he had shown was to have declined all offers of compensation.

He was going to pay his own travel and hotel expenses, he said. He must have felt guilty. But he was moved to take the boy under his wing, his scientific curiosity was piqued. A savant who both drew with photographic exactitude and could perform prime-number factorization – how absolutely riveting. To his own surprise he even decided to skip the Nobel Prize dinner. The young woman had made him take leave altogether of his senses.

*

Hanna Balder was sitting in the kitchen on Torsgatan, smoking. It felt as if she had done little else apart from sit there and puff away with a heavy feeling in her stomach. She had been given an unusual amount of support, but she had also been getting an unusual amount of physical abuse. Lasse Westman could not handle her anxiety. It detracted from his own martyrdom.

He was always flying into a rage and yelling, "Can't you even keep track of your own brat?" Often he lashed out with his fists or threw her across the apartment like a rag doll. Now he would probably go crazy too – she had spilled coffee all over the *Dagens Nyheter* culture section, and Lasse was already worked up because

or even move her head. She could feel the tears welling up and her heart pounding. But actually that had nothing to do with the blow. That morning she had received a call which was so perplexing that she hardly understood it: August had been found, had disappeared again and was "probably" unharmed – "probably". It was impossible for Hanna to know if she should be more worried, or less.

The hours had gone by with no further news. Suddenly she got to her feet, no longer caring whether she would get another beating or not. She went into the living room and heard Lasse panting behind her. August's drawing paper was still lying on the floor and an ambulance was wailing outside. She heard footsteps in the stairwell. Was someone on their way here? The doorbell rang.

"Don't open. It'll be some bloody journalist," Lasse snapped.

Hanna did not want to open either. Still, she could not very well ignore it, could she? Perhaps the police wanted to interview her again, or maybe, maybe they had more information now, good news or bad news.

As she went to the door she thought of Frans. She remembered how he had stood there saying that he had come for August. She remembered his eyes and the fact that he had shaved off his beard, and her own longing for her old life, before Lasse Westman – a time when the telephone rang and the job offers came flooding in, and fear had not yet set its claws into her. She opened the door with the safety chain on and at first she saw nothing; just the lift door, and the reddish-brown walls. Then a shock ran through her, and for a moment she could not believe it. But it really was August! His hair was a tangled mess and his clothes were filthy. He was wearing a pair of trainers much too big for him, and yet: he looked at her with the same serious, impenetrable expression as ever. She would not have expected him to turn up on his own, but when she undid the safety chain she still gave a start. Next to August stood a cool young woman in a leather jacket, with scratch marks on her face and earth in her hair, glaring down at the floor. She had a large suitcase in her hand.

"I've come to give you back your son," she said without looking up.

"Oh my God," Hanna said. "My God!"

That was all she managed to say, and for a few seconds she was completely at a loss as she stood there in the doorway. Then her shoulders began to shake. She sank to her knees and, forgetting the fact that August hated to be hugged, she threw her arms around him murmuring, "My boy, my boy . . ." until the tears came. The odd thing was: August not only let her do it, he also seemed on the verge of saying something – as if he had learned to talk on top of everything. But before he had the chance, Lasse was standing behind her.

"What the hell . . . Well, look who's here!" he growled, as if he wanted to carry on with their fight.

But then he got a grip on himself. It was an impressive piece of acting, in a way. In the space of a second he began to radiate the presence which used to make women swoon.

"And we get the kid delivered to our front doorstep," he said to the woman on the landing. "How convenient. Is he O.K.?"

"He's O.K.," the woman said in a strange monotone, and without asking walked into the apartment with the suitcase and her muddy boots.

"By all means, just come right on in," Lasse said in an acid

"Is this some kind of joke?"

"Not at all. You're leaving this house now, right now, and you're not coming anywhere near August ever again. You've seen him for the last time."

"You must be off your rocker!"

"Actually I'm being unusually generous. I was planning on throwing you down the stairs there. But I brought a suitcase with me. Thought I'd let you pack some shirts and pants."

"What kind of a freak are you?" Lasse shouted, both bewildered and beside himself with rage, and he bore down on the woman with the full weight of his hostility, and Hanna wondered if he was going to take a swipe at her as well.

But something stopped him. Maybe it was the woman's eyes, or possibly the mere fact that she did not react like anyone else would have done. Instead of backing off or looking frightened she

423

only smiled at him, and took a few crumpled pieces of paper from an inside pocket and handed them to Lasse.

"If ever you and your friend Roger should find yourselves missing August, you can always look at this and remember," she said.

Lasse turned over the papers, confused. Then he screwed up his face in horror and Hanna took a quick look herself. They were drawings and the top one was of . . . Lasse. Lasse swinging his fists and looking profoundly evil. Later she would hardly be able to explain it. It was not just that she understood what had been going on when August had been alone at home with Lasse and Roger. She also saw her own life more clearly and soberly than she had for years.

Lasse had looked at her with exactly that twisted, livid face hundreds of times, most recently a minute ago. She knew this was something no-one should have to endure, neither she nor August, and she shrank back. At least she thought she did, because the woman looked at her with a new focus. Hanna eyed her uneasily. They seemed on some level to understand each other.

"Am I right, Hanna, he's got to go?" the woman said.

The question was potentially lethal, and Hanna looked down at August's oversize shoes.

"What are those shoes he's wearing?"

"Mine."

"Why?"

"We left in a hurry this morning."

"And what have you been doing?"

"Hiding."

"I don't understand . . ." she began, but got no further.

Lasse grabbed hold of her violently. "Why don't you tell this psychopath that the only one who's leaving is her?" he roared.

Hanna cowered, but then . . . It may have been something to do with the expression on Lasse's face, or the sense of something implacable in the young woman's bearing. But then . . . Hanna heard herself say, "You're leaving, Lasse! And don't ever come back!"

It was as if someone else were speaking in her place. And after that things moved quickly. Lasse raised his hand to strike her, but no blow came, not from him. The young woman reacted with lightning speed, and hit him in the face two, three times like a trained boxer, felling him with a kick to the leg.

"What the hell!" was all he was able to say.

He crashed to the floor, and the young woman stood over him. As Hanna took August into his bedroom she realized for how long and how desperately she had wished Lasse . . .

. . . on his way home to his mother.

Thanks to the boy himself and to Lisbeth Salander his father's killer had been arrested, even though it was not yet established that he would survive his injuries. He was in intensive care at Danderyd hospital. He was called Boris Latvinov but had for some time been using the name Jan Holtser. He was a major and former elite soldier from the Soviet army, and his name had cropped up in the past in several murder investigations, but he had never been convicted. He had his own business in the security industry, and was both a Finnish and Russian citizen, and a resident of Helsinki; no doubt someone had doctored his government records.

The other two people who had been found at the summer house on Ingarö had been identified by their fingerprints; Dennis Wilton, an old gangster from Svavelsjö M.C. who had done time for both aggravated robbery and grievous bodily harm; and Vladimir Orlov, a Russian with a criminal record in Germany for procuring, whose two wives had died in unexplained circumstances. None of the men had yet said a word about what happened, or about anything at all. Nor did Bublanski hold out much hope that this would change. Men like that tend to hold their peace in police interviews. But then those were the rules of the game.

What Bublanski was unhappy about, though, was the feeling that these three men were no more than foot soldiers and that there was a leadership above them linked to the upper echelons of society in both Russia and in the U.S.A. He had no problem with a journalist knowing more about his investigation than he did. In that respect he was not proud. He just wanted to move ahead, and was grateful for all information, whatever its source. But Blomkvist's discerning approach to the case had pointed up their own shortcomings and reminded Bublanski of the leak in the investigation and the dangers to which the boy had been exposed because of them. On this score his anger would never subside, and perhaps that explains why he was so irritated at the head of Säpo's eager efforts to get hold of him – and Kraft was not the only one. The I.T. people at the National Criminal Police were after him too, and so were Chief Prosecutor Richard Ekström and a Stanford professor by the name of Steven Warburton from the Machine Intelligence Research Institute who wanted to talk about "a significant risk", as Amanda Flod put it.

That bothered Bublanski, along with a thousand other things. And there was someone knocking at his door. It was Modig, who looked tired and was wearing no make-up, revealing something different about her face.

"All three prisoners are having surgery," she said. "It'll be a while before we can question them again."

"Try to question them, you mean."

"I did manage to have a brief word with Latvinov. He was conscious for a while before his operation."

"Did he say anything?"

"Just that he wanted to talk to a priest."

"How come all lunatics and murderers are religious these days?"

"While all sensible old chief inspectors doubt the existence of their God, you mean?"

"Now, now."

"Latvinov also seemed dejected, and that's a good sign, I think,"

Balder's research.

"And Zander, the young journalist?"

"That's what I came to talk about. It doesn't look good."

"What do we know?"

"That he worked late and was spotted disappearing down past Katarinahissen accompanied by a beautiful woman with strawberry- or dark-blonde hair and expensive clothes."

"I'd not heard that."

"They were seen by a man called Ken Eklund, a baker at Skansen. He lives in the *Millennium* building. He said they looked as if they were in love, or at least Zander did."

"You think it could have been some sort of honeytrap?"

"It's possible."

"And this woman, might she be the same one who was seen at Ingarö?"

"We're looking into that. But I don't like the idea that they seemed to be heading towards Gamla Stan. Not only because we picked up Zander's mobile phone signals there. That revolting specimen Orlov, who just spits at me whenever I try to question him, has an apartment on Mårten Trotzigs gränd."

"Have we been there?"

"Not yet. We've only just discovered the address. The apartment was registered in the name of one of his companies."

"Let's hope there's nothing unpleasant waiting for us there."

Westman was lying on the floor in the entrance hall on Torsgatan, wondering how he could be so terrified. She was just a chick, a pierced punk chick who hardly came up to his chest. He should be able to throw her out like some little rat. Yet he was as if paralyzed and it had nothing to do with the way the girl fought, he thought, still less with the fact that her foot was planted on his stomach. It was something about her look or her whole being that he could not put his finger on. For a few minutes he lay there like an idiot and listened.

"I'm just reminded," she said, "that there's something really wrong in my family. We seem to be capable of pretty much anything. Of the most unimaginable cruelties. It may be a genetic defect. Personally I've got this thing against men who harm children and women, and that makes me dangerous. When I saw August's drawings of you and your friend Roger, I wanted to hurt you, badly. But I think August has been through enough, so there's a slight chance that you and your friend might get off more lightly."

"I'm—" Westman began.

"Quiet," she said. "This isn't a negotiation; it's not even a conversation. I'm just setting out the terms, that's all. Legally there are no problems. Frans was wise enough to register the apartment in August's name. But for the rest, this is how it's going to be: you have precisely four minutes to pack your things and get out. If you or Roger ever come back here or contact August in any way, I'll make you suffer so much that you'll be incapable of doing anything nice again, for the rest of your lives. In the meantime, I'll be preparing to report you to the police with full details of the abuse you've subjected August to. As you know, we have more than the drawings to go on. We have testimonies from psychologists and experts. I'll also be contacting the evening papers to tell them that I have material which substantiates the image of you that emerged in connection with your assault on Renata Kapusinski. Remind me, Lasse, what was it that you did? Bite her cheek through and kick her in the head?"

"So you're going to go to the ....."

..... month, you may be alright. I have my doubts – as we all know, the rate of re-offending for violence against women is high, and basically you're a bastard, but with a bit of luck, who knows . . .? Have you got it?"

"I've got it," he said, hating himself for saying so.

He saw no way out, he could only agree and do as he was told, and so he got up and went into the bedroom and swiftly packed some clothes. Then he took his coat and his mobile and left. He had nowhere to go.

He had never felt more pathetic in his life. Outside an unpleasant sleety rain lashed into him.

Salander heard the front door slam and footsteps receding down the stone stairs. She looked at August. He was standing still with his arms straight down by his sides, staring at her intently. That troubled her. A moment ago she had been in control of things, but now she was uncertain, and what on earth was the matter with Hanna Balder?

Hanna seemed about to burst into tears, and August . . . on top of everything else he started shaking his head and muttering. Salander just wanted to get out of there, but she stayed. Her work was not yet complete. Out of her pocket she took two plane tickets, a hotel voucher and a thick bundle of notes, both kronor and euros.

"I'd just like, from the bottom of my heart—" Hanna began.

"Quiet," Salander cut in. "Here are some plane tickets to Munich. Departure is at 7.15 this evening so you've got to hurry. I've organized transport to take you directly to Schloss Elmau. It's a nice hotel not far from Garmisch-Partenkirchen. You'll be staying in a large room on the top floor, in the name of Müller, and you'll be there for three months to start with. I've been in touch with Professor Edelman and explained to him the importance of absolute confidentiality. He'll be making regular visits and seeing to it that August gets good care. Edelman will also arrange for suitable schooling."

"Are you serious?"

"I'm deadly serious. The police now have August's drawing and the murderer has been arrested. But the people behind all this are still at large, and it's impossible to know what they might be planning. You have to leave this apartment at once. I'm busy with a few other things, but I've arranged for a driver to take you to Arlanda. He's a bit weird-looking, maybe, but he's O.K. You can call him Plague. Have you got all that?"

"Yes, but—"

"Forget the buts. Just listen: you mustn't use your credit card or your own mobile during the whole of your time away, Hanna. I've fixed an encrypted mobile for you, a Blackphone, in case there's an emergency. My number is already programmed in. I'll pick up all the costs of the hotel. You'll get a hundred thousand kronor in cash, for unforeseen expenses. Any questions?"

"It sounds crazy."

"Not to me."

"But how can you afford all this?"

"I can afford it."

"How can we . . .?" Hanna looked completely bewildered, as if she were not sure what to believe. Then she began to cry.

"How can we ever thank you?" she struggled to say.

"*Thank?*"

Salander repeated the word as if it were something incompre-hensible. When Hanna came to

put in some home or institution, I want you to fight back as hard and as ruthlessly as you can. Aim for their weakest point. Be a warrior."

"A warrior?"

"Exactly. Don't let anyone . . ."

Salander stopped herself. They were not perhaps the greatest words of farewell, but they would have to do. She turned and walked towards the front door. She did not get far. August started to mutter again, and this time they could make out what the boy was saying.

"Not go, not go . . ."

Salander had no good answer to that either. She just said, "You'll be O.K." and then added, as if talking to herself, "Thanks for the scream this morning." There was silence for a moment, and Salander wondered if she should say more. But instead she turned and slipped out of the door.

Hanna called after her, "I can't tell you what this means to me!"

But Salander heard nothing. She was already running down the steps to her car. When she reached Västerbron, Blomkvist called on the Redphone app to say that the N.S.A. had tracked her down.

"Tell them hi and that I'm on their tracks too," she said.

Then she drove to Roger Winter's house and scared him half to death. After that she drove back to her place and set to work with the encrypted N.S.A. file, without coming any closer to a solution.

Needham and Blomkvist had worked a long day in the hotel room at the Grand. Needham had a fantastic story for Blomkvist, who would be able to write the scoop *Millennium* so badly needed, but his feeling of unease did not abate. It was not just because Zander was still missing. There was something about Needham that did not add up. Why had he turned up in the first place, and why was he putting so much energy into helping out a small Swedish magazine, far from all the centres of power in the U.S.? Blomkvist had undertaken not to disclose the hacker breach, and had half promised to try to persuade Salander to talk to Needham. But that hardly seemed enough.

Needham behaved as if he was taking enormous risks. The curtains were drawn and their mobiles were lying at a safe distance. There was a feeling of paranoia in the room. Confidential documents were laid out on the bed. Blomkvist was permitted to read them, but not to quote from or copy them. And every now and then Needham interrupted his account to discuss various aspects of the right to protect journalistic sources. He was obsessively thorough about ensuring that the leak could not be traced back to him, and sometimes he listened nervously for footsteps in the corridor or looked out through a gap in the curtains to check that no-one was out there watching the hotel, and yet . . . Blomkvist could not help feeling that most of it was play-acting.

He became more and more convinced that Needham knew exactly what he was doing and was not even especially worried about someone listening in. It occurred to Blomkvist that Needham was playing a part which had the backing of his superiors – maybe he himself had also been given a role in this play which he did not yet understand.

Therefore he paid close attention not just to what Needham said, but also to what he did not, and he considered what he might be trying to achieve by going public. There was undoubtedly a certain amount of anger there. Some "bastards" in and

There were other aspects of the story he was not quite so comfortable with. Occasionally it felt as if Needham was wrestling with some kind of self-censorship. From time to time Blomkvist went down to the lobby just to think, or to call Berger or Salander. Berger always answered on the first ring and, even though they were both enthusiastic about the story, Zander's disappearance haunted their conversations.

Salander did not pick up all day, until eventually he got hold of her at 5.20. She sounded distracted, and informed him that the boy was now safe with his mother.

"And how are *you*?" he said.

"O.K."

"Not hurt?"

"Nothing new at least."

Blomkvist took a deep breath. "Have you hacked into the N.S.A.'s intranet, Lisbeth?"

"Have you been talking to Ed the Ned?"

"No comment."

He would say nothing, even to Salander. The protection of sources was even more important to him than loyalty to her.

"Ed isn't so dumb after all," she said.

"So you have."

"Possibly."

Blomkvist felt the urge to ask her what the hell she thought she was doing. Instead, as calmly as he could, he said:

"They're prepared to let you off if you'll agree to meet them and tell them how you did it."

"Tell them from me that I'm on to them as well."

"What's that supposed to mean?"

"That I've got more than they think."

"O.K. But would you consider meeting . . ."

"Ed?"

How the hell did she know, Blomkvist thought. Needham had wanted to be the one to reveal himself to her.

"Ed," he said.

"A cocky bugger."

"Pretty cocky. But would you consider meeting him if we provide guarantees that you won't be arrested?"

"There are no such guarantees."

"I could get in touch with my sister Annika and ask her to represent you."

"I've got better things to do," she said, as if she did not want to talk about it any more. He could not stop himself from saying, "This story we're working on . . . I'm not sure I understand all of it."

"What's the difficulty?" Salander said.

"First of all, I don't understand why Camilla has surfaced after all these years."

"I suppose she has just been biding her time."

"How do you mean?"

"She probably always knew she would be back to get her revenge for what I did to her and Zala. But she wanted to wait until she had built up her strength on every level. Nothing is more important to Camilla than to be strong, and I suppose she suddenly saw an opportunity, a chance to kill two birds with one stone. At least that's my guess. Why don't you ask her next time you have a drink together?"

"Have you spoken to Holger?"

"I've been busy."

"And yet she failed. You got away, thank God."

"I made it."

Blomkvist smiled to himself.

"Yes," he said. "You're probably right. Let's not trust him any more than we absolutely have to. I don't want to become his useful idiot."

"Doesn't sound like a role for you, Mikael."

"No, and that's why I'd love to know what you discovered when you accessed their intranet."

"A whole load of compromising shit."

"About Eckerwald and the Spiders' relationship with the N.S.A.?"

"That and a bit more besides."

"Which you were planning to tell me about."

"I might do, if you behave yourself," she said with a teasing tone, and that only made him feel happy.

Then he chuckled, because at that moment he realized precisely what Ed Needham was trying to do.

It hit him so forcefully that he had a hard time keeping up his act when he returned to the hotel room, and he went on working with the American until 10.00 that night.

CHAPTER 29

Vladimir Orlov's apartment on Mårten Trotzigs gränd was neat and

of communicating – claimed to have no knowledge of bloodstains or of Zander, so Bublanski and his team concentrated on getting more information on the woman who had been seen with him. By now the media had published columns and columns not only about the drama on Ingarö but also about Andrei Zander's disappearance. Both evening newspapers and *Svenska Morgon-Posten* and *Metro* had carried prominent photographs of the journalist, and there was already speculation that he might have been murdered. Usually that would jog people's memories and prompt them to remember anything suspicious, but now it was almost the exact opposite.

Such witness accounts as came in and were thought to be credible were peculiarly vague, and everyone who came forward – except for Mikael Blomkvist and the baker from Skansen – took it upon themselves to remark that they did not suppose the woman guilty of any crime. She had apparently made an overwhelmingly good impression on everyone who had encountered her. A bartender called Sören Karlsten, who had served the woman and Zander in Papagallo on Götgatan, even went on and on boasting that he was such a good judge of character and claimed to be absolutely certain that this woman "would never hurt a soul".

"She was class personified."

She was just about everything personified, if one were to believe the witnesses, and from what Bublanski could see it would be virtually impossible to produce an identikit picture of her. The witness accounts all depicted her in different terms, as if they were projecting their image of an ideal woman onto her, and so far they had no photographs from any surveillance camera. It was almost laughable. Blomkvist said that the woman was without a shadow of doubt Camilla Salander, twin sister of Lisbeth. But go back in the records for many years and there was no trace of her. It was as if she had ceased to exist. If Camilla Salander were still alive, then it was under a new identity.

Bublanski especially did not like it that there had been two unexplained deaths in the foster family she had left behind. The police investigations at the time were deficient, full of loose threads and question marks which had never been followed up.

Bublanski had read the reports, ashamed that out of some bizarre respect for the family's tragedy his colleagues had even failed to get to the bottom of the glaring problem that both the father and the daughter had emptied their bank accounts just before their deaths, or that in the very week that he had been found hanged the father had started a letter to her which began:

"Camilla, why is it so important to you to destroy my life?"

This person who seemed to have enchanted all the witnesses was shrouded in ominous darkness.

*

It was now 8.00 in the morning and there were a hundred other things Bublanski should have been attending to, so he reacted with both irritation and guilt when he heard that he had a visitor. She was a woman who had been interviewed by Modig but who now insisted on meeting him. Afterwards he wondered if he had been especially receptive just then, maybe because all he was expecting were further problems. The woman in the doorway had a regal bearing but was not tall. She had dark, intense eyes which gave her a slightly melancholy look. She was dressed in a grey coat and a red dress that looked a bit like a sari.

"My name is Farah Sharif," she said. "I'm a professor of computer sciences, and I was a close friend of Frans Balder."

sation with Professor Warburton."

"That's right. He's been looking for me too. But it's been so chaotic I haven't had time to call him back."

"Steven is a professor of cybernetics at Stanford and a leading researcher in the field of technological singularity. These days he works at the Machine Intelligence Research Institute, whose aim is to ensure that Artificial Intelligence is a positive help to mankind rather than the opposite."

"Well, that sounds good," Bublanski said. He felt uncomfortable whenever this topic came up.

"Steven lives somewhat in a world of his own. He found out what happened to Frans only yesterday, and that's why he didn't call sooner. But he told me that he had spoken to Frans as recently as Monday."

"What did they talk about?"

"His research. You know, Frans had been so secretive ever since he went off to the States. I was close to him, but not even I knew anything about what he was doing. I was arrogant enough to think I understood some of it at least, but now it turns out I was wrong."

"In what way?"

"Frans had not only taken his old A.I. program a step further, he had also developed fresh algorithms and new topographical material for quantum computers."

"I'm not sure I follow."

"Quantum computers are computers based on quantum mechanics. They are many thousand times faster in certain areas than conventional computers. The great advantage with quantum computers is that the fundamental constituent quantum bits – qubits – can superposition themselves."

"You'll have to take me slowly through that."

"Not only can they take the binary positions one or zero as do traditional computers, they can also be both zero and one at the same time. At present quantum computers are much too specialized and cumbersome. But Frans – how can I best explain this to you? – would appear to have found ways to make them easier, more flexible and self-learning. He was onto something great – at least potentially. But as well as feeling pride in his breakthrough, he was also very worried – and that was obviously the reason he called Steven Warburton."

"Why was he worried?"

"In the long term, because he suspected his creation could become a threat to the world, I imagine. But more immediately, because he knew things about the N.S.A."

"What sort of things?"

"There's one aspect I know nothing about. He had somehow stumbled upon the messier side of their industrial espionage. But there's another aspect I do have a lot of information on. It's no secret that the organization is working hard specifically to develop quantum computers. For the N.S.A. that would be paradise, pure and simple. An effective quantum machine would enable them to crack all encryptions, all digital security systems eventually, and after that no-one would be safe from that organization's watchful eye."

"A hideous thought," Bublanski said with surprising feeling.

"But there is actually an even more frightening scenario: were such a thing to fall into the hands of major criminals," Farah Sharif said.

"I see what you're getting at."

"S··· f····· I'm k··· t· k··· what you've managed to get

without trace. They probably have a number of identities.

"Worrying."

Bublanski nodded and gazed into Farah Sharif's dark eyes, which looked beseechingly at him. A hopeful thought stopped him from sinking back into despair.

"I'm not sure what it means," he said.

"What?"

"We've had I.T. guys go through Balder's computers. Given how security-conscious he was, it wasn't easy. You can imagine. But we managed. We had a spot of luck, you might say, and what we soon realized was that one computer must have been stolen.

"I suspected as much," she said. "Damn it!"

"But wait, I haven't finished. We also understood that a number of machines had been connected to each other, and that occasionally these had been connected to a supercomputer in Tokyo."

"That sounds feasible."

"We can confirm that a large file, or at least something big, had recently been deleted, and we haven't been able to restore it."

"Are you suggesting Frans might have destroyed his own research?"

"I don't want to jump to any conclusions. But it occurred to me while you were telling me all this."

"Don't you think the murderer might have deleted it?"

"You mean that he first copied it, and then removed it from his computers?"

"Yes."

"I find that hard to believe. The man was only in the house for a very short while, he would never have had time – let alone the ability – to do anything like that."

"O.K., that sounds reassuring, despite everything," Sharif said doubtfully. "It's just that . . ."

Bublanski waited.

"I don't think it fits with Frans' character. Would he really destroy the greatest thing he'd ever done? That would be like . . . I don't know . . . chopping off his own arm, or even worse: killing a friend, destroying a life."

"Sometimes one has to make a big sacrifice," Bublanski said thoughtfully. "Destroy what one loves."

"Or else there's a copy somewhere."

"Or else there's a copy somewhere," he repeated. Suddenly he did something strange: he reached out his hand.

Farah Sharif did not understand. She looked at the hand as if she were expecting him to give her something. But Bublanski decided not to let himself be discouraged.

"Do you know what my rabbi says? That the mark of a man is his contradictions. We can long to be away and at home, both at the same time. I never knew Professor Balder, and he might have thought that I was just an old fool. But I do know one thing: we can both love and fear our work, just as Balder seems to have both loved and run away from his son. To be alive, Professor Sharif, means not being completely consistent. It means venturing out in many directions all at the same time, and I wonder if your friend didn't find himself in the throes of some sort of upheaval. Maybe he really did destroy his life's work. Maybe he revealed himself with all his inherent contradictions towards the end, and became a true human being in the best sense of the word."

"Do you think so?"

"We may never know. But he had changed, hadn't he? The custody hearing declared him unfit to look after his own son. Yet that's precisely what he did, and he even got the boy to blossom

"That you're . . ."

He got no further, but neither did he need to. Farah Sharif gave him a smile which in all its simplicity restored Bublanski's belief in life and in God.

At 8.00 Salander got out of her bed on Fiskargatan. Once more she had not managed to get much sleep, and not only because she had been working at the encrypted N.S.A. file without getting anywhere at all. She had also been listening out for the sound of footsteps on the stairs and every now and then she checked her alarm and the surveillance camera on the landing.

She was no wiser than anyone else as to whether her sister had left the country. After her humiliation on Ingarö, it was by no means impossible that Camilla was preparing a new attack, with even greater force. The N.S.A. could also, at any moment, march into the apartment. Salander was under no illusions on either point. But this morning she dismissed all that. She went to the bathroom with resolute steps and took off her top to check her bullet wound. She thought it was finally beginning to look better, and in a mad moment she decided to take herself off to the boxing club on Hornsgatan for a session.

To drive out pain with pain.

Afterwards she was sitting exhausted in the changing room. She hardly had the energy to think. Her mobile buzzed. She ignored it. She went into the shower and let the warm water sprinkle over her. Gradually her thoughts cleared, and August's drawing reappeared in her mind. But this time it wasn't the illustration of the murderer which caught her attention – it was something at the bottom of the paper.

Salander had only had a very brief glimpse of the finished work at the summer house on Ingarö; at the time she had been concentrating on sending it to Bublanski and Modig. If she had given it any thought at all, then like everyone else she would have been fascinated by the detailed rendering. But now her photographic memory focused on the equation August had written at the bottom of the page, and she stepped out of the shower deep in thought. The only thing was, she could hardly hear herself think. Obinze was raising hell outside the changing room.

"Shut up," she shouted back. "I'm thinking!"

But that did not help much. Obinze was absolutely furious, and anyone other than Salander would understand why. Obinze had been shocked at how weak and half-hearted her effort at the punchbag was, and had worried when she began to hang her head and grimace in pain. In the end he had surprised her by rushing over and rolling up the sleeve of her T-shirt, then to discover the bullet wound. He had gone completely crazy, and evidently had not calmed down even now.

"You're an idiot, do you know that? A lunatic!" he shouted.

She was too weak to answer. Her strength deserted her completely, and what she had remembered from the drawing now faded from her mind. She sank down on the bench in the changing room next to Jamila Achebe. She used to both box and sleep with Jamila, usually in that order. When they fought their toughest bouts it often seemed like one long, wild foreplay. On a few occasions their behaviour in the shower had not been entirely decent. Neither of them set much store by etiquette.

"I actually agree with that noisy bastard out there. You're not

Salander did not answer. Her mobile was buzzing again in her black bag. Three text messages with the same content from a withheld number. As she read them she balled up her fists and looked lethal. Jamila felt that it might be better to have sex with Salander another day instead.

Blomkvist had woken at 6.00 with some great ideas for the article, and on his way to the office the draft came together in his mind with no effort at all. He worked in deep concentration at the magazine and barely noticed what was going on around him, although sometimes he surfaced with thoughts of Zander.

He refused to give up hope, but he feared that Zander had given his life for the story, and he did what he could to honour his colleague with every sentence he wrote. On one level he intended the report to be a murder story about Frans and August Balder – an account of an eight-year-old autistic boy who sees his father shot, and who despite his disability finds a way of striking back. But on another level Blomkvist wanted it to be an instructive narrative about a new world of surveillance and espionage, where the boundaries between the legal and the criminal have been erased. The words came pouring out, but still it was not without its difficulties.

Through an old police contact he had got hold of the paperwork on the unsolved murder of Kajsa Falk, the girlfriend of one of the leading figures in Svavelsjö M.C. The killer had never been identified and none of the people questioned during the investigation had been willing to contribute anything of value, but Blomkvist nevertheless gathered that a violent rift had torn apart the motorcycle club and that there was an insidious terror among the gang members of a "Lady Zala", as one of the witnesses put it.

Despite considerable efforts, the police had not managed to discover who or what the name referred to. But there was not the slightest doubt in Blomkvist's mind that "Lady Zala" was Camilla, and that she was behind a whole series of other crimes, both in Sweden and abroad. But it was not easy to unearth any evidence, and that exasperated him. For the time being he referred to her in the article by her codename, Thanos.

Yet the biggest challenge was not Camilla or her shadowy connections to the Russian Duma. What bothered Blomkvist most was that he knew Needham would never have come all the way to Sweden and leaked top-secret information if he were not bent on hiding something even bigger. Needham was no fool, and he in turn knew that Blomkvist was not stupid either. He had therefore not tried to make any part of his account too pretty.

On the contrary, he painted a fairly dreadful picture of the N.S.A. And yet . . . a closer inspection of the information told Blomkvist that, all in all, Needham was describing an intelligence

agency which both functioned well and behaved reasonably
decently, if you ignored the revolting bunch of criminals in the
department known as Protection of Strategic Technologies – the
self-same department, as it happens, which had prevented
Needham from nailing his hacker.

The American must have wanted to do serious harm to a few
specific colleagues, but rather than sink the whole of his organization, he preferred to give it a softer landing in an already
inevitable crash. So Blomkvist was not especially surprised or
angry when Berger appeared behind him and with a worried
expression handed him a T.T. telegram.

"Does this scupper our story?" she said.

those guilty to account. Anyone working for the N.S.A. must
have the highest ethical standards and we undertake to be
as transparent during the judicial process as we can, while
remaining sensitive to our national security interests," N.S.A.
chief Admiral Charles O'Connor has told A.P.

The telegram did not contain very much apart from the long
quote; it said nothing about Balder's murder and nothing that
could be linked to the events in Stockholm. But Blomkvist understood what Berger meant. Now that the news was out, the
Washington Post and the *New York Times* and a whole pack of
serious American journalists would descend on the story, and it
would be impossible to anticipate what they might dig up.

"Not good," he said calmly. "But not a surprise."

"Really?"

"It's part of the same strategy that led the N.S.A. to seek me out: damage limitation. They want to take back the initiative."

"How do you mean?"

"There's a reason why they leaked this to me. I could tell right away that there was something odd about it. Why did Needham insist on coming to talk to me here in Stockholm, and at 5.00 in the morning?"

"So you think that what he's doing is sanctioned higher up?"

"I suspected it, but at first I didn't get what he was doing. I just felt that something was wrong. Then I talked to Salander."

"And that clarified things?"

"I realized that Needham knew exactly what she'd dug up during her hacker attack, and he had every reason to fear that I would learn all about it. He wanted to limit the damage."

"Even so, he hardly presented you with a rosy picture."

"He knew I wouldn't be satisfied with anything too pretty. I suspect he gave me just enough to keep me happy and let me have my scoop, and to prevent me from digging any deeper."

"He's in for a disappointment then."

"Let's at least hope so. But I can't see how to break through. The N.S.A. is a closed door."

"Even for an old bloodhound like Mikael Blomkvist?"

"Even for him."

CHAPTER 30

25.xi

The text message had said <Until next time, sister!>

...

It was not the wording of the texts that had upset Salander so much as the thoughts it had brought to mind, the memory of what she had seen on the steep rock slope in the early morning light when she and August had crouched on the narrow ledge in falling snow, gunfire rattling above them. August had not been wearing a jacket or shoes and was shivering violently as the seconds went by and Salander realized how desperately compromised their situation was. She had a child to take care of and a pathetic pistol for a weapon, while the bastards up there had assault rifles. She had to take them by surprise, otherwise she and August would be slaughtered like lambs. She listened to the men's footsteps and the direction they were shooting in, even their breathing and the rustle of their clothes.

But the strange thing was, when she finally saw her chance, she hesitated. Crucial moments went by as she broke a small twig into pieces on the rock ledge in front of them. Only then did she spring to her feet right in front of the men and, taking advantage of that brief millisecond of surprise, she fired right away, two, three times. From experience she knew that moments like these burned an indelible impression on your mind, as if not only your body and muscles are sharpened, but also your perception.

Every detail shone with a strange precision and she saw each ripple in the landscape in front of her, as if through a camera zoom. She noted the surprise and fear in the men's eyes, the wrinkles and irregularities in their faces and clothes, and the weapons which they were waving and firing off at random, narrowly missing their targets.

But her strongest impression did not come from any of that. It came from a silhouette further up the slope which she caught out of the corner of her eye, not menacing in itself, but it made more of an impact on her than the men she had shot. The silhouette was that of her sister. Salander would have recognized her a kilometre away, even though they had not seen each other for years. The air itself was poisoned by her presence and afterwards Salander wondered if she should have shot her too.

Camilla stood there a moment too long. It was careless of her to be out on the rock slope in the first place, but presumably she could not resist the temptation of seeing her sister being executed. Salander recalled how she half squeezed the trigger and felt a holy rage beating in her chest. Yet she hesitated for a split second, and that was enough. Camilla threw herself behind a rock and a scrawny figure appeared on the terrace and started shooting. Salander jumped back onto the ledge and tumbled down the slope with August.

Now, walking away from the boxing club, thinking back to it all, Salander's body tightened in readiness for a new battle. It struck her that perhaps she should not go home at all, but leave the country for a while. But something else drove her back to her desk; what she had seen in her mind's eye in the shower, before reading Camilla's texts, and which was now occupying her thoughts more and more. August's equation:

$$N = 3034267$$
$$E : y^2 = x^3 - x - 20; P = (3.2)$$

From a mathematical point of view, there was nothing unique or extraordinary about it. But what was so remarkable was that August had started with the random number she had given him at Ingarö and taken that further to develop a considerably better elliptic curve than the one she herself had made. When the boy

ematics. She did not even take off her boots or leather jacket, she just stomped into her apartment and opened the encrypted N.S.A. file along with her program for the elliptic curves.

Then she rang Hanna Balder.

Hanna had scarcely slept because she had not brought any of her pills with her. Yet the hotel and its surroundings still cheered her. The breathtaking mountain scenery reminded her of how cramped her own existence had become. Slowly she began to unwind, and even the deep-seated fear in her body was beginning to let go. But that could have been wishful thinking. She also felt slightly at sea in such extravagant surroundings.

There had been a time when she would sail into rooms like these with perfect self-assurance: *Look at me, here I come.* Now she was timid and trembling and had difficulty eating anything even though the breakfast was lavish. August sat beside her, compulsively writing out his series of numbers, and he was not eating either, but he drank unbelievable volumes of freshly pressed orange juice.

Her new mobile rang, startling her. But it had to be the woman who had sent them here. Nobody else had the number, so far as she knew, and no doubt she just wanted to know if they had arrived safely. So Hanna answered cheerfully and launched into an effusive description of how wonderful everything at the hotel was. She was brusquely interrupted:

"Where are you?"

"We're having breakfast."

"In that case stop now and go up to your room. August and I have work to do."

"Work?"

"I'm going to send over some equations I want him to take a look at. Is that clear?"

"I don't understand."

"Just show them to August, and then call me and tell me what he's written."

"O.K.," Hanna said, nonplussed.

She grabbed a couple of croissants and a cinnamon bun and walked with August to the lifts.

It was only at the outset that August helped her. But it was enough. Later she would see her mistakes more clearly and make new improvements to her program. Deep in concentration she worked on for hour after hour, until the sky darkened outside and the snow began to fall again. Then suddenly – in one of those moments she would remember for ever – something strange happened to the file. It fell apart. A shock ran through her. She punched the air.

She had found the secret keys and cracked the document, and for a little while she was so overcome by this that she hardly managed to read. Then she began to examine the contents, and her amazement grew with every passing moment. Could this even be possible? It was more explosive than anything she had imagined, and the reason it had all been written down could only have been that someone believed the R.S.A. algorithm was impenetrable. But here it was, black on white, all that filth and dirt. The text was full of internal jargon and strange abbreviations and cryptic references, but that was not a problem for Salander since she was familiar with the subject. She had got through about four-fifths of the text when the doorbell rang.

Salander's brain started ticking. How had he managed to track her down? What should she do? The best she could come up with was to send the N.S.A. file off to Blomkvist on their P.G.P. link.

Then she shut down her computer and hauled herself to her feet to open the door.

What had happened to Bublanski? Sonja Modig was at a loss to understand it. The pained expression he had been wearing in recent weeks had vanished, as if blown away. Now he smiled and hummed to himself. It's true that there was plenty to be pleased about. The murderer had been caught. August Balder had survived despite two attempts on his life, and the details of Frans Balder's conflict and connection with the research company Solifon were becoming clearer.

But many questions remained, and the Bublanski she knew was not one to rejoice without good reason. He was more inclined to self-doubt, even in moments of triumph. She could not imagine what had got into him. He walked around the corridors beaming. Even now, as he sat in his office reading the dull report on the questioning of Zigmund Eckerwald by the San Francisco police, there was a smile on his lips.

"Sonja, my dear. There you are!"

She decided not to comment on the unwonted enthusiasm of his greeting and went straight to the point.

"Jan Holtser is dead."

"Oh no."

"And with him went our last hope of learning more about the Spiders."

"So you think he was about to open up?"

"There was a chance, at least."

"Why do you say that?"

"He broke down completely when his daughter showed up."

"I didn't know. What happened?"

"He has a daughter called Olga," Modig said. "She came from Helsinki when she heard that her father had been injured. But when I talked to her and she heard that he had tried to kill a child, she went berserk."

"In what way?"

"She stormed in to him and said something incredibly aggressive in Russian."

"Could you understand what she was saying?"

"Something like he could die alone and she hated him."

"So she laid into him."

"Yes, and afterwards she told me that she would do everything in her power to help us with the investigation."

"And how did Holtser react?"

"That's what I was saying. For a moment I thought we had him.

He was totally destroyed, had tears in his eyes. I'm not really big on that Catholic teaching which says that our moral worth is determined just before we die. But it was almost touching to see. This man who had done so much evil was crushed."

"My rabbi—"

"Please, Jan, don't start with your rabbi now. Let me go on. Holtser said what a terrible person he had been, so I told him that he should as a Christian take the opportunity to confess, and tell us who he was working for, and at that moment I'm convinced he came close. He hesitated and his eyes flitted from side to side. But instead of confessing he began to talk about Stalin."

"Stalin?"

an hour later."

"Anything else?"

"Only that someone we're beginning to think may be a super-intelligence has vanished and that we still have no trace of Andrei Zander."

"I know, I know."

"We've at least made progress on one front," Modig said. "You remember the man identified by Amanda on August's drawing of the traffic light?"

"The former actor?"

"That's right, he's called Roger Winter. Amanda interviewed him for background information, to find out whether there was a relationship between him and the boy or Balder, and I don't think she expected to get much out of it. But Winter seemed to be badly shaken, and before Amanda had even begun to put pressure on him he confessed to a whole catalogue of sins."

"Really?"

"And we're not talking innocent stories. You know, Westman and Winter have been friends since they were young men at Revolutionsteatern and they used to get together to drink in the afternoons at the apartment in Torsgatan when Hanna was out. August would sit in the next room doing his puzzles, and neither of the men paid him much attention. But on one of these occasions the boy had been given a thick maths book by his mother – it was clearly way above his level, but he still leafed through it frantically, making excited noises. Lasse became irritated and grabbed the book from the boy and threw it in the bin. It seems August went completely crazy. He had some sort of fit, and Lasse kicked him several times."

"That's appalling."

"That was just the beginning. After that August became very odd, Roger said. The boy took to glaring at them with this weird look, and one day Roger found that his jeans jacket had been cut into tiny pieces, and another day someone had emptied out all the beer in the fridge and smashed all the bottles of spirits. It turned into some kind of trench warfare, and I suspect that Roger and Lasse in their alcoholic delirium began to imagine all sorts of strange things about the boy, and even became scared of him. The psychological aspect of this isn't easy to understand. Roger said it made him feel like shit, and he never talked about it with Lasse afterwards. He didn't want to beat the boy. But he couldn't stop himself. It was as if he got his own childhood back, he said."

"What on earth did he mean by that?"

"It's not altogether clear. Apparently Roger Winter has a disabled younger brother. Throughout their childhood Roger was a constant disappointment, while his talented brother was showered with praise and distinctions, and appreciated in every possible way. I guess that bred some bitterness. Maybe Roger was subconsciously getting his own back on his brother. Or else . . ."

"Or else what?"

"He put it in an odd way. He said it felt as if he were trying to beat the shame out of himself."

"That's sick."

"Yes. Strangest thing of all is the way he suddenly confessed everything. It was almost as if he wanted to be arrested. Amanda said he was limping and had two black eyes."

"Peculiar."

"Isn't it? But there's one other thing which surprises me even more," Modig said.

"You haven't gone and fallen in love, have you?"

"It's just dinner," Bublanski said, blushing.

Needham did not enjoy it. But he knew the rules of the game. It was like being back in Dorchester. Whatever you did, you could not back down. If Salander wanted to play hardball, he would show her hardball. He glared at her. But it did not get him very far.

She glared back and did not say a word. It felt like a duel, and in the end Needham looked away. This whole thing was ridiculous. The girl had been unmasked and crushed after all. He had cracked her secret identity and tracked her down, and she should be grateful that he wasn't marching in with the Marines to arrest her.

"You think you're pretty tough, don't you?" he said.

"I don't like surprise visits."

"I don't like people who break into my system, so we're square. Maybe you'd like to know how I found you?"

"I couldn't care less."

"It was via your company in Gibraltar. Not too smart to call it Wasp Enterprises."

"Apparently not."

"For a smart girl, you make a lot of mistakes."

"For a clever boy, you work for a pretty rotten set-up."

"You got me there. But we're a necessary evil in this wicked world."

"Especially with guys like Jonny Ingram around."

He was not expecting that. He really was not expecting that. But he would not let it show.

"You have quite a sense of humour," he said.

"It's hilarious, isn't it? To have people murdered and to work together with villains in the Russian Duma making megabucks and saving your own skin, that's really comical, isn't it?" she said.

For a moment he could barely breathe. He could no longer keep up the pretence. Where the hell had she got that from? He felt dizzy. But then he realized – and that slowed his pulse a little – that she was bluffing. If he believed her even for one second it was only because in his worst moments he too had imagined that Ingram might be guilty of something like that. But Needham knew better than anyone that there was not a shred of evidence of such a thing.

"Don't try to bullshit me," he growled. "I have the same material you do and a lot more besides."

"I wouldn't be so sure of that, Ed, unless you too have the private keys to Ingram's R.S.A. algorithm?"

Needham looked at her and told himself that this could not be true. Surely she could not have cracked the encryption? Not even he, with all the resources and experts at his disposal, had thought it was even worth trying.

But now she was suggesting . . . No, it was impossible. Maybe she had a mole in Ingram's inner circle? No, that was just as far-fetched.

"This is how it is, Ed," she said in a new authoritative tone. "You told Blomkvist that you would leave me in peace if I told you how I carried out my data breach. It's possible you're telling the truth there. It's also possible that you're lying, or that you won't have any say in the matter anyway. You could get the sack. I don't see any case at all for trusting you or the people you work for."

"You're a tough guy," she said. "But you're also a proud bugger, aren't you? You need to make absolutely sure that no-one ever gets wind of my breach, whatever the cost. But as to that, I'm ridiculously well prepared. Every detail of it would be made public before you even have time to blink. I don't in fact want to do it, but I *will* humiliate you if I have to."

"You're full of shit."

"I wouldn't have survived either if I was full of shit," she said. "I hate this society where we're watched over all the time. I've had enough of Big Brother and authorities in my life. But I'm prepared to do something for you, Ed. If you can keep your trap shut, I can give you information that will put you in a stronger position, and help you clear out the rotten apples in Fort Meade. I'm not telling you anything about my breach – only because it's a matter of principle for me. But I can help you get your own back on the bastards."

Ed stared at the strange woman in front of him. Then he did something which would surprise him for a long time.

He burst out laughing. He laughed until he cried.

CHAPTER 31

2.xii–3.xii

Levin woke up in a good mood at Häringe castle after a long confer-

had enabled him to get Natalie Foss up to his hotel room in the small hours. Natalie was twenty-seven and sexy as hell, and despite the fact that he was drunk Levin had managed to have sex with her both last night and this morning.

Now it was already 9.00 and his mobile was pinging and he had more of a hangover than was good for him, bearing in mind all the things he had to do. On the other hand he was a champion in this discipline. "Work hard, play hard" was his motto. And Natalie, Jesus! – how many fifty-year-olds could pull a bird like that? But now he had to get up. He was dizzy as he lurched to the bathroom for a pee. Then he checked his share portfolio. It was usually a good way to start hungover mornings. He picked up his mobile and went into Internet banking.

Something must be wrong, some technical mishap he could

not understand. His portfolio had crashed, and as he sat there, shaking and skimming through his assets, he noticed something peculiar. His large holding in Solifon had as good as evaporated. He was beside himself as he went into the stock-exchange sites and saw the same headline everywhere:

THE N.S.A. AND SOLIFON CONTRACTED FOR THE MURDER OF PROFESSOR FRANS BALDER. *MILLENNIUM* MAGAZINE REVELATIONS SHOCK THE WORLD.

What he did next is unclear. He probably yelled and swore and banged his fists on the table. He vaguely remembered Natalie waking up, asking what was going on. But the only thing he knew for sure was that he kneeled for a long time over the toilet bowl, vomiting as if there were no end to it.

Grane's desk at Säpo had been tidied. She would not be coming back. Now she sat there for a little while, leaning back in her chair and reading *Millennium*. The first page was not what she had expected from a magazine serving up the scoop of the century. It was black, elegant, sombre. There were no pictures. At the top it said:

IN MEMORY OF ANDREI ZANDER

And further down:

THE MURDER OF FRANS BALDER AND THE STORY OF HOW THE RUSSIAN MAFIA GOT TOGETHER WITH THE N.S.A. AND AMERICA'S LEADING TECHNOLOGY COMPANY

Page two consisted of a close-up of Zander. Even though Grane had never met him, she was moved. Zander looked beautiful and a little vulnerable. His smile was searching, tentative. There was something at once intense and unsure about him. In an accompanying text Erika Berger wrote about how Zander's parents had been killed by a bomb in Sarajevo. She went on to say that he had loved *Millennium* magazine, the poet Leonard Cohen and Antonio Tabucchi's novel *Pereira Maintains*. He dreamed of the great love and the great scoop. His favourite films were "Dark Eyes" by Nikita Mikhalkov and "Love Actually" by Richard Curtis. Berger praised his report on Stockholm's homeless as a piece of classic journalism. And even though Zander hated

But I am also proud to have had the privilege of working with him. I have never met such a dedicated journalist and genuinely good person. Andrei was twenty-six years old. He loved life and he loved journalism. He wanted to expose injustices and help the vulnerable and displaced. He was murdered because he tried to protect a small boy called August Balder and, as we reveal in this issue one of the biggest scandals in modern times, we honour Andrei in every sentence. In his report, Mikael Blomkvist writes:

"Andrei believed in love. He believed in a better world and a more just society. He was the best of us."

The report ran to more than thirty pages of the magazine and was perhaps the best piece of journalistic prose Grane had ever read. She sometimes had tears in her eyes, but still she smiled when she came to the words:

> Säpo's star analyst Gabriella Grane demonstrated outstanding civic courage.

The basic story was simple. A group of individuals under Commander Jonny Ingram – who ranked just below the N.S.A. head, Admiral Charles O'Connor, and had close contacts with the White House and Congress – had begun to exploit the vast numbers of trade secrets in the hands of his organization for their own gain. He had been assisted by a group of business-intelligence analysts at Solifon's research department "Y".

If the matter had stopped there, it would have been a scandal which was in some way comprehensible. But the course of events followed its own evil own logic when a criminal group – the Spiders – entered the drama. Mikael Blomkvist had evidence to show how Jonny Ingram had got together with the notorious Russian Duma member Ivan Gribanov and "Thanos", the mysterious leader of the Spiders, to plunder tech companies of ideas and new technology worth astronomical sums of money, and to sell it all on. But they really plumbed the depths of moral depravity when Professor Frans Balder picked up their tracks and it was decided to eliminate him. That was the most astonishing part of the story. One of the most senior executives at the N.S.A. had known that a leading Swedish researcher was going to be murdered and did not lift a finger to prevent it.

It was not the account of the political quagmire that most engaged Grane, but rather the human drama. There Blomkvist's gifts as a writer were on full display. She shuddered at the creeping realization that we live in a twisted world where everything, both big and small, is subject to surveillance, and where anything worth money will always be exploited.

Just as she finished reading she noticed someone standing in the doorway. It was Helena Kraft, beautifully dressed as always.

Grane could not help remembering how she had suspected Kraft of being the leak in the investigation. What she had taken to be guilty shame had been Kraft's regret at the unprofessional way in which the investigation was being conducted – at least that is what she had been told during their long conversation after Mårten Nielsen confessed and was arrested.

"I can't begin to say how sorry I am to see you go," Kraft said.

"Everything has its time."

"Do you have any idea what you're going to do?"

"I'm moving to New York. I want to work in human rights.

memorial for Andrei Zander?"

"I'm afraid I have to do a presentation for the government on this whole mess. But later this evening I'll raise a glass to young Zander, and to you, Gabriella."

Alona Casales was sitting at a distance, contemplating the panic with an inward smile. She observed Admiral O'Connor crossing the floor, looking like a bullied schoolboy rather than the head of the world's most powerful intelligence organization. But then all the powerful figures at the N.S.A. were feeling put-upon and pathetic today, all of them apart from Needham, that is.

Needham was not in a good mood either. He waved his arms around and was sweaty and bilious. But he exuded all his usual authority. It was obvious that even O'Connor was afraid of him.

Needham had come back from Stockholm with real dynamite, and had caused a huge row and insisted on a complete shake-up throughout the organization. The head of the N.S.A. was not going to thank him for that; he probably felt like sending Needham to Siberia – immediately and for ever.

But there was nothing he could do. He looked small as he approached Needham, who did not even bother to turn in his direction. Needham ignored the head of the N.S.A. in the same way he ignored all the other poor bastards he had no time for, and plainly nothing improved for O'Connor once the conversation got going.

For the most part Needham seemed dismissive and, even though Casales could not hear what was going on, she could imagine what was being said, or rather, what was not being said. Over the course of her own long conversations with Needham he refused to say one word about the way he had got hold of the information. He was not, even on a single point, going to compromise, and she respected that.

Now he seemed determined to exploit the situation for all it was worth, and Casales solemnly swore that she would stand up for integrity in the agency and give Needham as much backing as she could if he ran into any problems. She also swore to herself that she would call Gabriella Grane in a final bid to ask her out, if the rumour was true that she was on her way over here.

Needham was not in fact deliberately ignoring the N.S.A. head. But nor was he going to interrupt what he was doing – yelling at two of his controllers – just because the admiral was standing at his desk. Only after about a minute did he address him and then in fact he said something quite friendly, not to ingratiate himself or compensate for his nonchalance, but because he really meant it.

"You did a good job at the press conference."

"Did I?" the admiral said. "It was hell."

"Well, you can thank me then, for giving you time to prepare."

"Thank *you*? Are you kidding? Every news site around the world is posting pictures of Ingram and me together. I'm guilty by association."

"In that case for Christ's sake keep your own people in line from now on."

"How dare you talk to me like that?"

"I'll talk however the hell I want. We're in the middle of a crisis and I'm responsible for security. I don't get paid for being polite."

"Watch what you say . . ." O'Connor began.

But he was completely thrown when Needham suddenly stood

Swedish magazine?"

"I've explained it to you a thousand times."

"Right, your hacker. Guesswork and bullshit is what I call it."

Needham had promised to keep Wasp out of this mess, and it was a promise he was going to keep.

"Top-quality bullshit in that case, don't you think?" he said. "That damn hacker, whoever he may be, must have cracked Ingram's files and leaked them to *Millennium*. That's bad, I agree. But do you know what's worse? What's worse is that we had the chance to cut the hacker's balls off and put an end to the leaking. But then we were ordered to shut down our investigation. Let's not pretend you went out of your way to stand up for me then."

"I sent you to Stockholm."

"But you called off my guys and our entire investigation came to a grinding halt. Now the tracks are covered, and what good would it do us if it came out that some lousy little hacker had taken us for a ride?"

"Not a lot, probably. But we can still make trouble for *Millennium* and that reporter Blomström, believe you me."

"It's Blomkvist, actually. Mikael Blomkvist. And be my guest. You'd really do well in the popularity stakes if you marched in on Swedish territory and arrested the world's most celebrated journalist right now," Needham said.

O'Connor muttered something inaudible and stormed off.

Needham knew as well as anyone that O'Connor was fighting for political survival and could not afford to make any reckless moves. He himself was fed up with working his fingers to the bone, and he loped over to Casales to chat with her instead. He was in the mood for something irresponsible.

"Let's go get hammered and forget this whole fucking mess."

Hanna Balder was standing in her snow boots on the little hill outside Hotel Schloss Elmau. She gave August a push and watched him whizz down the slope on the old-fashioned wooden toboggan the hotel had lent them. He came to a stop near a brown barn. Even though there was a glimmer of sunshine, a light snow was falling. There was hardly any wind. In the far distance the mountain peaks touched the sky and wide-open spaces stretched out before her.

Hanna had never stayed in such a wonderful place, and August was recovering well, not least thanks to Charles Edelman's efforts. But none of it was easy. She felt terrible. Even here on the slope she had stopped twice and felt her chest. Withdrawal from her pills – benzodiazepines – was worse than she could have imagined. At night she would lie in bed curled up like a shrimp and examine her life in the most unsparing light, sometimes banging her fist against the wall and crying. She cursed Lasse Westman, and she cursed herself.

And yet . . . there were times when she felt strangely purified and occasionally she came close to being happy. There were moments when August was sitting with his equations and his number series and he would even answer her questions – albeit in monosyllables and somewhat odd terms.

The boy was still an enigma to her. Sometimes he spoke in numbers, in high numbers to the power of even higher numbers, and seemed to think that she would understand. But something had indeed changed, and she would never forget how she had seen August sitting at the desk in their hotel room that first day, writing

it, even to Edelman, it meant the world to her. She began to feel proud too, immeasurably proud.

She developed a passionate interest in savant syndrome, and when Charles was staying at the hotel they often sat up after August had gone to bed and talked into the small hours about her son's abilities, and about everything else too.

She was not sure that it had been such a good idea to jump into bed with Charles. Yet she was not sure it had been a bad idea either. Charles reminded her of Frans. They formed a little family of sorts: she, August, Charles, Charlotte Greber, the rather strict but kind teacher, and the Danish mathematician Jens Nyrup who visited them. Their whole stay was a voyage of discovery into her son's remarkable universe. As she now sauntered down the snowy hill and August got up from the toboggan, she felt, for the first time in ages, she would become a better mother, and she would sort out her life.

Blomkvist could not understand why his body felt so heavy. It was as if he were trying to move through water. And yet there was a commotion going on out there, a victory celebration. Nearly every newspaper, website, radio station and T.V. channel wanted to interview him. He did not accept any of the requests. When *Millennium* had published big news stories in the past, he and Berger had not been sure whether other media companies would latch on to them. They had needed to think strategically, to make sure they were syndicated in the right places and sometimes even shared their scoop. Now none of that was necessary.

The news broke with a bang all by itself. When N.S.A. head Charles O'Connor and U.S. Secretary of Commerce Stella Parker appeared at a joint press conference to apologize publicly for what had happened, the last lingering doubts about the story's credibility were dispelled. Now a heated debate was raging on editorial pages around the world about the consequences and implications of the disclosures.

But in spite of all the fuss and the telephones which never stopped ringing, Berger had decided to arrange a last-minute party at the office. She felt they deserved to escape from all the hullaballoo for a little while and raise a glass or two. A first print run of fifty thousand copies had sold out the previous morning and the number of hits on their website, which also had an English version, had reached several million. Offers of book contracts poured in, their subscription base was growing by the minute and advertisers were queuing up to be part of it all.

They had also bought out Serner Media. Berger had managed to push the deal through a few days earlier, though it had been anything but easy. Serner's representatives had sensed her desperation and taken full advantage, and for a while she and Blomkvist had thought that it would prove beyond them. Only at the eleventh hour, when a substantial contribution came in from an unknown company in Gibraltar, bringing a smile to Blomkvist's face, had they been able to buy out the Norwegians. The price had been outrageously high, given the situation, but it was still a minor coup when a day later the magazine's scoop was published and the market value of the *Millennium* brand rocketed. They were free and independent again, though they had hardly had time yet to enjoy it.

Journalists and photographers had even hounded them during Zander's memorial at Pressklubben. Without exception they had

, but Blomkvist felt smothered.

people started to stream in,

number of friends of the magazine, among them Holger Palmgren. Mikael helped him out of the lift and the two embraced.

"Our girl made it," Palmgren said, with tears in his eyes.

"She generally does," Blomkvist replied with a smile. He installed Palmgren in the place of honour on the sofa and gave instructions that his glass was to be kept filled.

It was good to see him there. It was good to see all sorts of old and new friends. Gabriella Grane was there too, and Chief Inspector Bublanski, who probably should not have been invited, in view of their professional relationship and *Millennium*'s status as independent watchdog over the police force, but Blomkvist had wanted him to be there. Officer Bubble spent the whole evening talking to Professor Farah Sharif.

Blomkvist drank a toast with them and the others. He was

wearing jeans and his best jacket, and, unusually for him, he had quite a lot to drink. But he could not shake off that empty, leaden feeling and that was because of Zander of course. Andrei was constantly in his thoughts. The moment in the office when his colleague had so nearly taken up his offer of a beer was etched in his mind, a moment which was both humdrum and life-determining. Memories of the young man came to him all the time, and Blomkvist had difficulty concentrating on conversations.

He had had enough of all the praise and flattery – the only tribute that did affect him was Pernilla's text: <you do write for real, Pappa> – and occasionally he glanced over towards the door. Naturally Lisbeth Salander had been invited, and would have been the guest of honour had she turned up. Blomkvist had wanted to thank her for the handsome contribution to help close out the Serner dispute. But there was no sign of her. What did he expect?

Her sensational decrypted document had allowed him to unravel the whole story, and had even persuaded Needham and the head of Solifon, Nicolas Grant, to give him more details. But he had heard from Salander only once since then: when he had interviewed her – to the extent that was possible – over the Redphone app about what had happened at the summer house out on Ingarö.

That was a week ago now and Blomkvist had no idea what she thought of his article. Maybe she was angry that he had dramatized it too much – he had had no choice but to fill in the blanks around the meagre answers she gave. Or perhaps she was furious because he had not mentioned Camilla by name but had simply referred to her as a Swedish–Russian woman known as Thanos. Or else she was disappointed that he had not taken a harder line across the board.

It was impossible to know. Things were not improved by the

fact that Chief Prosecutor Ekström really did appear to be considering a case against Salander: unlawful deprivation of liberty and seizure of property were the charges he was trying to cobble together.

Eventually Blomkvist got fed up with it all and left the party without saying goodbye. The weather was awful and for lack of anything better to do he scrolled through his text messages. There were congratulations and requests for interviews and a couple of indecent proposals. But nothing from Salander. He switched off his mobile and trudged home with surprisingly heavy steps for the man who had just pulled off the scoop of the century.

severed. Ivan Gribanov, the Duma member, was under tremendous pressure in Moscow, Camilla's hit man was dead and her closest henchman Jurij Bogdanov and several other computer engineers were wanted by the police and forced to go underground. But Camilla was alive out there somewhere. Nothing was over. Salander had only winged her quarry and that was not enough. Grimly she looked down at the coffee table, where a packet of cigarettes and her unread copy of *Millennium* lay. She picked up the magazine and put it down again. Then she picked it up once more and read Blomkvist's report. When she reached the last sentence she stared for a while at the new photograph next to his byline. Then she jumped to her feet and went to the bathroom to put on some make-up. She pulled on a tight black T-shirt and a leather jacket and went out into the December evening.

She was freezing. It was crazy to be wearing so little, but she did not care. She cut down towards Mariatorget with quick steps, turned left into Swedenborgsgatan and walked into a restaurant called Süd, where she sat down at the bar and alternated between Irish whiskey and beer. Since much of the clientele came from the world of culture and journalism, it was hardly surprising that many of them recognized her. Guitarist Johan Norberg, for example, who wrote a regular column for *We* and was known for picking up on small yet significant details, observed that Salander was not drinking as if she enjoyed it, but rather as if it she had to get it out of the way.

There was something very determined about her body language, and a cognitive behavioural therapist who happened to be sitting at a table further in even wondered if Salander was aware of anyone else in the restaurant. She hardly looked out over the room and seemed to be preparing herself for some kind of operation or action.

At 9.15 she paid in cash and stepped into the night without a word or gesture.

Despite the cold, Blomkvist walked home slowly, deep in gloom. A smile only crossed his lips when he ran into some of the regulars outside the Bishops Arms.

"So you weren't washed up after all!" Arne, or whatever his name was, bellowed.

"Maybe not quite yet," Blomkvist said. For a moment he considered having a last beer inside and chatting with Amir.

But he felt too miserable. He wanted to be alone, so he carried on to the entrance door of his building. On the way up the stairs he was overcome by a vague sense of unease, maybe as a result of all he had been through. He tried to dismiss it, but it would not go away, especially when he realized that a light had blown on the top floor. It was pitch black up there.

He slowed his steps and sensed a movement. There was a flicker, a weak sliver of light as if from a mobile, and a figure like a ghost, a slight person with dark flashing eyes could be made out standing in the stairwell.

"Who's that?" he said, frightened.

Then he saw it was Salander.

He brightened at first and opened his arms, but she looked furious. Her eyes were rimmed with black and her body seemed coiled, as if prepared for an attack.

"Are you angry with me?" he said.

"Quite."

"What if I ask you in now?

"Then I suppose I'll have to accept."

"In that case, welcome," he said, and for the first time in ages a broad smile spread across his face.

A star fell outside in the night sky.

AUTHOR'S ACKNOWLEDGEMENTS

Mathematics at Uppsala University, as well as to Fredrik Laurin, digger-in-chief at Ekot, Mikael Lagström, V.P. services at Outpost 24, the authors Daniel Goldberg and Linus Larsson, and Menachem Harari.

And of course to my Anne.

DAVID LAGERCRANTZ is an acclaimed Swedish writer and crime journalist. He is the author of *Fall of Man in Wilmslow* (2015), a novel inspired by the life and death of Alan Turing, and co-author of the bestselling autobiography *I Am Zlatan Ibrahimović*.

GEORGE GOULDING was born in Stockholm, educated in England and spent his legal career working for a London-based law firm. Since his retirement in 2011 he has worked as a translator of Swedish fiction.

Stieg Larsson

THE GIRL WITH
THE DRAGON TATTOO

Translated from the Swedish by Reg Keeland

Lisbeth Salander gets under the skin of her targets like no-one else.
Those who underestimate her live to regret it. If they are lucky . . .

Mikael Blomkvist – disgraced journalist, womanizer – is everything
she ought to hate. But when she is hired by a security firm to
investigate him, her report on his life reveals an integrity that
fascinates her.

Then she discovers that Blomkvist, himself a brilliant investigator,
is cracking open the cold case of a missing girl – uncovering secrets
that have poisoned a family through generations.

And only one thing gives Salander greater satisfaction than
exposing a liar: stopping a killer.

MACLEHOSE PRESS

...hosepress.com

...terly newsletter

Stieg Larsson

THE GIRL WHO PLAYED WITH FIRE

Translated from the Swedish by Reg Keeland

Salander's prints are on the murder weapon. But Blomkvist knows
Lisbeth would never act without reason, and he cannot find one here.

The victims were his friends. But so is Salander.
And something much more dangerous is surely at play . . .

MACLEHOSE PRESS

www.maclehosepress.com

Subscribe to our quarterly newsletter

Stieg Larsson

THE GIRL WHO KICKED THE HORNETS' NEST

Translated from the Swedish by Reg Keeland

Lisbeth Salander is a threat to national security. Since she was thirteen, shady government forces have acted to keep her quiet.

Prone to violence, deemed mentally disturbed, she has had her freedom removed and her every movement watched.

Yet still, she is an unstoppable force for justice.

Salander has a bullet in her head. She is wanted for murder. She knows that the secrets and corruption at the heart of her country's government go right to the top.

And she will not take it lying down . . .

MACLEHOSE PRESS

ehosepress.com

arterly newsletter

Daredevils &
Desperadoes

Britannica: 100 Great Stories from British History.

Also by Geraldine McCaughrean

Britannia: 100 Great Stories from British History
Britannia on Stage
God's People
God's Kingdom
Stories from Shakespeare

100 World Myths and Legends
incorporating The Golden Hoard,
The Silver Treasure, The Bronze Cauldron *and*
The Crystal Pool

Knights, Kings and Conquerors
Rebels and Royals
Ghosts, Rogues and Highwaymen
Movers, Shakers and Record Breakers

Daredevils &

Geraldine McCaughrean
Illustrated by Richard Brassey

Dolphin Paperbacks

For Alice

This edition first published in Great Britain in 2002
by Orion Children's Books
a division of the Orion Publishing Group Ltd
Orion House
5 Upper St Martin's Lane
London WC2H 9EA

The stories in this volume were originally published
as part of *Britannia: 100 Great Stories from British History*,
first published by Orion Children's Books in 1999.

Text copyright © Geraldine McCaughrean 1999
Illustrations copyright © Richard Brassey 1999

A catalogue record for this book is available
from the British Library

Printed in Great Britain by
Clays Ltd, St Ives plc

ISBN 978-1-84255-059-5

Contents

Introduction

And where ....

So watch out for the liars and opportunists among the heroes, explorers and magnificos.

The Garter

helmets of warrior knights, the
formed a kind of heraldry, bright with colours and
chivalric splendour.

Then the Countess of Salisbury's garter slipped, slid
down and came off altogether, to lie on the marble
floor. Nobody could miss it. A page tittered. A gossip
pointed. And the music ended just as King Edward saw
it too.

Splendid in a quartered doublet of silk-lined velvet,
he made a low sweep of his hand, a flourishing bow to
his dancing partner, and his fingers scooped up the
offending garter.

The countess flushed a vivid red. The silk stocking,
which the garter had been holding up, wrinkled
unceremoniously round her ankle. Was the King going
to make some coarse joke? Humiliate her in front of
her friends and inferiors? Would this model prince
really do such a thing?

Edward pointed a toe and slipped his own foot
through the garter, sliding it up as far as it would go
round his manly calf. The crowd did not know if it was

a joke. Two or three nervous giggles erupted from the courtiers. King Edward, turning his leg this way and that, heel in, heel out, looked up sharply. "Shame on him whose thoughts are shameful!" he said. "*Honi soit qui mal y pense.*"

It was the kind of slogan noble houses were adopting the length and breadth of Europe, in the great race to invent a new, more civilized nobility: devices, mottoes, heraldic beasts, liveries, crests and honours. Some flattering duke jotted down the King's words in a commonplace book. The music struck up again and the countess, still pink with a mixture of embarrassment and pleasure, joined fingertips with the King once more. The slow, prancing geometry of the

forward his leg and

greatest in the land shall wear such a garter! Let it be awarded only to my most favoured subjects! Only the most esteemed and chivalrous men in the kingdom will share with me this honour, this privilege of wearing . . . *the Garter!*"

And so the Order of the Garter began – at a time when English pride was at its height, when it lay in the power of a king to grant everlasting glory.

The order of the Garter is the oldest surviving order
of Chivalry in Europe and was invented in the wake of
an English victory in the Hundred Years War with
France. Chivalry was reshaping the very nature of
bravery, virtue and love. The story is cast into doubt
by another in which Edward gave the signal for a
victorious battle charge by waving his own blue garter.
But whatever the origin of the award, it is now worn
by only twenty-four honoured recipients (plus royal
and overseas VIPs) at any one time, and only when
one dies is another appointed to this most prestigious
circle of all.

Dick Whittington

feed ...... seemed. "You should go ..." said a neighbour. "They say the streets there are paved with gold!"

So Dick set off to walk, thinking London must be just over the hill. A hundred hills later, he found himself in narrow streets, among high houses and the shouts and bustle of London. His poor sore feet found no golden pavements to walk on – not so much as a golden pebble. And his stomach was empty.

He got work scraping pots in the kitchen of Captain Fitz-Warren, a rich merchant. Though Dick could eat the scrapings, the cook was a cruel bully. Dick slept in an attic so overrun with mice that with his first sixpence he bought a cat. That cat was a good friend to Dick, and he came to love it . . . almost as much as he came to love Captain Fitz-Warren's daughter, Alice. Sweet, kind, beautiful Alice. "If I weren't me and you weren't you, I would marry you one day!" he used to say.

"Who knows what you might be one day," Alice would say in reply.

But the cook's cruelties were too much for Dick to bear, and one very early morning he and his cat ran away. He might have walked all the way home, had he not stopped to rest on a milestone at Holloway. Across the fields came the distant ringing of Bow Bells in Cheapside – a familiar enough sound – except that today he seemed to hear words among the clamour: "Turn again, Whittington, thrice Lord Mayor of London!"

At once, Dick ran back the way he had come, and

was busy scrubbing the kitchen floor before the cook even woke.

That day the house was all at sixes and sevens. Captain Fitz-Warren was setting sail. All kinds of people had invested in his voyage, hoping for huge ~~~~~~~~~~ cargo in distant

down the rats on board my ship."

Dick did not want to be parted from his friend, but at the last moment, he agreed.

Disaster! Captain Fitz-Warren's ship ran aground on the shores of a country where no one wanted or needed his valuable cargo. The caliph there had everything a man could desire: gems and silk, sherbet and oysters, palace walls clad in beaten gold.

One thing more the caliph had. Rats. His realm, his palace, even his throne-room swarmed with rats, because there were no cats in the whole land. When Puss saw the rats, he slew them by the dozen, by the tens of dozen, while the caliph watched in wonder. "For this cat I will pay three sacks of diamonds!" he declared.

Dick's fortune was made. With the proceeds, he became a respected London merchant and before long he was elected Lord Mayor of London – not once but three times. Bow Bells rang once again for Dick Whittington – on the day he married Alice Fitz-Warren.

Sir William Whittington of Gloucestershire had three sons but, when the youngest was still a baby, he was outlawed. The two older brothers sent Dick to London to be apprenticed to a distant relation, Sir Ivo Fitzwaryn. Sir Ivo was a mercer – a dealer in fabrics – and Dick's first job, at thirteen, was to stand outside his master's shop shouting, to attract customers. "What d'ye lack? What d'ye lack?"

From early morning till Bow Bells rang at eight, Dick learned his trade. They were eventful times. He saw John Wycliffe tried for heresy, saw Wat Tyler's rebels come flooding over London Bridge, saw the plague carry off 30,000 people in a single year.

They were fashionable times, too – times when the rich spent lavishly on clothes. There was no better time to be a mercer. The London mercers had money to spare, so became the bankers of the day as well, growing even richer from lending money.

By the age of twenty-nine Richard Whittington had £10 of his own to invest. At thirty-five he was an alderman and sheriff. King Richard II appointed him Mayor of London (there was no Lord Mayor then). His fellow Londoners re-elected him time after time.

Mayor Whittington invented street lighting, commanding every citizen to hang a lantern outside his door at night. He invented the public drinking fountain, too. He was the terror of dishonest tradesmen, prosecuting those who gave short measure, watered beer, overcharged or sold shoddy goods. He rebuilt his parish church, built almshouses for the poor, began a vast library . . . and lent King Henry V £60,000 towards the cost of fighting a war in France.

He entertained Henry and his new bride, Princess Catherine of France, to a feast more splendid than any ever seen before, warming the banqueting hall with three blazing fires of costly cedarwood and cinnamon. Queen Catherine clapped her hands in delight at such sweet-smelling, extravagant fires.

"Ah, but I shall feed them with something more costly still than cedarwood!" declared Sir Richard, and promptly tossed into the fire all record of moneys he had lent King Henry. "Thus do I acquit your Highness of a debt of £60,000" he said.

Henry was staggered. "Never had a prince such a subject!" he cried.

"Never had a subject such a prince," said Whittington with a gracious bow.

Whittington *did* marry his employer's daughter, Alice. But they had no children. So when the great man died a widower, his immense wealth was bequeathed to London – to rebuild Newgate Prison, to restore St Bart's Hospital, to put windows in the Guildhall, to found a college . . . and his library of books was given to the Greyfriars. He had many "cats" (for the word means a cargo-carrying sailing boat); but as to the furry kind – well, they leave no pawprints on the pages of history.

Say "Bread and Cheese"

1381

"When Adam delved and Eve span, who was then the gentleman?" John Ball asked the question in market squares all over Kent, and no one could answer him. Everybody is descended from Adam and Eve. So how come some people have become knights and barons, the rest starving serfs, taxed and oppressed by their so-called "betters"? Ball was a "Lollard". He wanted to end the feudal system. The people of Kent were eager to help him.

At Dartford, the cry was taken up by Walter the Tiler (or Wat Tyler).

Unlike Ball (an educated priest with strong religious beliefs), Tyler was a hooligan and a murderer. But the people followed him, like children following the Pied Piper. Joining forces with John Ball and a thatcher named Jack Straw, Tyler began to march towards London trailing behind him a growing army of protesters. Some just wanted to tell the young King their grievances; some wanted to bring down the old order, some simply a chance to pillage the city and cut a few throats.

Out of other counties came other columns of marchers. The citizens of London, faced with this flood of angry rebels, slammed the gates of London Bridge, to keep them out.

"Tell them to gather on the Thames shore at

Rotherhithe on Thursday, and I will speak to them," said King Richard.

He was only fifteen, but appeared calm as he and a ... of barons sailed down-river to meet the ... the huge crowd on the bank ... ... surged

w...

"Come ashore, a... . back.

The Earl of Salisbury stood up, rocking the boat. "Gentlemen, you are not properly dressed for conversation with a king!" As the barge pulled out again into mid-stream, the crowd muttered angrily, and headed for London. Finding the gates of London Bridge shut, they threatened to burn down the suburbs and take the city by storm.

Could they be fought off? The Lord Mayor was doubtful. The City itself was full of rebel sympathizers – maybe as many as 30,000 living *inside* the gates might rise up, too, if it came to a battle. Slowly, creakingly, the gates were swung open, and the mob surged across – hundreds of hungry men. Sooner than be plundered of everything, grocers and bakers hurried into the street to distribute food.

A mob is a mindless, savage beast. This one went through the city looting, setting fire to the homes of lawyers, courtiers and churchmen. They burned down the Savoy Palace, the house of the Knights Hospitallers and the Marshalsea Prison. It was a night for settling old

scores. Wat Tyler searched out an old employer who had
crossed him once, and hacked off his head.

His power-crazed army grabbed people in the street,
shaking them by the throat and screaming: "Say 'bread
and cheese!'" When times are hard, the poor and the

ignorant always blame foreigners for their troubles. Any trace of a foreign accent and they killed their victim. "Say 'bread and cheese!'"

"Brod unt cheess."

...foreigner!"

...murdered

kill them like flies. ...

a weapon, and we can muster – what? – ...

But the Earl of Salisbury shook his head. The mob must be appeased, soothed with kind words. "If we should begin to kill them, and not go through with it, it will be all over with us and our heirs. England will become a desert."

So Richard sent word telling the rebels to meet him at Mile End meadow where he would discuss their demands.

Only half the mob believed him. The rest were too busy cutting throats. Waiting till the gates of the Tower were opened and the King's party gone, Ball and Tyler and Straw sped across the drawbridge, scouring the maze of apartments and staircases for the people they hated most. They slashed the bed of the Princess of Wales. They beheaded the Archbishop of Canterbury, killed a prior, a friar and a sergeant-at-arms, and mounted their heads on poles to decorate London Bridge. Then on to Mile End meadow.

Tens of thousands of peasants from every county in England confronted Richard as he rode out to speak with the leaders of the Peasants' Revolt. Some of his pages and courtiers were so scared that they turned their horses and galloped away, abandoning the young King. But his nerve held.

"My good people. What is it you want and what do you wish to say to me?"

"We want you to make us free for ever," said a man nearby.

"I grant your wish," said Richard.

Just like that. An end to serfdom. An end to one man "owning" another.

It took the wind out of their sails. It defused the moment. It turned the mob back into a dignified assembly of loyal subjects. "Go home now," said Richard. "Leave two men behind from every village, and I will have letters written, sealed with my seal, for them to carry home. I shall send my banners, too, as proof that you have my authority."

Thirty secretaries were summoned to write those precious letters, and as each one was sealed and delivered, large numbers of protesters turned for home, saying, "All's well. We have what we wanted."

Not Wat Tyler. Not Jack Straw. Not John Ball, nor thousands of others. They had the City of London at their mercy, and were not going to leave till it was stripped bare. Still more peasants were converging on London, and the looters had no wish to share their plunder with newcomers.

Almost by chance, King Richard and sixty outriders came face-to-face with the vast, drunken mob at Smithfield. Fresh in Richard's mind were the horrors he had found at the Tower – those four headless bodies, the blood, the trail of destruction leading from room to room. And yet the words of the Earl of Salisbury were still ringing in his ears: ". . . England will become a desert."

When he recognized the King, Tyler gave a terse laugh and fumbled for his stirrup, to mount. He was

you see all those men ~~~~ ~~~~ ~~~~ command and have sworn to do whatever I shall order." He wanted the King's letters, he said – would not leave London without them in his hand.

"That is what has been ordered. They will be delivered as fast as they can be written." The fifteen-year-old King answered calmly.

But Tyler was hysterical, overwrought, wanting to prove what power he wielded. "Give me your dagger!" he told the King's squire. The squire refused, but Richard told him to give it up. "Now your sword!" demanded Tyler. The squire refused.

The Mayor blustered: "How dare you behave thus in the presence of the King!"

Richard remembered those four headless bodies, all that blood. "Lay hands on him!"

A sword struck Tyler so hard on the head that he fell. The royal party milled around, their horses blocking the crowd's view. A squire dismounted and finished Wat Tyler where he lay. Messengers rode off to the city for reinforcements.

Then the body was spotted. "They have killed our captain! Let's kill the whole pack of them!" The mob drew a single breath. Arrows were laid to ash-wood bows, and the crowd began to move, like volcanic lava, bubbling, seething. What happened in the next few seconds would decide the fate of everyone there.

"No one follow me!" said King Richard, and urged his horse towards the furious crowd. Rising in his stirrups, he yelled: "Gentlemen! What are you about? You shall have no other captain but me. I am your King!"

It was a startling gesture from a boy of his age. Thousands drew back from the brink. Some hotheads wanted to cut down the King, but hesitated, uncertain.

That hesitation gave time for several thousand armed men to ride, pell-mell, out of London, and reinforce King and court.

John Ball and Jack Straw crept away, hoping to hide.

"Let's charge, and kill them where they stand!" urged one of Richard's knights, but the King would not hear of it. There was no need. The balance of power had changed. King Richard was demanding the return of his banners, the handing back of his letters. And the people were passing them forward – banners and letters – giving up their passports to freedom.

In front of their eyes, Richard tore up the letters, crushed the waxy seals, and they stood and watched him do it – docile, cowed, leaderless. Like sheep they scattered. Like sheepdogs at their heels, new proclamations chased them out of town. Anyone not resident in London one year or more was to be gone by Sunday or lose his head.

As they streamed over London Bridge, three severed

heads grinned down at them from the top of poles: not the archbishop nor the prior nor the sergeant-at-arms, but Wat Tyler, Jack Straw and John Ball. On the various roads to London, thousands of peasants still ~~join~~ in the Peasant's Revolt heard that it

Who was in the wrong? Tyler and his murderous louts? The King and Parliament, with their broken promises? After the peasants returned home, every letter was revoked, every charter withdrawn. Even more hardships were heaped on the peasants. Large crowds were forbidden to gather. Richard II imposed his authority by marching around the country with an army of 40,000 men. The nobles were no more ready to set serfs free than to give away their own knives and forks. Property is property, after all.

In some regions, the Peasants' Revolt was not so easily snuffed out. There were risings all over the country, and nobles shut themselves up in their castles and trembled. But order was gradually restored by the usual means: battles, trials, beheadings; in Essex, 500 peasants were killed.

"A Little Touch of Harry

the Night"

From the French camp floated the noise of hammering home rivets, a minstrel singing, men laughing; banners of red-and-yellow light. But within the English camp there was hardly a sound, hardly a light showing. Six thousand exhausted men had walked through teeming rain 260 miles from Harfleur, with too little to eat and disease dogging them every step of the way. In the morning they would have to confront the army barring their road to Calais and escape. And the well-equipped French outnumbered them four-to-one. There did not seem much to sing about, as the rain teemed and the dark pressed suffocatingly close.

"Who goes there?" The sentries were jumpy.

"Friend."

"Whose regiment?"

"Sir Thomas Erpingham's." The cloaked figure moved closer, hood pulled forward against the filthy weather. The sentry let him pass and join a group of men sitting round a damp little fire.

"It's all right for the King," one was saying. "He

21

wants to win the throne of France, so we have to come here and die."

"Is that how you see it?" said the hooded stranger equably. He took a sip of ale, before passing his tankard on round the group. "I would have thought the King had a heavy burden to carry. He's the father of his men. He has to provide for them, pray for them, look after them . . . All those wives and children depending on him to bring home their menfolk –

that's a terrible responsibility for any man."

"Yeah, but tomorrow he'll be up there on his big horse on top of a hill somewhere, watching us get trampled by the French cavalry."

"Oh, why? Was Harfleur like that?"

"No. Not at Harfleur,

For a second the firelight caught his face and the sergeant's hand shot out and gripped the man alongside him. "Oh no! You know who that was, don't you? You know what I just done? I only went and called the King of England a saucy rogue to his face!"

Henry walked on, moving between the dim red circles of dying campfires like a meteor through the dimness of space, calling out greetings to those he knew by name. Some recognized him, even bare-headed and without his surcoat of leopards and lilies. The King was a tall, erect figure, with a long, straight nose and strong jawline. His voice was sometimes soft and soothing, sometimes bright and laughing, depending on the nature and needs of his men. He played dice with some, exchanged memories with others, broke bread with them, listened to their jokes. He did not sleep that night, but the following morning his men were less weary because of it.

Only then did he begin to speak of glory.

His sword was drawn as he spoke, rallying them, encouraging them, praising their valour and skill as warriors. The men farthest off craned to catch every last word. Henry invited all those who wanted to leave, to go with his blessing – but warned them that they would miss out on the glory, miss out on being part of the greatest battle ever fought. No one got up to leave. When he had finished, there was no more talk of dying under French hooves, no more lolling in the mud nursing belly aches and fear. Henry had his men mustered and ready while the French were still quarrelling about who would lead the charge.

So sure of victory were the swaggering French knights, that they bragged to one another: "I shall capture the English banner!"

"I shall take a thousand prisoners!"

"They haven't above 900 men-at arms! The rest are nothing but poxy archers!"

Their horses pranced and capered under them, so unruly that their commander could not apply his battle plan. They even managed to trap 3,000 of their own crossbowmen behind them, leaving them unable to fire on the enemy for fear of hitting French knights.

At mid-morning, with a shout from Henry of,

"Banners advance! In the name of Jesus, Mary and St George!" and with a blare of trumpets, the English trudged a half mile towards the enemy. When the French banners were just within range of the archers' arrows, the English halted and sank long, sharpened stakes into ~~the sodden ground, points outward.~~

the English archers could fire off twelve arrows a minute – metre-long arrows whose tips could pierce armour. By the time the French cavalry reached the longbowmen, 850 out of 1,000 were dead. The survivors rode on to the wooden stakes, or were pulled from their saddles and done to death by the archers. Riderless horses and fleeing French knights turned and galloped back the way they had come – trampling their own foot-soldiers.

The first line of French infantry finally surged up. But they were so tightly massed that they had no room to swing their weapons. They could only mill about, gasping for breath. The English archers threw down their bows and fell on them with swords and axes. Unaware of the disaster at the front, more French men-at-arms came marching up from behind. The first line, now trapped, could neither advance nor retreat. More Frenchmen died of being crushed, than of wounds inflicted by the English.

The aristocratic knights, in their heavy, ornate

man, changed ... into a sober statesman. He believed so ... claim to the French throne that he pawned the Crown Jewels to fund a war, and borrowed hugely from such people as Dick Whittington (see page 5). By tireless warring, by the astounding victory at Agincourt and by marrying Catherine, daughter of the mad old King of France, he secured both England and France for his son.

Undoubtedly, English chroniclers of the battle exaggerated the difference in casualty figures. But the events recounted here are not simply some patriotic invention of Shakespeare's. His play *Henry V* (1599) was based on "fact" – the chronicles of Hall and Holinshed. Henry V, king for only nine glorious years, was dead at the age of thirty-four.

"Hang on the Bell, Nelly!"

1460

"And this be the sentence of this court; that you be taken from this place and, at the sounding of the curfew bell, hanged by the neck until you are dead. And may God have mercy on your soul."

The young man standing between his guards sagged a little at the knees, and a young women in the court cried out, "*No!*" But the judge did not so much as look up. He had passed the death sentence so often before. In these days of war, death was commonplace.

This was the time of the Wars of the Roses. The young man – Neville Audeley – was a Lancastrian. In attempting to visit his sweetheart, Nell, he had been unlucky enough to fall into the hands of Yorkist troops. His only crime was to be on the wrong side in the wrong place, during an endlessly bloody civil war which had torn apart families, and pitted neighbours and towns against one another. Once, Neville had given Nell roses, but all she had left now were the thorns embedded deep in her heart.

There was hope, even so. Neville was the nephew of the Earl of Warwick, and his uncle had influence. A word at court, a favour owing, and the earl might just win a reprieve for his nephew. But court was far off in London, and there was so little time! To Neville, gripping the bars of his prison cell, it seemed that the sun was crossing the sky with the speed of a cannonball, bringing his death hurtling towards him.

"Time to go," said his gaoler, jangling the keys in the

"... of a reprieve?"

... paste

to put out their ...
Neville kicked out his life to the sound ...
church bell. I shall never hear the last stroke of that curfew bell, he thought to himself, as he set his foot on the bottom rung of the gallows ladder.

He searched among the crowd for Nell, but to his utter dismay she was not there. Where was she, his "little Nell"? Where was her sweet, encouraging face? It would have lent him such courage to catch one last glimpse of her. With her there, he thought he might at least have put on a show of bravery.

"For shame!" someone yelled. "He's only a boy! Hold off, hangman. There'll be a reprieve come for sure! He's Nelly Heriot's sweetheart! He's only a lad!"

But the hangman worked to the letter of the law, and the law said that Audeley must die on the first stroke of curfew. The belltower of St Peter's cast its shadow across the square, dwarfing the town gibbet. The bellringer stepped out smartly, squinting up at a corner of sky to judge the correct time. He was a very punctual man.

Up on the gallows, the noose around his neck,

Neville waited for the bell to chime. He listened so intently that he could hear the starlings roosting, a horse stamp in a stable, a cook scrape a spoon around a pot. There was a dull thud he mistook for his heart breaking. Too late now for a reprieve. No hope now of seeing his Nelly again.

Inside St Peter's, the bellringer tugged again on the rope, but again there was no sound. He swung his whole body weight on the rope's end, but it was as if the bell had been struck dumb. Had frost broken off the clapper? Had the rope become entangled in the rafters? He pulled with a will – strong, rhythmic heaves: nothing but silence throbbed out into the darkening sky.

Beneath the gallows, the crowd began to stir restlessly. Surely the curfew should have rung by now? Had a reprieve already come? Or did St Peter himself refuse to sound the death knell of this poor young man? His eyes blindfolded, his hands losing their feeling with the tightness of the ropes, Neville could not judge what time had passed. Still he strained his ears for the sound of the bell. But half an hour went by, and it did not ring.

Then, with a noisy commotion which startled

satisfy their curiosity as to why

As they got there, the bellringer had just finished climbing the long succession of ladders to the top of the belltower. He peered ahead of him in the shadowy belfry, mobbed by bats. At first he mistook the pale figure for a ghost. Then he saw it for what it was.

Nell had climbed up the tower and, despite the dizzying drop below her, leapt out to clasp the bell's huge clapper, wrapping her arms and legs around it like a lover, cloaking and muffling it with her clothing and hair. A hundred times and more the bell rope had swung her against the great brass wall of the bell, and yet she had not let go. Sickened by the motion, battered and bruised by the crushing impact, she had still refused to let the bell sound, refused to lose her grip, refused to die.

Half insensible, she refused even now to let go until the people called up to her through the wooden platforms of the tower: "He's safe! Your sweetheart is safe!" Only then did she allow her hands to be

31

prised from its clapper, and permit the bellringer to carry her down the tower across his shoulder. ". . . must not ring . . ." she repeated, over and over, without opening her eyes, ". . . must not ring tonight . . ." until, at the church door, Neville's kisses finally silenced her.

Originating in Chertsey, Surrey, this story was so
popular that it spread far and wide, balladeers taking
liberties with the details. It even crossed the Atlantic
to America where the song, still sung today, came
into being:

> *Hang on the bell, Nelly*
> *Hang on the bell!*
> *Your poor daddy's locked in*
> * a cold prison cell.*
> *As you swing to the left and you*
> * swing to the right,*
> *Remember the curfew must never*
> * ring tonight!*

The Princes in the Tower

1483

"Mother, Mother, who are the boys in the velvet coats who came to the Tower today with all those servants and fine baggage?"

"That is Prince Edward, my dear – king as shall be – and his brother Richard. Their father is newly dead of a fever, and soon Edward will be crowned. Think of that!"

"Poor souls," said Mary.

"Why do you say that? The Tower of London isn't all dungeons and guardrooms, you know. The state apartments are very fine."

"No, no. Poor boys to have lost their father, I mean," said Mary.

"Mother, mother, *when* is Prince Edward going to be crowned? I see him and his brother playing in the gardens and on the battlements, but the coronation never comes . . . They look sadder than they did. Only today I heard a servant call out: 'My Lord Bastard!'"

"Ah, child. There'll be no coronation now. It is held that Edward was born illegitimate. He cannot be king. Their uncle is crowned instead: King Richard III."

"Poor boys," said Mary.

"Mmm, but to be king at twelve, and to carry the whole weight of government on those narrow shoulders. It would have been a hard life for the boy."

"No, not to lose the crown, I mean," said Mary. "Poor boys, to be called such names by their own servants."

"Mother, Mother, why do the princes never play in the Tower gardens any more? I see them at the windows,

"To be squabbled over like a hand of ̶ dear."

"No, no. Not to be able to play out-of-doors, I mean," said Mary.

"Mother, Mother, where are the princes? I never see their faces at the window any more."

"Sshsh, my dear. No more questions. Best to keep silent in these wicked times."

"Tell me. I want to know. What has become of the princes?"

"Very well. I shall tell you what is said. They say that the King – King Richard, that is – gave the orders. He chose the most ambitious man at court, and told him, 'Do it.' James Tyrrell was eager to 'oblige' the King in anything. So he summoned two men, his keeper of horse, John Dighton and Miles Forest who looks after – looked after the princes."

"The boys were asleep together in the one bed, their arms tight round each other. Forest took hold of a feather pillow, Dighton another . . ."

"Oh Mother, no!"

". . . and they pressed the pillows over the boys' faces. The sleepers woke, of course, and struggled, but what could two little boys do against two grown men? After a while they stopped struggling. Forest and Dighton hid the bodies, and it was as if those little princes had never lived."

"King Richard did that? But why?" asked Mary. "He already had the crown! Why did he need to kill them?"

"Hush, child, speak lower. If he did order it done,

then it did him no good. Richard himself is dead – killed in battle – and there's a new king crowned. A Tudor king. King Henry VII. He says that Richard killed the princes in the Tower. So keep quiet, little child, and say no more. These are not times to question

The Wars of the Roses (1455–87) was a time of turmoil, with factions forming alliances, then betraying each other. The crown kept changing hands. That is why it is so difficult to arrive at the truth of what happened to the princes in the Tower.

Some 200 years after their disappearance a box was unearthed by builders. It contained the skeletons of two children aged about ten and twelve – probably, but not certainly, the princes. The bones were interred in Westminster Abbey.

After defeating Richard III at the battle of Bosworth, Henry Tudor set about systematically blackening Richard's name. All at once Richard was a hunchback, a child killer, a psychopath. (Shakespeare, living under a Tudor monarch, helped greatly in this reshaping of history, casting Richard as the arch villain.) Historians think Henry (whose own claim to the throne was not strong) might equally have ordered the killings. So might Henry Stafford, Duke of Buckingham, who may have been waiting his chance to usurp both Henry and Richard.

A Recipe for Simnel Cake

Take one fifteen-year-old. Lambe...
Spread thickly the rumour that *he* is the rightful
heir to the throne.
Whip up the Irish and a few English lords.
Raise an army.

Lambert Simnel was pretending to be the Earl of
Warwick.

The priest called Father Symonds had tutored
Lambert well. By the time he turned up in Ireland, he
carried himself like an earl, could speak intelligently
about affairs of state, and seemed to be acquainted with
all the lords and ministers of court. He was handsome
and pleasant, and people instantly warmed to him.
They listened with bated breath to the thrilling account
of his escape from the Tower of London, where wicked
King Henry VII had locked him up.

The Irish sank to their knees and paid homage. They
also swore to put this wronged boy back in his rightful
place: the throne of England.

In fact, Father Symonds was banking on the fact that

the Earl of Warwick had been murdered by King Henry. Secretly. Unwitnessed. What could the King say, then, when this "escaped Earl of Warwick" suddenly appeared to claim his rightful crown? "You are an impostor; I have already murdered the real Earl of Warwick"? Hardly.

And Father Symonds' obedient, talented protégé had managed to convince the Irish. Lambert Simnel knelt at the altar rail of St Patrick's Cathedral, Dublin. The crown was placed on his shining blond hair, and a fanfare acclaimed him Edward VI, *rightful* King of England.

There were only two drawbacks Father Symonds had not foreseen. In point of fact, Henry VII had *not* murdered Edward, Earl of Warwick: he was still alive! Secondly, Edward, Earl of Warwick, was *not* a handsome, intelligent, well-informed young man. He was a gormless ninny, as everyone knew who had ever met him.

King Henry fetched out the real earl, and paraded him through the streets of London, saying, "Speak to him! Anyone may speak with him! Ask him who he is!" It seemed a simple way to prove that the rumours from Ireland were all nonsense.

"Ah, well yes, he *would* produce an impostor," argued Father Symonds, "and pass him off as the real earl. But we know the real one, do we not? We have met the true Edward Plantagenet!"

Some believed him in all sincerity. Some simply *chose* to believe him since, to them, any usurper was preferable to the upstart Henry VII.

[illegible] instance, was [illegible]

through his mind, he [illegible] Lambert Simnel, and his face betrayed not a qualm, not a doubt.

Perhaps Father Symonds miscalculated. Perhaps, by the time he found out the Earl of Warwick was still alive, he was in too deep to turn back. Perhaps he staked too much on the unpopularity of Henry VII. The English lords who rose up in support of "King Edward VI" brought with them a few household armies; the Irish brought daggers and short swords. Altogether, they were no match for the army which came against them at Stoke. King Henry fought his rival for the throne, and won.

Lincoln was killed and Lovell fled, their hopes and fortunes dashed. Lovell made for his house at Minster Lovell, and hid in an underground room. "Lock the door and make it secret," he told a servant. "I have not been here, you understand? You have not seen me – or the King will have my head before the week's out!"

Father Symonds and Lambert Simnel did not slip so easily through the King's fingers. They were caught at once, and people winced to think what hideous punishment awaited them.

To everyone's astonishment, Henry VII, far from loosing the full might of royal justice on his enemies, seemed mildly amused by the whole affair. He invited the rebel lords to dine with him, and as they sat there, a serving boy came to serve them each with meat.

They looked once, they looked twice. An earl choked on his bread and grabbed for a cup of wine. It was! It had to be! The last time they had seen this boy, they had bent their knees and bowed their heads and sworn everlasting fealty to him and his descendants. It was Lambert Simnel. Henry had cut off neither his head nor his hands. "I have put him to work in the scullery," said Henry brightly. "He turned the spit where your meat was cooked tonight, so if it is underdone, you can blame – well, you may blame the King, I suppose!"

Lambert Simnel must have given satisfaction in the King's kitchen, for within a few years he had risen to the post of royal falconer.

There is a tradition that Lambert, while working in the King's kitchen, invented the Simnel cake one Eastertime. A spicy fruit cake, flavoured with almonds, he topped it with eleven marzipan balls, in token of the eleven faithful disciples. The twelfth was missed off, of course, because Judas, the twelfth disciple, betrayed Jesus. And nobody likes a traitor.

The Lambert Simnel epis... the way Henry VII handled it. Instead of appr... tyrannical cruelty of earlier ages, he used a lightness of touch which amazed and amused everyone. Afterwards, he was called "the Solomon of English kings".

In 1708, during building work at Minster Lovell mansion, a locked subterranean room came to light. Inside, the skeleton of a man sat with his head resting on a table, as if asleep. As the door opened, both clothes and bones crumbled to dust. Could this have been Francis, First Viscount Lovell? Did his servant run away, fearing arrest? Or was he simply too stupid to realize that a young man entombed below his own house needs food and water to survive?

The Faery Flag

1490

The wife of the fourth laird of the MacLeods led him by the hand to a bridge near Dunvegan, and kissed him on the cheek. "Twenty years I have been a wife to you, MacLeod," she said, "and twenty years I have kept secret my birth and parentage."

"What do I care where you come from or who your parents were?" he said bluffly. "You've been a good wife to me. Better than most."

"That's because I am different from most. I am a fairy," she said, "and being a fairy, I came only for a while. I must go back now to my land. But before I do, I have a present to give you, in token of the love that has been between us." And she gave him Britach Sith: "the Faery Flag". "If ever the clan of the MacLeods is in mortal danger, unfurl this banner, and the tide of fortune will turn. Three times its magic will come to your family's aid." Then she stepped away from him, over the parapet of the bridge, and disappeared like the spray of the water beneath.

Now the bold MacLeods are not people to ask help of anyone, especially the fairies. And though the fourth laird treasured the banner, at Castle Dunvegan – a memento of his faery wife – he never unfurled it. Nor did his children.

But a hundred years later, when a future laird was born, a slight, diaphanous figure was glimpsed within the castle walls one day, descending the stairs from the room which held Britach Sith. The baby's nurse saw the wraith cross to the cradle and (though she feared the child would be stolen away to the Land of Faery or replaced with a changeling) she could neither move nor

the fairy

nurse's brain like a splinter in a finger. Singing it, she found she had the power to soothe the loudest crying. Never again was a nurse employed to care for any heir to the MacLeod estates unless she had learned the faery lullaby from her predecessor. And yet still no human hand had unfurled the banner for its real purpose – to summon aid. The MacLeods were Scotsmen, and Scotland is a land of granite.

In battle, the Faery Flag was guarded by twelve of the finest men, each one holding a rope tied to the flagstaff, so that Britach Sith might never fall to the enemy. But what enemy could stand, anyway, in the face of the ferocious MacLeods, beards piled on their chest, red hair flying?

None but the MacDonalds.

At Glendale, MacDonalds as numberless as the thistles on the braes, came clamouring down to the noise of drum and fife, and hemmed in the MacLeods.

"The Faery Flag! Unfurl the Faery Flag!" came the cry, and the Twelve Finest unfurled the banner from its pole-head with a century of creases kinking its silken design.

Perhaps the sun came out to shine in the MacDonalds' eyes. Perhaps magic threads entwined themselves in the hearts of the MacLeods. Either way, before sunset, the glen was strewn with dead MacDonalds, and the day belonged to the MacLeods.

Back and back came the MacDonalds intent on revenge, numberless as the tics on the heather. At the battle of Waternish, thirty years later, the MacLeods of Clanranald once more faced destruction at the hands of their age-old enemy.

"The Faery Flag! Britach Sith or we die!" came the

cry, and the little silken bundle at the head of the flagstaff licked out like a dragon's tongue over the heads of the Twelve Finest.

Suddenly, the MacDonalds' charge faltered and stumbled to a halt, the men behind cannoning into

rout, and victory went to the

Many wars have washed over the purple hills of Scotland and stained the glens with blood. And many more MacLeods have travelled to dangers farther afield. But the Faery Flag has yet to be unfurled a third time. It lies folded within Castle Dunvegan, awaiting the third and last cry of "The Faery Flag! The Faery Flag! Unfurl the Faery Flag!"

Some believe the Faery Flag to have come to Scotland with the Norwegian king, Harald Hardraade, when he set out to conquer England in 1066. He flew a flag which he called Land-Ravager, a magic flag which, once unfurled, supposedly brought destruction to any enemy. On his journey south to fight King Harold, he lost Land-Ravager somewhere among the lochs and glens of Scotland.

Even in this century, during the First and Second World Wars and on battlefields far away from the braes, men of the MacLeod clan carried photographs of Britach Sith over their hearts. Some of them even came home again, their photographs as creased and tattered as the flag itself.

Tyndale's Crime

And now they've burned ...... they've burned him.

He studied at Oxford and Cambridge; he was a brilliant scholar – could speak five languages! His colleagues had nothing but good to say about the man. But when he set about translating the New Testament from Latin into English, for the common people to read, suddenly he was a criminal. He had to go abroad to get it done.

"If God spares my life, ere many years I will cause the ploughboy to know more of the Scriptures than you do," he told his learned colleagues before he went.

Even abroad they hounded him. Some villain overheard the printers talking about the new book they were working on: Tyndale's New Testament. "What a revolution this will stir up in England!" the printers said, and this eavesdropper thought, Revolution? Here's news the authorities will want to know about.

When they raided the printers, only the first ten sheets had been run off. But William was too quick for them. He had those ten sheets rolled up in his pack, and

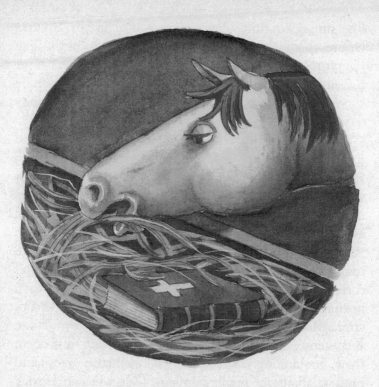

he was away to another city before they could lay hands on him.

He was in danger the whole time, every day of every year, but he pressed on with his work. Two editions were printed finally – one large, for reading aloud in public, one small enough to fit in a man's pocket. Anyone's pocket. Yours and mine.

He needed help, naturally, to distribute them. An association of European merchants, regularly travelling to and fro across the Channel in the course of their business, hid Tyndale's little printed Bibles among their goods. The books sold for two shillings, in shady corners and at back doors – black-market Bibles, selling like smuggled rum. There were 6,000 in the country before the bishops even knew what was happening. Everyone wanted one. *I* wanted one. I don't ever remember wanting a thing so much, or prizing anything so dearly as that parcel slipped into my hand one rainy

themselves – not share ~~~~~

under the feet of swine," was how they put it. We didn't care. We had the Word of God in our own hands at last, in our own language. My old mother learned to read, specially to be able to read Tyndale's Bible.

When they couldn't track down the printing presses, they bought up thousands of finished copies and burned them in great bonfires. But the more they burned, the more people wanted to know what it was they were missing.

So the King made it illegal to own a Tyndale Bible.

Troopers searched high and low, in bread ovens and mangers and haylofts. Anyone found owning a Bible or reading one was put in prison for a month. I was one.

It was Shrove Tuesday, 1527. There were six of us. They dressed us up in penitential robes and gave us candles to carry, and faggots of wood. And there was this great parade through the streets – a public humiliation. We had to kneel on the ground and beg forgiveness from the people for our "crime". Then we were led three times round a bonfire – had to fuel it with those faggots of wood – and they made us throw our Bibles into the flames.

It was like throwing my very heart, I can tell you. It's hard to put into words, but I hated myself for doing it. Tyndale had given us this great book and here I was, destroying his years of work, *apologizing* for the joy he had given me. Of course I never meant a word of what I said that day. But I said it, even so. Like the apostle Peter denying Christ three times, to save his skin.

And now they've thrown Tyndale himself into the flames. Do you want to know his last words, before they strangled him at the stake and set him alight? "Oh Lord, open thou the King of England's eyes." That's what he said.

Well, you can burn a man and you can burn his books. But the truth won't burn, no more than water or milk. Fifty thousand copies of Tyndale's Bible have come into this country since the presses started up in Belgium. They might as well try to gather up the stars as to keep all those out of the hands of the people. It can't be done. Look here, hidden behind this panel in the wall: here's proof. Hold it. Open it. Read it. They will never stop up God's mouth – not now He's able to speak to us face to face, in Tyndale's English.

as John ...y

had been available in English. But copies ...

been hand-written and cost the great sum of £30 apiece, so they were scarcely meant for ordinary people.

Though Tyndale's translations were suppressed (of the first 15,000 volumes imported to England only three or four are left in existence) King Henry VIII was forced to acknowledge a need for a Bible in English. He therefore authorized a new translation – and the Great Bible came into existence.

These beautiful, large-format volumes were chained to church pulpits and read out at weekly services. People flocked to hear them in such vast numbers that the nobility and clergy must have taken fright. Within a couple of years Henry passed a law forbidding anyone to own or read or listen to readings from an English-language Bible unless they were of noble birth or a member of the clergy. Ordinary people were once again shut out. Two more reigns came and went before they were allowed access to the Word of God.

The Ghost of Anne Boleyn

1536

When the old queen died, Anne Boleyn and her train of
ladies wore yellow dresses, in celebration. "Now am I
a queen indeed!" she said gleefully.

She had already won the heart of King Henry VIII
away from his wife of eighteen years; in order to marry
Anne, he had divorced Catherine. But now everyone
would regard Anne as the true queen – even those who
had questioned Henry's right to set aside his first wife.
All that remained was for Anne to give Henry a child –
a male heir – and their happiness would be complete.

She gave him a daughter – Elizabeth – but then
Catherine had achieved *that* much. No, no. What
Henry really wanted was a son, and Anne would give
him that, too. Already she was pregnant again.

Turning the handle of the door, Anne entered,
already shuffling the handful of pretty phrases which

she would deal the King if she found him there. Henry was there, but to her surprise, not alone. One of the ladies-in-waiting was sitting on his knee, giggling at some witty remark of his, her fingers sunk lovingly in

flinched: her

astonishment to shrill hysterics. One ...
round belly, the other to her forehead. She was hot. She was cold. Tears pricked behind her eyes. She felt sick. The roaring in her ears told her she was about to faint.

The shock of finding her husband with another lady sent Anne into labour much too soon. The baby she was expecting – a boy – was born dead. Afterwards, Henry shouted at her for allowing "the loss of his boy". Anne reproached him for being the cause. But Anne had seen him wear that expression before – when people had counselled him against divorce, when people had spoken up for the ex-queen. Henry might

just as well have shut the visor of a helmet: his face was all steel.

His love for Anne went out like a snuffed candle. All the fun had been in the chase and the wooing. Now he had seen another pretty face and he wanted to have it. Anne Boleyn was headstrong and gave herself airs. Saucy little Jane Seymour was far more agreeable, far more accommodating. No one had been able to stop him changing wives before – indeed his toadying ministers had smoothed the way to it. And if he could do it once, what was to stop him doing it again? The toadies would arrange it.

So he cut Anne Boleyn adrift.

There are always a ready supply of people who will say anything for money, or because they have been told to. A good lawyer can whip up a whisper of gossip – the smallest, spiteful rumour – into a mountain of damning evidence. Before long Anne was accused of being unfaithful to Henry with a whole host of men – even her brother. Accusations were flung like clods of mud, until the truth disappeared altogether. Henry had no interest in the truth – only the outcome. The Queen must die, so that he could marry Jane Seymour.

He un-married Anne. He un-queened Anne. He sent for a swordsman to cut off her head.

Getting up at two in the morning, she said prayers till dawn. Later, she sent for Sir William Kingston and said, "I hear I shall not die afore noon, and I am very sorry therefore, for I thought to be dead by this time and past my pain."

"The pain will be little," he said, his eyes fixed awkwardly on the carpet at her feet.

Anne nodded. "I have heard say the executioner is very good," she said, putting both hands round her throat, "and I have a little neck."

In the morning of 19 May 1536, Henry VIII went hunting in Richmond Park. He was restless and

Jane Seymour, he wore a ... fancy-dress intended for gala days.

But Anne Boleyn's spirit was not so easily done down. Her headless ghost leads a nightly procession of phantom knights and ladies through the Tower, down to the chapel of St Peter-ad-Vincula within the Tower's precinct, where her body was interred. And every 19 May, a ghostly coach drawn by four headless black horses drives up to the gates of Blickling Hall where Anne was born. In it sits a ghost, her severed head resting in her lap. Meanwhile her father's accursed spirit is chased by a pack of shrieking demons over forty Norfolk bridges from midnight till dawn: an everlasting penance for giving his daughter into the hands of a murderer.

ANNE BOLEYN

Never before had a woman's blood been spilt on an English scaffold. It was an unprecedented wickedness. When Jane Seymour died, after giving birth to a son, Henry married Anne of Cleves for political reasons, but had the marriage annulled (see page 67).

He beheaded his fifth wife, Catherine Howard on much the same charges as Anne Boleyn. His sixth wife, Catherine Parr, outlived him, her wifely duties reduced to tending a gross, diseased old man through his protracted final days.

Anne Boleyn's ghost appears in more places than any other. No fewer than five country houses attest to hauntings, not to mention the Tower. It was of her ghost that the song was written which runs:

> *With her head tucked*
> *underneath her arm*
> *She walks the Bloody Tower*
> *With her head tucked*
> *underneath her arm*
> *At the midnight hour . . .*

"Little Jack Horner

Christmas p

deeply depressed. What would become

he wondered; of the fish in the ponds, of the crops in the fields, of the books on the shelves, of the wines in the cellar? What would become of the tenants who rented their land from the monasteries, of the church plate and the saintly relics? And what would become of him, if the abbey ceased to exist?

He knew the answer to all but the last. Everything would go to the King – that insatiable, Godless villain, Henry VIII, who had set about disbanding holy communities a thousand years old. Perhaps during Jack's service the odd teaspoon or bottle had found its way into his pocket, but on the whole he considered himself an honest, loyal, hard-working servant. But where would loyalty and hard work get him if the monastery were dissolved? He would lose his position, his livelihood, his home. Would his master still employ him when that master became plain "Richard Whiting, Gent", rather than Abbot of Glastonbury?

Horner eyed the pie. Well, perhaps the bribe would work after all, and Glastonbury would be spared. Jack did

not hold out much hope. He had heard what happened to other monasteries – their treasures confiscated, their statues smashed, their monks turned out of doors. Jack failed to see how one Christmas pie was going to persuade the King of England to spare Glastonbury. Even this one.

Jack had helped to "bake" it. He had fetched the deeds from the abbot's great oak chest, rolled them tight and bent them round until all twelve fitted inside the pie dish. Then he had watched as the baked pastry lid went on. It was like the old nursery rhyme: "four-

and-twenty blackbirds baked in a pie" . . . Only this pie had twelve surprises inside it: the deeds to twelve manorial estates owned by Glastonbury Abbey. The bribe was supposed to persuade King Henry not to down the abbey.

" the inn-keeper

the more he drank, the deeper melancholy. What did the King of England want with twelve Somerset estates? What had he ever done to deserve them? Loyalty and hard work ought to count for something! Jack Horner clumped an angry fist down on the table. The pie jumped. Its pastry lid came loose.

The fingers of Jack's other hand went up to his mouth. What had he done? One corner of a deed showed white like a piece of tripe. Little Jack Horner glanced around the dimly lit inn. No one was looking. The document slipped out of the pie easy as winking. The pastry slipped back into place. Then, with trembling fingers, Jack broke the wax seal, pulled the ribbon . . .

Mells in Somerset.

It was the best estate of all the twelve. The plum. Horner knew its spreading beech trees, its stew ponds and hayricks, its skylines and rambling manor house. He closed both hands around the document and kissed it.

Well? Weren't eleven manors bribe enough for

anyone? King Henry would never know there had been twelve to start off with. If the abbey were dissolved, then better that Mells should be kept back. If Henry spared it – well, then, Jack would always return the deed to Abbot Whiting, and be thanked for saving it.

A log settled in the grate and Jack guiltily crammed the parchment under his jacket. It lay over his heart, muffling the quick beat. He tried to summon the landlord, but the voice cracked in his throat. He breathed deep and tried again. "Landlord! A drink for everyone here, and have one yourself!"

Drinkers looked around, smiling. Horner felt a glow of pleasure.

"Thank you kindly, sir, and who shall I tell folks is treating them?"

"Tell them: 'a man of property'. Tell them: 'the Master of Mells', my good man. Jack Horner of Mells in the county of Somerset."

rhyme, "Little Jack Horner ...
Christmas pie." Jack Horner was indeed steward to
the abbot of Glastonbury during the reign of Henry
VIII. Presumably the bribe of the Christmas pie
failed: Glastonbury was dissolved.

Corruption was rife in monastic communities of
sixteenth-century England. Whereas some monks and
nuns kept their vows, others led luxurious, immoral lives,
outside reach of the law. But what began as a necessary
"cleaning up" of the monasteries quickly got out of hand.

Since the crown seized the proceeds, Henry VIII
gained a fortune from each closure. He got greedy.
Soon his commissioners were using any excuse to shut
down monasteries, colleges, hospitals. The King's
officers then went in, stripped out all valuables and
took them to London. Locals rushed to take what was
left: masonry, doors, windows — anything portable.
Beautiful buildings were reduced to ruins. It has been
called the Great Pillage.

The Flanders Mare

1540

Henry rested his hands on his belly, and contemplated the two paintings. What a masterly painter Holbein was! And what a statesman Cromwell had been to track down two such handsome girls! Lutherans, too! A marriage to one of these princesses would endear him to half Europe, as well as filling that cold space in his life left by the death of his third wife.

Poor little Jane. He mourned her even now – even though he detested wearing black. At the cost of her own life, she had given him a boy child, a male heir, and for that he would always thank her. But a man cannot be expected to do without a wife; not a man of such royal appetites as Henry VIII. One more glance at the portraits, and Henry made his choice: the older girl, Anne. What though she could play no music? There are more important attributes in a wife.

Anne was wooed, and Anne was won, though not by Henry in person: he left all that to his diplomats. Anne was sent for and Anne came, crossing the Channel in the depths of winter. The closer she came, the more impatient he grew to see her. So, summoning seven gentlemen of about his own age, he told them to put on grey overcoats and saddle up: they were all riding to Rochester. Behind their obliging smiles, he glimpsed a certain unwillingness, given the filthy weather, but he just could not wait another moment to see his future bride! Henry, too, called for his horse to be saddled and for a grey overcoat to wear.

Eight anonymous gentlemen, all in grey, rode to Rochester, where Anne of Cleves had paused on her

crossing, when she first saw

mountain of bejewelled lard, sweating cheeks bulging through a square beard, eyes piggy with outrage. When she reverently fell to her knees before him, she could smell a whiff of disease from his lap and legs and feet.

What did Henry think when he first saw his bride? Nothing that could be put into words. He simply stared at that pock-marked face, that stocky body, that nose. The hands she thrust into his were dry as pigskin. When she spoke to him in some ugly, guttural language he did not understand, he could not get away quickly enough.

Thomas Cromwell would pay for this.

"Alas! Whom shall men trust? She looks like nothing so much as a great Flanders mare!" blared the King.

The official meeting of bride and groom at Blackheath scarcely went any better. Admittedly, inside a brocaded tent, with music and quantities of warmed wine within reach, Henry found it easier to be civil. But no one had the right to be as ugly as that! He felt duped. He had been sold a pup. Thomas Cromwell must get him out of this marriage or face the consequences.

The lawyers picked over the princess's life as if checking for nits. But though she had been betrothed as a child to someone else, the law said it was not enough of an impediment. Furthermore, the King's allies would be seriously offended if the wedding were called off. "Is there then no other remedy but I must put my neck into the yoke?" bayed the King.

Cromwell would pay with his: one neck for another. Even as Henry placed the wedding ring on Anne's finger, he was thinking how to be rid of her. She was, after all, his fourth wife, and a man who takes four wives can always take a fifth . . .

The wedding over, the bride was quickly dispatched to Richmond "for the good of her health". Her ugliness was a crime, pure and simple: a kind of treason. He owed it to his people to be rid of her. Besides, Henry had seen a face he much preferred.

Archbishop Cranmer, having just performed the marriage, dutifully listed all the reasons why it should be dissolved. Convocation declared it null and void. Parliament stifled its groans and passed a Bill to the same effect. All eyes turned on Cromwell, who had .... over-ambitious

would be that of the King's ..... precedence over her, except for the King's daughters and his future queen. And she should have £4,000 a year to live on.

Anne of Cleves sat in the window of Richmond Palace, one hand spread across her throat as she listened. She did not reply at once. Perhaps she was trying to choke back tears of disappointment. "You may tell the King I live only to please His Majesty, and will act according to his wishes – though I hope I may be allowed sometimes to see the Princess Elizabeth who has become most dear to me."

The French ambassador caught her eye. The smile was so fleeting that he thought he must have imagined it, and yet so dazzlingly happy that, for a moment, the ex-Queen of England had appeared truly beautiful.

Six months later, the King was paying a visit to his ex-wife. The servants listening at the door heard laughter all afternoon. The Lady Anne had acquired a good grasp of the English language, and the King was as relaxed as anyone had ever seen him. Plainly, Henry and Anne were finding each other the best of company. She was witty and clever, well read and well bred. Best of all she was a good listener. While she sewed, the King talked, describing events at court, scandals uncovered, visitors up from the country, the word from overseas.

"Do you suppose they might be reunited?" whispered a lady-in-waiting sentimentally.

"He must lack company – a sick old man like that, surrounded by toadies."

"Do you suppose he has come to claim her?" whispered an equerry.

But the King swept out again and left, he in excellent good humour, she waving brightly from the window till he was out of sight. The Lady Anne seemed greatly cheered by the visit. Perhaps Henry had let slip that he was secretly married already to Catherine Howard.

assemble a selection of pretty candidates for him to choose from. "It is impossible to bring ladies of noble blood to market, as horses are trotted out at a fair," retorted Francis. That is how Hans Holbein came to paint two pictures – of Anne and of her sister Amelia – so Henry could "view" them without committing himself.

Unfortunately, Holbein omitted the smallpox scars which pitted Anne's face, and painted a flattering portrait. Cromwell's agents abroad, anxious to bring about the alliance, also reported nothing but good. Thomas Cromwell, when he saw the King's reaction, tried to duck the blame, but when he could not extricate Henry from the marriage, went to the Tower and was beheaded in July 1540. This is the man who had helped Henry become supreme head of the Church.

The Staircase

1560

The Queen, her head on one side, contemplated the portrait being held up by two equerries. The man in the picture was handsome – dashing, even. "Hang it at the foot of my bed, where I can see it when I wake!" she said.

Elizabeth I was going through the motions – pretending to be contemplating marriage to yet another eligible suitor. This time it was an archduke – the man in the portrait. Before him there had been King Philip of Spain, the eldest Prince of Sweden, the Earl of Arran . . .

But those well acquainted with Elizabeth knew she cared nothing for any of them. She was not stirred by the archduke in the portrait, nor by any Spaniard, Swede or Scotsman. Elizabeth was in love with Robert Dudley, her master of the horse.

His relatively lowly station did not matter (a commoner can soon be made a baron or an earl), nor did his father's execution for treason. No, there was only one small impediment to Elizabeth marrying her true love: Robert Dudley already had a wife.

"The Queen is only waiting for her to die," wrote the Spanish ambassador in his letters home.

But why should Dudley's wife, Amy Robsart, die? A young woman in the prime of life? It was said by some that she was ill. Others said that she was all too healthy for Dudley's liking and that he was wondering how to change that.

Amy Robsart sat in the big dark house on Cumnor [illegible] to the fair in [illegible] continuing to breathe, blocked [illegible] success and happiness. That was why she had not refused the wine at dinner, even though she feared it might be poisoned.

Not that Robert would do such a thing. Oh no, surely not her Robert who, in marrying her, had promised to cherish her. But the Queen – ah, the Queen's wishes could creep like ivy into every last crevice of her kingdom. Amy could feel those wishes entwining her, dragging on her, sapping her strength. A loyal subject ought to help the Queen to happiness, rather than hinder her.

The big dark house creaked and rustled around her, its corridors, landings and stairs unlit. It was not her own house. It belonged to a friend of Robert's. And Robert was away at court, as usual, dancing, paying compliments, exchanging witty remarks with the Virgin Queen. The pain in Amy's chest grew worse. The trees on Cumnor Hill put their heads together and whispered – gossip and rumour, rumour and gossip.

*

Robert Dudley was out riding with the Queen when the messenger arrived from Cumnor. Terrible news, a tragic accident. "What has happened?" asked Dudley.

"It's your wife, sir. Found yesterday, sir. A tragic fall, sir. The stairs . . ."

Amy Robsart lay spread-eagled at the foot of the staircase in the house at Cumnor Hill, her neck broken, her feet bare, her skin as pale as her night-dress. The coroner's jury brought in a verdict of accidental death. In the dark, unfamiliar house, she had tripped and fallen.

The other possibility – that she had committed suicide – could not be put into words, for that would have meant a suicide's burial in unconsecrated ground.

The public, however, were in no doubt as to what had happened. Dudley had wished his wife dead and

[illegible] Robert Dudley

'A murderer in the arms of our Q[ueen]'

But they were all wrong. The truth was that Amy Robsart's suspicious death had made such a marriage impossible. Dudley was so unpopular now that Elizabeth would antagonize the whole country, her ministers and her allies by marrying him.

Concealed behind the red curls, the porcelain-white skin, the coquettish flirting, the bright, bird-like eyes, was a steely, calculating brain. If Elizabeth had ever considered marriage to the beautiful Robert Dudley, she shut her mind to it now. Love was sweet, but politics were crucial. Marriage to her, she proclaimed, "was a matter of the weal (well-being) of the kingdom". She would only marry if it were in the country's best interests.

She did indeed make Robert Dudley Earl of Leicester, and as he knelt before her to receive the accolade, she tickled his neck playfully and giggled. The courtiers turned to one another with raised eyebrows and meaningful looks. But they were entirely wrong. The earldom was intended to make Robert Dudley a fit suitor for a queen, but not Queen Elizabeth. She had suggested he should woo the troublesome Mary Stuart, Queen of Scots.

Elizabeth was Queen first, woman afterwards. She did not marry the man in the portrait, nor the Duke of Anjou, nor Emperor Charles IX, nor the Duke of Alençon, nor the Earl of Essex, nor any of the other suitors who wooed her. She was in her mid-twenties and yet she had no illusions left. She was a queen, and whoever smiled or bowed or sent her gifts or poetry or portraits was thinking chiefly of her crown, not her beauty.

She was a kind of staircase ambitious men wanted to climb.

country urged her to, and she assured her
would. She liked to keep suitors dangling for as long
as possible, for while a suit continued, she was in a
very strong position to negotiate.

Did Amy Robsart kill herself? Was she murdered
on her husband's orders? Or by Sir William Cecil, the
Queen's Secretary, who frowned on the romance and
knew the scandal would force Elizabeth to shun
Dudley? Or did Amy just trip in the dark and fall, her
spine breaking easily because of the breast cancer
which some say was already killing her? The truth will
never be unearthed now.

Robert Dudley took a second wife in 1573 and
married again, bigamously, in 1578. Elizabeth was
fleetingly furious with him, but relented and, despite
his poor military record, appointed him commander
of forces against the Spanish Armada in 1588.
That same year, however, he suddenly died: poisoned.
Rumour had it that poison meant for his wife had
somehow found its way into his own food.

Walter Raleigh Salutes the Queen

1580

It was no weather for finery. But Queen Elizabeth shone like the sun wherever she went (as she never tired of being told). So Walter Raleigh pulled on his finest shirt, with its wide, stiff ruff of pleated cotton at the throat. His manservant helped him into the stiff, bombasted brocade doublet and short-hose, then pulled the laces tight. (The bright lining showed through the slashed panels of the plump hose like segments of Seville orange.) He drew on his own pale, silvery, silk stockings and secured them with tasselled garter-ribbons above his knee. Then he slid his arms into the painted leather over-doublet and his feet into his new low-heeled, calfskin shoes which he fastened with ribbon bows. He buckled on his embossed swordbelt, then, last of all, swung round him his brand new cloak – a masterpiece of panned, piped, interlined, gilt-clasped, silver-corded velvet. Raleigh was about to meet the Queen of England for the very first time.

Magnificent as Raleigh looked, his outfit paled into shabbiness beside the Queen's finery. As she descended from her coach, the small boys who had chased three miles in its wake caught their breath and gasped. She was as marvellous as a galleon new-rigged, as an angel forest, overhung with cloud, overrun with mud. Elizabeth hesitated and looked around her, with obvious unease, skirts bunched within her two fists, to lift them clear of the dirt. Across her path lay . . . a large, brown puddle.

A cold, spitting rain fell on Walter's hair as he took off his hat and bowed low. A cold, reproachful blast of wind ruffled his cuffs as he unfastened his splendid cloak. Then, with a bull-fighter's flourish (but the careless expression of one who does such things every day) Walter Raleigh laid down his cloak. He laid it down over the puddle – it made a soft, velvety squelch – inviting the Queen to walk over it rather than dirty her shoes.

The sight of that handsome velvet cloak lying in the mud made even Elizabeth catch her breath. She stared for a moment as the cloth grew sodden and settled, then she turned a dazzling smile at the owner. The glance lengthened as she took in his dashing good looks, his exquisite tailoring. Then she stepped on to the cloak, as carefully as a skater stepping on to the ice of a pond. Momentarily, the crowd glimpsed the pale prettiness of her shoe.

The cloak lay ruined, soaked. But as Walter said, with a shrug, to any who mentioned it, that was a small sacrifice to please a queen. Even the beaux and coxcombs strutting in the Queen's wake held hand-kerchiefs to their noses and whispered among themselves that it was "cleverly done", even they admired the panache of it – the grand, chivalric flourish of it. Raleigh was a made man.

It is not known with any certainty whether the incident of the cloak actually took place – several towns lay claim to it – and whether it was this which first endeared Walter Raleigh to Queen Elizabeth I. Certainly he became a great favourite of hers after joining court at the age of thirty. She heaped gifts of land on him and sent him on various missions of exploration and conquest. But she never seems to have found him reliable enough to entrust with high office. He could not intrigue as well as those around him and eventually lost his head for treason.

The cult of Elizabeth's beauty gave rise to music, literature and art, even after Elizabeth herself, vain to the last, had decayed into a sad, painted old lady with rotten teeth and a flame-coloured wig. At the end, she sat up in a chair for three days and nights for fear, if she went to bed, death would lay hands on her.

Francis Drake and a Game of Bowls

1580-1588

The sun rose bright and cheerful, but the bride did not. Lizzie Sydenham put on her wedding finery with a heavy heart. Her mother and father greeted her with little cries of admiration and happiness – "Fancy! Our little Lizzie a bride!" – but she could not smile.

Even so, she knew better than to say, "I don't want to marry. I do not love this man." So she took the nosegay of flowers from her mother and stepped out of doors for the short walk to church. What good would be served by defying her parents' wishes?

Her one true love was oceans away, attempting the impossible, trying to sail around the world. If he were not already dead, it would take several miracles to bring him safe home. Her parents said Francis Drake was a nobody, a rough, coarse, low-born pirate, for all the gold, silver and pearls he had stolen in the Spanish Main. Lizzie did not believe it, but when, after years of waiting, Francis still had not come home to claim her, what else could she do but accept the respectable, unremarkable gentleman waiting for her now at Stogumber Church? Suddenly, something made her look up.

It happened so fast: there was no dodging aside, no

ducking down or turning to run. She stopped stock still, and with a massive thud which shook the ground and raised a spew of dust, a great round stone ball landed at her feet. It struck so hard that it half sank itself in the ___. The little wedding party stared.

her vow. When Francis Drake sailed into _____ harbour, and all the church bells in the West Country welcomed him home, Lizzie Sydenham stood waiting.

The rock was not a cannonball at all, of course. Nothing so ordinary. It was a meteorite. While Drake's little vessel the *Golden Hind* sailed round the world, a fragment of debris from an exploding star had been voyaging through the vastness of space, to land at Elizabeth Sydenham's feet. The Spanish said Sir Francis Drake had a drum with which he could summon up the wind. They said he had a mirror in which he saw the future. They said that he had sold his soul to the Devil for mastery of the seven seas. But then the Spanish were superstitious, and their captains preferred not to admit that any Englishman could get the better of them. Ever since Drake had sailed up the River Tagus to Cadiz, and burned the King of Spain's warships, they had called him "El Draco" – "The Dragon" – a beast of fire and destruction.

With Spain's fleet – its "Invincible Armada" – massing for war on the other side of the Channel, the

English themselves liked to think that Drake possessed magic powers. They told how he had *made* the entire English fleet, sitting on a cliff one day, whittling a twig. Every splinter had turned by magic into a ship on the sea below.

The Spanish, on the other hand, had felled an entire forest, to build their fleet.

When the Armada finally attacked, the English admirals – Drake, Hawkins, Frobisher and Lord Howard of Effingham – were playing a game of bowls on Plymouth Hoe, a grassy flatness overlooking the sea. The pleasant knock of wood against wood was interspersed with talk of strategy, and jokes about Spanish beards.

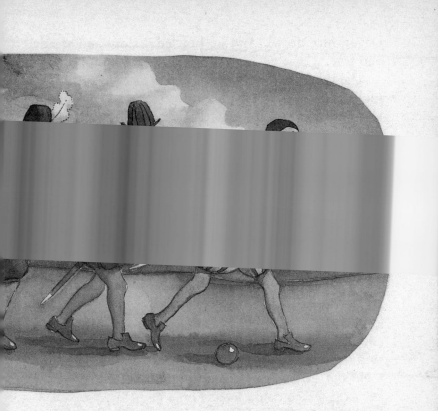

Suddenly there was a shout, and a look-out came pelting along the Hoe: "They're coming! They're coming! The Spanish fleet is sighted! They're coming!"

Snatching up gloves and sword belts, peering out to sea, the various commanders started for their ships at a run. There were crews to turn out, gangplanks to raise, ropes to cast off, anchors to weigh, drums to be sounded, wives to kiss goodbye . . . The fate of the country was about to be decided.

"Hold hard, friends, hold hard!"

They turned back. Drake stood just as before, a cluster of bowls at his feet. "Plenty of time to win the game and beat the Spaniards too!" he said, in his slow,

Devonshire drawl. And he bowled – slow and steady and true.

The other men walked back, laid aside their gloves, took their turns. Over the horizon a hundred topsails, like puffy white clouds, moved into sight. Crowds gathered along every quay and jetty and cliff, standing on tiptoe, craning their necks to see. But the English commanders finished their game before strolling sedately to their ships and giving battle-orders, for all the world as if they were ordering dinner.

The English ships were smaller, quicker and more manoeuvrable than the lumbering Spanish galleys and galleons. They could dart in close, loosing cannonfire and arrows. Drake used fire-ships, too – filled with kindling or gunpowder, helms lashed on collision course, while down below, the fuses burned . . . Fire ships wrought havoc among the Spanish fleet, blasting them out of the water or burning them down to their keels. El Draco could indeed breathe fire.

Even so, the Spanish sea captains believed that their honour depended on victory, and their honour was worth more to them than their lives. They fought with frenzied heroism, until blood ran in streams from their gunports and their ships foundered under them. Their commander-in-chief, the Duke of Medina Sidonia, was an incompetent, but they fought on despite him, till ammunition ran out on both sides, and the noise of battle fizzled into silence.

Then the Spanish beat north up the English Channel, planning to skirt the north coast of Scotland and sail home. That is the day, legend says, when Francis Drake went ashore, and danced with the witches and demons on a windswept clifftop, summoning up a storm.

Gales came in from the west. Damaged, leaking ships, manned by injured, hungry crews, wallowed lower and lower in the water. The storms, which raged for a fortnight, drove ships on to rocks, on to sandbars,

Sidonia was pelted with stones by the [...] disgraceful failure.

Drake went home to Lizzie. But ambition for gold and glory soon sent him back to plundering the Spanish Main. He died there, and was lowered to his eternal rest in the vaults of the sea.

DRAKE

The Spanish Armada of 1588 was doomed from the outset. Rotten provisions, leaks, storms, disease all conspired against King Philip's navy. The design of its ships was medieval and only suited to calm, clement seas. "Drake's gales" were phenomenal – historic events in themselves. But none of this lessens the achievements of the English in defeating the Armada.

In Ireland, where many of the wrecks took place, you can still see faces with Mediterranean features which suggest that not all the shipwrecked Spaniards died. And even after 400 years, not all the missing ships have been accounted for.

By the time the crisis was over, fever was rife among the English sailors. When Queen Elizabeth heard this, she deliberately delayed paying them off until so many had died as to save her a third of the bill.

It is said that Drake's Drum, kept now at Buckland Abbey, can be used to summon Drake back if ever England is in peril.

Lizzie's meteorite is still at her family home in Somerset. He married her in 1585, but she was his second wife, no patient childhood sweetheart.

the letter from Anthony Babington—
devoted, devout young man, but rash and passionate.
He said he was planning to assassinate Queen Elizabeth
and put Mary in her place.

So long as she did not actually *acknowledge*
his suggestion, she could not be accused of conspiring
with him. But surely a letter would be safe enough
hidden inside the empty casks which left Chartley
House?

Letters from her friends and supporters arrived in the
full casks, and her own left in the empty ones. It was a
fine, convenient arrangement and a great comfort to a
woman kept under house arrest for the best part of
twenty years. Mary folded the letter, and allowed her
hand to rest on it, trembling. She had just given her
consent to his assassination plot.

Mary Queen of Scots was Elizabeth's second cousin, a
Catholic and a serious nuisance. She threatened the
nation's stability. Every Catholic would have liked to
see Elizabeth dead and Mary crowned in her place.

Elizabeth, for her part, would have liked to see Mary dead and out of the way.

And yet they were cousins. Elizabeth must not seem unnaturally cruel to her own flesh and blood. It was a problem. Best if Mary should be discovered committing some gross act of treason, plotting some coup. So Elizabeth put her secret service to work, spying on Mary, keeping a watch on her and her friends, vetting all her visitors – intercepting all her mail.

So when Babington wrote to Mary of killing the Queen, and Mary wrote back, encouragingly, Sir Francis Walsingham, head of the Queen's secret service, read both letters. After all, it was he who had organized the business of the wine casks.

Mary was damned by that letter to Babington. Babington and his fellow conspirators were doomed men. Their plot gave Elizabeth just the excuse she had lacked all these years. Now she could put Mary to death.

In September, Babington and thirteen other conspirators were dragged through the streets of London on hurdles, face-up to the sky, to a scaffold of dizzying height where they were hanged, drawn and quartered.

Elizabeth's Council clamoured for Mary to be imprisoned at once in the Tower of London, but Elizabeth sent her to Fotheringay Castle instead – yet another secure house in the long line of comfortable prisons. At Fotheringay she was in the charge of Sir Amyas Paulet.

Tearfully Elizabeth received loyal deputations from her people calling for the death of the treacherous Mary. With great shows of unwillingness, she finally allowed herself to be persuaded. Mary was guilty of treason. Wild delight met the announcement, with church bells ringing all day and bonfires lit in the streets. Elizabeth's adoring public bayed for Mary's ˡ ᵇ ˡ All Elizabeth had to do was agree.

ˡⁱᶠ ᵇᵘᵗ ⁿᵒᵗ ᵛᵉʳʸ

would be to me," she muʳᵐᵘʳᵉᵈ ⁻⁻ ⁻
subject were now to kill Mary . . ."

Amyas Paulet, Mary's prison warder, refused to take this heavy hint. He wrote back that he would not "make shipwreck of his conscience without law or warrant".

And so the warrant was sent – oh, quite against Elizabeth's will – an abuse of trust (she said), a wicked flouting of her will! She had never intended it to be sent! The man responsible would pay!

Even so, on Tuesday, 7 February, a hand knocked gently on the door of Mary's apartments and a gentleman informed her, with great civility and courtesy, that, "Tomorrow morning, ma'am, you must die."

Mary spent the night praying, then in the morning dressed entirely in black with a veil of white lawn over her auburn hair. At forty-four, her former beauty had faded. Years of enforced idleness, sitting over books or embroidery or letters had made her portly, with a fat face and double chin. Her shoulders stooped. And yet it was a dignified, fearless figure who was led into the great hall of Fotheringay Castle to be confronted by a scaffold draped in black, two executioners, a huge axe.

Her servants were beside themselves with grief, trembling, sobbing, swooning. Though Mary wept at being parted from them, her sole companions for so many years, she told them to be glad, not sorry. "For now thou shalt see Mary Stuart's troubles receive their long-expected end."

The executioners tugged inexpertly at her clothing. She smiled: "I was not wont to have my clothes plucked off by such grooms." Then she knelt at the block and prayed in Latin: "Into your hands, O Lord . . ."

The axe fell; the room flinched with a single spasm at the noise of it. There was a ghastly moment of unforeseen horror. The head was not off! The axe man took a second stroke.

He lifted the severed head up for all to see . . . and

broke off, as the skirts of the dead . . . . . to stir.

Out at the hem nosed a little dog, whimpering and afraid. One of Mary's dogs. It trotted into the pool of blood between head and shoulders, and lay down, whining, inconsolable. Nothing could erase that image from the minds of those who saw it.

No more could Elizabeth's raging and protests and loud public regrets erase the impression that she had got her wish at last: Mary Queen of Scots was extinguished and Queen Elizabeth could sleep easy in her bed.

JAMES I

William Davison, Elizabeth's secretary (and innocent scapegoat) was accused of sending the death warrant to Fotheringay against Elizabeth's wishes. He was tried, fined and imprisoned in the Tower. No one seriously expected the sentence to be carried out, but Elizabeth insisted on it. Mary's perfidious son, on his mother's death, became King James VI of Scotland. When Elizabeth died childless (even though James was widely believed to be a secret Catholic), he became King James I of England, too.

The City of Raleigh

New World.

Roanoke Island, at first sight, seemed a far more promising place to begin. It rose out of the curved horizon, green and clad in trees. There were rumours of gold and pearls.

One hundred and seven settlers built a fort there. But instead of planting crops, they went hunting for gold. They quarrelled with the local people and ran desperately short of supplies. When a hurricane struck, they were so terrified that they begged a visiting ship to take them home. Sir Richard Grenville, calling at Roanoke, found no one there. He did his best to revive the settlement by landing fifteen men with enough provisions for two years.

In due course, Sir Walter Raleigh arrived with another group (this time including women and children). It was their task to found the "City of Raleigh" in this land called "Virginia" after the Virgin Queen Elizabeth. But where were Grenville's fifteen sailors? There was not a trace – except for one skeleton of a murdered man!

Undaunted, the settlers took over the deserted fort, built timber cabins, cleared land and planted it. A baby girl was born – she too was called Virginia. With just a few more supplies from England, the community would be able to survive the whole year round!

"I'll go myself and get them!" said John White, elected leader of the little community.

But when he reached home, he found that England had troubles of her own. War with Spain was brewing. The novelty of the New World had worn off, and nobody was interested in the troubles of a handful of settlers. It was two frustrating years before he could lead a relief expedition.

It was an anxious voyage for White. How many more children would have been born? Would tornadoes have struck? Or hostile natives? As the ship sighted land, the cheerful sight of rising smoke was a great relief to him.

Then he realized that the smoke was a forest fire, nothing more. The ship fired its guns to attract attention. John White leaned eagerly over the rail, to see which of his friends would come running down to the beach: Mary, Ananias or even Virginia.

No one came.

It was getting late and there was a heavy sea running. Not until the next morning did the captain send two boats ashore. One overturned in the surf and seven people were drowned. But the survivors scrambled

the people disappeared, but the

around like dead birds, fluttered by the wind. But there was no Mary, no Ananias, no little Virginia Dare.

There were no graves, either, no skeletons or bloodstains. John White took heart from that. "They have moved on. It was agreed among us: if a move was decided upon, they would leave word: a message carved on a tree – a cross beneath it if danger had driven them to it. Look for a sign. Look for a message!" And he ran from tree to tree, searching. "Over here! Make haste, there's something here!"

There carved in a tree were just three letters: C R O. What did it mean? There was no cross underneath, but then perhaps the person who carved them had been prevented from finishing. Anyway, what sense could be made from three letters: C R O?

John White said, "Croatoan. They have gone to Croatoan Island.

The Croatoans are friendly. I am greatly joyed. It means my friends are safe!"

And with quite extraordinary confidence in those three crude letters, he set sail again for England. Incredibly, he did not make for Croatoan Island or enquire any further. It was as if the people with whom he had been entrusted had simply gone on ahead of him to somewhere he could not follow.

The next time English ships happened to anchor off Croatoan Island, they found no trace of any English prisoners or settlers. Six expeditions Sir Walter Raleigh sent in search of the citizens of the City of Raleigh: they found nothing.

And yet 100 years later, Croatoans sided with the English in the War of Independence, saying that they had taken all their laws and religion from English settlers. Some had blue eyes, fair hair and beards. They told a legend at their firesides, too, of a little white maid who grew up into a beautiful woman, and then changed by magic one day into a white deer. Was that child Virginia Dare, born in hope, christened in thanksgiving, lost while the world was looking the other way?

When Captain John Smith landed at Jamestown in 1607, he heard tell that he was not the first: there were settlers already living inland. They had reputedly been taken there by Croatoan tribesmen. Some had been killed, some had escaped, including a little girl. It was also suggested that local agricultural processes and copper smelting had been learned from contact with white settlers.

Although the historical credit as "founding fathers" usually goes to the Pilgrim Fathers, they did not sail for the New World aboard the *Mayflower* until 1608, by which time the East Coast was quite well-trodden ground.

The Spanish Galleon
of Tobermory

1588

Not for the first time and not for the last, love came in a dream. Viola, the King of Spain's daughter, dreamed of a man, and his face was so fine and his whole bearing so kingly that she swore to find him, even if it meant sailing the world round. Past Scotland she came, to the island of Mull.

Her galleon, the *Florencia*, dropped anchor in Tobermory Bay, for the cliffs had the same ragged edges as in her dream. There indeed she found the man she had dreamed: MacLean of Duart. Viola thought her happiness would never end, that MacLean would marry her and make all her dreams come true. The man himself was hugely flattered. There was only one snag: MacLean of Duart already had a wife – a fiery Scottish wife who did not mean to lose her husband to the lady in the bay.

Wife MacLean took matters into her own hands, took a keg of gunpowder, too, and went aboard the *Florencia*. "Leave my man be, ye black-eyed hussy!" she told Viola. "Have ye not men enough in your country that you must come stealing ours?"

"I must go where my heart leads," said Princess Viola. "I was meant to marry MacLean: my dream told me so."

Wife MacLean left the ship – left, too, her keg of gunpowder and a slow-burning fuse. Not all the Northern Lights on Midsummer Eve ever lit up the Hebridean skies like the explosion which rocked the galleon *Florencia* that day and scattered her to the four

Instead, word reached the King of Spain, ⸻ with such spitting wrath that men fled him like a keg of gunpowder.

"Get you to Mull!" he told his trusted sea-captain. "Kill the man MacLean, his wife and all his children! Kill his dogs and cats and the birds in his chimneys! Kill his servants and kinsmen and neighbours! Break down his walls and burn every blade of grass on Mull, for he has robbed me of my daughter, lovely as any dream!"

When MacLean of Duart saw the Spanish man o' war drop anchor in Tobermory Bay, his big stomach quaked and his heart beat so wildly that all thought of Princess Viola fell out of it. "See what ye have done, ye foolish wife!" he whispered.

But his wife squared her square shoulders and stuck out her several chins. She summoned all of the eighteen witches of Mull, and pointed to the ship in the bay. Like frogs all hopping into the one pond, the eighteen witches of Mull pooled their eighteen magics, pooled their curses, pooled their worst of wicked spells. Above the bay, they spread their arms, their feather-white shawls. Eighteen seagulls flew out to sea, circling and soaring, screaming fit to chill the blood of any fiery Spaniard.

The wind too began to scream, like a million gulls, and the waters of the bay swirled. The ship's mast turned like the spoon in a mixing bowl. Then down went the ship, confusing sea foam with rich Spanish lace.

When the storm was spent, not a trace remained of the captain or his ship. Within a matter of years, only the ghost of a memory survived, faint as any dream.

A galleon *Florencia* probably did explode and sink in Tobermory Bay on the Hebridean island of Mull in 1588. It was one of the ships of the Spanish Armada sent by Philip of Spain to invade and conquer England. Defeated by Drake, scattered by storms, the fleet struggled to reach home by sailing round the coasts of Scotland and Ireland: many were lost on the way. The Scots and Irish, being Catholic, should have been sympathetic towards the bedraggled Spanish. But in those days, shipwrecks were a ready source of booty, and shipwrecked mariners were not encouraged to survive.

News of the sea battle waged between England and Spain in the English Channel must have been very slow to reach the Hebrides. Even then it would have had precious little significance for the inhabitants of Mull. It is hardly surprising, then, that this local legend grew up to account for the galleon's visit in a more romantic way.

The Theatre that Disappeared

He pulled himself up to his full height (which was not great): "Is this not the Age of Poesie? And are we not the finest of a fine profession, speaking verse of genius, holding up to humanity the bright likeness of its image?"

He tried again: "My father built this theatre! It is the oldest and most visited in London – yeah, in the kingdom!"

He even tried darkest tragedy, and he was famous for his tragic roles. "And wilt thou see us cast upon the mercy of the rude winds? Hoist up upon the shoulders of misfortune for want of a house over our untousled heads?"

But the landlord only crossed his arms, pursed his lips and scowled. "I say the lease is up and that's an end. You actors can take your theatricals, Richard Burbage, and shift yourselves off my ground. The Theatre is closed, and there's an end!"

Burbage threw an arm across his eyes and struck the pose of a man betrayed by fate. But when he took his arm away, the landlord had gone. He was standing alone in the street. Tugging down his doublet, he replaced his hat at a rakish angle and squared his stocky shoulders. "Very well, you wish the Theatre gone, do you? Then go it shall!" he said under his breath.

He went in search of his elder brother, Cuthbert, and told him to hire a cart. "A big cart. Better still, five carts. Then find John and Francis and Will – everyone who's sober. We have work to do." And as the light faded and the streets emptied, a caravan of carts negotiated the narrow lanes of London, southwards towards the river.

Lying in bed the next morning, the owner of the land, north of the city walls, where the Chamberlain's Company had acted night after night, mused on the value of the Theatre, now that its lease had expired. There was not much to be done with a circular building

open to the elements in the centre. Cock fighting, perhaps, or a bear pit. Boxing, even. But all those were lewd and Godless pastimes and attracted lewd and Godless people . . .

His wife threw open the window and emptied out

"What's gone?"

"The Theatre. It has . . . walked in the night."

"Fallen down, you mean?" He ran to the window, the noises of early-morning London rising up like starlings to circle his head. But there in a cityscape he knew as well as his wife's bumpy profile, was a hole. Where, the day before, the Theatre had stood lay a heap of thatching, a snow of plaster, and wattle enough to fence a field. All the timber uprights, and joists and beams and benches, all the barge boards and staging and duck boards and doors had gone, loaded aboard the Burbages' carts and trundled away in the night, southwards over the river.

The landlord's mouth opened and shut, opened and shut, but he knew no poetry with which to express his feelings. He was, after all, neither a theatrical man nor a poet.

SHAKESPEARE

The Theatre, London's first purpose-built permanent theatre was built by Richard Burbage's father James, in 1576. When the lease expired, Richard, Cuthbert, and the rest of the "Chamberlain's Company" of actors, took its timbers to Southwark (maybe not in just the one night) and used them to build a new theatre. Several of them, including William Shakespeare, went into business together, sharing the profits. The building they put up was much the same octagonal shape as the Theatre had been – a wooden O. This was the Globe Theatre, up and running. It made Shakespeare and his fellow shareholders rich men.

Richard Burbage played all the great Shakespearean roles – Hamlet, Othello, Lear, Macbeth, Richard III. But perhaps his greatest role was in creating the Globe Theatre, during the Golden Age of dramatic art.

In 1613 the Globe burned down during a performance of *Henry VIII*. It was rebuilt, but closed thirty years later when the Puritans suppressed the theatres as sinful. In 1997 it opened again, reconstructed in all its Elizabethan glory.

Gunpowder, Treason and Plot

His fellow troopers cheered, and the officers puffed out their cheeks in admiration at his cool, reckless courage.

That was at Calais. They made him a captain for his bravery at Calais. Everyone said there was no better explosives man in the Spanish army than Guido Fawkes of England.

He was still abroad eight years later when his old friend, Thomas Winter, came looking for him. He had a job for Guido – a job for a good explosives man. This time, however, Guido would be striking a blow for his religion – a blow for Catholicism, which England had suppressed with fire and sword for half a century. This time the target was Parliament.

The plot had already been hatched before Captain Fawkes joined it. In April conspirators met at the house of Robert Catesby, a tall, fair-haired man seething with indignation at the plight of English Catholics. King James (that worthless Scots popinjay) would gather, with all his lords and ministers, in the Lords' Chamber of the Palace of Westminster for the State Opening of

Parliament. One explosion would put paid to the whole pack of them!

This was no rash, spur-of-the-moment piece of mischief. The conspirators gave themselves nine months to prepare. Thomas Percy, a white-haired, respected gentleman with influential friends, managed to secure a small house right alongside the palace. The cellar lay hard up against the cellars of the Lords' Chamber. All they had to do was tunnel through and lay the charge.

From May to December no one lived in that house but Guido Fawkes – or rather "John Johnson", for that was what he called himself.

December
All those days of waiting, doing nothing: for a man of action like Guido it was a torment. Then one December night, eleven men came to the door, darkly dressed, hats pulled down, spades and adzes and picks hidden under their clothes; also food and ale enough for a fortnight.

Down in the cellar they began to dig – not with great ringing, noisy blows, but with quiet gouging and grubbing and boring. They dug till their hands bled and their backs refused to straighten, but the tunnel progressed with ridiculous slowness.

"At this rate we shan't be through in time for the opening of Parliament!" Catesby fretted.

On 7 February it was announced by the town criers that the parliamentary session had been postponed indefinitely. The men in the cellars fell on each other's aching shoulders and laughed with relief. Time for a rest! Extra time for the tunnel to be finished! God must be on their side . . . but then they had known that all along.

That night, Guido Fawkes and Robert Keyes went

across the river to a lock-up in Lambeth. It was dark, and no one saw the two men furtively transferring barrels to a nearby rowing boat. They had chosen a moonless night to row their gun-powder across the Thames to Westminster.

on their heads?

It was neither. The rushing noise continued. "John Johnson" ran outside into the street. There stood a wagon being filled with coal. The noise was of coal being shovelled out of a room *above* their tunnel – a room they had never even known existed! The coal merchant's vault must lie *directly below* the Lords' Chamber. They had never needed to dig a tunnel – only to secure that vault and pile their gunpowder there!

The tunnel was abandoned. God must truly be on their side – but then they had never doubted it.

Percy managed to rent the place. Spring and summer drifted by, with "John Johnson" caretaker now of a coal-dusty vault. One by one, thirty-six kegs of gunpowder were transferred from their hiding place to the alcoves of the cellar.

October
In one week the hall above would be plush with ermine robes, glittering with coronets, crowded with Protestant statesmen.

Of course there would be Catholics, too. In among the elder statesmen would be good Catholic men, like Lord Monteagle. It upset the conspirators, of course it did. Catholics kill Catholics? Still, it could not be helped.

Perhaps someone thought it could. For Lord Monteagle received a letter – unsigned – advising him not to attend Parliament on 5 November, if he wanted to avoid an "unseen blow". Monteagle read and re-read the letter, then sat tapping it against his lips, wondering what it could mean, what to do with it, who should see it . . .

4 November
It was time for Guido Fawkes, their explosives expert, to stack the kegs, lay the fuses and lie in wait to light them. The other

conspirators dispersed – some were already in the Midlands, ready to raise up the revolution in the wake of the bombing. Fawkes was cock-a-hoop. Sir Robert Cecil, Secretary of State, had ordered a search of the cellars, but his incompetent men had found nothing!

Tramp tramp tramp. There was against stone, a jangle of keys; dancing yellow lantern light sprang into the vault. So sure was Robert Cecil about the letter Monteagle had showed him that he had ordered a *second* search. This time his troopers saw the kegs at once. Then they saw, standing against the far wall, the dark figure of a tall man. He did not struggle as they bound his wrists.

They manhandled him all the way to the King's bedchamber, shouting questions in his face, punching and kicking him. But the man from the cellar gave only his name: "John Johnson".

November
Though the others fled, Sir Robert Cecil seemed to know exactly where to find them. Fawkes refused to name them, but they were tracked down anyway, within three days. They rushed out of doors, swords in hand, and three were gunned down: Catesby and Percy killed by a single bullet.

The gaolers broke Fawkes on the rack. It startled

them how long he held out, but in the end, a man can be made to confess to anything on the rack.

He was the last to die. His fellow conspirators had all died traitors' deaths when Fawkes was led out to execution. But the crowd were still in good voice, taunting and jeering. "Traitor! Coward! Murderer! Villain! Devil!" Their hatred and disgust knew no bounds. They would savour his agonizing death: hanged, cut down alive, disembowelled, quartered, and only then beheaded. Guido could barely climb the ladder; the rack had crippled him. But shakily he reached the top, the hangman, the noose.

Whispering a prayer, he jumped from the ladder. His neck snapped. The crowd groaned. The villain had cheated them! He was already dead, and they had been robbed of an afternoon's entertainment.

Guido Fawkes, now referred to as Guy, was born Protestant, but converted to Catholicism after his widowed mother married a Catholic country gentleman. Full of religious zeal and a love of adventure, he left England in 1593 and went to fight in Catholic causes in Europe. He was thirty-five when he died.

In 1606 Parliament decreed that 5 November should be kept as a day of thanksgiving for their deliverance. But the burning of a guy on Bonfire Night is a later, Victorian addition to the festivities.

Britannia

Rebels and Royals
  (the Vikings to the mid 14th century)

Daredevils and Desperadoes
  (mid 14th century through the Tudors)

Ghosts, Rogues and Highwaymen
  (17th and 18th centuries)

Movers, Shakers, Record Breakers
  (19th and 20th centuries)

Also by Geraldine McCaughrean
Illustrated by Richard Brassey

Britannia

100 Great Stories from
British History

In one volume illustrated in full colour on every page, this unique book comprises a hundred stories from the very beginnings of British history right up to the end of the twentieth century. Many are more legendary than historically accurate, and Geraldine McCaughrean has chosen them simply because they are wonderful stories that have been known and loved for generations and give us a sense of our past.

A panel giving the facts behind the stories accompanies each one, and there is an introduction, an index, and a list of recommended reading.

Britannia on Stage

class, but she has also provided a frame... ...
several plays can be acted together to make a
whole performance. There are simple stage
directions and suggestions for a few basic props
and costumes, and a programme note on each
play gives the background to the story.

Very lively, with lots of action and a chance for
as many or as few children to perform as
necessary, the plays are also a great read, and
the line drawings by Richard Brassey are as
entertaining as his pictures for the original
Britannia.